REVENGE IS SWEET

KALI SWEET URBAN FANTASY, BOOK 1

MISTY EVANS

Beach Path Publishing LLC

Revenge Is Sweet, Kali Sweet Urban Fantasy Series, Book 1

Misty Evans

AUTHOR NOTE

Author Note:

This series is one of my all-time favorites. Years of writing, editing, and rewriting have gone into it, and I loved every minute of it.
I've included a Glossary of Terms at the end of the story.
I hope you enjoy Kali's world as much as I do!

ONE

We save what we love. I love humans, even though I'm not one, and while I can't save them from themselves, I *can* protect them from supernaturals like me. My name is Kali Sweet and I'm a vengeance demon. I run Sweet Investigations and work for the Bridge Council, the supernatural world's version of the Justice Department.

A week before Halloween in the Windy City, the trees were leafless skeletons against a murky sky, bare branches dripping rain. One storm was done, another moving in, and the atmosphere was tight and leaden. In two hours, the Chaos Demons rock band would take center stage at The United Center, a.k.a. the Madhouse on Madison, and the place was already jumping. Fans clogged the parking lots, security was heavy. High-pressure shoebox lights laid a haze around the building. A breeze kicked up, scattering a confetti of wet leaves around my feet.

Head down and clinging to the shadows, I passed two tour buses, both emblazoned with the Chaos Demons graphic

Greek god logo. Despite the cool night air and approaching storm, scantily clad female groupies surrounded the buses. Hanging around the women were assorted tattooed and pierced males trying to look badass. A few appraised me, eyes gleaming and heads tilted with interest, but not so much as a snicker or a whistle accosted me. While I looked like a male fantasy come to life in my short leather skirt, thigh-high boots, and Red Riding Hood cape, they knew a true badass when they saw one.

As I passed one of the ginormous plate glass windows in the front, the dull roar of drums, electric guitars, and keyboards thumped against it like a lion trying to roar its way out. The band was warming up, the lure of music tantalizing. I wanted nothing to do with the Chaos Demons, but my MP3 player was tucked in the pocket of my cape, along with my weapons, tempting me to listen to my latest playlist. Tonight, though, I had to keep my senses clear and my wits on high alert. Music would only distract me.

I kept walking.

One of the things I love about humans is their power to create. Music, literature, movies... their ability to invent and design new worlds fascinates me. I covet that ability, perhaps valuing it more than they do.

Finding the service door I was looking for at the rear of the building, I also found a six-foot-five, two-hundred-and-sixty-five-pound security guard blocking it. Beefy hands settled on his nonexistent waist when he saw me. "Kali Sweet. What'chu doin' here, girl?"

"Hi, Hone." A cross between a Hawaiian fire dancer and a sumo wrestler, Hone could intimidate an entire NFL team. Me? I saw a teddy bear under the immense brawn and glowering attitude.

Even though he knew who I worked for and my status

among the supernatural crowd, I'm a stickler for doing things by the rules. I flashed him my badge and gave him my most professional face. "Bridge Council business."

Security guard, bodyguard, bouncer, you name it, Hone had been my muscle on a couple of jobs in the past, some for the Council, a few for Sweet Investigations. The outer package was just for show—he could read minds, and that's what made him the better fighter, no matter who he was up against.

He scratched the top of his buzzed head. "Here? Tonight? Before the concert? It's not one of the band members, is it? Boss ain't gonna like that. Bad for profits if the lead loses his voice right before the show."

If I ever got hold of him, the lead singer of the Chaos Demons would lose more than his voice. But that wasn't Council business, that was personal, and I wasn't allowed to exact personal revenge. Ever. Period.

Hone's boss still wasn't going to like me. "I'm delivering a warning tonight, and it isn't to one of the band members."

Hone studied me for two seconds before he guessed my mission. "Nudra? No. Way."

I nodded, and Hone's gaze swept the shadows behind me, looking for my backup. "You alone?"

Two little words, but his tone suggested it was a crazy idea to face the vampire king without some muscle. I fingered a short stake, sharpened to a nice point, inside my cape. "Nudra and I are just going to have a brief conversation. That's all."

I had the coming encounter planned out in my head down to the last detail. I'd deliver the Council's message with my usual Italian flair mixed with a touch of American snarkiness, and Nudra would try to seduce me with his vampiric East Indian charm. When that didn't work, he'd threaten me with his typical vampire king bluster. In the end, though, no blood would be shed. I'd wrap things up and be back on the South Side to celebrate my friend Neve's birthday before she finished her first beer.

Moving aside, Hone opened the door for me. "Nudra doesn't like the Council stepping on his toes."

Vampire kings craved power as much as they craved human blood, and they always considered themselves above the laws of both human and supernatural worlds. "I'm the messenger this round, not the enforcer."

"You know what they say about shooting the messenger?" Hone's teeth flashed a bluish white in the dim glow from the overhead light. He waved me through the door with a dramatic flourish of his enormous arm, looking like Chicago's most dangerous doorman.

"Things go bad..." He tapped the side of his head as I passed through the door. "You call me."

Nice to know his loyalties lay with me even though he worked that night for Nudra. Human or supernatural, times were tough. Jobs were scarce. I'd drink a gallon of holy water before hanging a sign around my neck that said, "Will work for vamps", but I didn't blame Hone for taking any job he could get. "You still treating Renee well?"

He laid a hand over his heart. "Aphrodite set me up with the perfect woman. Renee's amazing. We're talking about getting married."

Told you he was a teddy bear.

I squeezed his arm. "I'll tell Di. She'll be thrilled, and we'll both be expecting a wedding invitation."

"You got it."

When the door shut behind me, my happiness over Hone's good news fled, my confidence wavering as a sense of dread attached itself to my back like a horny teenage boy. I hadn't confronted a vampire of Nudra's level in fifty years. My last experience with one had ended in a lot of blood. Mine, his, and a couple of humans. The memory still made me sick to my stomach.

Evading inside security, I circumvented the elevators and took the stairs. My heeled boots sounded like gunshots on the concrete, echoing in the stairwell. I silenced them with a touch of my fingers, the magic coating the boot soles before I made my way to the management level where the offices were located. The *tha-wump-wump-wump* of drums and the whine of guitars vibrated over my skin. A hard-driving rock song was hard to resist, but this one, like all the songs the Chaos Demons had built their successful career on, made me want to gouge my eyes out while jumping up and down barefoot on hot coals. Thinking about Radison Beaumont in any capacity, his role as lead singer of the Chaos Demons no exception, always resulted in the same visceral response.

Big girl panties, Kali. After nearly three hundred years, I shouldn't even remember *il pistolino's* name, much less how much he'd hurt me, but hearing the music the half-human, half-chaos demon created, feeling it vibrate over my skin, was like the touch of his fingers on my body all over again. My pulse throbbed in tune with the drum and my heart squeezed with the same sharpness as when Rad had left me.

In some ways he never had. Every night, the past and Rad haunted my dreams. Only one dream, actually. The only dream I ever have. Rad kisses me, swearing his love for me against my lips as he peels off my corset. Me, heart thumping and hands shaking, swearing mine in return. But just at the moment our physical union affirms our emotional one, Rad snaps his fingers and a silver dagger appears in his hand. He shoves the blade through my heart and I wake, screaming his name. Every. Single. Night.

Which is why I worked nights instead of days. A few years

ago, I'd hoped changing my sleep and dream patterns would throw my subconscious into new territory. Didn't work. Every day, it's the same rerun. Rad, love, silver dagger.

Shows you what the heart, even one belonging to a demon, is capable of.

Shoving all thoughts about Rad into the hole of scorn I'd dug for him years ago, I refocused my thoughts. Warning or not, I was about to go head-to-head with a vampire king twice my age. You didn't get to be that old without having a few tricks up your sleeve. Best to stay focused and on my guard. My magic allowed me certain advantages with supernaturals, but vamps were in the *super* supernatural category and could match me in almost every one of them.

The hallway was carpeted, the air tinged with human excitement and the scent of the Undead—old blood and musty dirt. Under those smells, my demon nose picked up the smell of gun oil and acrid metal, probably from the demons Nudra used for security. Two sets of elevator doors were on the right, three closed office doors across from them. Framed concert posters as big as the refrigerator in my kitchen hung in between the doors. Taylor Swift, Gaga, Black-Eyed Peas. Not my taste, but big names brought in lots of cha-ching.

An elegant eighteenth-century table with a marble top dominated the end of the hall. A giant cut-glass vase filled with blood-red orchids and corkscrew willow limbs sat on top looking like a floral monster ready to grab unsuspecting visitors. Knowing Nudra's perverse sense of humor, it might well have been.

Of course, the door closest to the floral arrangement had the name Raj Nudra inscribed on it in flowing Old World script. I took a deep breath and centered myself, making sure I stayed out of reach of the willow branches.

Show no fear. Act like an equal. Those two rules had kept

me alive for centuries. I called up my power by rubbing the tip of my ring fingers against my thumbs and mentally stating my mantra, *Vengeance is mine*. A warm glow, invisible to anyone but me, suffused my body from head to toe.

Ignoring the dread leeched to my back, I flung the door open without knocking.

TWO

Raj Nudra, Vampire King of the Central United States, was waiting for me.

Seated behind a mammoth black desk, Nudra appraised me with flat reddish-brown eyes. Two of his minions flanked his sides, arms crossed, weapons in plain sight. Low-level demons, good for muscle but who couldn't think their way out of a coffin.

Nudra leaned back in his chair, long black hair falling across his shoulders as his feminine lips curved up into a smug smile. "Calina Dolce, what brings you here? Hoping to score front-row seats to the concert?" He pointed to a couple of tickets on his desk and then to a bright orange lanyard with a plastic ID protector. "Or perhaps a backstage pass? Word has it, you were once sweet—no pun intended—on Rad Beaumont. If you're looking to hook up again..." He let the suggestion hang in the air.

No one had called me Calina Dolce since I'd left Rome in 1910. Kali Sweet was more modern, more American, and it didn't remind me every day of what had happened to my family and friends. Didn't make me catch my breath in fear when someone called me by it, or make my gut cramp with guilt when I saw it written on a random envelope in the mail pile.

I shut down the bloody memory the name called up. Now wasn't the time to revisit the past. In fact, it was never a good time to visit the past. Under the circumstances, I recognized Nudra's one-two punch. He'd caught me off guard with his use of my old name and knowledge about my relationship with Rad. He had anticipated my visit and planned accordingly.

Blood-sucking bastard.

Rule one when dealing with vampires, always have a ready escape. Leaving the door open, I removed my Bridge badge from the inside pocket of my cape, regaining my composure as I did so. The weight of the shield reassured me. The way the overhead light bounced off the gold reminded me of the responsibility I held. Nudra was king of a bunch of Undead vamps. Big deal. I was a member of the Bridge Council and the best damn vengeance demon on the face of planet Earth.

I shoved my badge in his face. Sniffed the air as if he stunk —which he did—as I flicked the hood off my head. *Italian flair, check.*

Offense taken, he straightened ever so subtly as I glared down at him. "You've crossed the line with humans again, using them as blood slaves. Trafficking them across state lines and selling them to the highest bidders. That's two strikes this year. One more, and..."

"You'll send me to my coffin for a time-out?"

East Indian charm, check.

"One more, and the next time you see me, I'll have pliers in my hand."

His flat eyes sized me up, and then he *tsked*. "Such an inhumane way to remove my fangs."

What he was doing to humans wasn't? What an ass. I

fished the written warning out of my back skirt pocket and tossed it on the top of his desk. "They're not for your fangs, buddy boy." *American snarkiness, check.* "They're for your balls."

I grabbed my crotch to emphasize my point before backing toward the door. Rule number two, never, *ever* turn your back on a vamp, especially when threatening his vamphood. "I take your balls, you lose your sex drive, and with that gone, your bloodlust will decrease by ninety-nine percent. You'll stop preying on human girls and boys, and a king with no sac is nothing but a figurehead, so you can wave bye-bye to all this power you've amassed. The Council will divide up your territory among the other American vampire rulers and your fortune will be doled out to the blood slaves as restitution."

While his DNA gave his skin a warm tone, the vampire disease paled it. The result was a taupe-y gray, making it impossible to discern whether or not my words were sinking in.

Nudra leaned forward in his chair. "How surprising the Council sends you, its heart and soul, to do its dirty work." Instantly, I felt his power rising around both of us. Sexual power, blood lust, and desire, all mixed together. "I could use someone like you in my organization. Someone with your strength, your influence. That zest for humans you have fits perfectly with mine. The compensation, of course, would be exemplary. You would have everything you ever wanted."

There was only one thing I wanted, and no one, not even God Himself, could give that to me. Once a demon, always a demon.

I stopped in the doorway. "My name is Kali Sweet." Holding up two fingers, I made snipping motions. "Don't forget it or I'll tattoo it into your skin when I cut off your balls."

I moved quickly into the hallway, my nerves jangling as loud as the music in the walls, and continued to back toward the stairs. Threatening a vampire king was stupid, but running a human blood slave business was unforgivable, and if it had been me making the call, I would have staked him on the spot. The Council, however, existed for this very reason. Vigilante justice created more problems than it solved.

No surprise, Nudra's minions darted out of the office after me a few seconds later, weapons drawn. *Vampire king bluster, check.* Guns won't kill me, but bullets will slow me down. And they hurt like hell.

Adrenaline pumping, I hit the bar of the stairway's door hard with my backside to push it open. I didn't want to engage the minions, but I reached for my trusty whip— named Volante because she could fly—curled around my left arm like a bracelet, anyway.

I'd just turned to run down the stairs when I smacked into a solid wall.

Where did that come from, my brain screamed as the impact sent me backward onto my butt, my spine hitting the cold concrete wall and knocking the wind out of me. A guitar landed at my feet, making an odd twanging noise as if someone had run unskilled fingers over the strings.

A familiar, surprised-sounding voice said, "Kali?" and I looked up to see my daily nightmare standing there in the flesh.

Radison Beaumont, in too-worn jeans and a too-tight black T-shirt, gave me a slow once-over with his beautiful gold-colored eyes before his lips quirked to one side in a smile that sent my already hammering heart into overdrive. Beating like a battering ram inside my chest, it rang in my ears and drowned out the bass drum echoing in the stairwell.

My skirt had flipped up to reveal an expanse of skin between the top of my boots and my underwear and Rad's gaze lingered between my legs a second too long before lifting to meet mine. Dozens of warnings went off in my head, but damn if I could find my voice or my extensive repertoire of Italian curse words. I couldn't even find my breath. He looked a little older than the last time I'd seen him, but still perfect to me in every way. Thick black hair, a little too long and mussed, those gorgeous eyes, flawless skin and teeth. Not to mention faultless proportions. Like they'd done every other time I was in the near vicinity of him, my body, mind, and heart staged a coup. Traitors.

While it seemed like an eternity before he spoke, it was in reality only another beat of my heart. He held out one long, perfect hand and in his eyes, I saw it was more than an offer to help me to my feet. It was an olive branch. A peace treaty. "I can't believe you're here. Did you come to see m—" He caught himself, thought better of it. "Did you come for the concert?"

It would have been easy, so easy, to slip my hand into his. To forget the past under the spell of those mesmerizing eyes and allow him to help me up. Instead, I pushed myself off the ground, keeping my back against the wall, and shoved my skirt down into place.

Before I could answer, Nudra's minions barreled through the door and nearly knocked Rad and me both down the stairs. As the first one reached for me, Rad snapped his fingers and the guitar on the ground jerked upward, tripping the demon and sending him flying face first onto the top stair. Being half-chaos demon, causing trouble was as easy as breathing to Rad.

He turned on the second bodyguard, the clean ocean smell of a summer squall rising in the stairwell, and the demon held up his hands and stepped back. Smart. He must have known Rad could bring the entire building down on him if he wanted to. The demon disappeared through the door, a soft clicking sound resonating in the now silent stairwell as the latch snapped into place. My breathing sounded too loud in my ears. The demon at my feet groaned but didn't move.

As if nothing had happened, Rad turned to me, a smile tugging the skin over the fine bones of his cheeks. Two dimples sprang to life. "Your hair. It's...different."

"Seriously?" I righted my cape, which had twisted to the left when I fell. I kicked the demon on the stairs out of the way. "That's the best you've got after standing me up at the altar three hundred years ago? My hair is different?"

"It was two-hundred eighty-five years and three days ago." His golden eyes darkened and he grabbed me around the waist, jerking me up against his rock-hard body. The summer squall smell intensified. His gaze dropped to my lips and I was suddenly seventeen again. "And this is the best way I can think of to say I'm sorry."

Before I understood what he was about to do, *il pistolino* lowered his half-demon, half-human lips to mine and kissed me.

THREE

Bam, bam, bam. A pounding on my front door woke me the next morning. I'd made Neve's party, given the birthday girl the latest tech gadget on the market, laid a vengeance whooping on a lowlife trickster demon, and managed to be on the rooftop of my place in time to watch the sunrise, where I mentally cursed Rad and his lips in my native Italian, as well as American, lexicons.

Peeling open one eye, I checked the digital clock on the nightstand. Nine a.m. Who the hell would be at my door on Sunday morning at nine frickin a.m.? Anyone who knew me understood that I was DND—do not disturb—until noon at the earliest, and only then for an emergency. Especially on Sunday, my only day off.

Bam, bam, bam. Persistent, I'd give them that. Whoever stood at my front door didn't know me or didn't like me and wanted to piss me off. Either way, my day was off to a bad start. And their day? Their day was about to go straight to hell. Literally. Rule number one when dealing with a vengeance demon: don't mess with her beauty sleep. I wasn't sure what rule number two was, but the early draft had something about not kissing her after you'd ripped her heart to shreds and thinking bygones were bygones.

Even without caffeine to aid my thinking, I wasn't taking chances on who might be on my doorstep. My run-in with Nudra had him at the top of my list. Like the demon body-guards last night, not all of his minions were Undead. They could walk around in the daytime like I could, even if they preferred not to. Reaching under the bed, I removed a stake from my extensive weapons stash. Stakes are effective at chasing off everything—the living, the Undead, door-to-door salesman, bill collectors—you name it. Must be that whole Buffy thing, and really, I have to give the girl credit. Supernaturals and humans alike see a stake and run the other way.

As I trod down the marbled steps from my loft to the front foyer, I ran one hand through my tangled hair and shoved the stake into the waistband at the small of my back. At the enormous French doors, I rose on tiptoe to look through the peephole I'd installed when I moved in.

A man stood on the other side, head bowed in what looked like defeat over a drink carrier. Twin paper coffee cups, stamped with my favorite green and black logo, rested in the drink carrier in one hand. In his other hand was a box with a bright red lid. The dark hair, broad shoulders, and callused fingers caused my heart to pick up its pace. At the same time, irritation burned in my suddenly queasy stomach.

What the hell was Rad doing here? Of more concern, how did he know where I lived?

I dropped back flat-footed, the smell of full-bodied coffee with just the right amount of cream filtering through the doorway. For a second, I leaned my forehead against the solid wooden door and told myself to ignore him and go back to bed.

Pretend I wasn't there. Hope he was defeated enough never to come back.

Bam, bam, bam.

Startled, I jumped back, hand flying to the spot over my heart. Persistent SOB. No wonder the pounding sounded so loud. He wasn't knocking on the door with his fist, he was kicking it with a booted foot.

No defeat there. Rad had always loved a challenge, and right now that's what I represented. He wasn't going to give up.

Hell's blood. Just what I needed—Rad Beaumont deciding I was his new challenge.

The deadbolt made a loud *thunk* as I slid it back. Rad's head snapped up, face bright with expectation as I swung the door open. Both dimples locked in as he smiled so big, he looked like a frickin lottery winner.

I fingered the stake, still hidden in my waistband. *You're about to win the lottery all right, buddy boy, but not the one you think.*

That smile of his could melt icebergs. My lips tingled, remembering his kiss in the stairwell. It had been soft and sweet, the way a make-up kiss should be, and I'd had trouble remembering my name at one point.

But I'd ended it with a flick of my whip to his ankles, jerking him off his feet before walking away. His voice, calling me back, had echoed down the stairs after me and followed me the rest of the night, trailing its way into my damn dreams, along with him and his silver dagger.

I pursed my traitorous lips. "What do you want, Rad?"

If he was surprised by my Goth Hello Kitty pajamas or my bed-head appearance, he didn't show it. "How is it you live on consecrated ground?"

My loft sat inside an old abandoned church that yearned to be a castle. The great hall was oversized and had high ceilings for effect that echoed horribly. The layout here was rectangular, three times as long as it was wide. The windows were slim but tall, allowing a generous amount of natural light. The hearth was large enough to roast a person in, standing up.

A big showdown between good and evil had happened in this church around the time of the Civil War. Evil had won, the place had been abandoned, and the lone ground still consecrated was the sanctuary, which I steered clear of. Now, the only evil on the premises was me, and I was evil in that nice-demon sort of way. "I'm special."

Rad gave me a look that told me he knew I was lying, but wouldn't pursue the subject further. He held out his offerings. "Sorry about last night. You... surprised me. I brought coffee in hopes we could talk, you know, about...stuff."

Right. *Stuff*. Not going there, no way, no how. "What's in the red box?" I was hoping it was chocolates. Or pastries. Something good to go with the coffee.

"Kings in the Corner. It's a card game like we used to play at Court. The one you liked so much."

The Italian Court in the heart of the Roman Empire. I hadn't thought about that in centuries. An unbidden memory of Rad in his scarlet and black court clothes and jaunty French hat flitted across my mind. He'd been the scandal of the Queen's entire inner circle when he'd arrived as the French ambassador, flirting tirelessly with all of us. He'd taught me a dozen different ways to cheat at cards, and even though I refused to cheat my friends, I admired his ability to cheat my court enemies. It wasn't the only thing I'd admired about him.

Along with his ability to cheat at cards and get away with it, he'd cheated me out of the life I'd dreamed about. Reaching out, I snagged one of the coffees, raised it in salute, and slammed the door in his face.

For the next five days, he showed up each morning with

two coffees and some sort of gift. One day it was a vampire hunter video game he thought I would like, then a puzzle depicting the coast of Italy. On Saturday, he offered me tickets to his Milwaukee concert that night. Each morning, I took the coffee and shut the door in his face.

To my horror, I started anticipating his knock. I told myself it was only because I was determined to be more bullheaded, and more resolute and dogged than he was. I wasn't one to play games, but this one became addictive and I found myself looking forward to our next sparring match as well as a *gigante* cup of coffee hand-delivered to my door.

Di, my best friend and traitor *straordinario*, informed him about my work/sleep schedule and he'd been coming later every day, so by the time the next Sunday afternoon rolled around and he hadn't shown up, I wasn't concerned. He'd probably been up all night after the concert and then had the bus trip back to Chicago. Maybe getting a taste of his own medicine would cure him of waking me up before two p.m.

It was four when I finally heard a knock. A part of me was relieved. He'd finally come. And that's when I knew, this had to stop. Rad was a cheat, a liar, and a heartbreaker. Hadn't I learned my lesson the first time?

I peered through the peephole, disgusted with myself for letting him get a toehold in my life again. But it wasn't Rad on the step, it was Di and her latest boyfriend, a young grad student from one of the universities. She was dressed in jeans and a cute double-breasted jacket. Her boyfriend was dressed like a Harvard professor.

I opened the door. "Hey, what are you two doing here?"

Aphrodite tugged the professor-wannabe across the threshold. "We're going antiquing at Navy Pier. There's a Halloween theme this weekend. Want to come?"

Professor stared blankly at the wall, obviously not interested in my company. The Goddess of Love had a fear of commitment and men came and went like a boyfriend version of Netflix. This was only the second time I'd seen him with Di, and like most of her boy toys, the professor didn't like me.

Whatever. "Wow, that sounds like fun, but I have..." I fell back on my usual excuse for being antisocial, "Bridge business to take care of this afternoon."

Di studied me for a second. "Rad hasn't shown up yet, has he?"

Definitely had to stop playing his stupid game. "Rad who?" Without waiting for her usual tirade about my lack of a love life, I shoved her and the professor out the door. "Go, enjoy antiquing. I'll see you tomorrow at work."

Shutting the door on her protests, I leaned against it, lost in thoughts of Rad. So stupid to let him get back under my skin and mess with my head. Sloppy of me. And sloppy was one thing I couldn't afford. I'd learned that the night my family died at the hands of The Slayers, the Roman Church's demon hunters.

The Slayers' official name was a bastardized Latin term, The Noctifectors. A literal translation had to do with night and bringers of night (or death in this case). Most supernaturals simplified Noctifector to Noct and American supers called them The Slayers, again probably because of Buffy.

The biggest reason I'd been so effective at staying alive all these years, even with the Noctifectors slaying supernaturals all around me, was because I didn't do sloppy. I didn't let anyone, especially not Rad Beaumont, get under my skin.

After another minute of berating myself, I started back to my living area to watch TV and stew. Two steps from the door, a knock, hard and persistent, stopped me in my tracks.

Rad.

Knowing it was a bad idea, I threw the door open anyway,

ready to tell him to take a long hike off Navy Pier, but again, it wasn't *il pistolino* waiting for me on the stoop with that iceberg-melting grin on his face.

Two men, dressed in black from head to toe, filled the entryway, necks thick as the church bell tower's support beams, bodies massive as the benches inside the sanctuary.

The metallic vinegar stench filled my nose. Mercs—demon mercenaries. I jerked back fast, ready to slam the door and run for my weapons stash. Logic, however, took over.

Mercenaries didn't come to the front door in daylight. They didn't knock politely and stand at relaxed attention on your front stoop. Maybe they were out of work and looking for me to hire them. I tried not to freak, but my pulse flipped the bird at logic and raced as if I were sprinting. "Can I help you?"

The front merc flashed a strained smile. He held a flashlight in his right hand and thumped it against his leg as if bored or striving for patience. "King Nudra requests your presence tonight at his home."

There was so much wrong with this request, it took my brain two seconds longer than it should have to backtrack to the flashlight. I reached for the stake out of habit and realized I didn't have it.

Merde.

Still, there was no reason to panic. The mercs were playing nice.

I touched a ring finger to one of my thumbs, ready to raise my defensive powers, anyway. I never play nice when dealing with bloodsuckers who violate Bridge law. "Well, you can tell Nudra to pack sand."

I started to shut the door when Merc No. 1 jammed his free hand against it. Instantly, my magic formed a protective shield around me, but he raised the flashlight and a bright arc of silver light danced between two prongs on the end of it.

Not a flashlight. Stun gun.

Correction, stun *baton*. "He said you'd be difficult."

A crackling noise filled the air and a million volts of specialized silver electricity hit me at once, knocking me ass over hellhounds to the ground. Not even my protection magic could repel that. Pain seared my nerve endings, muscles contracting into a solid, rigid mass. My eyes rolled up in my head and my brain hula danced inside my skull. The last cognizant thought I had wasn't about Nudra or mercs or dying at the hands of a vampire king.

My last thought before I passed out was, *Where the hell is Rad?*

FOUR

When I woke, my brain cells were still scrambled and it took several minutes for them to come online. Even then, I wasn't sure they hadn't sustained permanent damage from the stun baton's silver wattage, because for some reason, they were convinced I was in an eighteenth-century torture chamber.

I took inventory again. Dim light from sconces bolted to stone walls. Check. Assorted chains, whips, and saws hanging from hooks. Check. The coppery smell of dried blood and the sharp smell of disinfectant. Under both, the lingering taint of fear.

Check and check.

A stainless steel surgical tray, draped with a white cloth, stood beside me.

Yep, it had been a while since I'd been in one, but this was straight out of my Old World past. The shelves lined with quart jars of blood were a nice touch, though. Queen Maria would have been impressed.

Not a big fan of torture, nausea cramped my stomach. I

tried to move, but my body—from forehead to ankles—was belted to a bumpy, wooden table by leather straps. The rough leather chafed my skin and the wood, bulging and rippling underneath me, bruised it. Cool, damp air sucked at the visible skin between the straps, so while I couldn't lift my head to look down at myself, I surmised I was naked.

Even my fingers were individually secured to the table, splayed apart so I couldn't touch any of them together. No touch, no magic.

No way out.

Nudra.

This wasn't bluster anymore, this was the real deal, and unless he'd transported me back to Rome or some other ancient location, I had to be in his house. Under the other smells, I detected the scent of lawn chemicals. Green grass and a well-cared-for lawn equaled suburbia. Nudra's residence was listed on the Council's file as downtown Chicago. Maybe my brain cells *were* fried, or Nudra was even kinkier than I thought. A vamp king and lawn chemicals. Too weird.

On my checklist for the torture chamber, I could have checked off the creaky door when the man in question, or vamp in this case, entered the room. From what I could see from the corner of my eye, his conservative Madhouse suit had been traded in for a red silk shirt and harem pants.

Harem pants. The sight was so unsettling, that I shut my eyes against it.

"Playing possum, Calina? That's beneath you."

Forcing my chin to move against the strap holding it, I told him to suck off and then screw himself in Italian. It was less effective without the hand gestures. "Kidnapping a Council employee violates Code 6A, Section Two of the Bridge Mandates. Punishment is imprisonment."

He chuckled and I heard the rattle of stainless steel—or was it silver?—surgical implements near my head. I cracked open one eye to see if he was doing what I thought he was doing and sure enough, I wished I hadn't looked.

In one hand, he held a silver dagger similar to the one in my dreams of Rad, turning it over and over to catch the scant light from the nearest wall sconce. "I asked you nicely to join me and you refused. Now, I'm afraid, I can't be nice anymore." He smiled, evil intent evident, as he placed the tip of the knife at the outside corner of my left eye. A fierce burning took up residence where it touched my skin and I forced myself not to react. "Unless you've had a change of heart?"

Completely immobile, unable to use my powers, and staring at a silver dagger that could do substantial permanent and painful damage to me...the logical side of my mind thought it prudent to reconsider his offer. Since it was Sunday, no one would notice me missing and no one would come looking for me any time soon, either. What to do...what to do...

Hmm, maybe he didn't understand Italian. "Fuck you."

He removed the dagger and the repulsive reek of burned skin filled my nose. The demon inside me woke at the pain, arching against it. I coughed and shoved her back behind the bars I'd imprisoned her with.

But Nudra skimmed the sharp tip down the side of my neck, trailing a stinging sensation with it, and my demon's claws came out. "Once you have blood slaves, you'll change your mind. You'll wish you had come to me sooner."

Blood slaves? Me? Nudra had been sniffing too many lawn chemicals. "I'm not a vamp. I'm a demon. We don't use blood slaves and I would never take one even if we did." The demon inside me disagreed, but I ignored her. "What you do to humans is horrific. You're an atrocity. I should have staked you when I had the chance."

The silver tip sank into my neck, drawing blood and Nudra

licked his lips. Warm blood rolled down the side of my neck and onto the table. The demon I was struggling to subdue roared her anger. "A blood slave will give you what you want. The ability to feel what humans feel. To experience what they experience. That connection...it's the closest you'll ever come to being one of them."

A self-defense mechanism, my blood was repulsive to other supernaturals as well as humans. "A human would have to drink my blood to become my slave, and my blood smells and tastes like gasoline to them."

The dagger moved lower to my exposed stomach and cut me again. Deeper this time, causing me to flinch even though I had steeled myself not to. He laughed as if proud of himself. My demon laughed too. Game on. "Not anymore. I injected you with some of my blood. My blood." He pounded a fist on his chest. "You taste like me now, my dear sweet demon. Humans can't resist you. Once they've tasted your blood, they'll be addicted."

My world jumped the shark, as they say, and everything inside me went very still. Including my demon. This was bad —the kind of bad you don't recover from. Only a few supes can create blood slaves—vampires and a few with top-shelf blood, like archdemons and such, and it generally requires a few installments over time. Demons don't want, nor need slaves and find them to be a nuisance. If we want blood, we kill the human and drink our fill. Vampires are a whole other story.

The room swam in front of me. My career with the Council, my life as an enforcer, was over. Everything I'd worked so hard for was gone.

The door to the room creaked, followed by the shuffle of feet. Once again I was afraid to look but compelled to anyway. An older woman and a young man stood inside the door, eyes locked on me. Locked on my blood. Their nostrils flared and I swore under my breath.

Humans.

Magic tingled in the air around them, but it was weak. Barely a blip on my internal radar. They'd messed with it, but it didn't live inside them like it did me and the Undead vamp king.

Nudra drew the knife over my hip and sliced down my inner thigh. I locked my lips together, refusing to give voice to my internal scream. My demon spun in her cage, but there was no letting her out now. She didn't discriminate between supernaturals and humans. If I let her take over, the humans would die along with Nudra. Everyone in a two-block radius would be turned into dog food as well.

Seeming satisfied with his work, Nudra motioned the others over. "Victoria, Arman, this is your new mistress, Calina Dolce. Drink her blood and it will give you the power you desire."

The older the demon, the more potent the blood. The older the vamp, the more controlling. My blood was powerful on its own. Another reason it was nauseating to any creature who tried to ingest it. A demon with that much power was a nuclear bomb times ten. Mixed with Nudra's vamp blood, it was twice as potent, maybe ten times more so since we were both so old.

The woman slid in between me and Nudra to bend her head over my stomach. Nudra stroked her hair as her lips touched my skin.

"No!" I yelled, but she didn't stop and the vampire king looked down on me with half-closed eyes as if her drinking my blood excited him.

"Victoria is head of the Satrina Arcanum." He drew a deep breath and let it out slowly. In his office, I'd felt his power rising. This time it was stronger, flooding my senses with a cloying need. "She desires to summon hell's Queen to come forward and walk the Earth again.'

Satrina was another name for Lilith, Hell's Queen and the mother of demons. In essence, she was my mother. As old as the Earth, older than any creature I'd encountered. She was Adam's first wife but had refused to obey him, so God threw her out of Eden and cursed her womb so she would never bear human children. She bore demons instead.

And while I may have admired her audacity, I sure as shit didn't want her walking the Earth again, mother or not.

Arman, more boy than man, met my gaze before he leaned down to kiss my neck. Soft lips, cool as spring water, touched my burning hot skin. He drew back for an instant, licked his bloody lips, and smiled at me. Inside me, my demon smiled back. His eyes were cat eyes, greenish-gold and titled up at the corners. So young. So stupid.

I fought against the leather straps restraining my forehead and chin. "Whatever Nudra told you, it's not true. Whatever he promised, it'll never happen." The argument was useless. Arman dipped his head for a second helping of the Kali liquid dinner special.

As if I'd been stunned by the merc's baton a second time, my body went rigid from the simultaneous assault of him and Victoria feeding off me. A lightheadedness washed over me, and with it, a strange sense of euphoria, accomplishment, and success.

Victoria and Arman's feelings were now my feelings. Nudra's as well. He was drawing emotion from the mix of our bloods. Drawing power. I glanced at his face, and sure enough, his eyes were closed in vampire ecstasy.

Feeling my hateful gaze on him, he opened his eyes. "Arman wishes to control his werecat side." He reached across Victoria to touch the kid's hair.

"Were...cat?" My voice shook, partially from rage and partially from the incredible feel of wild, undisciplined, and ferocious human emotions electrifying every organ, every cell inside me.

"Cheetah. Anything that crosses his path triggers his animalistic nature. He runs it down and attacks. Can't live among humans because he can't control the animal inside. With your blood, he will."

I knew all about controlling the animal—or in my case, demon—inside. I felt for the kid, but drinking my blood wasn't the answer to his problem.

No, no, no. I struggled once more against the bonds, the table under me seeming to come to life and drive the wooden lumps and bulges deeper into my skin and muscles. With sudden clarity, I realized the table was made of the wicked corkscrew willow branches like the ones in the vase outside Nudra's office.

Black dots danced in front of my vision. A dull roar filled my ears. I started babbling and turned to my foul-language life preserver in an attempt not to blackout. Nudra chuckled, clearly amused.

The creaky door sound interrupted. A voice said, "Master, there's been a security breach on the south wall."

My brain yelled, *yes,* and did a fist pump. Maybe someone had figured out I'd been kidnapped. Hell, at that point, I'd take a frickin raccoon tripping a security wire just to give me a minute to think without Nudra getting off on me.

The vamp king grabbed Vicky and Arman by the back of their necks, breaking their holds on me and shoving them toward the door and the minion standing there. "Take them to the guest wing and lock them in one of the bedrooms."

Before they disappeared, he looked me over like a prized pet. Then he leaned over and licked blood from the inside of my thigh. Disgust rocked me from head to toe. I hated him more in that moment than I'd ever hated another supernatural.

His flat eyes now shone with lust and excitement. "With my blood now in your veins, you belong to me. You're my blood slave, just like Victoria and Arman are yours. Which means we have much yet to share."

Blood bonds couldn't be broken unless the master or slave died. There weren't enough curses or hand gestures in the world to convey what I wanted to say to him. I opted for a statement of fact. "I will kill you before this day is over."

"How very Hollywood of you." He wagged a skinny finger. "But I'm your master now, my little vengeance demon. Remember?"

He sauntered out, confident in his Undead world, and I hated him all the more. I was now a vampire king's bitch. That would certainly score points with the Council. How had I let Nudra get the jump on me? I was always careful, especially with vamps because they were so unpredictable. This time, though, I'd blown it, and it was all because I'd been so eager to see Rad.

Damn him all to hell.

Whether from Nudra's blood coursing through my veins, the loss of my own blood from Vicky and Arman's dinner feast, or the sheer loathing I had for myself, my vision became a blur of black dots again.

Fight it, I told myself, but control over my body drained away with every drip of my blood onto the table. I forced words to form on my tongue. "Help me," I called out, in case the raccoon was nearby.

The only sound was the echo of my voice back at me. I closed my eyes and the black dots took me under.

FIVE

"Kali. *Ka*-li."

Someone was shaking my shoulders. I cracked an eye open and Rad's face swam into view. He was disheveled, clothes caked with mud, face streaked with dirt, hair wet and starting to curl at the ends.

Admittedly, he'd never looked better.

"What..." My lips were dry and stuck together. I wetted them. "How'd you find me?"

"Saw a black SUV speeding away from the church when I showed up. Took me a minute to figure out you'd been kidnapped. I tried to follow, but they lost me outside of Oak Park. I had to track down your precious Council and get them to help me locate you."

"Oak Park? Where are we?"

"Naperville. Nudra's compound. You wouldn't believe this place." He looked me over and grimaced. "You're supposed to keep that red stuff on the inside, you know."

Il saccente. Smart ass. "No shit, Captain Obvious. Unstrap me."

He did and never once ogled body parts he shouldn't, which I appreciated because I was so out of it, he could have groped me and I wouldn't have lifted a finger. He cut the straps with the silver dagger, then stuck it in his back pocket. Racked with a bone-deep cold, my body shook violently as he assisted me in sitting up.

Removing his shirt, he slid it over my head and worked my arms through the sleeves, my limbs as floppy and weak as a string puppet. The shirt was wet and muddy but warm with his body heat. The salty smell of a warm ocean enveloped me.

Best. Shirt. Ever.

When I pushed off the table, my knees buckled and I went down. Rad caught me before I hit the stone floor. "Not so fast there, hot shot."

"Is the Council here?"

"They sent me ahead to confirm you were being held against your will. I'll call them."

"Forget it." I brushed hair out of my eyes with shaking fingers, and though it killed me to do it, I wrapped my arms around his neck. I needed to get my wits about me before I faced the Council. "Just get me out of here."

He lifted me with ease, securing his arms under my shoulders and the backs of my knees. We were headed for the door when we heard shouts outside and the handle turned. Rad snapped his fingers, sending the ancient deadbolt into place and jamming the door.

Jostling me as he ran to the opposite end of the chamber, he headed toward a raised wooden platform with a coffin in the center. Dim light reflected off the top of the highly polished black lid of the coffin. Blood-red satin curtains on the wall behind it created the illusion of a dramatic headboard. Surely Nudra didn't sleep here, did he?

"What are you doing?"

Rad set me on the floor, one arm around my waist to steady me. "Hiding." He lifted the coffin lid. White satin and fresh grave dirt sat inside. "Get in."

Normally, the very idea would have sent me screaming in the other direction. Delirious, I laughed out loud instead. The doorknob rattled behind us. "Why don't you snap your fingers and blow the roof off or create a hole in the wall? We need to get out of here?"

With one quick movement, he picked me up and tossed me into the coffin. The smell of moldy dirt hit my nose. Gross! Rad shook his head. "Already tried. Nudra's got some kind of anti-magic ward on the roof and walls. All the beams and foundation. It's tamper-proof."

He launched himself into the coffin, pinning me up against the satin before dropping the lid. Dark and musty, it smelled like Nudra. Rad had me weak and at his mercy with that damn silver dagger in his pocket. My body shook harder.

"Shit, Kali," he whispered in my ear. My back was to his front and he spooned his body against mine. His arms went around me, solid and reassuring.

"I can't help it," I whispered back. "Nudra injected me with his blood. I'm having a bad reaction."

"He did *what*?" Rad ground his teeth, jaw working against my skull behind my left ear. "I'll kill him."

"If anyone gets to kill him..." My teeth chattered hard. "It's me."

Rad gave me a squeeze and sighed. "So when did you get the white streaks?"

We were lying in a vamp's coffin, trying to avoid bodily harm, and he wanted to revisit the subject of my hair. Nudra wasn't the only one I was going to kill as soon as I got my strength back. "Two-hundred eighty-five years and..." I counted up the days. At least my brain wasn't fried if I could still count. "Nine days ago."

He turned my body, maneuvering me to face him. Not an easy job considering our close confines and my dead weight. "You bleached your hair because of me?"

I couldn't hear anything outside the coffin, but something told me that wasn't necessarily a good thing. "I didn't bleach anything. It just...happened." The morning after my first Rad nightmare to be exact. "On its own."

That shut him up.

Or something else did. He leaned down, sniffed my neck where blood still oozed from the knife wound, and then without warning, he nuzzled my skin. An arc of white-hot electricity danced between our chests. Literally. It lit up the inside of the coffin, illuminating Rad's naked and well-defined chest and bouncing off the handle of the knife sticking out of his back pocket. The light reflected in his eyes, and I saw lust, deep and dangerous, spark to life. "Man, you smell good."

Oh, shit. He was half-human. "Rad, whatever you do, do not—"

Too late, he licked my skin.

SIX

Average shelf life for demons is not much longer than it is for humans. Not because we're susceptible to disease and old age, but because we live with the seven deadly sins. You know, gluttony, pride, lust. While humans can, and do, send themselves to hell for dabbling with sin, demons *are* the sin. Each of us embodies at least one. It's in our DNA. We can't escape it. Humans have the opportunity to overcome their vice and make it to heaven. Demons, not so much.

The moment Rad's lips touched my neck, I tried to pull away from him. I did. But the confines of the coffin wouldn't allow it. The instant my blood touched his lips, he was a goner.

Bigger problem? So was I.

Never mind I already had two blood slaves, as his tongue licked the side of my neck, the energy sparking between us exploded into a colorful light show of lust so bright, that I knew the entire coffin had to be glowing. We were sure to get busted, but I didn't much care at the moment. Inside my body, it was the same. Rainbows, unicorns, puppies—the best orgasm I'd ever experienced.

One after another, sensations exploded under my skin. Emotions tore through my chest with an intensity that left me shaking all over again. I felt what Rad felt and it was joyful, intoxicating chaos.

Happiness, excitement, lust...

Love.

Those last two were killers. One playing with my heart, the other my body, and neither of which I had an ounce of control over. A concentrated warmth flooded my chest and the light seeping under my lids intensified with it. For half a second, with Rad holding me close and his lips trailing fire over my skin, I swear I experienced heaven.

And then he blew it all to hell.

His lips nuzzled my ear. "Kali, I need to tell you something."

Hell's blood. Rad was about to brush against a pain much too raw to discuss in an evil vamp's coffin. Too deep to discuss, period. "Not. Now." *Come back,* I mentally called to the light and the warmth. *Please, come back.*

No dice. Heaven was gone.

"This is important. About us and what happened...before." He licked my neck again. "Damn, you taste so good. Smell good too. Like chocolate pastries and vanilla ice cream."

I'm so *not* vanilla ice cream. Jeez. "That's the blood, Rad. I'm infected, remember? The human in you is now addicted to..." I swallowed hard. "Me."

The coffin lid flew up and Nudra, angry but smug at finding our hiding place, pointed a bright silver sword at my neck. "How charming. Radison Beaumont and Calina Dolce making out in my coffin." His gaze locked with Rad's. "She is a prize, isn't she? I can't wait to have her alone myself."

Rad's free hand moved but Nudra pinned the point of the sword against my heart. "Snap those fingers and she dies."

He kept his gaze on Rad but spoke to me. "Get up, my dear."

The sword point bit into my skin through the shirt. I pushed against Rad's chest, signaling him to stay put. Finagling my other hand hidden behind my backside, I touched my fingers together. Nothing. No magic anywhere.

No wooden stakes either. Ugly, here we come.

Nudra took my hand, guiding me out of the coffin. All the while, he kept the sword trained over my heart and his gaze locked on Rad.

There was only one thing to do. I fake-fell over the side of the coffin, swiping the silver knife from Rad's pocket. Nudra's sword drooped for a second as he automatically tried to stabilize me.

Shifting my weight, I fell into him, and having mastered Bambi eyes long before Disney did, I gave him my best innocent look. "I'm so weak."

"Of course you are. The new blood slaves have drained you. You need more of my blood to make you strong again."

"I need your blood, all right." With one swift motion, I stabbed the vamp king in his heart with the dagger. Wouldn't kill him, but it startled him enough, I had time to yell, "Stake!" at Rad.

He snapped his fingers, causing the willow torture table to fly into a million curly pieces. Lucky for us, Nudra's anti-magic spell was only on the house's structure, not its contents. Solid branches flew through the air, and the moment I snagged one, the warm sensation came flooding back to my chest.

Nudra swung the sword at my neck. I ducked, dragging the dagger down with me and cutting him from heart to belly button. His eyes went wide and he stumbled backward, blood and guts spilling a trail. The smell of his blood filled my nose.

One good thing about not being human? Vamp blood reeks.

The sword sailed toward my head. Too late, I threw up an arm, knowing I would lose it, but thinking in that split second it was better than losing my head.

Nothing hit me. Rad flew out of the coffin, blocking the sword before it made contact. It clattered on the stone floor, Nudra's face showing fear for the first time. "I'm your master, sweet Calina Dolce. You cannot murder me."

Even when nauseated, drained of blood, and wearing nothing but a wet, muddy T-shirt, I still have standards. "Nudra, by the order of the Bridge Council, I hereby..."

With vamp speed, he swept my legs with his. I fell hard, but my aim was true. I nailed him with the willow stake square in his already bleeding heart.

Just before he went poof, I smiled into his astonished vamp eyes. "My name is Kali Sweet and I'm nobody's blood slave."

Nudra disintegrated into a pile of ashes and the stake bounced to the floor.

Both of us breathing hard, Rad and I looked at each other. "We make a good team," he said, reaching down to help me up.

"We are *not* a team."

I swayed on my feet, adrenaline leaving as fast as it came. He swung me up into his arms, ignoring my weak protests. "The band and I are throwing a Halloween party tomorrow night downtown at the Blackstone." His lips quirked and it was a good thing no icebergs were in the near vicinity or I would have drowned. "Wanna come?"

I blame Nudra's blood for what happened next. The demon inside me purred. The warm sensation in my chest intensified, and maybe, just maybe, the polar icecap there melted a teeny, tiny bit.

But not that much. "No."

Rad looked pained. "Kali. Please."

I shook my head but then laid it against his naked chest.

Damn, but he smelled good. Not in that weird blood slave way, or even in his chaos demon manner, but in a nice warm, human male way. "Just take me home, Rad."

He did. And the next day, he brought me coffee. Nothing else. Just coffee. Rang the doorbell, left it on the doorstep.

I was due at the Bridge office at seven that evening to give them my report on Nudra. Forget I'd gone against orders and killed a vamp king, once they found out I had three blood slaves, I was doomed. So on the drive through downtown to the Bridge office, I took a detour.

The party was in full swing on the tenth floor outdoor terrace of the Blackstone, costumes as plentiful as beer and groupies. For once, my short skirt, thigh-high boots, and red cape looked completely appropriate. Hone and Renee waved at me from the bar while Chaos Demons' music filled the air.

I located Rad, standing alone on the edge of the terrace, staring out over the city. I sidled up to him, hoping the city lights and dark expanse of the lake would calm my racing heart.

They didn't.

He gave me a goofy grin and the icecap heart inside me melted a fraction more. "You came."

I shrugged, trying for nonchalance. "The lesser of two evils."

He grabbed a nearby guitar and held it up like a peace offering. "Want to hear the song I'm working on?"

At that moment, I wanted nothing more than to feel Rad's music ripple across my skin. I moved closer to pick up the smell of warm, human male. It was there and so was that look in his eyes. Hunger, passion, desire.

Peace offerings. More dangerous than a wooden stake any day.

"Yeah," I said, wild human emotion clogging my throat. "I'd love to."

We left the party in full swing, a couple of groupies giving me jealous glares. Inside Rad's suite on the top floor a minute later, I stood on the balcony, the breeze from the lake raising gooseflesh under my clothes. What was I doing here?

Being sloppy again, that's what.

The tinkle of glass sounded behind me. The suite was big, open, and glamorous. Thick carpet, high thread-count sheets, fancy furniture, and a complete bar. You couldn't get more North Side if you tried.

I moseyed back into the living area and Rad handed me a flute of champagne. The bubbles tickled my nose as I sipped. He was pretending not to watch me as I gave myself a tour of the suite, ending once again at the balcony. The air temp was dropping and the sounds of the party echoed through the night. I closed the glass doors with slow, deliberate movements before I turned to find Rad, guitar in hand, standing a few feet away. He was no longer pretending he wasn't watching me.

He reached for my hand and led me to the couch. There he took the glass out of my hand and set it on the enormous glass coffee table. He tugged the cape off my shoulders, his fingers hesitating ever so slightly when they grazed my neck. His gaze slid to my left eye where Nudra had laid his silver dagger against my skin, burning it. "How are your cuts?"

Demons heal fast. The dagger, being pure silver, had left some damage though. I had a triangular scar, silvery like its source at the corner of my eye. A long slender scar on the inside of my thigh. The other cuts weren't as deep and had already healed, leaving thread-like silver lines behind. "Almost gone."

"What did you tell the Council?"

Our eyes met. Because he was my blood slave, I could see his bone-deep desire to take my blood shining in his eyes. I could feel his craving, as palpable as my own, coursing through me. His need called to my blood, his emotions entangling themselves with mine, and my own desire kicked low in my stomach. My pulse jumped. "Nothing. Yet."

His hands slid under the cape at my shoulders, sliding the red garment down my arms and letting it linger around my waist to keep me close to him. "I could go with you, talk to the Council. Tell them how I found you, what I witnessed. They won't blame you, K. It's not your fault, what Nudra did."

I shuddered at his touch. At his too-close body and the need rolling off of it. The way he called me K like he'd done during intimate moments three hundred years ago.

Career, Kali. Focus. "I got sloppy. The Council doesn't allow sloppy."

The blood lust was evident on his face but so was pure old human desire. He wanted to kiss me. Wanted to wipe away my disgust with myself and my fear of facing the Council. Instead, he tossed my cape on the end of the couch and handed me the champagne. "Everyone makes mistakes. They'd be stupid to cut you off for this."

Not stupid. Smart. I was in violation of six different Bridge laws. Since I was purposely blowing off my official debriefing, make that seven.

Focusing on my job was the last thing I wanted to do even if it kept me from jumping Rad right then and there. "Are you going to play me that song or not?"

I sat on the couch. Rad sat on the coffee table. I expected something hard and fast, but as he strummed his fingers across the strings, a soft melody rose from the guitar, so sad it made my eyes sting with tears.

The music wove invisible threads around me, flowing over my skin, filling my senses. I closed my eyes and rode the swells his fingers produced as he walked them up and down the chords. A throbbing set up camp between my thighs.

Rad sang softly, his deep baritone heating my blood while

the image of his fingers touching the strings, selecting the just-right notes to harmonize with his words, floated under my eyelids.

Listen to my music
Listen to my heart
I finally found my way
No words of mine can ever say
How much I miss you...

More fingerwork, chords pouring out from under them the way he'd played my body once. I rested my head on the couch, the throbbing between my legs building with the music. I wanted him, with all his humanness and creativity. Wanted his music inside me as well as out. Knowing I was a screw-up to let him worm his way back into my life and yet wanting nothing more than to feel him moving, hard and needy, against me. To feel his lips on my throat, his fingers making music with pieces of my body.

After all this time
After all the wrongs
I still care...
Listen to my music
Listen to its heart
Open yours, if you dare

I dared all right. Not opening my heart, because I was too cold after all these years to believe I even had a heart anymore. But lowering my defenses enough to let him in.

Just for tonight. I need to forget what a screw-up I am.

The last of the guitar notes faded away. I opened my eyes. Rad was looking down at the guitar, eyes hidden under his dark lashes as he avoided my eyes. With all his success, was he still afraid of criticism? Or was he afraid I'd slap his face? Throw my champagne on him, and in effect, throw his song and its apology, back at him?

What I was about to do was damning, but then I was already damned. The demon inside me hummed. Easing forward, I took the guitar from his hands, set it aside, and replaced it with my own hands, sliding them together with his and interlocking our fingers. His gaze rose up my thighs, lingered on my breasts. Climbed to my neck.

I crawled into his lap, hating myself for being so weak against my lust, but not caring.

For half a second, our eyes met, hands still clasped. Then Rad leaned his face into mine, stretching our arms out wide, and kissed me.

Slow and erotic, the kiss rocked me. He wanted me, not just my blood, and he wasn't about to rush this, even though we'd been apart for nearly three centuries. His emotions fueled mine, but mine were in a bigger hurry.

So long. It had been so damn long. I parted my lips and whimpered into this mouth, a primal begging. *More.* I needed more.

Rad tensed at my whimper. No longer willing or able to draw the seduction out, his mouth firmed on mine, forcing my lips farther apart. He released my hands, driving one of his into my hair, the other pressing against my lower back and dragging me against his broad chest. My breasts, already heavy with desire, flattened against him and it was his turn to moan.

Grasping my ass, he stood, carrying me while his lips continued to assault mine. I wrapped my arms around his neck, legs around his waist, oblivious to where we were going but knowing it was his bedroom.

Once there, he deposited me on the edge of the king-size bed. Covered in an artistic graphic black and red patterned duvet, the soft satin was cool against my thighs. Rad kneeled between my legs, flipping my skirt out of the way and running his tongue just above the top of my boot across my healing scar.

I shuddered and sank my fingers in his hair, urging him to do more. He obliged, finding the sweet spot hidden under my panties and kissing me there, his warm breath and lips scorching me through the satin material.

I wanted my panties off. I wanted everything off. Pushing him back, I told him so. "Take off your clothes."

He kissed me once, twice, three times, before standing. As I unhooked my skirt and slid it and my panties off my hips, he lifted his T-shirt over his head.

Muscles flexed. Behind him, a mirror on a dresser reflected his well-toned upper body. Mm mm. There was a lot there to admire.

But as my eyes took it all in, there was also something there that stopped my heart cold.

A tattoo between his shoulder blades. A dagger, the three points of the hilt forming an elaborate cross with the blade. A rune I'd known all my life. A rune that terrified me.

Noctifector.

Hell's blood.

I backed up, hitting the bed and stumbling away from him, running into the nightstand with the back of my legs.

Rad dropped his shirt to the floor. "K, what's the matter?"

Stunned beyond words, I pointed to the mirror. Muscles undulated under the Noctifector dagger as he shifted to follow my finger. "You're...you're a..."

He caught sight of himself, flinched, and slowly swung his gaze back to mine. "It's not what it looks like. I swear."

It was exactly what it looked like. He'd joined the specially trained and highly secret unit of the Roman Catholic Church's police force. "How could you?" I whispered. "You're half demon."

He stepped toward me and I cursed myself for leaving my cape and its weapons in the other room. Volante was inside the cape too—one of the rare occasions I wasn't wearing her on my arm. The only weapon at my disposal was a lamp. Unfortunately, it was bolted to the wall.

"It was a long time ago." He took a step toward me. "I didn't have any choice."

"Don't come any closer." I raised my hand in a stop gesture and sidestepped the nightstand. From the corner of my eye, I calculated my odds of clearing the bedroom doorway before he grabbed me. My skirt and panties were on the floor, but leaving them behind would be a small sacrifice to saving my life. "Nice, Radison. You're more deceitful and calculating than I imagined. What was this? One last fling before you killed me?"

He held a hand out, much like mine, only in a way meant to calm me. "You've got it all wrong, K. Let me explain."

We were way beyond explanations. I touched my ring fingers and thumbs together, raising my protective magic. "What is there to explain? You're a Slayer. A demon killer. You've turned traitor."

"I would never kill you, you know that."

The bloody images of my family the night they were murdered by the Noctifectors flashed in front of my eyes. The cloying smell of betrayal clogged my nostrils. "The night we should have been celebrating our marriage, my mother, father, and baby sister died at the hands of the Nocts. Did you kill them? Was that your initiation?"

"Of course not. I had nothing to do with the strike against your family."

He might have been more believable if he hadn't broken eye contact right before he claimed innocence.

"*Faccia di merda*. You bastard." I would have flicked my fingers and retrieved my skirt and panties, but I couldn't afford to use magic for anything other than protecting myself and getting the hell out of there. Even though they were human,

The Church's slayers were the most highly skilled assassins on planet Earth. They had to be in order to take on demons, vamps, and other evil entities.

Skimming the wall and skirting furniture, I worked my way toward the bedroom door, never taking my eyes off his hands. One finger snap and I could be crushed under the weight of the roof, suffocated by a sudden lack of air, boiled alive from the inside if he decided to heat my blood that high.

I thought about my dream. Rad sticking the dagger in my heart. That wasn't just my subconscious symbolizing his betrayal. It was a premonition. "You always were a selfish prick, but I can't believe you'd betray your own kind."

He stopped moving, dropped his hand. "If I'd wanted to kill you, Kali, I could've done it in Nudra's coffin. I could've done it on your doorstep."

His voice was flat and devoid of emotion. As if he was suddenly very tired.

Join the crowd. I was too. Tired and devastated at his betrayal all over again. Devastated at my own incompetence. My inability to see what was right in front of me. I hadn't just been sloppy, I'd been a complete idiot. My throat tightened. "So why didn't you?"

"Because I'm still in lo..."

"Don't you dare," I seethed. I lowered my voice, rage eating at my heart. "Don't you dare bring love into this. You *never* loved me."

Along with the rage, an emotion I couldn't quite name bloomed inside my chest, tears stinging the edges of my eyes. Before I could blow any semblance of control, I fled, grabbing my cape as I ran through the living room, smashing the champagne glass on Rad's guitar. He called my name and I heard his footsteps behind me right before I yanked the door to the suite open. I tied my cape around my hips as I fled, running hard for the stairwell and brushing those damned tears off my cheeks.

The moment the heavy hotel door closed behind me, cutting off Rad's voice, I regained a small amount of composure. I half-ran, half-jumped down six flights of stairs, thankfully not coming into contact with anyone else. Once I was sure he wasn't following me, I slowed. The adrenaline overload nailed me, along with the emotions tied up in my chest, and I sank onto a stair, back against the wall, and gritted my teeth.

There was only one thing left to do. One place left to go. I'd screwed my career over, but there was a light at the end of the tunnel. Rad was a demon hunter, working for The Church, the Bridge Council's long-standing arch-enemy. The supernatural world had its own justice system and didn't appreciate the human world interfering, especially since the Roman Catholic Church saw everything in black and white. A demon was evil, no matter what, and that's why they'd instituted the Noctifector unit. To kill all forms of evil.

So why recruit Rad into their leagues? It went against everything they stood for.

Except The Church was smart. And Rad was half human. Maybe they thought they could save his soul while he infiltrated places their all-human assassins couldn't. He could insert himself into demon organizations, demon families, and all the while, planning to kill them as soon they trusted him.

Like *my* family.

Black rage coiled inside me. I gripped the stair railing and hauled myself off the step. It was time to go see the Council and salvage my career.

Radison Beaumont was going to hell.

And I was the one going to send him there.

SEVEN

My first code as a vengeance demon is *don't take anything personally*. My second code is *don't get emotional*. Speeding through downtown Chicago, I broke both codes. This was personal and I was highly emotional.

I punched in Rebel Radio on my Audi's stereo, needing to blank out the emotions and stop reliving the past. Beating myself up over my failure then and now wasn't going to keep me alive or salvage my job as the enforcer. Beating someone else up...well, that was a horse—or in this case, demon—of a different color.

AC/DC thumped the speakers as I raced the TT out of downtown and south along the lake. Traffic was light, as light as it usually got on Lakeshore Drive, and I could have topped a hundred easily without having to weave much, but a few verses of *Highway To Hell* and my controlled, calculating side resurrected itself. It was Halloween after all, bringing out Chicago's Finest along with the looney and deranged. A speeding ticket would be the icing on the suckfest of my evening.

Besides, code number three, *don't call attention to yourself,* seemed especially important tonight since my emotions were close to the surface. Any time my emotions got the better of me, my demon surfaced, and that was never a good thing.

The Bridge Institute was glamoured. To the human eye, it looked like nothing more than a large shipping warehouse sitting on Lake Michigan's edge. The glamour included bays of semi-trucks, several multi-storied buildings with skywalks running between them, enormous diesel fuel tankers, and assorted parking lots dotting the buildings' perimeters. Between the frontage road and the Institute, a large chunk of open ground, complete with park-like grass and trees, obscured the view. The entire area was gated off, increasing security.

Seconds after I drove up to the entrance, the gate swung open. Good sign. The Council hadn't deemed me an enemy yet and revoked my access. Damon, Yasmin, and Kirill had no doubt given up on me attending the meeting by now and were probably furious, but they had yet to figure out I was no longer qualified to walk on Institute ground.

I raced the TT past the green park, the unglamoured Institute rising before my demon eyes. The building's footprint equaled that of the shipping warehouse but this was more Spanish castle than sparse metal structure. Younger than me by a few centuries, the Institute was technically Chicago's oldest building, although it would never receive landmark designation or be included in any human history books.

After parking the car behind the main building, I pressed my hand to the stone carving next to the entrance door. The usual emanations of the occupants inside vibrated into my skin. Nothing alarming or out of place. As a demon, my magic originates with the Earth, so by placing my hand on the stone, I could hear and feel what was happening inside. The stone, in turn, recognized my identity and granted me access. The door's locks and charms released and I entered the building.

Inside, a long, semi-dark hallway, lit only by wall sconces, greeted me. This entrance wasn't for guests so there was no grand foyer, no chandeliers, no sweeping stairs to the second floor like there was in the front. Just a blood-red carpet runner that needed vacuuming and a dozen matching closed doors on either side of the hall. At the other end was an enormous bay window, looking out over the lake, and a functional set of stairs.

The Council's conference room was on the third floor, but as I stood looking at the stairs leading up, my fingers shook. I was too keyed up to face the heads of the Council and I'd be damned if I'd let Damon or Yasmin see me wearing my cape as a skirt. No need to scream *incompetent* with my clothes as well as my actions.

So I headed down to the basement training rooms.

Cole, the War demon in charge of US Bridge Security and Defense, was working with three young demons. Really young. Twelve or thirteen at most. Pubescent demons had the hardest time adjusting to the human world. Some were sent by their parents to tame their wild side. Others were recruited by the Institute because they had unique powers or combinations of powers. The minority were scooped up off the streets. Typically their parents had been killed by the Noctifectors or possibly by other demons. There were always wars waging inside the supernatural community as well as the human one. Occasionally, kids got caught in the crossfire. Those who couldn't be placed with demon families were adopted by the Bridge Council and trained to fight.

The kids Cole was training had a desperate look in their eyes. A desperation I'd once had. The Institute had trained me, too, years after my family was wiped out. I was too old to need parents, but I had skills Damon wanted to capitalize on. And I had a bone-deep desire to keep humans safe from true evil.

Combined with a hatred of the Nocts, I was the perfect student.

Cole was showing one boy a chokehold position when I entered. He took one look at me and released the boy. "Work on your palm strikes," he commanded, not even glancing at them as he made his way to me.

His dark brown hair was pulled back in a low ponytail. He was bare-chested, the normal smattering of dark curls there shaved off and showing his beefy upper body and ridged six-pack to full benefit. If rage hadn't still been percolating in my blood, I might have said something cute and flirty to him. As it was, I didn't have to say anything for him to pick up on my mood.

His low-slung cargo pants and bare feet made alternating slapping-swishing noises on the gym floor. His gray eyes narrowed, taking in the placement of my cape and his energy tightened in response to mine. "Slummin' again with the wrong people?"

"I need to burn off some energy."

His lips tilted down, questions running amok behind his eyes, but he knew me. Knew I didn't interrupt his training sessions unless I was at the emotional breaking point. My demon needed release. The rest of me did too.

"No weapons. Hand to hand."

I nodded, terms accepted, and went to the locker room to change.

When I returned, the kids were gone. Cole punched a punching bag bare-knuckled. Poor thing. The punching bag, not Cole.

He didn't look at me. "If I win, you tell me what happened."

"And if I win?"

"You take me to Outback for dinner and then tell me what happened."

Men and their steaks. "Confessions aren't my style. You know that. Too ugly."

Cole stopped the swinging punching bag with one hand and met my gaze. "There is nothing ugly about you."

There was nothing ugly about him either. His once-straight classic Roman nose ran in a crooked line from one too many breaks that even his demon blood couldn't heal. Various bullet wounds and knives had left marks on his shoulders, arms, chest, and stomach. Across his back, fat silver scars laced up his spine. Those were the worst. Not ugly to me, but a symbol of survival. To others outside the Institute, the ragged scars crisscrossing his skin labeled him damaged goods. He'd been caught and tortured by Tonya, an arrogant Erinyes who used her brass-studded scourge to turn Cole's back into hamburger. Tonya'd poured holy water into the wounds, disfiguring his gorgeous back and nearly killing him.

In the end, I'd killed her slow and sweet, and doctored him back to health. Since then, he'd been head of the Bridge's security and defense department, his capture and torture at Tonya's hands turning the demon who'd once been a gladiator into an unstoppable force of nature. I credited him for saving my ass once or twice as payback.

Barefoot now, I stood several inches shorter than him. He knew facts about me, but not all of them. Nothing about Rad or my penchant for letting *il pistolino* screw up my life. "We gonna fight or what?"

"That bad, huh?" He sniffed the air, narrowed his eyes. "You smell like Chaos demon."

My nerves buzzed. I flexed my hands into fists. "If I don't get release in the next minute or two, I'm going to wipe Chicago off the hell-forsaken map."

He stepped closer and ran a finger down the side of my face. That close, I could see flecks of sapphire dotting his gray eyes. "There are better ways to release pent-up emotion, Kali."

This from the man who lived to fight.

On any other night, I might have taken him up on his offer. But when it came to my demon, the only cure for rage was violence.

So I punched him in the stomach.

EIGHT

Cole was faster than me, but only by a millisecond. He sucked in his stomach and my fist connected with his rock-hard abs. My knuckles lost that fight, burning with pain.

For the next half hour, we feinted, wrestled, and knocked each other silly. I took out my frustrations with Rad, Nudra, as well as with myself, on Cole, and he loved every minute of it, giving as good as he got. It was the best damned time I'd had in a while.

My demon was happy too. I let the bitch out of her cage but kept her on a leash. I never, ever gave her total freedom, even when fighting Cole for grins and giggles. Doing so would be akin to setting off a hurricane in the Madhouse on Madison. I wouldn't just destroy a few things, I'd obliterate them. People too. The demon inside me was a bomb waiting to go off.

Cole didn't know I kept my demon on a leash when we fought. Nobody knew my daily struggle with her. That's the way I preferred it. Like a dog, she needed regular exercise and the constant training and steam-releasing sessions with Cole were part of her care and feeding.

He pinned me against the stone wall of the gym, one hand restraining both my wrists over my head. We were breathing hard, his chest pressed against mine, his lower body still inviting me to take my aggression out in a more naked manner, when the gym door rumbled open behind us.

A man cleared his throat. Loudly. Amazing how much Damon, our boss, could convey in such a simple sound. Irritation. Disappointment. Impatience.

I peeked over Cole's shoulder. Damon stood in front of the door, one hand in the pocket of his dress pants. The other loose at his side. He looked fresh from the shower crisp and probably smelled like it too. "Crap," I murmured.

Cole released me, took a step backward, and bowed. Our session was over, and in the warrior's world, that meant showing respect to your opponent. He'd spent half a dozen centuries fighting in coliseums, dojos, and back alleys, but he was still a gentleman.

In my line of work, contrary to popular belief, I rarely engaged in hand-to-hand combat. I relied on my magic if I needed to stop someone or protect myself. Cole had told me on many occasions that I relied on it too much. That someday I'd run into a supernatural whose magic was stronger and more skilled than mine. He was right, which was one of the reasons—outside of keeping my demon under control—I continued to train with him. He was the best at his job.

Rubbing my shoulder—Cole had practically dislocated it—I bowed back. Our faces were close together again and he whispered, "You owe me dinner."

After our showdown, I owed him more than that. "You're on. If Damon doesn't kill me first."

"Kali." Damon's voice echoed in the gym, commanding as always.

I rose, nodded at Cole, and slowly sauntered over to my

boss, gaze on the floor. Stopping a few feet in front of him, I wiped sweat off my forehead and glanced at his face.

His intense dark eyes were almost black as he sized up my sweat-soaked and bloody T-shirt—I'd smashed Cole's nose and he'd fattened my lip, so the stairs were a mix of both—ripped pants and bare feet. He was dressed in a gunmetal gray Italian silk suit, white dress shirt, and merlot-colored tie. Black calfskin shoes peeked out under the perfectly pressed hem of his pant legs.

It was hard not to admire his style.

When our eyes met, he gave me an eat-your-heart-out look. Lust swirled around us and a lump formed in my throat. Like most demons, lust is my greatest vice. Flirting, and the sex act itself, embody pride and gluttony, the desire to covet, the insatiable yearning to satisfy that which can never be truly satisfied.

Thanks to Rad, it had been a damn long time since I'd been satisfied.

I licked my fattened lip. If I could combine Damon and Cole into one being, I might find a way to quench my darkest cravings. No Chaos demon necessary.

Damon's power was as sexy as his Italian suit. He used that fact, as he used all his superior Archdemon skills, to full advantage. Sensing my desire, he studied me with smug satisfaction, but his eyes said, *never gonna happen.* "Do you have presentable clothes in your locker?"

"Presentable?"

"Business attire."

Thanks to going three rounds with Cole, I was less emotional and back in control of my demon as well as the rest of me. Nevertheless, plunking my neck on the chopping block, even if I did have an ace up my sleeve, was unappealing. "It's after midnight. Can we reschedule the debriefing for tomorrow?"

He flicked his wrist, glanced at his Rolex. "You've got ten minutes to clean up and get your ass in my office. And no wearing your cape for a skirt."

Busted. He'd been watching for me, had seen me sneak in.

Turning on his calf-skinned heel, he shoved the gym door open, then turned back, nose twitching. "Take a shower while you're at it. You smell like a bloody Chaos demon."

He walked out and the door slammed shut behind him. Cole's voice sing-songed to me across the floor. "Told you so."

Running past him, I cuffed his shoulder. "Shut up or no Outback for you."

He chuckled and I sprinted into the locker room.

Ten minutes, hell.

I'd be spit-shined and sitting in Damon's office in five.

NINE

Damon didn't look up from the file he was reading when I knocked on his open door. "Seven minutes and twenty-seven seconds." He flipped a page over. "And no red cape in sight."

So I hadn't made it in five minutes but I'd still come in under ten. I stood in the doorway, waiting for him to motion me in. He kept reading the file.

Fine. Two could play that game. I stood there, expressionless, emotionless, and wondering what the hell he was up to.

A minute ticked by as my boss, who'd been in such a damned hurry to get me there, ignored me. I let my gaze drift over the cool, calm interior of his office. After getting rid of all my rage at Rad, my head was clearer, my demon nicely suppressed. I was prepared to take my punishment, and if necessary, make a deal.

Finally, Damon glanced up. His eyes skimmed me from head to toe. My hair was scraped back in a high ponytail. I was wearing my best black pencil skirt, white shirt and a jaunty red and yellow scarf around my neck. Italian flair, check.

He leaned back in his chair, his gaze landing first on my badge which I'd hung on my skirt's high waistband and then on my four-inch red platforms. The shoes were a little over the top for business attire, but conservative black pumps didn't exist in my wardrobe at home or at work.

Plus, the red matched the scarf.

"Let your hair down," he said. "You look like a child playing dress up."

Annoyed he wasn't more impressed with my outfit, I reached up and removed the hairband, letting my wet hair fall around my face. I stuck the hairband on my wrist, right under my Volante bracelet. "Does it matter?"

"Appearance always matters." He pointed one sturdy finger at a chair across from him. "Sit."

I eased into the chair, the tight skirt hindering my movements slightly. "Yasmin and Kirill skipping the debriefing?"

Damon retrieved the file. "Tell me about Arman and Victoria."

I blinked my surprise. Held my breath. How did he know?

He glanced at me, saw my hesitation. "Your blood slaves. What do you know about them?"

"Not much," I stammered, awed by his ability to find out my mother of all secrets in less time than I could spit. He was worse than my mother had been when I started dating boys. That woman had had eyes in the back of her head, and spies on every street corner, building and room within Rome's city limits.

"Why did Nudra pick these two to be your blood slaves?"

I swallowed, called up what the vamp king had told me. "Arman is a shifter who can't control his shapeshifting. Victoria is a witch. Leader of the Satrina Arcanum. She wants to raise Lilith from hell. Nudra convinced them that with my blood, they could both get what they wanted."

Damon nodded once, making a note on the file. "Shouldn't be hard to track them down."

"Track them down for what?"

He gave me a hard look as if I were purposely being dense. "You can't work for the Bridge Council if you have blood slaves, Kali."

My stomach fell to my feet. "You're going to have them killed?"

His stare continued to bore into me.

"They're human!"

"Barely. A werecat and a witch deep in the occult are not worth risking everything we've worked for."

"Arman is half human. Victoria is all human. Their judgment may be skewed by sin, but they can be redeemed. They don't deserve to die because of Nudra's manipulation."

"It's them," Damon said, his voice cold and detached. "Or you."

Talk about manipulation. For several long moments, I couldn't find my voice. Then I rose from the chair, snapped the badge off my waistband. "Fine. I tender my resignation."

I tossed the badge on the file in front of him, walked to the door.

"Kali."

I pulled up short, kept my back to him.

"This is why you're so valuable to the Council."

"The Council put their faith in the wrong demon this time."

"I don't think so. Your willingness to give up your career, which clearly you enjoy and are good at, to save two humans is exactly why you're so valuable."

Facing the Archdemon, I kept all emotion off my face. "What do you want from me? I screwed up. Me." I pointed a finger at my chest. "I will not let you murder two humans because I was sloppy."

His leather chair squeaked softly as he sat back. The side of his lips twitched. In Damon's world, that passed for a smile.

He fiddled with the edge of my badge. "Here's what's going to happen. Nudra's vampire counterparts from the other three regions of the United States are waiting for us in the conference room along with Yasmin and Kirill. You and I are going to the conference room and unruffling their feathers. During the next few minutes, I'm going to barter with them and make a deal or two. No matter what I say, you will go along with it. No questions asked. You will not show surprise or hesitate for one second to back me up, no matter what I offer or agree to."

I didn't like where this was going. "And in return?"

"I'll handle your blood slave problem with the other Council members."

"Handle it how?"

"The two humans will be spared. That's all I'll promise."

I considered telling Damon about Rad, discarded the idea. "Do the vamps want revenge on me?"

"Quite the opposite, I believe."

What the hell did that mean?

He tossed the badge to me. I caught it in mid-air. Sensing my confusion, he explained. "The regional managers hated Nudra as much as you did, and now they're looking for a new leader to take his place. A trailblazer. Someone who's in the good graces of the Bridge Council."

The bad feeling I had worsened. "What does that have to do with me?"

Another twitch of his lips. Damon stood, straightened his cuffs and buttoned his jacket. "Let's go make a deal."

TEN

D amon opened the office door, saw I was still frozen to the spot, and shut it again.

I thought he would ask me what was wrong, and there were so many things wrong, I didn't know how I would answer.

But he didn't ask. Instead, he dropped his gaze to my fat lip.

Even in my platforms, I was several inches shorter than his six-one height. He grabbed my chin with one hand and tilted my head up to get a closer look at my lip. "Why do you allow Cole to use you as a punching bag?"

I tried to pull away, but he tightened his hold and held me in place.

Which pissed me off. "We're both sadists. We enjoy inflicting pain on each other."

"What pain did you inflict on him?"

"I broke his nose for the third time."

His lips did that twitchy thing. "A cheap shot."

I'd show him a cheap shot if he didn't turn loose of me. "And why is that?"

"Cole's nose has been damaged so many times, it's physically his weakest spot. You strike me as more of a...creative... sadist."

As he said the last two words, he brushed his thumb across my lip. The sensation burned, his dark magic pouring out and entering the tender skin, knitting the split back together. Heat shot across my jaw and down my neck, pain and pleasure suffusing my body at the same time. My breath caught in my chest.

Talk about a sadist. "You're going to feed me to the vamps, aren't you?"

His thumb still rested on my bottom lip ever so lightly, and as I said the words, my upper lip came down on top of it. An erotic tingling sensation ran down my spine.

Damon lifted his gaze and our eyes locked. "I'm going to do what's best for the Bridge Council and this institution."

"So that's a yes."

He caressed my lips one last time before releasing my chin and stepping back. His eyes had gone hard, detached. "Do you know what faith is, Kali?"

Disappointment was evident in his tone, and I understood the real question behind what he was asking. "Faith requires trust."

One brow arched. "You don't trust me?"

I'd surprised him. A rare event. "I don't trust anyone but myself."

That wasn't quite true. I trusted Aphrodite, and my human friend Neve, and even JR, my office tech guru, who was three kinds of crazy human.

But trust Damon? No way. I believed in him, believed in his ability to keep the Bridge Council on track and fighting the good fight, but he'd throw me under the bus if push came to shove. No questions asked. "At the moment, I'm seriously questioning your stability as head of the Council," I said, stomach clenching at my outright honesty. "You let Undead enter the Institute, which is totally against protocol."

Maybe I imagined it, but some kind of emotion flashed behind his eyes. "I'm hurt you don't trust me."

Now it was my turn to be surprised. The badass Archdemon was showing his hand. "If that's true, which I highly doubt, then you've just exposed *your* weakest spot." I swept past him, opened the door. "And don't think I won't use that against you in the near future."

I smiled, big, letting him know my inner bitch was still alive and active.

His lips did more than twitch this time, curving up on one side. My threat meant nothing to him, but he admired my bravado. "Remember our deal."

How could I forget? I fingered Volante on my wrist. "Give me a stake, and I'll take out all three of the regional managers, right here, right now."

"That wouldn't be prudent."

Party pooper. "Fine. Let's get this over with."

I started to walk into the hallway but Damon reached over and grabbed my hand. He drew me up against his body, eyes staring deep into mine as if he were reading my mind. Caught in his stare and totally confused by his actions, I stammered, "What are you doing?" right before he lowered his head and pressed his lips to mine.

The world stopped. The protest on my lips died. One of his hands pressed against my lower back forcing my body to mold to his. He took my mouth with power and command, kissing me with the expertise of an Archdemon who's been around a long, long time.

Every nerve ending in my body lit up like it was on fire. Pleasure, pain, hate, love, passion, his dark magic ripped through my blood, filling me with all of it. The wood-smoke smell of his

demonness filled my senses, drugging me. Cloyingly sweet, it
dulled the fight in me, suffocating any urge I had to pull away.

Shame on me, but the demon inside me sprang to life, and I
wrapped my arms around his neck, letting the heady smoke
drag me under. When his tongue demanded I part my lips,
I did.

And then I remembered Rad. Remembered Damon was
about to sacrifice me to the vamps in some kind of power play. I
was nothing but a pawn. To both of them.

And I was tired of being played.

I broke the kiss against my body's advice and shoved
Damon away. "Get your hands off me."

He grinned, wiped my lip gloss from his lips with a folded
white handkerchief. His eyes sparkled with satisfaction and he
patted my cheek as he passed me on the way to the hall. "Definite weak spot."

Dazed, I stood there for a moment, staring at his back as he
walked away. Then my anger kicked back in. Slamming his
office door, I stomped down the hallway after him, but with
each step, I closed my emotions off. Walking into a room with
three vamps and two extremely tight-assed Council members
required I be in top form.

No emotion.

Nothing personal.

Show no fear.

Act like an equal.

When Damon and I entered the conference room,
everyone rose. Introductions were made, Yasmin sending me a
reproachful glance from under her heavy eyelashes as I shook
hands with each vamp. I ignored her.

The room reeked of cigar smoke and graveyard dirt. The
Eastern regional manager, Rafael DeMarco, had the Godfather

image down pat. Salt and pepper hair slicked back from his face, ginormous bloodstone ring on his left ring finger, Cuban cigar firmly tucked between his thick lips. Along with the hair, the crow's feet in the corners of his eyes suggested he'd been turned later in life.

Juliana Ballou Jackson was a Creole beauty pageant queen. Big hair, double strand of pearls around her neck, significant hourglass shape under her designer dress. Youthful-looking package, but she gave off the air of someone who'd been older when she'd been turned as well. Her brown eyes sized up my clothes before evaluating the rest of me and she gave me a respectful nod. Guess my 'business attire' passed the vamp's elitist requirements.

The last regional manager, Toel Maze, was a mix of surfer dude and Dumb and Dumber. Strawberry blond hair, blue eyes, over-the-top enthusiasm. The word 'dude' was prevalent in his vocabulary and his clothes were a mix of organic cotton and hemp. A shark pendant hung from a black cord around his neck. His pupils were so dilated, I was afraid he'd vamp out on me. Especially when his gaze strayed to my cleavage and couldn't seem to find its way back up to my face while we shook hands.

Damon unbuttoned his jacket, pulled out a chair at the head of the table. "Kali and I apologize for keeping you all waiting. It is Halloween, after all. A busy night for us, especially our enforcer."

The Undead vamps bought the smooth lie, nodding at me with due respect. Yasmin did a modified eye roll and Kirill looked uninterested in the goings-on of one of the hired help. He was far more interested in the plate of gourmet brownies in the middle of the table. Couldn't say I blamed him. The brownies smelled so good, I considered snagging one myself.

"Dude," Toel said, giving me a goofy grin. "Kali, like *Cali*-for-ni-a, huh? Bitchin."

Bitchin. His pronunciation was off, but I wasn't going to correct him. With his type, it wouldn't do any good.

I took a seat at the opposite end of the table, more to distance myself from the vamps than to demonstrate my powerful position with the Bridge Council. Which, in reality, I didn't possess. I was an important asset, but I wasn't powerful in this room of powerful archdemons.

The vamps didn't know that, however, and Damon gave me an approving nod. He obviously liked me playing boardroom dress-up.

Rafael, the Godfather, removed the cigar from his lips. "I'd like to hear what happened at Nudra's compound."

Ugh. Like I wanted to tell that story as the opening act. I was going to have to tell it anyway, at least parts of it, in order to satisfy Yasmin, Kirill and Damon. Might as well get it over with.

Yasmin shifted in her chair to better face me and crossed skinny arms over her flat chest. "Yes, Kali, I'd like to hear that story as well."

Point to Damon's chief of staff. Pleasant and annoyingly earnest, she sounded believable to all but me.

So I pinned my gaze on the highly-polished table and relayed all the ugly details. The only one I left out was Rad licking my neck and becoming a blood slave along with Victoria and Arman. Why? I don't really know. It seemed too...personal. He was mine to deal with, rules about me seeking my own vengeance, a minor detail.

When I was done, a heavy silence hung as thick as Rafael's cigar smoke in the air. Raising my eyes, I found everyone staring at me. Even Kirill. Rafael and Juliana looked slightly disgusted. Toel looked excited, whether from the story or my cleavage, was up for debate. Yasmin swallowed hard and Kirill set down the brownie he was eating. Only Damon looked pleased.

Bastard.

Nudra had not only broken multiple Bridge laws, he'd also violated a few of the vamp kingdom's. He'd put the entire population in jeopardy by attacking a Bridge employee. The already uneasy truce between the vamp community and the Bridge Council was now at risk of exploding into a full-scale war. One the vamps wouldn't win.

"Please accept our abject apologies, Ms. Sweet." Juliana's voice was soft and feminine with a southern drawl.

She bit the inside of her cheek and batted her lashes at Damon. A nervous habit, or was she flirting with him? "I trust the board will not hold the rest of us responsible for Raj Nudra's renegade ways."

Damon sat back in his chair, crossed his legs at the ankles, and gave the vamp a cold, hard stare. He had Juliana and the other regional managers right where he wanted them. "Unfortunately, there is no one else to hold responsible."

"We're prepared to make reparations," Rafael said, waving the cigar around. "To Ms. Sweet and the Bridge Council."

A light shone in Damon's hard eyes. "We're listening."

Rafael, Juliana and Toel exchanged a look. Rafael stubbed out his cigar in the glass ashtray next to him. His fat fingers drummed the table. "The Council has always been fair to us. East Coast, Southern States, West Coast, we're all in agreement to your laws and regulations."

"But, dude." Toel turned his head toward Damon, then back to me and then back to Damon. The head jerking made me dizzy. His small brain had to be rattling around like a marble inside a hollow bowling ball. "Nudra was a dick dragger, y'know? Fucker controlled everything crossing East to

West. Now the donk's gone, fat waves for all of us, from the Benny—" he pointed at Raphael "—to the Big Kahuna." He pointed at himself.

Damon raised one brow at me, suggesting he didn't speak Idiot and needed a translation. I was no beach bunny, but I thought it was pretty clear. "Nudra's demise benefits all of you."

Toel met my eyes, puppy dog love shining in them. "Dude, you surf?"

Really, how in Hades had he ever become a regional manager?

Resisting the urge to knock him upside the head, I addressed the other two vamps. "The Central United States is a big territory. Who's going to run it now?"

Juliana once again batted her eyes at Damon and spoke in her soft, syrupy voice. "We have a proposition for the Council."

Damon made a show of looking at Yasmin and Kirill. They both nodded agreement to hear her out. Damon motioned for her to go on.

She smiled and it lit up her face. It was a vamp smile, though, all manipulation and no true emotion. Unwillingly I shivered. "I'm here for a few days to make the transition easier for the next Central regional manager, but the southern region is the largest in this country with the largest vampire population and I can't be absent too long. Finding the right candidate to replace Nudra is not a task we wish to rush, but we do need to move quickly and efficiently."

Rafael, seeming impatient for the punch line, leaned forward. "Temporarily, we'd like Ms. Sweet to take over and work with the House Master in Chicago. The Master has agreed to teach her everything she needs to know."

Each large city had a house for its upper and midlevel managers and was run by a specially appointed Master. The place also acted as a safe house, a retreat and a political meeting ground for that region's Undead. The Master oversaw the house. The Regional Manager oversaw the politics. Best case scenario, they worked together like the Senate and House of Reps to set rules and guidelines for the Undead population.

Rafael glanced at me, saw my startled reaction, and rushed on. "The arrangement would only be for a short time. Until we find a suitable replacement for Nudra."

Toel bobbed his head, a sloppy smile on his face. "Hella cool, dude!"

Hella cool. Sure. "Absolutely not."

At the same time I spoke, Damon said, "We'd have conditions, of course."

I glared at him and shook my head no. I even touched the ring finger and thumb of my left hand together under the table and started to throw a curse at him. Sensing my magic, he raised both brows in warning.

A sharp pain penetrated my frontal lobe, the sound of his voice ringing in my head. *Remember our deal.*

I pressed fingers against both temples and fought the sudden sick feeling in my stomach, brought on, not by his psychic push, but by a startling realization.

That's why he'd kissed me. Not because he was attracted to me or I was some sort of weakness for him. He'd planted his dark magic inside me so he could read my thoughts.

Damon was a *psuhke* demon. All archdemons were. He could read your body, mind and soul, if you had one, but only if he'd touched you physically in some way. Lesser demons and humans he could read with a simple touch. Demons like me, and other more powerful supernaturals like vamps, he had to touch intimately. A kiss was the most common means of implanting his *psukhe* seed.

Yasmin's gaze ping-ponged between us as if she realized

what was going on. I mentally called him a bastard in Italian and then my brain, already trained to think of someone else associated with that word, went in a bad direction.

Rad.

Too late, Damon caught the thought. The corners of his eyes pinched. *Radison Beaumont?*

Kirill, who'd returned to eating, paused long enough in mid-chew to state the obvious. "Won't work. She's not a vamp."

"She has Nudra's blood in her," Rafael countered. "She has blood slaves. For all intents and purposes, she's one of us now."

I bolted up from the chair, unable to take any more. "I am *not* one of you. I despise your kind, and I would never, ever consider such a deal."

All three vampires blanched. So did Yasmin and Kirill.

A muscle in Damon's jaw jumped.

Oops.

Again, pain exploded inside my skull. *Sit down and apologize.*

I grabbed my head with both hands, practically falling into the chair. After a second, the pain subsided and I could think again. I cleared my throat, raised my face to the others. The lives of two humans were in my hands. "I'm sorry. Nudra's blood has affected me in strange ways, my temper being one of them." I forced a half-assed smile. "I've been saying and doing crazy things all night."

Damon backed out of my head, turned to Juliana. "What benefit does the Prince of the Undead gain by allowing Kali to head the central region?"

"Ms. Sweet is a powerful demon who's been alive longer than most of us and knows how to run a business. She has all of the qualifications we look for in a leader." Juliana smiled at me, acting as if nothing was amiss. "Our sire seeks to strengthen the bonds between the Undead nation and the Bridge Council."

Damon didn't buy it, threw out his own theory. "The Noctifectors have devastated your numbers worldwide in recent years. By reopening the central corridor under Bridge-supported authority, you hope to duck under our protective umbrella. Am I right?"

Everyone in the room knew he was. If Juliana had been human, she would have blushed. Instead, she conceded with a tuck of her chin. "We lost over eleven-hundred of our race in the United States last year."

Free of Damon's crushing magic, my brain once again engaged. "I thought stupid humans were flocking to your doors after the recent popularity of vamp books and movies."

"Ka-biff! We don't touch the hype-outs." Toel tried to look serious. Failed. "Against policy."

Rafael played with his cigar, rolling it over and over in the ashtray. "In the past ten years, our numbers had been cut in half in North America. Even more in Europe."

Color me impressed. And more than a little surprised. I had no idea the Noctifectors had grown so efficient in the vamp war. Hated to admit it, but I had to give them props.

"The Noctifectors are becoming increasingly problematic," Damon said. "For a bunch of humans, they're extremely competent at killing us off."

Not all of them were human. At least not one-hundred-percent human DNA. Maybe they were more half-demons like Rad helping them out and that's why their proficiency had doubled. A theory I should run by my boss and the other directors. But not until I had hard facts.

Lucky for me, Damon wasn't listening to my thoughts at that moment. Juliana had leaned toward him and was giving him an earnest look. "A new alliance between our two camps would give you a stronger front against our common enemy while allowing us to rebuild our ranks."

Damon rocked his chair in thought. "We provide specialized training to fight them, and you in turn provide soldiers to perform preemptive strikes?"

Juliana and Rafael nodded their heads. Damon smiled.

Apparently, I wasn't the only getting thrown under the bus tonight. Wait 'til Cole found out he was going to be training vampires in Noctifector defense techniques.

I'd heard enough. My head still hurt from Damon's mind invasion and my stomach hurt from being used. I wanted another shower, my Hello Kitty pjs and at least twelve straight hours of sleep. Plus, I had to figure out what to do about Rad and I had three new cases for Sweet Investigations sitting on my plate.

Rising, I pushed back the chair and adjusted the badge on my waist. "I'll consider the offer, but just know, along with the Council's demands, I'll have my own set of conditions."

I made it to the door before Damon spoke. "Wait for me in my office, Kali."

Damn.

Without looking at him, I walked out.

ELEVEN

Inside Damon's office once more, I kicked off my shoes and wiggled my toes in the plush carpeting. Then I paced.

Outside his huge window, it was still pitch dark over the lake. It would be a few more hours before sunrise. Normally by this time of night, I had my Bridge business done and was on to the next case for Sweet Investigations. I hadn't done anything for SI since before my run-in with Nudra. Di would be up to her pretty goddess eyeballs soon if I didn't get back to work.

Lying on top of Damon's desk was the file he'd been pretending to read when I'd entered earlier. As I crossed back and forth from his red leather sofa at one end of the room to the towering bookcase filled with ancient tombs of demon literature at the other, my eyes kept staring at that file.

The laws of physics are clear and understandable to most of us. A body in motion tends to keep moving. A body at rest stays at rest. In my opinion, Einstein forgot one critical law of physics, though. An open file on your boss's desk can't be ignored.

A quick glance out the door showed the coast was clear.

The Bridge Council and the vamps were still negotiating. I sat in Damon's massive office chair, sighing as the cushioned seat wrapped around my butt and hips. The conference room chairs were hard and angular. Compared to those, Damon's chair was bliss.

I was still mad at him for planting that kiss on me. For intruding on my thoughts and threatening the life of my blood slaves. For agreeing with the vamps to let me run the central region until they found Nudra's replacement. For telling me how to wear my hair.

Grabbing the hair band off my wrist, I reinstated my ponytail. A small measure of control.

The file folder was one of those that held the papers by the top with metal prongs. The top pages had been flipped over, concealing the most important subject matter, but the name on the file tab made my heart skip a beat.

Calina Dolce

The heading on the open page read, *Familia*, and the parchment paper it was written on was old. The ink on the page, faded.

Under the heading was a list of my family's names, each accompanied by a birth and death date, cause of death, and miscellaneous facts about their jobs, hobbies, demonic activities. All of it was in Italian with a few notes in Damon's tight handwriting scrawled in the margins in English.

No surprise Damon had a personal file on me. He had files on all Bridge employees, even outside contractors like Hone. Personnel files were computerized, but most of us had been around long before computers took over the world, and paper files still existed.

The parchment paper, faded ink and precisely written Italian made a rare, funny homesickness rise in my chest. But seeing the names of my family made my chest tighten uncomfortably.

The unwelcome but familiar image of their bloody bodies rose in my mind. Crucified and decapitated—even my four-year-old baby sister.

That Rad could be part of that was unthinkable. I'd hated him for nearly three hundred years for breaking my heart, but I would never in a million years have believed him to be so vindictive and malevolent.

He'd been a playboy his whole life, using his good looks and charm to cheat at cards and woo gullible girls like I'd been all those years ago into thinking he loved them. But kill people? Kill humans? The incongruity struck me as another law of physics. Rad was a musician. He created things. He didn't destroy them.

Rad was not a murderer.

It wasn't in him, not the human side or the demon one. Those of us who had that particular gene in our DNA, that particular seed for the ultimate violence, recognized it in others. Cole had it. Damon had it. I had it. Even Hone, if pushed far enough, had it.

Radison Beaumont didn't.

But in order to be branded with the Noct tattoo, he had to have killed a demon.

I leafed through more pages of my file, fearing what I would read even though I'd lived it, but unable to resist the pull of the information. A second page caught and held my attention. The demon who'd written down the collection of facts about my life had included a detailed sketch of my family at the scene of the Noctifector's slaughter. A regular eighteenth-century crime scene investigator.

My stomach lurched and I flipped the pages closed. My

memory was one thing. Seeing the drawing of my parents and dead sister, their bodies crucified to beams in our home, my sister nailed to the floor, their heads hacked from their necks, was more than I could handle. I'd been there in the aftermath and no drawing could capture the gut-wrenching devastation I'd felt. If I hadn't been out searching for Rad, thinking there had to be some good reason he'd left me at the altar and all I had to do was find him and work it out, I would have been there to save my family.

Or more likely, I would have died too. Noctifectors were skilled assassins, but they were still human. They struck fast and hard and unexpectedly in large numbers, overwhelming most demons. My family was important to the Italian Court and Queen Maria, part demon herself. We were always careful about security, but that night, my parents had been most concerned about me. They'd let their guard down. I was to blame in more ways than one for their deaths.

The office door opened, startling me. Kirill gave me a bored look. "You're staying here for the next forty-eight hours until the coronation. I'll have Lainie make up a bed in the dorms for you."

The Institute provided temporary housing for the kids who needed family placement and anyone in training. It also provided lodging for various Bridge members from other countries when they traveled to the States. The second floor contained twenty rooms and a cafeteria. Lainie, a low-level demon nanny, was like the house mother.

"Coronation?"

"If you're going to be queen, even temporarily, you have to be crowned."

Nudra had called himself King of Chicago, but I hadn't realized he'd actually been *king* of Chicago. "You can't be serious."

"Serious as the nine levels of hell."

So not wearing a crown. "Why do I have to stay here for the next forty-eight hours?"

"Because," Damon burst in. unbuttoning his jacket and looking as tense as I felt. He motioned me to get out of his chair, not missing the fact I'd been ogling my file. "Until you're crowned, your life is in danger."

"From who?"

"Whom," Kirill corrected, finding a spot on the red leather couch and spreading his portly body out on it. "Who, whom. Subject, object. Confuses a lot of people."

Damon was standing next to the chair, towering over me and waiting for me to get up. I didn't move. "Becoming queen puts me on someone's kill radar?"

Brushing the sides of his jacket out of the way, he set his hands on his waistline. "There were Undead in line to take Nudra's place. Vamps as underhanded and cutthroat as he was. They won't like you usurping their rightful place, no matter what the regional managers and the Prince want."

"So they'd start a war and go against their boss's orders so they can take over Nudra's spot. Are they stupid or just insane?"

"Greedy." Kirill nodded his head. "I'd take you out, too, if I was them."

Damon was still irritated I was in his chair. "Until you're crowned, you're fair game. Once you're queen of the Central United States, they can't touch you. It's part of the blood oath. Once they've sworn allegiance and given you their blood offering, they can't raise a hand against you."

Blood offering? This just kept getting better and better. "Please tell me I don't have to drink the blood of several thousand vamps."

Kirill laughed like I was an idiot. "Not drink it. Bathe in it."

So glad I asked. "I can't do this queen thing. I get sick at the sight of blood and I absolutely hate vampires. No way in heaven, hell or purgatory I'm bathing in vamp blood or wearing a freakin' crown."

"You have to," Damon said. "The Council's already given its word."

I shot up out of the chair and slapped him. Hard. His head barely moved to the side. My handprint showed red against his dark Spanish skin and he rotated his jaw slightly before meeting my eyes. "What the hell was that for?"

"That," I said, practically growling with anger, "was for kissing me and planting your psychic seeds inside me so you could read my mind."

Kirill sat up straighter. "You kissed her?"

Damon rubbed his cheek, lips curving in a smug smile. "You give my kiss more credit than is due."

My hand stung and I wanted to shake it out, but I refused to give him the satisfaction of knowing I'd hurt myself slapping him. "I lowered my defenses because of that kiss and you took advantage of me. And you wonder why I don't trust you."

"I only meant to heal you. My magic entered your body and now we share a link. I didn't realize it would be a psychic one until we were in the conference room and you threatened me with your magic. My natural defenses picked up on it and opened the connection between our minds."

Such. A. Liar.

Kirill chuckled. "How interesting." There was an appalling excitement in his voice. As if Toel were behind his demon face saying, *Hella cool, dude!* "How close do you have to be to her for it to work?"

"I don't know." Damon was looking at me differently now. As if he were reconsidering the labels he'd pegged me with in his mind. "Over the next forty-eight hours, we'll have to test it out."

I was already connected to far too many people. Victoria, Arman, Rad. And now Damon. My skin itched.

I had friends, yes, and I felt a deep connection to them. But not like this. This was something else. Something invasive. Unnatural. As if everyone knew my secrets, could see into my soul, even though I technically didn't have one. I'd never felt so exposed in all my life, except for the first time I'd slept with Rad and confessed my love for him.

"I'm not staying here." I stepped around Damon, which wasn't easy since he was blocking the way. "Let the vamps come after me. I'll kill every one of them."

I made it past the desk, past Kirill on the couch before Damon spoke. "You'll be dead before sunset tonight."

"Seems I'm not the only one with a lack of faith in this relationship."

He removed his jacket and hung it on the back of the chair, then sat down. "Word will spread in the Undead community as fast as Kirill, here, spread plague in Europe."

I glanced at Kirill. "You caused that? The Black Death?"

The demon grinned manically. "The Plague of Justinian in the sixth and seventh centuries as well. One of my best pieces of work." He saw my consternation, the grin falling off his face. "That was before I changed sides, of course. Before I came to work for the Bridge Council."

Remind me to stay on his good side.

Damon mentally replied. *Kirill doesn't have a good side.*

"Stop that," I said to him, rubbing my head where the sharp pain of his invasion radiated. "Stop raping my mind."

He cocked his head at the term. "I insist you stay in the Institute until the coronation."

"I have a job outside of being the Bridge enforcer and I have a life, believe it or not, outside of this institute. I'll be safe at my place. I know how to protect myself."

"Like you did with Nudra?"

Score one for the Archdemon, damn him. "I got sloppy. It won't happen again."

Damon and I stared at each other, neither willing to give an inch. Finally, he sighed. "This is against my better judgment, but I'll allow it on one condition. Cole stays with you as bodyguard."

That was easier than I expected. I didn't need or want the warrior hanging around my place, but if that got Damon off my back and allowed me some freedom, I'd take it. Besides, Cole was fun to hang out with. "Deal."

"No beating each other up."

"What fun is that?"

Damon reached for the phone, shaking his head. Under his breath, he murmured, "Sadist."

TWELVE

Forty-eight hours. I had forty-eight hours to figure out how I was going to get out of becoming vamp queen of the entire Midwest.

What a freakin' nightmare.

Cole and I walked out of the Institute, heading for my car. The grounds were secure with magical protection and warning systems as well as the latest high-tech human security system, but that didn't keep him from taking his bodyguard job seriously. As he walked beside me, scanning the tops of buildings and even the trees in the park, his body hummed with tension. His nose was already healed, and in fact, looked straighter than before. "Safer to stay here, Kali. Safer and smarter. Easier for me to protect you here than at your church."

"You know where I live?"

"Is it supposed to be a secret?"

"Actually, yes. There are, like, two people in the whole hell-damned world, outside of Damon, who know my address."

He grinned, teeth flashing in the shadows as our footsteps echoed on the cold asphalt. "Make that three."

Cocky, but in a cool way. Not like Damon. "I have two days to figure out how to stop the vamp's coronation and still save a couple of humans in the process. I can't do that here."

"Is that also a secret?"

"Yes."

We'd reached my car. Cole walked me to the driver's side, held out a hand. "Give me the keys."

I waggled my eyebrows at him. "You're uber sexy when you take charge."

He smiled, but it was strained with patience. "Come on, Kali. Give me the car keys."

"Un, unh." I shook my head and dangled the keys out of his reach. "Nobody drives the TT but me."

"Bodyguards don't ride shotgun."

"You're dying to get your hands on her, aren't you?"

"That obvious, huh?"

I ran my hand over the top of the TT's sleek side. "She's a thing of beauty. Hard to resist."

"I'll let you beat me up any time you want. Just let me drive her this once."

He was still scanning the area, giving me pleading glances in between. I sighed and held out the keys. "All right, but just this once."

He leaned over and pecked my cheek. "Awesome."

We got in and he cranked the ignition. Megadeath exploded from the speakers. He scrambled around, looking for the volume control and once he found it, turned the radio down so low, it was nothing but background noise.

"You don't really like that stuff, do you?" he asked.

Metal rock could not be appreciated at anything less than full volume. I cranked it up again. "Best music. Ever," I yelled over the grind of guitars.

He shook his head, shifted the car into drive and we took

off, tires squealing along with Mustaine singing, "Peace sells, but who's buying?"

After a few miles, I was confused by Cole's series of turns. "This isn't the way to my house."

"I know that."

We were still yelling over the music. Disgusted, he poked the off button. Sudden silence, as loud as the music had been, descended.

"Hey," I complained.

"Fucking stuff gives me a headache."

"I know you're getting off on driving my car, but are you ever going to take me home?"

He glanced in the rearview. "I'm making sure we don't have a tail."

"I'm not that kind of demon. No tail. No horns. Just a wicked sense of justice and a mean temper."

Cole rolled his eyes, but I could see he thought it was funny. I pinched his arm. "I appreciate you doing this, you know."

He didn't answer, just punched the radio back on.

Half an hour later, we pulled into the drive that went around the back of the church to the parking lot and main entrance area. A weak solar light, the only one that hadn't been broken by vandals, cast a muted glow over the area. The wide concrete porch and steps were shadowed, but we could see their outlines. In the flash of the headlights, a figure moved, jumping up from a seated position on the porch.

"Who's that?" Cole said, hand on the gearshift, ready to back up and get out of there.

My eyes adjusted to the varying shadows and I could see it was a woman. She seemed to be wearing a long, flowing robe, but the hood was down and her frizzy hair flew in all directions. I remembered that hair, the way Nudra had stroked it while she was feeding off my stomach. What the hell? Did everyone know where I lived?

"Victoria."

"You know her?" She was moving toward the car and Cole drew a weapon from the inside of his coat. "She a friend?"

So not a friend. I tapped his hand, suggesting he put the gun away. "She's human. Don't kill her. Let me see what she wants."

Cole parked the car, left the engine running. Turned off the radio. "Got your protection mojo up and working?"

I touched my fingertips to my thumbs and magic formed a strong protective barrier around me. "Check."

A shadow moved behind Vicky and we both tensed. Cole swore under his breath. "Who the fuck is that?"

As the witch reached the car, I could see she was upset. I could also see the figure behind her—a man—walking into the muted light. Broad shoulders, dark hair, sexy saunter.

"Hell's blood," I muttered, reaching over and taking Cole's gun. "How good are you at burying bodies?"

Cole flicked his eyes to me holding the gun, back to Vicky, who was yelling at me from the outside of my window in between sobs. Great, just what I needed, an emotional witch and a Noctifector. "Unless he's a vamp, that gun won't kill him, y'know."

"I know," I said, "but it will hurt like hell when I drill him in the heart with a dozen holy water bullets."

He smiled a knowing smile. "The Chaos demon?"

"I'm going to need my keys back."

"Why is that?"

"Because after I'm done shooting *il pistolino*, I'm going to run him over. More than once."

THIRTEEN

"I raised her, but then she killed everybody in my coven. Everyone but me!" Vicky tugged at the ends of her kinky hair and paced back and forth between the car and Rad, not looking at any of us. "Why did she do that?"

The area I live in is considered a dump even by South Siders. When the battle between good and evil went down here in the mid-1800s, the leftover magic formed a repulsive barrier to humans. They stay away from the church and the nearby graveyard and say it's haunted.

Fine by me. I like privacy. Which is why I've also added a little gothic glamour to the place to also give humans an icky sensation if they get too close.

That Vicky had found my residence bothered me immensely. That she'd gone and raised an entity from hell bothered me more. I didn't think she had it in her, even with mine and Nudra's blood, to be able to do such a thing. Shame on me for underestimating her Underestimating what my blood mixed with a vamp's could do. "Are you sure it was Lilith and not some other demon?"

The gun in my right hand hung loose by my side. I'd wrapped my cloak around my shoulders once more and Volante coiled securely around my left wrist, her handle in my palm.

Rad kept his distance; he and Cole staring each other down. Even in the demon world, males give off *don't piss with me* signals. Similar to human testosterone, the magical variety permeated the air and crawled into my nostrils. Rad's stormy scent bucking up against Cole's metallic one. Air and earth colliding. The hair on the back of my neck prickled from their combined magical energies.

"Of course it was Lilith!" Vicky's voice echoed off the high stone walls of the church and several trees in the graveyard bowed their limbs as if a strong wind had just blown through, but I didn't feel even the slightest breeze.

"She ate their souls for strength," I told the witch. "She needs a lot of souls to take human form and walk the Earth after being in hell for so long."

Vicky faced me, eyes wide. She took two steps in my direction before Cole moved in front of me, cutting her off. "Why didn't she take my soul?" She looked around him, clutching the front of her dress and crinkling the fabric into a fisted bunch of cotton. "I raised her. Am I not good enough for her?"

Cole scanned the area, giving Rad another *my dick's bigger than yours* look. "We need to get inside. Now."

I couldn't leave Vicky in the parking lot but I wasn't hip on bringing her inside my home either. Stupid witch didn't have a coat on and had to be freezing in the early morning air.

November first. All Saints Day. A good day for demons to stay inside under the covers.

Walking around Cole, I started for the door. Vicky followed on my heels and Cole brought up the rear. As I passed Rad, I raised the gun and pointed it at his heart. "Get off my property."

He was wearing a black leather jacket that hung down past his hips. His hands were hidden deep in the jacket's pockets. "We need to talk."

No telling what weapons he had stashed in and under that coat. "*Vaffanculo.*" I used my favorite hand gesture. "We have nothing to talk about."

He stepped toward me and Cole immediately intercepted him, placing a big hand on his chest. "Lady doesn't want to talk to you. I suggest you go back to the hole you crawled out from."

Rad didn't back up, didn't even look at Cole. He started to draw his right hand from its pocket and Cole immediately had a blade at his throat.

Cool. A wrist blade. It hid under Cole's sleeve and slid out with the flick of his wrist. I'd used a similar knife on a few occasions, but most of the blades felt too heavy to me when I wasn't using them. I preferred my whip. Lightweight, easy to pass off as jewelry or a belt, and Volante was nearly a sentient being who fed off my wishes and desires when I was battling someone. As far as weapons went, she was a beast. I could wound or kill with a slash. I could choke someone or simply remove a digit with her. I could blind someone with the tip or tie them up using the entire length.

Rad dropped his gaze to Cole's. "I have something of Kali's. Right pocket."

Cole nodded for Rad to remove it. "Slowly."

Rad did so and held up a swath of black material. My skirt hung from one gloved finger. He looked back at me, raised the skirt higher. "Thought you might want this back."

I snatched it off his finger, not missing Cole's raised brow, and hoping Rad didn't pull out my underwear next. He didn't and I started for the church again. Victoria babbled softly to herself as she followed me.

"You know, if she did raise Lilith, you're going to need my help," Rad said to my back.

Cole had released him and was walking backward toward the church door, keeping Rad in full view while watching for other intruders. I paused at the French doors, laying my hand on the stone next to them. Earth magic communicated with my demon. Nothing but the usual vibrations and hums and the door unlocked at my touch.

"I don't ever want anything from you again," I told Rad. "You're lucky I don't kill you right now."

Cole shoved the door open wide. "Get inside."

"I'm not leaving here until we talk." The set of Rad's shoulders told me he wasn't kidding. Not only did I have a hysterical witch on my hands, I also had the most stubborn Chaos demon in history ready to camp out on my back porch.

Everyone was looking at me. Even Cole. His look told me he'd kill Rad for me, but he wanted all of us inside the safety of the church before he did it. Out here, he couldn't be my bodyguard and Rad's assassin at the same time. The minute he focused on killing Rad, he'd leave me vulnerable.

Rad had that effect—making me vulnerable every time he was around—no matter what the situation. "Fine. You can come in."

I led Victoria and Rad to my living room, a sunken area with curvy couches and a fireplace. It had taken me years to do all the work myself, but I was damned proud of it. Magic can be an awesome thing when it comes to remodeling a gothic church into a home.

Shrugging off my cape, I kept Volante on my arm and Cole's gun in my hand. Rad leaned one arm against the fireplace mantel, head down and looking at me from under his dark eyelashes. Cole, meantime, went room to room, avoiding the sanctuary, and making sure the place was secure. I knew it was, but if it relieved his sense of duty to confirm it, who was I to deny him the thrill.

Victoria sat on the edge of one cream colored couch and looked at me expectantly. "Why didn't she take my soul? Why?"

Suicidal much? Gaw. Witches. "When you raised her, you formed a sort of umbilical cord connecting the two of you together. You're what holds her here. If she killed you and ate your soul, she'd end up right back in hell."

There was a long, silent pause as Vicky digested what I'd said. She smiled as if deciding she was even more skilled than she'd imagined. People like her sold their metaphorical souls every day, obsessed with a goal that sacrificed their humanity the closer they came to obtaining it. "I'm her master."

"No," Rad said, as Cole came back into the room. "You're her slave, now, like the rest of the demon world. You get a free pass until she figures out how to stay here without you."

Cole took a sentry position where he could see the door to his left, the tall stained glass windows to his right, and me in front of him. "We can't let that happen."

"No, we can't," I said, staring at the witch. Too bad she was human or I would have severed Lilith's Earthly connection with one flick of my wrist.

A pregnant pause now filled the room as Vicky realized what I was thinking. She rose from the couch slowly as if afraid moving too fast would startle me and make her an easier target. "I think I'll go now."

"You're not going anywhere." I tossed Cole his gun and Vicky flinched. Exasperation at this new predicament got the better of me. What luck, I now had to protect Victoria while trying to figure out how to exorcise Lilith and stop the vamp coronation. Oh, and have a heart-to-heart with the man who'd screwed me over, not once, but twice.

I'd experienced a lot in three hundred years, but this night was one for the record books.

Rad pushed off the mantel. "Maybe I should make coffee. Where's your kitchen?"

Snatching up my cape, I motioned him to follow me. Time to take care of the least of my problems. It didn't feel like the least, but in the big picture, Rad was inconsequential. Our relationship, screwed up as it was, was minor compared to the mother of demons running loose on Earth and Damon forcing me to be a vamp queen.

In the kitchen, I opened the pantry door. At one time, it was the priest's study. Being a hermit, I had taught myself to cook and I was pretty good at it. I didn't even use magic. "There's a fancy espresso machine in a box on the top shelf in the back."

He took off his coat, slung it over a chair. "You don't have a regular coffee maker?"

"Is that a problem?"

He shrugged, found the espresso machine and whistled softly under his breath. "The Jura J9 one-touch. Sweet machine."

"Di gave it to me for Christmas last year."

"And you've never used it?"

We were having a conversation like normal people did. Like friends did. We were not normal people and we certainly weren't friends. I wasn't sure what we were, but a demon killer, let alone one who'd broken my heart and betrayed my family, would never in this lifetime be my friend.

I bit back an explanation. I didn't owe him anything, not

even a simple explanation. "I want you out of my house and out of my life. Go back to your life as a rock star and leave me alone."

He set the box down, opened it with a flippant rush. "Why not kill me along with Victoria? Solve two of your problems right here, right now."

"I'm considering it, but you're both human to some degree, and I don't kill humans. Never have and I never will. Besides, I never kill anyone in my home. Cleanup's a bitch."

He smirked, started to say something. I held up a hand to fend off whatever else was on his mind. "There are beans in the freezer. Once you've made coffee for Victoria and Cole, see yourself out. We clear?"

"Give me a chance, Kali."

"A chance?" I walked forward so I was in his face. I'd worn my platforms home, but we were hardly eye-to-eye, which pissed me off even more. I hated looking up at him.

Stupid of me to get so close, being he was obviously a good demon killer, but I was angry. Angry and tired and freaking out under my cool exterior. "You had your chance two hundred and eighty-five years ago and you left me at the altar and joined the Noctifectors. Don't you dare ask me for another chance."

I left him standing there with the J9 half out of the box and a sad look on his face, his emotions swirling and the scent of a summer storm prevalent. In the living room, I tipped my chin at Vicky and spoke to Cole. "Don't let her out of your sight."

"You can't hold me here against my will," Vicky said, indignant and oh, so human.

Cole and I ignored her and he acknowledged my request with a nod. "Where you going?"

"Upstairs." In the distance, the whir of the bean grinder told me Rad was following directions for once in his life. Miracles would never cease. "I need to think."

"What about the Chaos demon?"

I picked up my skirt and balled the fabric in my fist. "He'll be leaving shortly."

"You don't want me to kill him?"

"When the time comes," I muttered, "that'll be my job."

FOURTEEN

Chicago is a gray city six months out of the year. Gray sky, gray lake, gray buildings. When the sun breaks through the winter gloom, the sky sports a beautiful, sharp blue canvas, but even then, the lake and the buildings remain gray. And no matter what time of year, there's a pall that hangs over this entire part of the state. Most humans can't see it, but I can. A lot of evil has been done here.

Those nights I made it home by sunrise, I sat on the highest roof line of the church to watch. The building had been modeled after a castle in Ireland, complete with crenellations and a bell tower. On a normal morning, I sat in the tower and watched the sun rise to catch the array of colors and appreciate something most humans took for granted.

That morning, I had to stay inside for more reasons than one. Staying out of the line of pissed vamp fire was the least of them. I could think better on the roof and being forced to remain inside made my skin itch. I needed fresh air and sunshine, not the claustrophobia of stone walls and too many beings downstairs.

Changing out of my business attire, I exchanged the skirt and blouse for pants and a long sleeve turtleneck. I spread my cape on the bed, rearranged the weapons inside and then checked my stash under the bed. I was low on holy water and stakes and I wanted one of those stun batons like Nudra's mercs had used on me. That thing packed a punch and there was one person in particular I wanted to use it on. Later, after I sorted out a couple of things, I was going shopping. Nudra's office at the Madhouse would be my first stop. His residence, the second. I bet he had some fun weapons hidden in both places.

Lying on the bed and staring at the high ceiling, I stroked a long stake from my armory. Premium cherry wood, it was hard and strong and sanded to the smoothest finish to make sliding into a heart even easier.

Cherry makes a heavy stake, too heavy for carrying in my cape, but this one was utter perfection in home security. Best of all, I got the premium cherry stakes from an eco-friendly supplier right there in Chicago. From growing to harvesting to manufacturing, the wood had been handled with a focus on sustainability. The Earth was precious. Another point most humans didn't appreciate. Spend a little time in hell and you're glad for anything that isn't.

Of course, if Lilith was truly walking the Earth again, sustainability was a moot point. She would give a whole new meaning to deforestation and global warming.

As I stroked the smooth wood under my hands, there were a couple of things bothering me. Besides the biggies. How had Victoria found where I lived? What was Arman doing with his new powers? Why hadn't Rad killed me when he'd had the chance?

I could smell the bold, rich scent of fresh coffee floating up from downstairs. I couldn't remember the last time I'd eaten and I hadn't even had a sip of water after my workout with Cole. Sliding off the bed, I stood in the long hall, listening for Rad's voice and hearing nothing. I sniffed the air, but only the coffee aroma filled my nose. No salty ocean scent, no briny squall smell.

He was gone.

Grabbing my cape, I went downstairs, straight to the kitchen. A cup of steaming coffee waited for me. At the sink, I took a couple of sips and stared out the window at the grave-yard. Gray and purple shadows stared back. A mass of ancient scrub oaks, scrawny pines and leafless maples created a canopy over the old grave markers, most of which had long ago been covered in grass and moss. Wild grape vines and tangled brush created a natural fence, keeping humans out. A magical barrier I'd constructed a hundred years ago when I settled here kept the ghosts in. In other words, a magical condom.

"I still don't get why you want to live in a church." Rad's voice startled me so bad I dropped the cup in the sink, shat-tering it. He didn't seem to notice. "Can't the Bridge Council set you up in nicer digs? With everything you do for them, you're entitled to a better place than this."

I couldn't look at him for fear I'd unload every weapon in my cape and then some. Instead I stared at the busted cup and seethed as the coffee spread and stained the white porcelain. Why was he still here? How dare he criticize my home? I wanted to yell but my voice came out low, controlled. "What are you still doing here?"

Rad heard the dangerous undercurrent in my tone. "You have every right to be mad, K, but I'm not leaving until I've said what I came to say."

Mad? "I'm beyond mad. I'm furious. Nothing you say will change that."

Behind me, the phone on the wall rang, its loud blare

seeming to jump between us like a barrier as thick and impenetrable as the fence around the graveyard.

The thick stone walls of the castle made cell phone reception difficult. Add my magical shield and glamours, and it was impossible. Hence, a landline was necessary.

As I lifted the handset, Cole and Victoria entered the kitchen, eyes on me. Typically the only two people who ever called me at home were Di and JR. Occasionally Damon. Caller ID said, "office", so it had to be one of my Sweet Investigation employees. "Yo," I answered.

Di's voice came through the line in a strained whisper. "Why aren't you here yet?"

The hairs on the back of my neck rose. "What's going on?"

"Lilith, as in *the* Lilith of hell fame, is sitting in the waiting room. Said she's here to see you."

I grabbed the edge of the sink with my free hand, swallowed the sudden metallic taste in my mouth and tried to sound casual. "Did she say why she wanted to see me?"

A muffled sound came from Di's end, like she was cupping a hand over the phone for a second. I heard the squeak of a door shutting, then she came back on. "She says she has a job for Sweet Investigations. You're the only one she'll deal with."

A job. Oh fuck. "Listen, Di, here's what I want you to do. Get out of there, now. Is JR there?"

"No. I had to send him to Chloe's for some blood."

"What?" Holy hell and then some. Chloe was a Tempter demon who ensnared supernatural creatures as well as humans and took their blood. Similar to a vampire but she never turned the humans into the Undead or killed them. She simply ran a blood bank that supplied the entire Northern Illinois region, and she did it with coerced volunteers. If you needed O-neg for a ritual or you were a vamp in the twelve-step no-feeding-on-live-humans program, Chloe was your girl. Anyone who came

REVENGE IS SWEET   97

to her to buy was also asked to give. If you needed a pint of blood for your ritual, you had to donate the same. The Bridge left her alone for the most part because her services, while unconventional, kept a lot of supernaturals from killing humans or each other for blood.

Her place was located in a skeezy section of downtown and housed under a strip club that also catered to the supernatural crowd. Easier to ensnare the volunteers she needed for her business, but not exactly the place to send my techhead office assistant. My *human* techhead office assistant. "What do you need blood for?"

"Her Highness requested warm blood instead of coffee or tea."

I leaned over the sink in case the two sips of coffee I'd had made a hasty comeback. Cole stepped closer to me, a deep frown on his face. Rad was frowning too.

The only one in the room not worried or scared to death was Victoria. She was smiling, a strange and eerie light in her eyes. I moved the mouthpiece away from lips and glared at her. "How did Lilith know about me and Sweet Investigations?"

Vicky gave me a condescending look. "She asked how I managed to raise her, what help I had. I might have mentioned you."

"Did you mention where I lived or just where I worked?"

"Neither. I told her your name, that's all. Yours and Nudra's."

"Wait a minute," Cole said, eyes darting back and forth between us. He'd heard through the Bridge grapevine that I'd had a run-in with Nudra and the vamp ended up dead. He didn't know about the blood slave issue, though. "What exactly happened at Nudra's compound? You didn't...he didn't..."

"I'll explain later." I spoke into the phone again. "Di, you have to get out of there right now. Lilith is the mother of demons. She can level that entire place with the blink of an eye."

"Chill, Kali. I know who she is, and I've got everything under control. When JR gets back with the blood, I'll send him home, but I'm staying. She's not getting run of the office with no one here, and I'm not leaving you alone with her. If you're coming in, that is."

She was so stubborn. One of the reasons I adored her. "Don't even look at her, okay? Nothing. Eyes averted and don't ask her any questions. She'll peel the skin of your body in strips. And then she'll start the real torture."

"Pul-leez. I'm a goddess for heaven's sake. I can handle her."

There was stubborn and then there was stupid. I loved Di, but sometimes she could be so naïve. "You're the frickin' goddess of love! You get into a pissing contest with Lilith and she'll deep fry you."

"Kali, Kali, Kali. The only true weapon against evil *is* love. I'll be fine. You're the one I'm worried about. You definitely don't have enough love in you or around you. You really should open your heart to Radison. Give love another shot."

So not what I needed right now, a lecture on my love life. "This is not some Harry Potter movie, Aphrodite. Love will not conquer evil and leave you with a cool scar on your forehead if you challenge her. You could end up in hell with her pulling your guts out one intestine at a time and roasting them over hot coals while you watch."

Although her voice was still lowered, it now took on a hint of amusement. "You seem to know Lilith quite well."

I'd been born on Earth and had never visited the depths of hell. It wasn't exactly a vacation destination, even for demons. "I've never met her, but I know fellow demons who've gone to hell and come back. I've heard stories. Believe me, this is no game. You spit cupid arrows and write love sonnets, Di. Lilith eats babies for breakfast."

"Fine. I'll put Resident Evil on the Blu-ray in the waiting room and when JR gets back with her blood, I'll give her some in a fancy glass and clear out." She sighed as if I were the one being irresponsible. "You'll be okay?"

I glanced at my two bodyguards and the witch whose ass I was going to kick. "Just leave as soon as you can. I'm on my way."

FIFTEEN

S weet Investigations was dark when Cole and I arrived. Rad had taken Victoria home in his Porsche and Cole had called Hone to babysit her. Rad was meeting us as soon as he could get there.

I was stupid, but the fact he insisted on helping me deal with Lilith made me feel ever so slightly better. As if his presence could protect me. What a joke. Nothing and no one could protect me if the queen of hell was sitting in my office waiting for me.

The lack of lights should have been a relief. Maybe she'd left and Di and JR had gone to their respective homes. Should I have been relieved Lilith had tired of waiting for me and was roaming the South Side? No, but for half a second, when I saw the SI office windows were dark, I was giddy at the prospect of not having to face my creator.

True, I had an Earthly mother and father, but Lilith was the reason demons existed. She was our God. Demons were supposed to worship her. Like most humans with their gods, we did a poor job of it.

"I don't like this," Cole said as I parked the Roadster in my dedicated spot around back. Muse was singing about an uprising from the speakers. Caught up in my thoughts, I hadn't even noticed Cole had switched radio stations on me.

I'd told him the deets about the blood slave thing and after that, there wasn't much to say. He hadn't even teased me about it, which meant one of two things: he was as freaked out about it as I was or he was planning a way to kill me as soon as Damon gave him the go-ahead. Cole knew Bridge law as well as I did. A demon like me with control over humans was a danger to everyone.

The sun was shooting early morning rays over the building and parking lot. Di's black VW Beetle—her love bug, as she called it—sat next to us, its fuchsia interior practically glowing.

Sweet Investigations anchored a one-story mini complex with a mainstream coffeehouse at the other end and Louie's bail bonds-slash-check cashing station between us. A steady stream of patrons entered and exited the coffee shop, some using the drive-up and circling the parking lot in their cars once they had their caffeine fix, others standing in a line that stretched out the door and onto the sidewalk out front. The check cashing business wouldn't be open until six, but bail was often needed at the wee hours of the morning, especially on a holiday weekend, so a single light glowed inside Louie's place as well.

But Sweet Investigations was pitch black except for the scattered rays of light making their way past the towering hotel behind us.

"I'm not exactly excited about this myself." I switched off the radio and hit one of the buttons on the remote transmitter JR had programmed for me. At home, I didn't have a garage, so I'd had him program the transmitter for the office instead. I preferred locking and unlocking doors with the touch of my hands so I could get a feel for what was happening inside, but the SI office wasn't made of stone, so my natural earth magic didn't work. The remote control in the car could lock and unlock the doors and turn the lights off and on. All with me sitting safely inside the TT.

Another nifty trick JR had wired up involved the unlock feature. When I unlocked the back door remotely, a set of lights would automatically come on and the security alarm would disengage for one minute. If I didn't enter the building and punch in my code, the door would lock, the alarm would reengage and the lights would go out.

This time, however, when I hit the button, nothing happened with the lights. Even if the lock and alarm were working, the lights weren't.

Bad sign.

Cole took a phone out of his jacket pocket and pushed the touchscreen.

"What are you doing?"

He scanned the area, waiting for the phone to connect. "Calling in backup."

"No." I grabbed his arm and pulled the phone away from his face. "This is my problem. I'll handle it."

"You'll handle Lilith? How exactly? The way you handled Nudra?"

Low blow. I took the phone from his hand, disconnected the call before someone at the Institute answered. "I have to find out what she wants. Then I'll figure out what to do with her. Probably an exorcism. But before that, I need to know what she's planning."

Cole scoffed. "You really think holy water and chanting is going to work?"

"Not the Christian version of exorcism. A pagan one."

"Pagan, huh? Never heard of that."

Not many had. A lot of modern day pagans didn't believe in the Christian version of the devil. Just because you didn't believe in something didn't mean it ceased to exist. "Pagans were banishing demons long before Jesus was crucified and the Church took power, but that was also before YouTube and 20/20 made exorcism cool."

He looked at me, eyes detached. "That Chaos demon, he's your blood slave too. He going to help you?"

I started to answer in the negative, stopped. Rad was a Noctifector, blessed by the Roman Catholic Church, and a demon who controlled a great deal of elemental power. Mix the two together and throw in me performing an exorcism and that combination might be the tipping point for sending Lilith back to hell. "Rad owes me. Big time." Skepticism reflected in Cole's eyes. "And if Rad doesn't come through with the banishing, I'll feed him to Lilith."

Cole took his phone back, slid it into his pocket. "Just so we're clear, I'm only protecting you from the vamps, not the queen of hell."

"Fair enough."

We exited the car and stole up to the back door, Cole watching my six. Both of us had weapons at the ready but concealed from prying eyes since a regular stream of cars kept passing by. Volante was coiled around the wrist of my left hand, hidden under my cape. My right held a stake. Wouldn't do me a bit of good fighting Lilith, but if a vamp attacked, which was unlikely in such a public space, I was ready. I almost hoped one would. I needed to release some tension and was itching for a fight.

The door was unlocked from the remote. Out of habit, I pressed my hand against the outside wall, just in case the building materials had enough natural products in them to give me a hint of Lilith's dark evil waiting inside. A slick heat warmed my hand and burned its way up my arm. The fires of hell burned hotter and dark magic flowed slower. This was just an echo of her. She'd been there but didn't seem to be any more.

That could be good or it could just mean the building wasn't giving up its secrets.

Cracking the door open, I peered around the frame and squinted into the dark hallway. My eyes adjusted quickly, seeing only the usual shadows. I drew in a breath, taking in the smells of cheap commercial carpeting, plastic and metal cabinets, and stale office air. The computers and other equipment droned softly in the background.

But there...teasing my nostrils...the scent of smoke. Smothering smoke.

There was no actual smoke in the air. The residual scent resembled that of a candle being snuffed out, not the queen of the underworld lying in wait for me.

I stepped inside, motioned Cole in after me. On cat feet, we stole down the hall, my nerves fraying. Was Lilith masking herself to trick me? Where was Di?

A rustling sound came from the front. Cole and I exchanged a look and picked up our pace. At first glance, the reception area looked perfectly normal. Blinds hung over the windows, blocking out the early morning light. Three chairs sat next to the windows, two end tables stacked with magazines and the previous day's Chicago Tribune interspersed between them. The reception desk, with its elevated countertop, and chair which no one ever sat in, was clean and neat, a multiline phone, a message tablet and a couple of Sweet Investigations ink pens tucked in one corner.

I felt for the light switch, got no response to flipping it. Could simply be a power outage, but why did both my neighbors still have juice? Lowering the stake, I made my way past

REVENGE IS SWEET   105

the countertop to check the front door. As I stepped into the narrow waiting area, my foot hit a soft but unmovable object.

My stomach dropped. I knew what it was before I even looked down.

At my feet, curled in a fetal position and shaking from head to toe, lay Aphrodite, goddess of love and my best friend.

SIXTEEN

"Di!" I dropped to my knees and grabbed her. Her body convulsed under my hand as if she were having a seizure. In the dim light, I couldn't see if she was hurt, but her extremely pale skin and blond hair stood out enough for me to make out her face and her closed eyes.

She moaned, and her teeth chattered. Running my hand along her face, down her throat and across the exposed skin of her arm under her shirt sleeve, I found she was as cold as the November breeze outside. Damn it. Hadn't I told her not to mess around with Lilith? I undid my cape, weapons and all, and covered her with it.

Cole stood above us, keeping one eye on the dark office and one eye on me. "What's wrong with her?"

"I don't know, but she's freezing."

I smoothed hair back from her face and continued to run my hands over her limbs and torso, looking for a wound, anything, that would tell me what had happened. Her pulse beat erratically but with force under my fingers. "Talk to me,

Di. I know you're in pain, but I can't help you if I don't know what's causing it."

I probably couldn't help her anyway. I was a demon, full of dark magic, not white. I couldn't heal a fly, much less a goddess. Rain down destruction? Spread pestilence? I was your girl. But heal someone? No.

She was still shaking hard. Lying down next to her, I gathered her in my arms and spooned our bodies together. Being a demon is good for one thing. I radiate heat like a tropical sun.

Reassuring her as much as myself, I whispered in her ear. "Di, it's me. Kali. I'm here, and I'm going to take care of you."

As she lay shaking in my arms, I tried to figure out what Lilith had done to her. Poisoned her? Given her some funky disease? Goddesses had kickass immune systems. Di had never been sick or even hungover after a night of tequila and cabana boys. Had to be something else.

"Ev...il," Di said, teeth still chattering. Her body, though, was no longer shaking so hard.

"Lilith did this to you." It wasn't a question. "She's as evil as it gets."

Di shook her head and jabbed a thumb at her chest. "In... me."

Understanding snapped into place. "She injected you with evil."

A jittery nod. "Can't handle...it."

"Fight it, Di. Fight it with everything you've got."

"Can't."

I squeezed her tighter. "Yes, you can, and you will. Don't give me that pansy-assed, I can't do it crap. You're the strongest goddess I know." She was the only goddess I knew, but there was no point in splitting hairs. "You're the strongest *woman* I know."

"Need...love."

A tear squeaked out of the corner of my eye and fell into her hair. "You know I love you. Not in the gay human way or even the gay demon way, but you know I love you like a..." I swallowed and forced the words out. "Like a sister."

A small smile tightened her cheek under my chin. "Love...you...too."

She relaxed another smidgen in my arms. Seemed like a good sign. "BFFs forever, right?"

Cole looked down and caught my eye, cocked an eyebrow at me. "While I'm totally digging the girl-on-girl action here, we need to move to a more secure location."

I kicked out and hit him squarely in the side of his knee, making him yelp and nearly fall. "And Neve loves you, JR loves you, and probably the professor loves you even if he doesn't realize it yet. For thousands of years, men and women alike have worshipped you. You're one of the most loved figures in all of human history."

She sighed deeply. "Who's...the professor?"

"That college boy you brought by my place last week."

"Oh." She sounded sleepy now. "He's only after me...for my...body."

Damn, it was good to hear her joking again. I laughed, both from amusement and from relief. "And you're only after him for his brains, right?"

This time she laughed, a slight sound, but a good one. I loosened my hold and touched her skin in different places. Not normal, but warmer than when I'd first found her. "Feeling any better?"

"Yes." She yawned. "Just tired."

"Can you tell me what happened?"

"Lilith wouldn't wait for you. I tried to stop her from leaving."

"I told you not to engage her in any way." A new, ugly thought struck. "Did JR make it back?"

"No."

Merde. She'd sent him to the blood bank nearly an hour earlier. He should have been back before then. Had he seen the lights were out and figured Di and Lilith were gone? My gut told me no. I removed my cell phone from my cape and punched the speed dial button for JR. The call went directly to voice mail, and I swore under my breath.

Keeping my cape tucked around Di as I sat up, I looked at Cole. "Let's take her back to my place. She can sleep, and I can keep an eye on her there. I'll send Rad to find JR."

"No." Di pushed up on an elbow, then fell back down.

"Whoa, there. Take it easy."

Rolling onto her back, she pressed her fingers against her temple. "Not your place."

"I don't want to leave you alone yet, and my place is safer. Your place doesn't even have a deadbolt on the door."

"Your place isn't safe," she said, voice stronger.

"Why not?" Cole asked.

Three things happened at the same time. A *bam, bam, bam* at the front door only a few feet away made me nearly jump out of my skin. Cole's cell phone blared, echoing on the heels of the knock, and Di sat up and grabbed my arms. "Lilith is there."

SEVENTEEN

Inside the office's break room, Cole, Rad, Di, and I stared at the floor. None of us sat at the small, square table that looked dingy in the growing natural light from the hallway's single window, even with my red cape tossed on it. Cole was on his phone near the door, talking to Damon. Rad lounged against the sink. Di leaned on the fridge, and I paced the two feet of open space across from her, toying with the end of my ponytail—a nervous habit.

I lowered my personal protective magic a notch in order to fuel the protective circle I was sustaining around the building. The entire complex, actually. The humans next door weren't in direct danger from Lilith or the vamps, but demons and the Undead cared little about collateral damage. I couldn't take the chance that any humans would get hurt in the crossfire.

Usually, I wouldn't have needed to shift my energies and focus from one to the other, but that morning, I was drained. The past twelve hours had taken its toll on me, mentally, physically, and emotionally. I prided myself on stamina, but this was a little much.

The single bright spot at that moment was the coffee in my hands. Once again, Rad had come through in the coffee delivery department, stopping at the coffeehouse before knocking on the front door of Sweet Investigations.

The first sip had nearly made me swoon. It was hot, creamy, and oh-so-perfect. *Thank the sweet fires of hell for Rad and his obsession with coffee.*

The thought made me nearly drop my cup, Rad's half-lidded gaze intensifying as he watched me. A few hours ago, I'd wanted to kill him. Now, I was grateful because he'd brought me the perfect cup of coffee?

Yes, dammit. It was wrong, but I had to admit, it was also true. It's amazing what you're willing to forget over a simple act of kindness. All was not forgotten but temporarily dismissed, in this case.

"Finish your story," I said to Di. "You tried to stop Lilith from leaving. She shot you full of evil and took off. Why do you think she'd go to my house?"

"Like I told you on the phone, she said she had a job for you. Since Victoria had raised her, she planned to put her time on Earth to good use, but she wasn't waiting around. Said she couldn't trust anyone else to do the job properly. While she was talking, she started acting like a junkie needing a fix. She said she couldn't wait for you or JR, and she would find you at home when she was ready."

Ready for what exactly?

She doesn't know where I live, crossed my mind, but Lilith wasn't human. She was my creator. I was tied to her like she was to Vicky. My umbilical cord was much thinner, but she could still use her senses to find me like a bloodhound tracking a rabbit. "She is a junkie. For souls. She needs lots of them to stay here on Earth."

"What about the blood?"

"An appetizer. The blood JR was bringing wouldn't have sustained her for long."

Thinking of JR, I speed-dialed his phone. Once more, it went directly to voice mail. I left him the third message of the morning.

Rad played with his cup, turning it in circles. "What kind of job would Lilith need you for? One she only trusts you with?"

Di and I exchanged a knowing glance. What else did supernatural and human women come to me for?

"Vengeance," we said at the same time.

Rad whistled softly. "Who would be ballsy enough to piss off the queen of demons, and why wouldn't Lilith seek her own revenge?"

Both were good questions. Ones I didn't have answers to.

Cole was listening intently to Damon, sneaking an occasional glance my way. Jamming a hand through his short hair, he finally said, "Right," before disconnecting and slipping the phone inside his jacket. "Boss says I'm to bring you back to the Institute, pronto."

"Un, unh. No way. Besides Lilith being on the loose and looking for me, I need to find JR. I need to protect Di. I can't do any of those things at the Institute."

"You don't need to protect me," Di said. "I'll be fine."

"Fine like you were when I arrived?"

She stuck her tongue out at me.

Rad straightened. "She can come with me, and we'll find JR."

I narrowed my eyes at him. How damn gallant could one half-demon be? "Don't you have band practice or a concert in Canada or something?"

"North American tour doesn't start until next month. I'm free."

Oh, goodie. "What about your *other* job?"

He didn't need me to spell out I was talking about his demon hunting. "No assignments at the moment."

"What other job?" Di asked.

Cole huffed. "Kali, let's go."

Good to know I wasn't an assignment on Rad's docket, but on the other hand, why *wasn't* I? While in the overall scope of good vs. evil, I might be a peon I was high enough up in the demon hierarchy, freakin' Lilith wanted to hire me. "Tell Damon to screw himself. I'm not hiding out at the Institute. I'm not safe there from Lilith anyway. I'm not safe anywhere."

"Don't make me hurt you," Cole said with a hint of jesting in his eyes.

I smiled, but there was no humor in it. "The only way for me to handle this mess is to confront it head-on. I'm not hiding behind Damon's skirts. Lilith wants me to do a job, and that's what I'm going to do."

"There are other vengeance demons around," Cole said. "She can find someone else."

"But I'm the best." I set my coffee cup down, the rich flavor now bitter in my mouth. "And the queen of demons only accepts the best. She's not going to kill me until the job's done."

Cole, Rad, and Di looked at me like I was one hellhound short of a six-pack. Rad shook his head. "And when the job *is* done?"

I opened my mouth to reply and saw Cole go rigid. "What is it?" I whispered.

He raised his gun and threw my cape at me. "Weapon up. We've got company."

EIGHTEEN

The doorknob jiggled. Cole stood on one side of the door, me on the other. His gun pointed at the ceiling, and his head tilted toward the wall as he listened to whoever was on the other side. Rad had taken up a post at the front entrance, watching out the windows in the waiting room in case anyone tried coming through that door. Di held her pepper spray and stood in the hall, ready to do battle from either direction. For what good it would do, she chanted a love spell at the same time.

We could have seen who was outside on my security camera monitors if the electricity had been working. As it was, we were blind to who or what was trying to get in.

I put my nose to the door and drew a whiff as I heard the sound of metal on metal. Was someone trying to pick the lock? Touching the door handle, I tried to sense if our assailant was magical or human. No buzz of energy and only the faint feel of heat.

Filtering through the steel door, I caught the scent of a

sweaty human. The sharp tang of fear. The musky smell of male deodorant that had failed about two hours ago.

The doorknob jiggled again, followed by a soft rapping of knuckles. "Kali? Di? Anybody in there?"

I waved off Cole, a sudden lightness filling my chest. "It's JR."

We unlocked and opened the door, JR practically falling inside as we did so. His hair, usually flat and straight, was spiked in random places. His glasses were askew. A dirty streak smudged his fair skin from chin to ear, and his clothes were torn and soiled.

"What happened to you?" I asked, relocking the door and turning on the alarm.

JR was shorter than me by an inch or so and scrawny to boot, but he was a whiz at all things tech-oriented, which Di and I weren't. Plus, he had a master's degree in religious studies. He'd read and analyzed texts thousands of years old and had a library rivaling Damon's. He could spout the history of Rome with more accuracy than I could, and I lived through several centuries of it.

Besides Neve, JR was the only one-hundred-percent human who knew I was a demon, and also, like Neve, didn't treat me any differently because of it.

He pushed his glasses back into place, glanced at Cole, and then stared at my chin. JR never looked anyone in the eye. When I first met him, the idiosyncrasy annoyed me until I realized he was extremely shy, even with people he knew. "Vampires. At least, I think they were. They wanted the blood."

His eyes met mine for a split second. He shuffled his feet, crossed his arms over his chest, uncrossed them, fiddled with the edge of his coat. "They were waiting for me when I came out of Chloe's and jumped me. Asked me if the blood was for you and if you would drink it." He shuddered.

Rad and Di joined us, Di throwing her arms around JR and hugging him. "You're okay."

JR blushed, and Di looked him over. "Good grief. Did you roll in the dirt or bathe in it?"

His blush deepened. I motioned everyone into my office. The break room wasn't big enough for all of us.

My office was sparse but filled with things I loved, especially an early seventeenth-century Italian desk that had been my father's. The dark wood was scarred, mainly from me, but it held a wealth of good memories and my father's strong presence. As I settled into my office chair, I ran my hands over the ornate drawers and worn top and felt grounded again.

Cole stood guard at the door, frowning in thought. "Why would the vamps want to know if you're drinking blood?"

"Maybe they heard about my run for vamp queen and think I need the blood to keep up appearances."

Di, who was sitting on my sofa, went bug-eyed. "Your run for what?"

Rad was also giving me a curious look. I waved them off. "It's a temporary assignment from the Bridge Council to form a new alliance with the Prince of the Undead and his minions. I'm carrying Nudra's blood and have a couple of blood..." I cut myself off and looked at Rad. He didn't give anything away, for which I was glad. "The coronation ceremony is in two days, and a few vampires might be upset about me becoming queen, even if it is temporary."

JR stared at his shoes. "They took the blood, and the blond guy took my cell phone. Bastard. That was the next-gen xCelsar. The public doesn't have it yet. Hell, the CIA doesn't even have it yet."

JR was friends with some scary-smart people. He was always getting ahold of gadgets that the rest of us didn't know existed.

"Why would they want his phone?" I said to Cole and Rad. "Just because it was different?"

Rad shrugged. "Vamps like bling."

Cole didn't seem to care about the phone. "What'd these assholes look like? How many were there? The blond, was he the leader?"

"I think so." JR scrunched up his face. "I don't know. Guy was an idiot. Called me dude about a hundred times and talked like he'd toked too much in the back of the surf shop."

I sat forward. "Did Blondie have blue eyes and a shark tooth necklace?"

JR's eyes skimmed my chin. "Yeah. You know him?"

I smirked, sat back, and shook my head. "That little fuckweed."

Everyone was eyeing me, curiosity on their faces, so I gave them an explanation. "Toel Chase. He's the vamps' West Coast regional manager. Vamp king, in other words. I thought he was enamored with me, but that's too weird that he would jump JR and steal the blood we intended for Lilith."

JR looked at the doorway and fiddled with his glasses. "Where is Lilith, by the way?"

"She's gone," Di said. "Probably waiting for Kali at her house."

Yeah, and didn't that make my already shitty day even better. I wasn't sure who I most wanted to deal with: Toel or Lilith. Both had messed with my friends, and I didn't take that lightly.

Thinking about my friends, a new thought popped into my head. "Did you have a contact list on that phone?"

My tech guru nodded.

"Can you track the phone on your computer? Find out where Toel and his friends are?"

"Why?" Cole asked. "You going after a vamp for stealing a cell phone?"

"My friend Neve and other innocent people are in that address book. If Toel's trying to get to me, that's the perfect way to do it. I underestimated him once. I won't do it again."

Cole shrugged as if I was giving the vamp too much credit. "He sent JR back."

"As a message. To let me know he's gunning for me."

My bodyguard glared at me, impatient. "My orders are to bring you back to the Institute, not track down this Toel freak."

"I'm not hiding inside the Institute while my friends are in danger."

Di raised a hand to interrupt. "You mean I can't go home because this vampire might try to rough me up?"

Sunlight spilled through my east-facing office window. Di was still pale from her ordeal with Lilith. "Toel's clock is missing a few gears. He might do more than rough you up."

"I'm a goddess. What can he do?"

I raised a brow. After her ordeal with Lilith, I was surprised she'd ask such a question. "Humor me. I don't know how strong he is or what kind of powers he has beyond the usual vamp ones. Like I said, I won't underestimate him again."

"She can stay in my suite at the Blackstone," Rad said to me. Then he faced her. "Should be up to your goddess standards."

Di's eyes widened. "I love the Blackstone. That would be so cool." She glanced at me and winked. "What a nice guy."

Cole and I both rolled our eyes as Rad gave Di his stupid grin.

"And where will you stay, Mr. Nice Guy?" I asked.

He met my gaze. "With you."

Never one to enjoy confrontation, JR stood up. "I'll grab my laptop and triangulate the cell phone's location using the GPS chip."

I tore my gaze from Rad, who really needed to be taken down a peg or two, and nodded at JR. "While you're at it, see if you can locate a residence for a shapeshifter named Arman."

"That's it?" JR frowned. "No last name? No work address? Not even the type of car he drives?"

He'd done more with less information, but I let it slide. After all, JR'd been sent out to retrieve Lilith's blood and then accosted by a vamp king. Neither of which were listed in his job description. "Arman's a werecheetah. Can't control his cat side. Lives here in the Chicago area, but could be the burbs. I'd guess his age is seventeen."

JR looked put out as he headed for his own office. "I'll see what I can do."

"Thank you," I called after him and picked up my landline phone's handset—no dial tone. "Di, use your cell and call Neve. Tell her what's going on. She needs to lay low, get out of town, visit her mother in Jersey, or something. And then check with JR as to who else was on his contact list."

Knowing my tech-head, there weren't many contacts—his friends were as limited as mine—and most of those were other tech-heads like him, working at the Pentagon and for various countries around the world out of their mothers' basements. "All of them need to be on the lookout for Undead, especially those living in the tri-state area. Toel probably won't bother with anyone farther away than that."

"Got it." She left the room.

"Cole, call Hone and have him take Victoria to the Institute. She'll be safe there."

He snatched his cell from his pocket, and I could see he was annoyed that he'd been using that more than his gun in the past few hours. "You think the vamp will go after her?"

She was my blood slave. Killing her and Arman would undermine me in more ways than one. Losing my connection to them would weaken me physically since they'd taken my blood. Not having blood slaves would shake my tenuous run for Nudra's spot. Not that I wanted to be a vamp queen, nor did I want blood slaves, but Toel didn't get to harm humans because he was out to overthrow me before I'd even claimed the throne.

Plus, the vamp just pissed me the hell off.

Foiling his plans, being one step ahead of him, and making him look stupid was the best vengeance I could think of. "He doesn't want me taking Nudra's place for whatever reason, but killing me is a lot harder than killing those I'm connected to. He doesn't necessarily want to piss off the Bridge Council, either, and killing me would do that. Better to come at me from the side than head-on."

"The Institute doesn't allow humans inside."

Suits. Always up to their asses in rules. "Tell Damon he needs to make an exception."

Cole stared at the screen on his phone. "Reception in here sucks."

"I can ease up on the magic."

"No." He walked to the window and held up the phone. The bars on his screen must have multiplied because he lowered the phone and hit a speed-dial button.

Rad leaned on my file cabinet, confident and sexy as ever. Damn him.

"What do you want me to do?" he asked.

It was his turn to receive an arched you-really-have-to-ask-that-question brow.

Didn't faze him, of course. He continued to recline against the cabinet, looking good enough to eat. "Besides get lost," he amended.

I was at war with myself. He could help me send Lilith

back to hell, but he was a Noctifector and could send me back with her. Working with the enemy was stupid, sloppy, and downright mental.

He was also my blood slave. Toel might make a midnight snack of him before I could kill him. What to do, what to do...

"I think getting lost covers it."

"Here," Cole said, shoving his phone at me. "Boss wants to talk to you."

This should be fun.

I took the phone, and before I could utter a word, Damon started in on me, his voice dark and clearly angry. "How in the name of Hades did a common witch raise Lilith from hell?"

The question of the hour. "Doesn't matter. What matters is that Lil wants me to do a job for her. Once that's over, maybe she'll go back to hell on her own."

"If she doesn't?"

"I'll find another way to send her back."

"What kind of job?"

"I'm on my way to meet her and find out."

A long pause. I could almost see Damon scrubbing his face with his free hand. "What happens if she kills you?"

"You'll need to find a new vengeance demon to do your dirty work."

The tone of his voice dropped a notch, but his anger was even more apparent. "This is not a joke, Kali. Lilith is loose on Earth, and we have no way to stop her. One wrong move, and the world is annihilated."

Just a little pressure. Yeesh. "I know, Damon. Our only chance is for me to find out what she wants and do the job. Get in, get out, send her on her way."

"Where are you meeting her?"

"I think she's at my house. While I go check that out, I want you to take my friends and blood slaves into the Institute for safekeeping."

"Humans are not allowed inside the Institute."

I'd known he would say that, and I had a handy-dandy argument. "Toel Chase is threatening me and anyone associated with me. You want me to take Nudra's place, you offer sanctuary to my friends and slaves, or I walk now."

"Toel Chase?" His tone was incredulous.

"Hard to believe that idiot could have played us, but he did. So what's it going to be? Are you keeping my friends at the Institute, or am I walking away from our deal?"

"I don't kowtow to blackmail."

"But you can use it against me to get what you want?"

There was a long, heavy pause. "How long will it take you to get to your place?"

So Damon, changing the subject to avoid my spot-on accusation. "I'll be there around nine. Nine-fifteen, if traffic is bad. As soon as I know what Lilith wants, I'll let you know, but I want your promise you'll take care of my friends and the blood slaves."

"Meet me around back in the cemetery before you go into the church."

"What?"

He hung up. Disconnected silence met my ear.

"Dammit." I set the phone down before I threw it against the wall.

"What's up?" Rad asked.

I took a finely sharpened pencil out of my pencil holder and jammed the sharp end into my ink blotter. Cole took his phone as if he suspected I would use it as a substitute for Damon's face. The first time I jabbed the sharpened point into the blotter, the graphite tip broke. The second time, the pencil shattered into three pieces, reminding me of the last White Sox game JR and I had attended. Konerko blasted a homerun out of the Cell, even though his bat broke in half. I loved that guy. Too bad he retired.

"Damon's meeting us at my place," I told Cole, brushing aside the splintered wood. It was time to focus and get the show on the road. Time to stop taking everything personally and let the training kick in. People, both human and supernatural, were depending on me.

Rising from my chair, I withdrew money from my cape and handed a twenty to Rad. I wasn't meeting my creator on an empty stomach. While I would have preferred a hamburger and fries, it was a little early for the lunch menu. "I want a pumpkin spice latte, iced, not hot, and two chocolate chip scones." I handed him two more bills. "And whatever everyone else wants, get it. It's going to be a long day. We leave in ten minutes."

Annoyed at being my errand boy, he nevertheless nodded. Cole asked for another coffee, black.

He smirked after Rad left the room. "Remind me not to get on your bad side."

I wrapped my cape around me, double checked my weapons. "You're not on my good side."

"How much are you going to torture him before you forgive him?"

Keeping my head tipped down so Cole couldn't see my lying brown eyes, I snugged the cape tighter. "I will never forgive him."

"You gonna bust Damon's balls too?"

I looked up, locking in my usual detachment. "If necessary."

"Ouch." He grimaced. "You are one tough bitch, Kali."

I guess that said it all.

NINETEEN

An eerie orange glow hung over my house and the surrounding area. Not from the sun but from something far more sinister. Something unnatural. A glow like my mother had long ago described to me about the blazes of hell.

Contrary to the warm glow, a frigid cold breeze wormed its way under my cape as I entered the cemetery. Cole walked in front of me, Rad behind. There were times I might have enjoyed being the center of a man sandwich, but in the foggy morning air, walking through this particular cemetery, this wasn't one of them.

My breath puffed white before my face, mixing with the heavy fog, and my nerves were strung taught. Was Damon already here? I tried to sense him, read his mind like he had mine. I called to him mentally, but there was no reply. None of his smoky smell teased my nose as I tromped through overgrown vines and crunched grass and weeds, frozen with morning dew, under my boots.

Like I needed him looking over my shoulder and calling the shots. There had been times in the past when he'd given me an assignment, and we'd disagreed over the execution of it, but he'd never overridden my judgment. Which was one of the reasons I continued to work for him. He accepted that my ways were sometimes unconventional, but I got the job done and stayed alive in the process.

Supernaturals who worked for the Council lived at the Institute and worked only for the Council. I was the sole exception. When I'd signed on after arriving in America, Damon had offered an invitation to live at the Institute, and I'd politely turned him down. He'd never insisted, which had surprised me, and he seemed to understand my need to live alone and work outside the Council's perimeters.   He stayed out of my personal business and gave me a lot of rope when it came to doing my job as his enforcer. I put Bridge jobs ahead of SI jobs and gave him one hundred and ten percent on every Bridge assignment.

The lines between personal and professional weren't so clear this time. Victoria was my blood slave and one of the reasons I'd agree to become the vamp queen of Chicago. She'd raised Lilith without my consent and created the single greatest problem for both humans and supernaturals the Earth had known since the beginning of creation. She was my responsibility, and I'd put all of us, including the Bridge Institute, in a precarious situation.

Inside the cemetery, we were closed off from the world. There was no bird song, not even the sound of cars on the streets nearby. The magical barriers I'd erected around the perimeter reached out, scuttling over my skin, my hair, my face, reminding me of a pet dog begging me to throw a stick for him to fetch.

Natural earth magic was strong inside here. Dark earth magic. Dark human souls as well. A massacre had occurred on this ground. Not just in the manner of a fight pitting good against evil, but a massive-scale sacrifice had been made. A sacrifice I surmised had been to Death himself.

In the center of the graveyard was a portal to other worlds. Whoever had sacrificed so many souls here had opened that portal, and there was no telling what had come up from it. Somewhere along the line, the portal had been sealed, but when I'd found it, the seal was weak. One of the reasons I'd bought the abandoned church and the grounds was to secure that portal and keep it from ever opening again.

Kali. Damon's voice pierced my skull from temple to temple. *Come to the southeast corner.*

"Ugh." I grabbed my head with my hands. "Don't do that."

Cole spun on his heel, thinking I was being attacked. Rad grabbed my elbow. "What is it?" they asked in unison.

"Nothing. Damon's over there." I pointed to the right, and sure enough, Damon came into view through the fog hanging over the monuments and between the trees and vines.

Rad kept his hand on me and tried to help me over a toppled grave marker. I jerked away, annoyed at his hovering and mad he refused to go away and leave me alone. Apparently, he hadn't heard chivalry was dead. This wasn't the Middle Ages. This was modern-day America. Besides, if I could handle evil supernaturals on a daily basis, I could damn sure step over a piece of marble without help.

Petty, I know, but I was in no mood for niceties as we walked toward Damon. If I was being honest with myself, Rad's presence rattled me more than Lilith's. He was up to something. I just didn't know what.

Damon narrowed his eyes slightly when the three of us stopped before him. He still had on his suit under a long black trench coat. I wondered what weapons he had stored inside the coat's folds. Maybe none. He was an Archdemon, after all.

He openly appraised Rad. "What's he doing here?"

Rad held out a hand and gave Damon his goofy grin. "Radison Beaumont. Here to help."

"Ignore him," I said. "Maybe he'll go away."

Damon took my advice, making no move to shake Rad's hand. He gave Cole a nod and spoke to me. "She's in the church. I can sense her. What's your plan?"

The plan was deceivingly simple. "Go in. Find out what the job's about and pray it's something I can do quickly and efficiently."

"You think she wants revenge on someone."

"That's my specialty."

"There's no reason she can't do it herself, now that she's topside."

All this talk wasn't helping my nerves. "We can stand out here all day and speculate, but the only way we'll know for sure is if I go in and talk to her."

"I don't like it." Damon's hands were sunk deep in his coat pockets. I suspected he was keeping them there in order not to grab me and haul me back to the Institute.

"None of us like it." Me, especially. "We don't have a choice. If I ignore or run from her, she'll send me to hell and probably wipe out Chicago in the process."

Silence ensued, everyone lost in thought.

"What about Victoria?" I asked. "Did you let her and Hone into the Institute?"

"Hone is babysitting the witch at her house. She'll be safe there for now."

Cole had his back to us, keeping an eye out for danger of any and all kinds. Rad stepped closer to me, shoulder to shoulder, facing Damon. His scent overrode Damon's and the graveyard's. "I'm going in with Kali."

I stepped sideways, putting space between us again. "You certainly are not."

Rad spoke to Damon, ignoring me. "I know things about Lilith. I can help Kali and back her up at the same time."

Damon studied him as I huffed and swore under my breath. "What kind of things?"

"I've studied the queen of demons in-depth," he said. "We don't have time for me to relay all that to Kali, but I can go in with her and help her sidestep potential landmines."

As a Noctifector, Rad had to know more about demons than demons did. He probably knew how many times Lilith pissed in a given twenty-four-hour period.

But I didn't care if Rad could pull monkeys out of his ass and polka at the same time, I still wasn't facing Lilith with him by my side.

He's in love with you, Damon said.

"Gah." I grabbed my head, even though, surprisingly, this time, the pain was minimal. His words, though, angered me. "Stop talking to me inside my head!"

Cole whipped around, surprise evident on his face as he pinned our boss with a curious stare. "You have access to her mind?"

The War demon knew what it took for Damon to plant his *psukhe* seed in me, and he wasn't too happy about it. Rad knew, too, and was equally annoyed. Demon testosterone flooded the air.

Great. Just fucking great. That's what I needed right now, a pissing contest between these three over my honor. "For Satan's sake, all of you, stop it."

Damon seemed amused and superior about the whole thing. *Is Cole in love with you, too?*

"No," I yelled. I stomped a few feet away, needing to put distance between us. "Enough talk. I'm going in."

Rad started toward me, and I yanked a stake from my cape

and held it at throat level. "Unless you want your singing career to end right here, right now, you stay put."

Rad stopped in his tracks, raising his hands as if I were robbing him.

Told you. Stakes work on *everything*.

Damon moved toward me, amusement still dancing around the corners of his mouth. He laid a hand on mine, pressuring me to lower the stake. "Take the Chaos demon with you. He could be of use. If he does anything you don't like, you have my permission to end his singing career, pathetic as it is."

"Hey," Rad said.

Cole snickered.

Before I could argue, Damon added, "I'll monitor your thoughts while you're inside. If Lilith threatens you in any way, send an SOS, and Cole and I will come in, magic blazing."

That he would even think of taking on Lilith in my defense brought me up short. "You'll die. Both of you."

"Faith, Kali. I didn't get where I am as an Archdemon and head of the Bridge Institute without knowing how to deal with impossible situations."

I'd dealt with impossible situations all my life as well. Score one for the team, rah-rah, and all that, but having him, Cole, and Rad there didn't necessarily relieve my stress or doubts.

Once again, I reminded myself to shut down the emotions. I had a job to do, plain and simple. Only this job wasn't just about the vengeance being sought. If this job went south, a lot of humans and demons, including me, could die. "Have faith, Damon. I won't need you."

TWENTY

L ilith was righteously scary. Before Rad and I walked through the church's main entrance, I laid my hand against the stone like always to unlock the door and check for intruders. I already knew there was an intruder, but I hoped to get a sense of where she was and what she was doing. The heat radiating from the stone scorched my skin, blistering it instantly.

"Ouch!" I drew my hand back and shook it.

Rad reached for the injured hand. I jerked away, hiding it under my cape. "Not now," I said under my breath and cursed myself for not leaving him behind, regardless of Damon's orders.

As I started to open the French doors when, teeth bared, a hellhound materialized out of the air in front of me. Head level with my chest and his eyes devoid of intelligence or emotion, he was a killing machine. Like Mary's little lamb, he followed Lilith wherever she went.

Why I hadn't thought of that made me want to smack my

forehead. Lilith traveled with a pack of hellhounds at her command, even in hell.

The dog raised his nose and sniffed at my neck. Under my cape, I fingered the handle of my whip.

A sudden tornado of leaves swirled around the entrance, and Rad said something in an old language I didn't recognize. With slow reluctance, the hellhound shifted away from the door and once more became invisible. The swirling leaves stopped in midair and fell to the ground.

Okay. Maybe having Rad with me wasn't the worst thing.

I let out the breath I'd been holding and heard Rad do the same. So even though he knew how to make them heel, the Noctifector wasn't any more used to facing hellhounds than I was. The knowledge pleased me for some odd reason.

Inside, Lilith sat in front of my fireplace in my favorite over-sized chair, a roaring fire burning bright, and Victoria seated at her feet.

Victoria? Hone was supposed to be babysitting her at her place. Had Vicky escaped his watchful eye? Couldn't be. Hone would have called me.

Unless he couldn't.

My stomach tightened. Impossible that Victoria had gotten the drop on Hone, but then again, she'd raised Lilith from hell. Still, a more likely scenario popped into my mind...

Lilith had freed Vicky.

I dared not look at Rad, knowing I'd see the same thought reflected on his face. Instinct made me reach for my phone, but I couldn't call Hone at the moment. If Lilith had gotten to him, there was nothing I could do to help him. I still sent a mental message to Damon. *Check on Hone and hurry.*

Moving into the sunken living room, I realized Lilith was wearing my clothes. Not just any clothes, but my favorite

Versace dress, made by the late designer himself. What the fuck? Not only had she taken over my home, but my wardrobe as well?

Of course. It made no difference; I was short and curvy, and she was tall and model-thin. She embodied sin on all levels, coveting whatever was mine and taking it for her own. Her powers made whatever she wanted work for her.

Bowing my head, I kneeled before her, the sick feeling in my stomach rising. "My queen."

"*Alciscor*," she purred, calling me by an old-world term for vengeance. Evil magic rose and engulfed me, heightening my senses. Pride, desire, anger...every sin in hell and on Earth passed through me with exquisite force just from the sound of her voice. "You're a difficult one to locate. Rise and let me have a look at you."

Never look Lilith in the eye, my mother's warning rang in my head. *Never question her.*

I did as instructed by both the queen of demons and my Earthly mother, saying nothing and keeping my face blank. I pinned my gaze on Victoria, who openly stared up at Lilith with unabashed devotion. Witch or not, she was human and had no understanding of the demon hierarchy except in relation to her occult teachings. Which from what JR had told me the few times we'd discussed cases involving witches, warlocks, and associated occult religions, was far from accurate.

Lilith, however, didn't seem to mind Victoria's breach of the rules. Her long, thin fingers stoked Victoria's kinky hair, talon-like nails catching here and there. Lilith's fingers never stopped, though. Strands of Vicky's hair fell to the floor, yanked out by the roots courtesy of Lilith's rough treatment. The witch didn't even flinch.

Freak.

Lilith patted the top of Vicky's head and stood. I kept my

gaze on the Versace as Lilith circled me, her blistering heat skimming my skin through my clothes and making me want to scratch. Sweat broke out along my hairline.

The red dress was too short for her and much too loose through the chest and hips, causing it to drape erratically in those places. All that glorious fabric, tucked and sewn and molded precisely and specifically for my body, was now tainted by her touch.

Was I really mourning my dress at that moment? Hell yes. Even if Lilith's sinful presence hadn't been causing an uproar inside me, I would have taken a moment to hate her simply for ruining that work of art created especially for me by a master human.

As it was, jealousy and wrath heated the blood in my veins as hot as Lilith's essence heated my skin. I had to control what I was feeling, shut it down, no matter how intense the desires were. Too much emotion, and my demon would rear her pretty head.

Light from the flickering fire reflected off Lilith's blue-black hair, perfectly straight and looking like she'd stepped out of a salon. Her face was youthful, her skin unwrinkled. I'd heard rumors that she'd turned wickedly hideous in hell. That she looked like one of the monstrous creatures running around torturing lost souls there.

If that was true, her trip topside had rejuvenated her. How many souls had she eaten since Victoria had raised her? My fingers itched to raise my magic.

Easy, Kali. You can't help anyone if you lose your cool.

Lilith ran a finger down my cheek, the knife-sharp nail drawing blood. I didn't move, didn't make a sound.

But my demon woke.

The finger made its way to my chest, the nail slicing the strings that held my cape around my neck and cutting through the red fabric until it fell off my shoulders and pooled in a circle at my feet. I'd released my grip on the whip. It was still curled around my wrist like a bracelet, but without my cape, I felt naked, exposed.

Defenseless.

Which is precisely what she wanted.

Disappearing behind me, she chuckled under her breath, and a hot spike of pain ran down my spinal cord. My demon punched the walls of her prison. With my hair in its usual high ponytail, the base of my skull was exposed. Lilith sunk her nails into the skin there and clawed her way down my back, shredding my turtleneck and filleting my skin.

I sucked in air to keep from crying out. I would act the dutiful demon but not grovel at her feet over a bit of pain. Torture had never broken me in the past—as the Italian queen had witnessed firsthand—and it wouldn't break me with this queen either.

The demon inside me bared her teeth.

Blood ran down my back, hot and sticky. Both of my blood slaves heaved audible breaths. Rad had hung back in the shadows at my command. Lilith knew he was there but hadn't acknowledged him. Now he stepped forward, his damn chivalry mixing it up with the call of my blood. With his emotions spiking, his need to protect me made the shade on the nearby Tiffany lamp wobble. The scent of his anger, strong and briny, assaulted my nostrils.

This pleased my demon, and she backed off.

He inserted himself on one knee at Lilith's feet. "Radison Beaumont, here to do your bidding, my queen."

If he hadn't distracted her at that moment, she would have stripped me naked and probably continued to fillet my skin in order to deduce whether I was worthy of her expectations for the job she wanted done. With Lilith, reputation and experience only went so far. She wanted to see how strong you were, hence the torture. Strength was power, and most demons were weak.

I was many things, but weak wasn't one of them. She would have enraged my demon to the point I couldn't have subdued her, and then all hell would have broken loose.

Rad's distraction worked. Lilith looked down on him, assessed his good looks and bowed head, and lust filled the room. It slammed against my body with the force of one of Cole's punches, and I nearly doubled over.

Maybe I *was* weak, at least when it came to the Chaos demon.

She stroked his hair, rubbed a lock between her fingers, and trailed a hand over his broad shoulders. From the corner of my eye, I saw her smile. Wicked. Evil. Seductive. "Well, well, what do we have here?" She sniffed the air and closed her eyes as if the smell was orgasmic. "A Chaos demon with a soul."

Dammit. She was going to eat that soul if I didn't do something to prevent it. I stepped forward, willing to divert her again. "I was told you have a job for me."

She ignored me, grabbing Rad's coat collar and hauling him to his feet. He looked her directly in the eyes and smiled—that iceberg-melting smile—and all I could think was, *oh, shit.*

Lust trumped protocol, at least in this case. Lilith took in that charming grin, and another wall of desire hit me. My nipples hardened to tight peaks. A hungry ache swelled between my legs. To my left, Victoria moaned, no more immune to Lilith's rising lust than I was.

Rad responded, too, but he was no longer looking at the queen of hell. His leather coat was unzipped, and Lilith shoved it off his shoulders, raking her hands over his chest, down, down, until she hit the bulge of his jeans. She squeezed, and he barely moved, restraining himself almost as well as I had.

The whole time Lilith mauled him, his gaze was locked on mine. The Tiffany lamp shook harder. The pictures on the walls of the living room vibrated as if an earthquake was happening. The fire in the fireplace spit ashes high into the air. Lust, hunger, thirst...Rad's eyes told me everything he wanted to do to me, everything he wanted me to feel.

The passion and yearning reflected in those gold eyes nearly felled me.

I told myself to look away, to break the connection, but my body refused. I didn't want to break the connection. In fact, I wanted to push Lilith aside and take Rad right there in front of her. Mark him as mine.

Lilith began popping the buttons of his shirt, and I regained control of my body's traitorous desires. If she got him naked and saw the Noctifector tattoo between his shoulder blades, he'd be dead.

And revenge aside, the only one who got to kill him was me.

"My queen." My voice shook, and I cleared my throat. I was so horny and so jealous I could barely form words. "You're not safe here."

She shoved Rad's shirt open and scored his chest with her nails. Blood rose and ran down his hard, lean stomach muscles. But my words finally penetrated her lust and caught. She swiped a finger through Rad's blood, licked it off as if it were cake frosting, and eyed me. "Why is that, *alciscor*?"

"The Noctifectors are after me. They've grown almost unstoppable in recent years. If they show up here and find you, they'll do whatever it takes to capture you."

It wasn't far from the truth. Lilith feared nothing except, if my guess was correct, being exorcised back to hell. She was here, walking around on Earth, enjoying herself. Eating souls to restore her beauty and vigor, stealing designer dresses, seducing my ex-fiancé. Good times.

The Noctifectors could put a crimp in her party. While they'd need a miracle to send her back to hell, they could still imprison her. She'd get a refresher course in torture. Lilith liked torture, but only if she was doling it out.

"Do the Noctifectors know I'm here?" The lust receded, wrath taking its place. She wasn't angry at me, only at our mutual enemy.

I stopped myself from glancing at Rad. The earthquake had passed. He was in control of his emotions again. "They know," he answered her.

"Will they come after me?"

Dumb question. A wanted poster with her picture on it was probably circulating the world's Noctifector break rooms as we spoke. "Yes, my queen," he said. "Capturing you would be their greatest accomplishment to date."

She paced the room, touching my things here and there, watching the fire. Rad was still staring at me like he wanted to jump my demon bones.

Lilith faced me. "Where is it safe for me, *alciscor*?"

I spoke without thinking. "The Bridge Institute."

Damon yelled in my brain. *What?*

I locked my knees, so I didn't stagger from his voice vibrating in my head. "It's the safest place for you, but will limit your freedom."

She didn't like that. "And why aren't you in the Institute?"

"I was until a few hours ago when I got the call saying you wanted to see me."

As if remembering why she was there in the first place, her anger increased. "I want revenge."

Don't ask any questions. My back burned where she'd cut

me open. I used the pain to stay focused. "I'll be happy to seek it for you. All I need to know is who you want revenge on."

She returned to the chair, sat, and buried her talons in Victoria's hair once more. Then she sighed deeply, staring at the blood on Rad's chest. The flames inside the fireplace jumped, and sparks flew.

"I want revenge," Lilith said, her voice full of contempt, "on Lucifer."

TWENTY-ONE

O utwardly, I didn't react. Inside, I choked. She had to be kidding.

Only Lilith didn't kid. She was dead serious.

Rad's expression changed to *holy shit.*

My thought exactly.

Taking revenge on Lucifer was a ridiculous idea. A deadly absurd idea. There were methods, although few, that would return Lilith to hell and bind her there once more. Lucifer, on the other hand, was a fallen angel. Earth was his playground, hell, his kingdom. He could not be barred from here or exorcised and forced to leave. Neither could he be imprisoned in hell. He was free to move between worlds, reigning chaos and temptation everywhere.

In other words, I might be able to banish Lilith, but I could never banish the devil. And if I pissed him off, the only place safe from his wrath for me would be heaven.

Fat chance I'd receive a warm welcome there.

Damned if I do. Damned if I don't. "I live to do your bidding, my queen."

Rad's eyes grew to half-dollars, letting me know he thought I was crazy not to refuse. Of course, I was crazy. But who said no to Lilith? Only those with a let-me-spend-eternity-in-hell wish.

I pinned my gaze on her throat, sizing up my odds of slamming a stake there. Wouldn't kill her, but it would give me a moment's satisfaction before she roasted me over the fire in the fireplace.

It's the little things, after all.

"Lucifer believes he's in love with a witch." She sunk her nails into Vicky's head, and finally, the woman flinched. "I want you to make her life miserable."

Wait. She wanted me to take revenge on Lucifer by screwing with his mistress? I nearly laughed with relief. Piece. Of. Cake.

Lilith must have sensed my relief. "I'm told the witch now bares the Mark of Cain."

Back up the vengeance boat. Piece of cake...*not*.

No wonder Lilith was coming to me instead of cutting the witch off at the knees herself. The Mark of Cain was a warning. Messing with the witch would provoke the wrath of God. The ultimate vengeance.

What had the witch done to earn God as her bodyguard? "The Mark will make things more difficult."

Lilith laughed without humor. "That's why I came to you, *alciscor*. They say you're the best."

Great. No backing out of this.

This, however, was what I got for being a top-notch vengeance demon. Work your ass off, and you still get screwed. "Give me her name and location, and I'll find her."

Lilith rose from the chair with a smug smile as she crossed to stand in front of me. Like a good demon, I continued to keep my eyes averted. "Her name is Amy

Atwood. She lives near here in a town called Eden." She leaned in, licked blood from my cheek, and kissed me on the lips.

Lilith's lips scorched mine and sent a sharp, stinging sensation through my body. I fisted my hands to keep from punching her, her magic zipping along my nerve endings and energizing my demon with enough wattage to make me nearly scream. A deal had been struck. A contract, sealed.

I was so screwed.

When she was done mauling my lips, she stepped back. "My coat, Victoria."

Leaving so soon? What a shame. I shoved my demon back a few steps and took a deep breath. Vicky raced by me to get to the mink trench, tossed on the opposite sofa. I wondered briefly who Lilith had killed for it.

"It would be best, my queen, if you keep a low profile. Stay at the Bridge Institute for now."

Vicky held the coat while Lilith inserted her arms into the sleeves. "Do not worry about me, *alciscor*. No one will bother me."

Her gaze flicked to Rad, and once again, lust swirled around all of us. I shivered with the impact of it, the ache between my legs once more going into overdrive. My demon egged me to give into it. "You—" Lilith motioned at Rad "—come with me."

No, my brain screamed. "He's my blood slave."

It just popped out, but there it was. Not an argument. Those weren't allowed. Just a statement of fact.

Lilith's curious gaze turned to me. "You're not a Child of the Night."

"No, but he is my blood slave, as is Victoria. They were given to me by an old vampire king before he died. I'm to take his place, and to fulfill my promise, I must take their blood at regular intervals, and they must take mine. Victoria and Rad should not leave my side."

Vicky, never one to worry about her own safety, piped up. "I can leave her side. She hasn't fed on me."

I gave her a damning look. *Shut up, you moron.*

Lilith sized up Rad. "And you? Has my *alciscor* fed on you?"

"Yes," he lied, eyes half-lidded with desire. "She's my master, and I can't leave her."

The bedroom eyes were overkill, but it worked. Lilith hated being denied anything. She also knew the world was filled with handsome human men and equally beautiful human women eager to do her bidding. Her lust dropped off as fast as it had come.

"Find the witch," she said to me. "Make her so miserable tht she never wants to see Lucifer again. Then we'll discuss your reward."

Living to see another century would be rewarding enough.

She climbed the three steps out of the sunken living room and made her way to the entrance, Vicky on her heels.

Damon, I mentally called to him. Vicky jumped forward to open the door. *The queen is leaving the building. You might want to follow her.*

When an Archdemon grunts at you, even mentally, you know he's too pissed to speak.

The moment the door snapped closed behind Lilith, I started shaking, well aware I'd just skated through the most serious meeting of my life. My knees buckled, and I went down in a heap inside the cape still lying at my feet. The demon inside me paced, scratched at the walls, and hissed her displeasure.

The next second, Rad was beside me, examining my wounds and pressing a kiss into my temple. "You did good, K."

I shook from the adrenaline bleeding off, from corralling my inner demon. Shook from the touch of Rad's hand. I wanted to crawl into his lap and stay there. Block out Lilith and Lucifer and the witch causing problems for them. Block out that Hone might be dead, that Toel was gunning for me. That I had to become a vamp queen in less than forty-eight hours.

He curved a hand over my cheek and drew my head to his shoulder. I should have pushed him away, but I didn't. I was so tired. For a few minutes, I wanted to stop thinking and just feel. Release the hold I had on my emotions and let my defenses down.

Nestling my face into the crook of his neck, I breathed deeply and let his stormy ocean scent wash over me. His shirt was still open, and I placed my hand over his heart, my fingers touching the wound Lilith had left there. He tensed from my touch, his desire, thick and fierce as an ocean wave, swelling around us.

The lust Lilith had elicited a few minutes earlier was gone. We didn't need it. Humans call it sexual chemistry, but demon or human, it doesn't matter. We're all hardwired to respond sexually to certain pheromones, specific triggers. It doesn't matter what logic tells us; we lust after the wrong people at the wrong times.

This was one of those times and one of those people.

Because he was my blood slave, I not only felt my own desire sizzling in my veins, I felt his as well. A drenching, warm rain of need and craving. A demanding pressure filling me from the inside out. I licked his neck, tasting his salty skin and letting his human and demon emotions lift me higher. He pressed a hand over mine, where it rested on his chest, and kissed me, slow and deep.

It was nothing like Lilith's searing kiss. Nothing like Damon's probing one. Rad's lips were greedy and demanding but strangely reassuring. The kiss was about him and me, not a contract, not control.

I kissed him back. My head spun, my brain spewing arguments, but I ignored them. What if I let the lust take over? I could free myself from the tension, doubts, and responsibilities weighing on my shoulders for a little while. I'd have better control over my inner demon.

And right now, that sounded like a damn fine idea. The world wouldn't end if I took an hour or two for myself, right?

With Lilith on the loose, that was an unfortunate possibility.

Shutting down my brain, I kissed Rad harder. The world was going to end one of these days anyway. Why couldn't I find a little solace before it did?

My imagination went wild as I imagined pressing Rad down to the floor and straddling him. Removing the rest of our clothes and reacquainting myself with his beautiful body. Riding him until I could blot out everything else. I wanted to hear him cry out my name. Wanted to hear him beg me for mercy. Wanted...wanted...

A deep voice and metallic smell brought my imagination to a screeching stop. "Damn, it's hot in here."

Cole.

I jerked out of Rad's embrace and stumbled into a standing position. I hadn't heard my bodyguard enter. How long had he been standing there? My pulse pounded in my ears, my breath coming out in jerky huffs. "We were just..um.."

"Yeah, I figured that out." He scowled at Rad. "Damon thought I'd better interrupt you before you did something you'd regret." He put air quotes around *something you'd regret*.

Rad rose to his feet, brushed off his jeans, and rebuttoned his shirt. Lilith had sheared most of the buttons off, so it was pretty much a lost cause. Not that I minded seeing his chest.

I picked up my cape and fiddled with the weapons. Running my hands over them calmed me. "Any word on Hone?"

Cole pointed at his temple. "Bump on the head, probably a mild concussion. He's at the hospital."

He was alive. Good. "And what about Lilith?"

"Damon put two Tracker demons on her. They'll report hourly and inform him if she does anything requiring the Bridge Council to act."

Like eating souls and killing humans wasn't enough? "Have there been any news reports of unusual activity? Mass, unexplained deaths?"

"Not as much as expected. Damon went back to the Institute to monitor everything."

Which meant I could get back to work without him breathing down my neck.

Rad touched my waist. "We should doctor your back," he murmured in my ear.

My wounds were painful but not life-threatening. His either. He wanted to get me alone so we could talk. Or resume what we'd started. He looked exhausted, as if the confrontation with Lilith had taken as much out of him as it had me.

Cole wasn't fooled by Rad's pretense. "Damon wants you back at the Institute, Kali. Right away."

"No dice." I started for the stairs. I had work to do. A lot of it. "Call JR and tell him I want security cameras, infrared, the whole works, installed around the church and the cemetery, and call Damon and tell him I want two more bodyguards besides you—Merc demons—on twenty-four-seven duty until the coronation. I also want my security system to feed into the Institute rather than a human service, and I want Yasmin to set me up with a firewall like she's got around the Institute grounds."

I didn't wait to see if Rad was following me upstairs or if Cole was already dialing. I headed straight for my bedroom, hung up my cape, and started making a list. I needed JR to locate Lucifer's witch, I still wanted to check Nudra's weapons stash, and I needed the lowdown on Toel so I could shut him down before his game shifted into high gear. I also needed to send Hone flowers.

A noise behind me made me turn.

Rad, looking dangerous and hungry, stood in the doorway.

"I need to feed," he said, taking two steps forward and promptly passing out at my feet.

TWENTY-TWO

"Rad!" I dropped to my knees beside him and patted his face. Got no response. He was pale, and his breathing was too slow and faint for my liking.

Rolling him onto his side, I checked his waistband. Sure enough, a silver dagger was hidden there in a leather sheath. I drew it out and frowned. It was identical to the one Nudra had used to cut me.

There was no time to worry about it. I shifted Rad so his head was in my lap, took a deep breath, and scored my wrist with the sharp blade.

Blood bubbled to the top of my skin and pooled on my wrist. It ran over the sides and dripped onto Rad's lips. My stomach did a flip, and I looked away for a second to get hold of my queasiness before I parted his lips so the blood could drip into his mouth.

He'd gone several days without feeding on me, but so had Arman and Victoria, and neither of them were beating down my door in need of more. Why was Rad already feeling the effects?

He stirred and, without opening his eyes, grabbed my wrist in a two-handed vice grip and brought it to his lips. He sucked my blood with such ferocity I nearly cried out. A sudden surge of pleasure rushed up my arm and into my chest, tingling my nerve endings in its wake. The room spun, and I dropped the dagger.

The memory of Victoria and Arman drinking my blood trickled into my brain, but only long enough for a couple of synapses to fire. They had both drank deep, robbing me of a good deal of blood. Rad had only had a taste. That's why he'd gone belly up so soon.

As Rad took another deep pull of my blood, a second surge ripped through me, this one dropping to the spot between my legs, renewing the ache there. A new memory took front and center. The best damn orgasm I'd ever had after Rad had licked my skin in Nudra's coffin. The sparks that had flown. The light I had seen that seemed like heaven.

Rad moaned low in his throat and opened his eyes, the golden orbs filled with blood lust and something more. That yearning desire I'd seen earlier. That promise of heaven if we gave in and came together.

In one agile move, he flipped me onto my back and pinned both my wrists to the floor. He kneed my legs apart and ground himself against me. "I want you, Kali. So bad. So bad, it hurts."

The scratches on my back screamed a silent pain, lost in the pleasure of Rad's body on top of mine. I wanted him, too. I wanted this. The demon, the human, the blood slave. Shit, at that moment, even the Noctifector. I wanted all of him pounding into me, unable to stop himself. Unable to control his feelings for me.

I wanted it all: the good, the bad, the terrible.

Which sucked. Even after everything he'd done to me, I couldn't stop my lust for him. Couldn't stop wanting him. I was sick. Sick with love and hate and desire. Sick with guilt. Every time I let him in, I paid the price. Every time I said yes to him, my life got more screwed up.

I searched for some comeback, some argument. "It's just the blood lust," I reasoned, but it sounded unconvincing and feeble to my ears. Half-hearted and meaningless.

Must have sounded that way to him, too. "No." He released one of my wrists and wiped his lips with the back of his hand. "It's not the blood, Kali. It's you. I want...you. Every piece of you. Body, heart, and soul."

There was a point I could argue. "I don't have a soul."

His eyes burned pure gold. "Yes, you do."

He grabbed the dagger and sat up, his weight trapping my hips. He touched the tip of the dagger to my throat through the turtleneck, and I sucked in my breath. Now he was going to kill me?

I twisted, trying to buck him off. It did no good.

My wrist stung, bleeding less, but that arm, my strongest, was now weak. I raised my other arm and swung my fist at the blade.

He grabbed my hand, continuing to hold the blade tip at my neck. "Trust me."

I swallowed the lump in my throat. I was going to die, just like I'd dreamed. Rad would stick that silver dagger in my heart and end it. "Never."

Something changed in his eyes. A sadness flashed there and then a look that said he liked a challenge. Oh, yes, he liked a challenge, all right. And once again, I was it.

He released my hand and grabbed the turtleneck's fabric under my chin.

And then, ever so slowly, he cut it away.

Down my chest, between my breasts, and over my stomach, the ribbed cotton gave way under the sharp edge of the blade.

He peeled the material back, revealing my bra and bare skin. His fingertips lightly skimmed my stomach, stroked the pulse beating wildly at the base of my throat, traced the contours of my breasts above the line of red lace they were nestled in.

The rediscovery of something he'd once been familiar with seemed to produce a level of reverence. At the same time, the furniture in the room began vibrating. The pictures on the walls shifted on their hangars. The knickknacks on my dresser rattled against each other. "You're beautiful."

While I'm as prideful as any demon, I've never been comfortable with intimate flattery. Not that I didn't like hearing it, I simply never knew how to respond. So I reached for my American snarkiness, but my voice came out weak and shaky. "You probably say that to all the women you bed."

"Only the one I should have married."

My heart missed a beat, then fired off a heavy *thud*. He had me where he wanted me, and instead of taking advantage of my body, he was torturing my mind and heart with meaningless explanations and excuses about that day so long ago. A part of me wanted to forget and forgive, but I never would. That day, that night, couldn't be undone, and even two hundred and eighty-three years later, I grieved for my family. Grieved for what could have been with Rad. Even if I exacted revenge on him, the horror of the past could never be erased.

I looked away, unable to respond. Sensing my distress and cooled ardor, Rad didn't say another word. The mini-earthquake in my room didn't subside, though. He leaned down and teased my lips with his. Softly, slowly, asking for permission to take me away from my thoughts. Asking permission to take me higher than I'd been that night in the coffin when he'd shown me heaven.

I opened my lips, giving him access. His tongue swooped in, making the kiss turn hotter, wetter, and deeper. His free hand snaked up my side, released the front catch on my bra, and kneaded one breast, tugging and tweaking the nipple until I moaned.

He kissed the healing cut on my cheek, trailed kisses down my neck and over my collarbone his mouth eventually landing on the other breast. I arched into him as his tongue and lips circled the tender flesh, sucking it into his mouth and pulling on it like he'd pulled at my wrist earlier.

Digging my nails into his shoulders, I clung to him as he took his mouth to my other breast. His tongue and lips nearly brought me to orgasm. A minute later, I raised my hips so he could tug my pants over my hips and down my legs. He tossed them aside, grabbed the knife, and started to cut off my bikini underwear against my protests.

"Kali!" Cole's voice in the doorway startled me, and in the next instant, Rad's weight left my hips as Cole jerked him off and slammed him against the wall.

Interrupting a Chaos demon in the throes of lust is never a good idea. To give Cole credit, what he saw when he walked in on us wasn't a pretty picture. Blood from my wrist covered both of us and smeared the floor. Rad looked like he was raping me, holding me down, and cutting my clothes off...and with a silver dagger no less.

Of course, Cole had barged into my bedroom, which was rude, but he *was* my bodyguard and took the job seriously. Unfortunately, he'd now interrupted Rad twice, and the Chaos demon's anger flared—I felt it flash through me lightning quick —with the same intensity of his passionate lovemaking. The knife, still in Rad's hand, swiped at Cole's neck. At the same time, the other sent an uppercut to Cole's diaphragm.

Cole hadn't survived the Roman Empire's gladiator games by being slow or unskilled. He ducked, swiveled, and punched, and the dagger hit the floor and skidded to a stop at my feet.

"Stop it," I yelled, knowing one or both of them would end up hurt beyond repair, but they continued to kick, punch, and slam each other into the walls and my furniture. I scrambled up, realized I was naked, and grabbed the comforter off my bed to wrap around me.

The fighting continued for another minute, the demons equally matched until Rad snapped his fingers, and the lamp on my nightstand sailed across the room and crashed into Cole's head.

Now that was dirty pool. The warrior staggered, and Rad landed a kick to the back of his knee. But even as Rad's foot connected, Cole grabbed Rad's leg and flipped him onto the ground.

"*Fermati!*" I yelled, and this time they stopped. Both looked at me and blinked as if they'd forgotten I was even there.

That's demons for you. Fighting or fucking, they give one-hundred-and-ten percent.

"Both of you stop it this instant. I'm fine, Cole. He wasn't trying to hurt me. I'm going to take a shower now." *A very, very cold shower.* I shook my head at both of them and padded toward the bathroom. "Do not kill each other."

Realizing his *errore colossale,* Cole rubbed the growing bump on his head and glared at Rad. "I thought he was trying to kill you."

Another snap of Rad's fingers and the dagger flew into his hand. "Interrupt us again, and *giuro davanti a Dio,* you'll be the one I take this knife to."

Thank the hell fires that Rad's shirt was still on, covering his Noctifector tattoo, or Cole would have fought him to the death regardless of my yelling. I left the two of them bickering, shutting out their voices behind the heavy wooden bathroom door, and had a quiet, sad laugh.

I'd been alone for so long that it freaked me out, having not one but two men in my house, and both of them trying to look out for me. I'd been taking care of myself since I was seventeen and doing a damned good job of it, but on some level, it was nice to know I wasn't facing Lilith, Toel, and the whole vamp thing alone.

The cold shower didn't cool my sexual hunger. In fact, it seemed to do the opposite. After a few minutes, I switched the water to hot and scrubbed vigorously from head to toe, avoiding my cuts and letting the steam and water relax all the tight muscles. My back stung, but the pain distracted my thoughts. I'd wrapped my wrist before getting in, and the bandage was soaked, but it'd kept the soap and shampoo out. The cut didn't smart so much as buzz with the phantom memory of Rad's lips.

How many times would I have to bleed myself for my slaves? How many places on my body would I have to scar for them? How could I stand the feel of Vicky and Arman's mouths on me again?

At the unpleasant thought, goose flesh rose on my skin in the shower's steam.

I'd have to talk to Chloe and figure out a more civilized way to bank my blood. Rad drinking directly from my body turned me on. Vicky and Arman putting their mouths on me made me sick to my stomach.

Some vamp queen I'm going to make.

I shut off the shower, dried off, and applied my favorite skin lotion. I hadn't brought clothes, but the bathroom was connected to the walk-in closet I'd spent six months building to a precise layout. Beautiful garments and killer shoes were one of my indulgences.

I dropped the towel on the tiled floor and had just started for the closet when the bathroom door opened, and Rad walked in. He closed the door behind him, looked me over from head to toe, and flipped the lock.

No one was going to interrupt us this time.

His hands skimmed my naked skin, and he danced me backward, pressing me against the stone wall. One hand at the nape of my neck, the other at the small of my back, he lowered his lips to mine. I sunk my hands into his hair, tilting my head to kiss him deeper. Then I pushed the shirt off his shoulders and undid his jeans.

He was as ready as I was, his erection popping out as I shoved the pants down his hips. He'd never been one for underwear, and for once, I was glad. Taking him in hand, I stroked him hard, over and over, enjoying his murmurs and deep-throated groans, even as he massaged and pinched my nipples and drew the same noises from me.

Two-hundred-and-eighty years ago, when he'd taken my virginity, he'd been a considerate lover. He'd tasted and teased and taught me all about pleasure in slow, highly erotic, and very romantic lessons. That had been so long ago that I felt as if I was offering him my virginity all over again. But there was nothing tender or remotely romantic about this coupling.

Lifting me by the ass to position me so our bodies fit together, he rammed me against the stones, impaling me from the front as he did so. I arched and cried out, wrapping my legs tight around his waist and meeting every one of his thrusts with my own.

Sparks, like before, lit the dim room, our bodies somehow electrified. The bottle of lotion flew off the shelf, along with other toiletries. Towels left their places and danced in the air. The shower curtain fluttered, and the stones at my back vibrated with the intense magic.

An explosion of sensations rocked me, skittering under my skin and heightening my lust. I closed my eyes, finding Rad's rhythm and matching it, the sharp edges of the stones reopening the wounds on my back. Pleasure and pain taking me higher.

Rad buried his mouth against my neck and suddenly stopped our hurried coupling, hips pressing mine tight against the stones. Both of us were heaving air, our chests surging and falling against each other. I tried to buck him to get him moving again, but he refused to relinquish his position, licking my collarbone while he pulsed inside me, tensing and releasing, tensing and releasing.

He stroked a thumb between my folds, and the nerve endings there swelled and heaved. I begged for release, but he continued to tease me until I was nearly crying. Then he took one more hard drive into me, and everything in my body maxed out, peaking in a rush and shattering into a thousand pieces.

Once I came down from the high, him still pinning me against the wall, he began slow, deliberate in and out strokes. My legs were too heavy to hold up, and he propped his arms under my knees to keep me fully exposed and at his disposal. Exquisitely sensitive, I nearly sobbed, but the feeling was a sweet pain. He was so hard, so perfect, I glanced down between our two bodies to see him. Stroke after stroke, he went all the way in and drew all the way out until my pleasure built again.

I sensed the moment his climax began. Felt how he became harder, tighter. Our eyes locked, past, present, and future tied up in impossible knots, but truth evident in them. This was our pinnacle, not only physically but emotionally as well. Our hearts, our lives were tangled and at odds, and there was nothing we could do to change that.

One final plunge and I hit the apex with him, both of us hanging onto the other for dear life. He throbbed and pulsed inside me, my tender flesh hugging him tight, and if I'd had a soul, I would have sold it to keep him right there forever.

TWENTY-THREE

Rad put me to bed after that. Alone. I slept most of the day and woke at sunset to the delicious scent of pasta primavera teasing my nose. Mm mm. My favorite.

However, the best thing upon awakening wasn't the tray of food next to the bed. I'd slept dream-free. No Rad, no silver dagger, no waking up screaming. It was the best sleep I'd had in centuries. I felt like a new demon.

Physically, anyway. The past still tortured my mind—recent as well as distant. Giving into my desire for Rad hadn't been smart, and the ghosts of my parents and sister hung on me, the old guilt of not being able to save them now mixed with the new guilt of knowing Rad had something to do with their deaths.

The church's upper-story windows were a mix of stained glass and transparent. My bedroom boasted one of each. The stained-glass window showed a depiction of Christ's temptation. As I shoveled down the pasta, I stared at it.

Jesus, alone and weary in the desert, struggling to find his footing in an unknown land. My world had been flipped upside down in the past week, and a part of me wished I could turn back time to the night I served Nudra his warning papers. I would do it all so differently.

Everyone learns from disaster, humans and demons alike. When my family was murdered, I'd had to find new footing in this unknown land and resist giving in to the temptation to take the easy way out. To turn loose of the vicious demon living inside me and harm anyone stupid enough to get in my path. Through the years, I'd discovered one undeniable fact about life...you either deal with it on your terms, or it deals with you on its terms.

Personally, I prefer the former, and I suspect Jesus did too.

Knowing I'd hit my grief ceiling and there was no point in castigating myself further over the past or present, I finished eating in the twilight of my room. Then I washed my face, brushed my hair into a ponytail, and put on my usual work clothing ensemble before heading downstairs.

Rad and Cole were watching a Bears game on the flat-screen TV in my den, arguing over which player should be the first-string quarterback. When I walked in, Rad dragged his attention away from the TV and whistled low under his breath. He looked like he wanted to eat me. "How was the pasta?"

The Chaos demon didn't care whether I enjoyed his cooking. He was referring to what had happened earlier in the day. "Needed salt. Otherwise, it was...satisfying."

"More salt." He grinned. "I'll remember that."

A two-way radio sat on the coffee table along with the TV remote. "Why aren't you watching the front door?" I asked Cole, picking up the radio.

I'd moved into his line of sight, and he shifted and motioned me out of the way. "No need. JR's got the new security system in place. He's tweaking it now and keeping an eye on the video coming in."

He and Rad both let go of a sudden yell of disgust as one of the Bears missed a pass. Cole continued as if nothing had happened and grabbed the radio out of my hands. "Damon sent the Merc demons you wanted. I positioned one on the roof, and the other is on perimeter duty. I trained both of them, so I know they're the best."

"What about the firewall?"

"Yasmin's working on it." He used air quotes around *working on it*. Which meant she wasn't working on anything other than being a bitch.

"JR's a god among techies," Rad said. "That security system is sick."

They both clapped when the Bears completed a touchdown. A few hours ago, they'd wanted to kill each other. Now they were best friends, all because of a Sunday afternoon football game? Men. "Did either of you offer to help JR with all that work?"

Cole waved me off. "He wouldn't let us."

"He's kind of...well...freaky," Rad added.

I grabbed the remote and shut off the TV. They both protested loudly. "I happen to like freaky, especially when it saves my ass." I tossed the remote on the coffee table. "Sorry to break up your bromance, but we have work to do."

JR was set up in my home office, madly typing away on a massive curved keyboard and watching a bank of six screens, each divided into quarters showing different sections of the church's perimeter, parking lot, and cemetery.

He didn't look up when we came in but started talking to me as if I'd been standing there all along. Clicking keys, he rattled off specs and terms that meant nothing to me, even though they sounded impressive. "Twenty-four vision bullet cameras, night vision, and infrared, turbo view HD, vandalproof, 5G and higher phone compatible, high compression resolution—"

"Why aren't any of them positioned on the sky?" I asked.

JR stopped typing and looked at my chin. "What?"

"The sky." I pointed at the screens and did my best bat imitation. Vampires didn't turn into bats as folk tales suggested, but they had mad skills when it came to climbing trees and jumping tall buildings. "We're looking for vamps and they often come by sky."

"Oh." He fiddled with a few keys. The evening sky suddenly filled all four quads of the screen labeled Number Five. "How's that?"

On screen three, a dark shadow emerged near my car. At the same time, the computer's speaker sounded an alarm, and Cole's radio sputtered to life.

"Alpha one, this is Falcon," a gravelly voice announced. "We have a perimeter breach on the south side. Permission to engage? Over."

I squinted at the screen. The sun had gone down, and the parking lot's solar lights didn't give off enough illumination to show a lot of detail. JR's cameras enhanced what light there was. The person was small, almost childlike, and had a gangly, girlish walk as she approached the front of my car and looked up at the church. An odd sensation tugged at me as if I knew her. Not like I *knew her* knew her, but my body recognized her. My blood recognized her.

Vampire.

"Don't engage," I told Cole. "Tell him to stand down."

"One of your friends?" Rad asked.

He must not have felt the pull of her blood. That was good. "She's just a kid. Not a friend, but not an enemy."

The vampire girl hopped up on the hood of my car, hung her arms over her bent knees, and continued to stare at the church. I narrowed my eyes. My car was not a couch. "Then again, looks like I have to kick her ass."

Cole's finger hovered over the radio's talk button. His voice was edged with impatience. "Engage or not, Kali?"

"Ask your mercs to scan the area and see if they see anyone else."

Cole relayed the message, and JR reset the computer's alarm. Silence fell as we waited for a response.

"Negative," Falcon, the rooftop merc, responded.

"Negative," Jack Rabbit, the on-the-ground merc, dittoed.

"Everyone hold position." I adjusted my cape and grabbed a stake from one of the inside pockets. "I'm going out."

Rad and Cole protested, but I shut them down. Cole relayed my instructions to the mercs, and I went out the front door, Rad on my heels like a trained dog. Jack Rabbit fell in with us, keeping his focus on the nearby street and trees, semi-automatic with a hundred rounds of holy water ready to fire.

The girl slid off of my car, kneeled, and bowed her head as I approached. I shot a look at Rad, and he shrugged.

I stopped a few feet from her. Far enough away, she couldn't get the jump on me, close enough I could get the jump on her if necessary. I estimated she'd been turned at the ripe age of thirteen or fourteen, and didn't that suck? Who would want to be pubescent forever?

I could smell grave dirt and old blood on her. The idea of staking a girl sickened me, but she was a vamp and the action might be called for. "Who are you, and what do you want?"

She rose but kept her head down. "I'm Madison, and I'm here to help you."

"With what?"

She met my gaze. Her eyes were bright with determination, but her cheeks were sunken, and she looked like she was three days past feeding time. "With becoming queen, of course."

She was ballsy. And desperate. Never a good combination. "And how can you help me with that?"

"I can tell you who's going to stop the coronation and how he will do it."

That piqued my interest, even though I already knew it was Toel. I wanted to hear more, but information always came with a price. "Why would you do that, Madison? What do you want in return?"

She smiled a girl's smile, anticipation evident. "To be your assistant."

When I didn't immediately respond, her smile faltered. "You need me. You're not a vamp, and a few of them are *waaay* pissed that the Prince is even considering letting you into the nest."

She pointed a thumb at her chest. Her hand was shaking. "I know everything that goes on here in Chicago in the vamp world. That's why they call me The Mouse. I get in lots of places undetected, and I see and hear *every*thing."

It was a good shtick. And she needed to feed soon, or she was going to drop. I wavered, part of me wanting to bring her inside, warm her up, and order blood for her from Chloe.

In my line of work, being compassionate is wise. Wanting to save someone is not.

She was a vamp, and it wasn't my job to save her, like it or not.

Taking a deep breath, I threw her a bone anyway. "Prove it."

Her face lost its confident set, but she held her ground. Her eyes were so sunken that she appeared more like a zombie than an Undead teenager. "What do you want to know?"

I liked her, vamp or not. She reminded me of me. An opportunity had presented itself, and she was damn well going to take it. "What's the name of the vamp who wants to stop the coronation?"

"Toel Maze. He's the—"

I raised my hand to stop her. "Rule one, Madison. Never give away more information than you're asked for."

She blinked, opened her mouth, shut it again.

"Rule two." I brought the stake out from under my cape and showed it to her. "Never trust anyone."

Panic hit. She started to run. Anticipating that reaction, I flicked Volante out, catching The Mouse around the ankles and flipping her face down on the ground. A second later, I jammed my knee into her back and pinned her there. "And three. Never walk into a situation without a solid escape plan."

She raised her head, tried and failed to buck me off. Then she spit on the ground. "Fuck you and your stupid red cape too."

I definitely liked this girl.

TWENTY-FOUR

"How did you find my home?" I'd tied Madison's hands behind her with plasticuffs, and she now sat at my kitchen table. Not that I wanted yet another stranger inside my house, but I couldn't cross-examine her in the parking lot without risking everyone's safety. For all I knew, Madison was a pawn in some game Toel was playing.

She stared at the table, belligerence radiating off her even though she shook with cold and hunger. "It was in *The Vampire Quarterly* under Lives of the Rich and Demon Spawn."

More likely, Toel had put it out on the vamp hotline, a carefully connected mental phone tree between the upper-level vamps, who then spread the word to their underlings. Nice of him.

I crossed my arms and leaned my butt on the table. "Why are you so strung out? When was the last time you fed?"

Her gaze danced up to my neck and shot over to Rad's. Being half-human, he smelled better to her. "I can't feed on humans. Grosses me out. I *was* human six months ago." Her eyes came back to mine, pain-filled but still wild with blood lust. "And I can't kill animals either. I'm a failure at this vampire shit."

She dropped her head, and I couldn't gauge whether she was sincere or a good actress. "So buy blood from the blood bank."

"I don't have any money."

That was obvious. Nothing she wore cost more than twenty dollars, even when it was new. Which it wasn't. The knees of her jeans were threadbare, and not from some designer's scissors. Her jacket was soiled and torn. "Did you come here to apply for a job, or so I would kill you?"

Her head snapped up. "I'm only fifteen. I don't want to die. But I don't want to live like this either."

Fifteen. Yowza. Older than I'd thought but still damn young. "Nudra turn you?"

"How'd you know?"

"*Demon Quarterly* under Stupid Teenage Girls for the Taking." I grinned, but she didn't seem impressed by my obvious charm.

"I went to a concert last month and ended up a vamp."

"Hell of a concert."

"Yeah." She glanced at Rad. "Aren't you the lead singer of the Chaos Demons?"

He nodded.

A small smile broke her parched lips, and fandom shone in her red eyes. "That's so cool. I have all your songs."

She sounded exactly like what she should be...a fifteen-year-old girl...and my heart sank a little.

One, two, three, four...I counted off the seconds, waiting to see if she'd volunteer anything else about Nudra or Toel. She didn't. Normally, I would have played the waiting game a while longer since I was good at waiting. But duty called, and I was on a tight timeframe, growing tighter by the minute. Madison wasn't getting any younger or less dangerous. "Where's Toel staying while he's in town?"

"Untie me, and I'll tell you."

Fast learner. I admired her human-like spunk and determination. "Unbind her," I said to Rad.

He drew his silver knife from its resting place in the small of his back and walked over to her.

Cole, who'd been standing guard by the back door, protested. "She's going to vamp out on us any minute."

I was surprised she hadn't already. For a recently turned vamp, she had terrific control. I was jaded enough to think she was playing me. If she was, she wasn't going to like the end result.

Nodding at Rad to cut off the plasticuffs, I toyed with the stake on the table. "Being a vamp, you're preternaturally fast, but I'm a demon, which makes me faster. I'll dust you before you touch any of us."

She rubbed her wrists where the plastic had left its mark and then pressed the heels of her hands into her eye sockets. "The surfer vamp is at Nudra's compound in Naperville."

Well, well, what a surprise. Nudra's ashes weren't cold yet, and Toel had moved in.

JR appeared in the doorway. "I've got an address for that witch you're looking for."

Finally, something was going my way. "Lay it on me."

He handed me a piece of paper, saw Madison eyeing his neck, and tossed a set of keys at me as he backed toward the entryway. "I programmed the GPS in the Land Rover to take you to her front door."

The paper held more than Amy Atwood's address. There was information about her workplace—some ice cream shop she'd inherited from her grandmother—and a few incidentals. Social security number, bank account balance—which was anemic—a list of her friends and enemies, including their addresses and phone numbers.

I needed to give JR a raise.

"Let's roll." I grabbed my stake, motioned for Madison to get up, and started for my garage. "Follow me."

My company car sat in the garage most of the time. I rarely had passengers and rarely needed a bulletproof SUV. Damon insisted I have it, though, and for once, I was glad he was such an obnoxious boss. I led the group to the underground garage—another of the magical renovations I was quite proud of—and unlocked the doors. "Rad and Madison in the back. Cole, you're up front with me."

Cole looked like I'd slapped him. "You're putting Guitar Boy in charge of the vamp?"

"Guitar Boy?" Rad opened the doors for me and Madison simultaneously and gave Cole a disgusted look. "I founded The Chaos Demons, I'm lead singer, and I write all the songs."

"Chaos Demons." Cole snorted. "How original."

I climbed in and started the Land Rover. "Get in, Cole."

Rad sat behind me and made a snarky noise in the back of his throat. "Shouldn't your bodyguard drive, or did he fail driver's ed?"

The two of them kept up the sarcastic banter for the next several minutes. I would have told them to shut up, but I glanced in the mirror and saw Madison smiling, her gaze ping-ponging between them as they mocked each other in that stupid competitive way males had. Her smile made me think of my sister, and my heart felt a little lighter.

Once I'd hit the interstate heading north, though, I'd had enough of Cole and Rad. On my insistence, JR had tinkered with the Land Rover's music system, setting up an internal MP3 player and loading all my music onto it. I hit the button, flipped through the album covers on the touchscreen, and selected three of my favorites. Shinedown, Creed, and Alter Bridge. Then I hit shuffle and cranked the volume.

As soon as Brent Smith's voice filled the interior, singing, "I dare you," my nerves calmed. Music always had that effect on me. I could lose myself in the lyrics and somehow think more clearly.

Cole let a couple of songs go by and noticed I'd passed the turn for the expressway. "Thought you were going after that witch," he yelled over the music.

"Later. First, we get Maddy some blood. Then I'm going to show Toel who he's messing with.'

"You got a plan, or are you just going balls first into a goatfuck?"

"I've got a cherry-wood stake with Toel's name on it."

Madison stared out the window, seemingly unconcerned about her fellow vamp, probably because she was jonesing so badly for blood. Rad kept one eye on her, the other on my reflection in the rearview. "You're going to kill another vamp king?"

"Toel Chase is going to be an example of why no one messes with Kali Sweet."

Ten minutes later, I parked the Land Rover in front of the strip club above Chloe's underground blood bank. Parking downtown in this area was nonexistent unless you were into parking garages and long walks. Madison was jittery to the point of climbing the walls. "Hang on, I'm going to get you fixed up."

Dozens of junkies, hookers, and other assorted low-lifes hung around on the sidewalk in front of the club. A line formed at the door. Among the humans were vamps and demons, shapeshifters and fairies. A few witches and warlocks. Every one of them could cause us trouble.

Cole watched them through the bulletproof window, caressing his gun. "What's wrong with the back entrance?"

I touched my fingers and thumbs together, raising my protective magic. "We're using the front and making a real entrance. Time to show the Undead world I know how to play the game, and I'm not backing off because a few of them don't like me."

"Why...are you...doing this?" Madison asked. "Getting me blood?"

I glanced over my shoulder at her. "You're coming to work for me, aren't you? As my assistant?"

She nodded, lips trembling in a half-smile.

I double-checked my weapons and let the handle of my whip slide down into my palm. "Cole, take my six. Rad, drive around the block a few times. We'll be out in less than five. If anything hanky goes down, contact the Bridge Institute, but do not come in guns blazing on your own. Got it?"

No one but Madison looked happy. Too bad. I wasn't Santa Claus. "Let's move."

We all got out. Rad squeezed my arm, just a brief squeeze, like a lover sending a *be careful* message. I didn't like it, that intimacy, but I should have thought of that before I fed him my blood and let him bareback me against the bathroom wall.

I shook off his hand, raised my chin, and headed for the door. Madison fell into step behind me, Cole bringing up the rear. As I bypassed the line of waiting customers, I heard the Land Rover drive away.

I didn't need to flash my badge at the bouncer. He knew my face, my red cape, and my reputation. I flashed it anyway, even though I wasn't there on Bridge business. This whole vamp mess was partly Bridge business and partly personal. It was getting harder and harder to draw the line between the two.

Smells hit me at the same time the bass-thumping techno

dance music did—neither of which I liked. Stale beer, human sweat, cigarette smoke. The flashing lights, combined with the awful music and even worse scents of the Undead, shapeshifters, and low-level demons, gave me an instant headache. The women on stage moved with the music, but in a distant way, as if they were only going through the motions.

I raised my hood over my head, keeping it far enough back to see from my peripheral vision but close enough to my face to form a barrier between me and the filth around me.

People, even those drunk and high, cleared a path when they saw me coming. The few that didn't found themselves face-planted on the disgusting beer and who-knew-what-else stained floor. I avoid hurting humans as a general rule, but that night, anyone and everyone who didn't move out of my way or tried to get close to me or Madison ended up sucking carpet.

A Cupiditas demon ran the place. The term was misleading. He was no cupid but a demon who spilled avarice, desire, and the urge to party as easily as his customers spilled their beers. His usual hangout was behind a two-way mirror on the second floor, where he kept a private room and a harem of women to service him. I made sure he saw me, the weight of his gaze landing on me even through the heavy mirror.

Good. He was a raging gossip. Word would spread I was out and on the hunt before The Mouse tipped up her first bottle of A positive.

By the time I meandered through the club and found the door in the back that led downstairs to Chloe's, I was sure I'd made the impression I wanted on a whole group of people who would spread the word like wildfire. I was confident, in control, and ready to take on anyone who wanted to mess with me.

And I was only getting started.

TWENTY-FIVE

The moment we entered Chloe's, Madison's skittish eyes landed on the refrigerators of bottled blood, and she nearly fainted. Whether from hunger or because blood grossed her out, who knew, but I guessed the former was more like it.

Chloe met us personally at the bar, her short dark hair emphasizing her beautiful cheekbones. "Kali. What a nice surprise." She gave me a lascivious smile and tapped her long, red fingernails on the glass bar top. Her Southern accent deepened. "Come to pay your debt in person?"

JR hadn't donated blood when he'd picked up the stash for Lilith. He'd had Chloe put it on my tab. The Tempter demon didn't want my blood and couldn't have it, but she did want me. In her bed or wherever else she could get me. Not because I was such a catch. Tempter demons prided themselves on seducing and bedding everything supernatural.

I wasn't into females, so I plied her with weekend spa retreats to pay off the occasional bill. "I need you to set up my friend here with whatever she wants."

Madison was still staring dumbfounded at the rows of

refrigerated blood. Chloe made a sad face at me over my refusal to entertain her flirting. Then she winked at Cole, standing by the door, gun hanging loose at his side, and grabbed Madison's arm to lead her behind the bar. "What's your poison, sugar?"

"I'm...I'm not sure," Madison said.

Chloe shot me a worried look. A vamp in this bad of shape who didn't know what blood type she preferred? I shrugged. Like I could be of any help?

Chloe patted Madison's arm. "My, my, baby vamp, you are a young one. Let's try a few samples and see what you prefer."

"We don't have time for samples, Chloe." The rarer the blood type, the more vamps liked it. "Give her a six-pack of your best AB neg."

The Tempter demon frowned but went to a unique cooler directly behind the bar with a temp gauge hanging visibly behind the glass. "This blood is rich," she said, setting the bottles on the bar. "Maybe too rich for her in her current state."

I unscrewed the lid of one bottle and handed it to Madison. "Drink up."

She was too far gone to refuse. Her throat constricted and released as she guzzled the blood.

When she was done, she slammed the bottle on the bar and took several gulping breaths. Her hands, now resting on the bar, were steady.

"You throw up in the Land Rover, and you're cleaning it," I warned.

Her eyes were no longer red when she looked at me, and her cheeks seemed fuller. Almost human. "Deal."

She reached for a second bottle, but I stopped her. "You can have more after we're sure you're keeping that down."

Chloe secured the other five bottles in an insulated pack and gave me a written bill. I had plenty of money, but I handed it back. "Charge it to the Bridge Council."

"No can do." She shook her head. "That blood is the rarest I've got. Cash only, upon delivery."

Begrudgingly, I drew out my stash and counted ten hundred-dollar bills onto the bar top. "I'll need that receipt."

She swept the money off the bar, stuck it in her low-cut cleavage, and stamped the paper bill paid before handing it back to me. "What about your tab?"

Grabbing the insulated pack, I nudged Madison toward the door. "The Peninsula still your favorite weekend retreat?"

One side of her luscious mouth curved up. "You know it is."

"I'll have a weekend pass waiting for you."

"Thanks, sugar."

Cole, Madison, and I snaked our way back through the club and out the front entrance. Rad, whose timing had always sucked, pulled the Land Rover up to the curb a second later, surprising me.

He didn't, however, relinquish the driver's seat. "Where to?"

His clean scent was welcome after the strip club, and causing a scene in downtown Chicago with what appeared to be my personal driver wasn't the best way to leave the premises. Instead of sliding into the shotgun seat, though, I got in the back with Madison.

"Nudra's compound," I told Rad, ignoring Cole's look of disgust at having nowhere to sit but up front with Guitar Boy. "It's time to shake the Undead world up a little."

TWENTY-SIX

As Rad drove through the dark Chicago night, I made phone calls. First to Damon. "Since I'm Nudra's replacement and I killed him, do I have any rights to his possessions under Bridge law?"

Madison had already confirmed that under vamp customs, I had a right to claim Nudra's house and possessions, including his blood slaves since I'd already been named his successor by the Prince of the Undead. I hoped to have the Bridge Council's stamp of approval as well.

Damon's deep voice was pensive. "There's no precedence in this case. However, you were forced to remove Nudra from his position because he threatened your life. Bridge law indicates the Council then assumes his possessions and distributes them as we see fit."

"Great. As of this minute, Nudra's compound is mine. Draw up the papers. I want everything legal."

"I'll discuss it with Kirill and Yasmin."

You do that. "I need to exterminate a few pests running

around the compound. Got anyone on call tonight trained in vamp removal?"

"Kali, exercise caution. Killing more vampires will strain our new agreement with the Prince. Stay home and keep your head down until the coronation."

"I need soldiers, Damon, not a lecture, and in my opinion, the Prince is getting the better deal in your arrangement. Send whoever you've got with vamp experience to Nudra's compound within the hour."

Damon protested. I ignored it. Highway lights whipped past the SUV as Rad wove in and out of traffic at the pace of a race car driver. When Damon finally stopped bitching at me, I asked, "What's Lilith up to?"

"She's keeping a low profile. Unlike you. Why were you at the blood bank?"

He'd already heard about my visit to Chloe's. Word traveled faster than a speeding vampire. "Paying a bill. Why isn't she causing more trouble?"

"Perhaps your warning about the Noctifectors did some good."

More likely, she was worried Lucifer would find out she was gunning for his girlfriend. "I only have two options when it comes to sending her back to hell, you know."

Damon sighed a tired sigh. He didn't like the idea of me killing Victoria even though he'd used her as a means to manipulate me, but he was even less excited about me trying to exorcise Lilith. Odds were, I'd end up taking a trip to the pit with her. "I'm aware." There was a rustling sound of papers in the background. "I will not allow you to sacrifice yourself for the human witch."

Not your call, buddy boy. "We'll cross that bridge later. Any word on Hone?"

"No."

"Did you check on him?"

"Today has been extremely busy, Kali, and Hone is not my employee. He's a hired contractor."

He was also my friend and had been doing the Bridge Council and me a favor by babysitting Vicky. "You suck at interpersonal skills, you know that?"

I hung up on him and dialed my home. JR picked up on the first ring. "Which hospital is Hone at? I need the phone number."

The clicking of the keyboard echoed between us. "He's at Mercy. I'm sending you the number now."

Sure enough, my cell phone beeped with a text message. "Thanks. How about getting me diagrams and blueprints of Nudra's compound? I need to know the layout."

"You'll have a set shortly."

"Send them to Cole's phone too. Find anything on Arman yet?"

"Guy's in the wind. I've got nothing."

Merde. That couldn't be good. "Keep trying."

"Right, boss."

The third call went to the hospital. According to the nurse, the bump on his head wasn't terrible, but Hone was being held overnight for observation. Hunh. Hone was letting them keep him overnight for a little bump on his noggin?

The nurse patched me through to his room. When he picked up, I razzed him. "You getting soft on me, Hone? Letting a witch get the jump on you?"

"Kali Sweet, what'chu doin' callin' me when you got the queen of hell visitin' Chicago?"

"Vicky told you what she did, huh?"

"Right before she knocked me out."

Hone was a human with psychic abilities. Witches like Victoria were human but had either traded their souls for dark magic or had been born with a gift for controlling the elements. The gifted ones could use air, water, fire, and/or earth elements to manipulate their world. Those who'd sold their souls could raise certain classes of lower demons to do their bidding. A few natural-born elemental witches went to the dark side and amassed enough power to match that of many supernaturals.

Evidence suggested Victoria was one of these, but my gut said differently. She didn't ooze dark magic or even elemental power. The only thing my senses got off her was plain ol' blind human determination.

Maddy was sleeping, head propped against the window. Cole and Rad were listening to a nighttime radio talk show. My fingers itched to change the channel as the host tried to work callers into a frenzy over the latest political scandal. "How exactly did she do that? Knock you out?"

"Damn witch was supposed to be sleepin'. So I'm watchin' Smackdown on cable and wham! There she was, in front o' me, all misty and...well, she looked like a damn ghost. She said words I didn't understand, and suddenly, I couldn't move. Like I was paralyzed, y'know? Whacked me over the head with a baseball bat."

Misty and ghost-like. Hmm. Sounded like astral projection. What other tricks did Vicky have up her sleeve? "You didn't read her mind?"

"Never heard a mental peep from her before she clobbered me."

The words Hone hadn't understood were a spell to immobilize him since she couldn't have taken him on without handicapping him first. "I'm sorry she put you in the hospital. I miscalculated her abilities."

"You and me both."

"When is the doctor sending you home?"

"Don't matter what he says. I'm gettin' out o' here tonight."

"You sure that's a good idea?"

"Hell, yes. Got me a witch to find."

Didn't we all? "Did the head knock dampen your abilities any?"

"Not one bit. Didn't hurt nothin' else either. MRI and all that bullshit came back negative."

Good. "I'll make you a deal. You help me with a small vamp problem I need to take care of this evening, and I'll handle your revenge on Victoria pro bono."

He hesitated. "No offense, but I wanna put my hands around her neck myself."

So did I, but she was still human. Hone's advantage was he was human, too. Human-on-human violence wasn't my territory. "I can't stop you from going after Vicky on your own, but she's hanging with Lilith now. You won't be able to touch her and could end up in the boneyard instead of the hospital."

Another pause while he thought it through. "I feel ya, Kali. I'll give it some thought. Meanwhile, where's this vamp problem?"

I gave him the compound's address. He agreed to meet us there in an hour. "Gotta take Renee home first. She's been here with me the whole time."

"Bet she's not too happy about me putting her man in danger."

"She's cool," he said. "Knows it goes with the territory."

"I'm still invited to the wedding?"

"Absolutely."

We exchanged goodbyes, and I hung up. I didn't want or need Hone for his muscle at the compound. At least, I hoped I wouldn't need him to dust any vamps. What I did need were his mind-reading skills. And maybe if he threw a few vamps around, he'd burn off some of his anger at Vicky.

Then again, if Hone took Vicky out, that would sever her

connection to Lilith and send Lilith packing, solving several of my problems in one fell swoop. I didn't condone human-on-human violence, but it was a fact of life. Unfortunately, Hone wasn't a killer. He wanted revenge for Vicky, making him look weak and taking advantage of him, but that wasn't enough to trigger his killing instincts. Besides, if Lilith planned on sticking around, she'd protect her anchor to Earth. Hone would be dust before he could lay a finger on Vicky.

I rubbed my forehead. One problem at a time. First, I'd deal with Toel and make sure he didn't touch any of my friends ever again. Then I'd deal with Lilith and both her witches.

And then, if I was still standing, I'd deal with the vamp coronation.

I looked up and saw Rad watching me in the rearview.

Oh, yeah, and after taking care of the Undead, witches, and the queen of hell, I'd deal with his happy ass, too.

TWENTY-SEVEN

We drove through neighborhoods with two-story brick Tudors, well-manicured lawns, and inviting parks. Nudra's two-acre property was set back on a cul-de-sac and took up half of a block with a park on one side and a forest preserve behind it. A high-stone wall surrounded the grounds, blocking the street view of the house as Rad did a drive-by.

The wrought iron gate stood open, though, so I caught a glimpse of the long drive, lined with oak trees, and a circular parking area near the front of the house. A massive water fountain took center stage with half a dozen luxury and sports cars parked between it and the front entryway.

Since I'd been knocked out the last time I'd entered, and too messed up when I'd left to notice the ostentatious Hollywood look of the place, I was more than curious. Fancy houses weren't uncommon in this area, but fenced and gated properties were.

The drive-by didn't give me any real sense of the property's grounds. Good thing JR had come through with diagrams and satellite pictures. The house was a mansion, even by Chicago standards. Over five thousand square feet of brick and stone, an outdoor tennis court, and an indoor swimming pool. Porticos, a Juliet balcony, and extensive landscaping covered the front. One of the porticos led around to the north side and a five-car garage.

The cars in that garage were listed on the inventory JR had sent and read like a Maddy list of the Top Five Cars of the Rich and Famous. Several of them piqued my interest. An Aston Martin, a Lamborghini Gallardo, a Porsche Carrera GT, a Bugatti Veyron, and a Ferrari Enzo. Cole and I would have one hell of a good time test driving all of those.

None of the cars on the list matched the ones parked out front. Those belonged to Toel and his friends. Since the gate was open, I suspected he was expecting more.

Either that, or he was expecting me.

Rad turned the Land Rover around and parked up the street. "Security is tight inside the fence's perimeter. Cameras over all the entrances were mounted on trees around the house. Last time I was here, the place was reinforced with structural magic, and the hired help was armed." He glanced at me in the rearview. "We were lucky to get out last week without more bloodshed."

The statement carried a warning. If we went in tonight, blood was going to flow.

I fiddled with the satellite image JR had fed me. "What about the sky? Any cloaking over the house?"

Cole snorted. "You gonna fly in, Kali?"

I was walking in through the front door. My backup, however, needed a less detectable entrance. "Nudra's security is all ground-oriented. Seems he was more worried about human criminals than supernaturals. Our best plan of attack may be to slip in from the roof."

Madison woke up and yawned. "Where are we?"

I opened the insulated case of blood and handed her a bottle. "Nudra's compound. Drink up. You're doing recon for me."

She didn't hesitate to take the bottle but gave me a funny look. "Recon?"

"Toel's throwing a party to win some of Nudra's followers over to his side is my guess. You're a vamp. I want you to sneak in, have a looky-loo, and report back to me. How many Undead are there, what are they doing, where are they clustered? Anything you hear or see that can help me."

She glanced at her clothes and back at me. "I'll stick out like a palm tree on Lake Shore Drive."

"I thought you were The Mouse."

A touch of indignation raised her voice. "I am."

"Then get in and get out without being noticed, Mouse."

Three Cadillac Escalades rolled up and pulled in behind us. One by one, the passengers filed out, demon soldier after demon soldier. All dressed in black, all wearing their Bridge badges conspicuously.

When Damon sent the cavalry, he didn't mess around.

They lined up on the sidewalk, and Cole hopped out to inspect his troops. Each one popped in a high-tech earbud that doubled as a microphone as Cole went down the line, and most had some sort of visible weapon. Those that didn't were probably more dangerous.

I climbed out of the Land Rover, bringing Maddy with me. Rad hung back, watching the surrounding area with a trained eye.

The soldiers had tight, skillful magic simmering under their skins and were hyped with controlled anticipation. They hung out with weapons day in and day out, honing and fine-tuning their bodies until they were as dangerous as the guns, knives, and other killing tools they used. Thus, the smell hanging in the cold night air made me think of the inside of an armory.

"Maddy's with us," I told them, making sure each of them looked her in the face and registered her features. "She's going to sneak in and gather intel, then give me the lay of the land. When things go down, if she's inside, you don't touch her, you protect her. Understand?"

The soldiers nodded and grunted affirmations. A few of them were familiar. We'd worked previous jobs together. The rest were strangers but still part of Cole's elite fighters. All well-versed in combat, I knew every one of them hated vamps as much as I did.

Oh, yeah. This was going to be fun.

Still, I wanted to be clear about the situation. "Anything happens to Maddy, and I'll hold you all responsible."

A female soldier stepped forward and handed me a folded set of papers. "Director Soule asked me to give these to you."

Damon's formal title sent a shiver down my spine, especially in the female's Basque accent, which sounded like his. He'd probably brought her to America with him, and if so, she'd been around a long time. I wondered why I hadn't run into her at the Institute. "Thank you."

Unfolding the papers, I felt Damon's magic on them. Yasmin and Kirill's as well. There was a bunch of legal jargon and their signatures, but bottom line, the papers were a decree naming me sole proprietor of Nudra's compound, possessions, bank accounts, and blood slaves.

I refolded them and tucked them in my cape. Cole and I gathered the group into a huddle. It was dark out, and the neighborhood was quiet, but we didn't need to draw more attention than necessary. "Did you bring any rope?" I asked Cole's second-in-command.

The male was basketball-player tall, black as the night, and held his magic so tight, a bowling ball would have bounced off it. I'd never worked with Jimmy, but I'd seen him in the gym. He was a crack Brazilian jiu-jitsu practitioner, and once he had you down, you weren't getting back up in one piece.

At the mention of rope, his dark eyes flashed with excitement. "Rope, harnesses, crampons, carabiners, we've got it all. What are we climbing?"

"You won't need the rope to climb, only to repel down from the trees around the house onto the roof." I showed him the satellite shot on my cell phone screen. "You'll infiltrate on the upper level, round up any occupants there, and restrain them until I give the signal." I grabbed Maddy, who was standing on the sidewalk looking nervous. "The Mouse is going to get us a headcount and tell us where the majority of people are. While she's doing that, I need half your squad to get into position around the backside of the perimeter where the largest trees are located. The other half stays here with me."

I looked at Maddy. She was pale, even for a vampire, but it wasn't because of blood loss. She was scared. "You up for this?"

Her hands disappeared into the sleeves of her jacket, and she bounced lightly on her toes. "Do I have a choice?"

I shook my head. "Not if you want to work for me."

"Here," Damon's Basque female handed her an earbud from a pocket in her tight-fitting jacket. "Put this in your ear. No one will see it, and we'll be able to talk to you through it and give you guidance if you need any. It also has a mic, so we'll be able to hear anything you say, even if you're whispering."

Maddy looked impressed. Hell, I was impressed. I gave the female soldier a grateful nod and patted Madison on the back. "I'll give you ten minutes, not a second more. Go through as much of the place as you can, but don't take unnecessary risks. Tell us what you see, who you see, and anything that looks out of place or unusual. Then get your butt back out here, got it?"

She gave me a determined nod, the old Maddy surfacing. "I won't let you down."

I watched her disappear into the shadows and set the timer on my watch. Cole, the Basque female, and Jimmy all did the same to their watches. Jimmy counted off half his men, motioned them to follow him to the last Escalade, and started handing out repel rope.

A mid-sized Ford eased down the street. Hone.

"I'll be right back." Walking away from the rest of the soldiers, I waved Hone over. He parked and rolled his giant body out of the poor car. I swear the shocks squeaked from the strain.

It was good to see him. "You ready to read a vamp king's mind for me?"

His head was bandaged, but he'd snugged a black knit cap over it. After hiking up his pants, he adjusted the cap, covering a strip of white bandage peeking out near his temple. "Another vamp king? You crazy, girl?"

Hone and I had a system when I was interviewing perps. If the perp told the truth, Hone kept his hands at his sides and his eyes on the perp's upper body. If he put his hands behind his back or lowered his eyes to the perp's shoes or the floor, I knew the idiot was lying. Even the clever criminals never guessed my bodyguard could read minds. "Crazy as a Mockery demon."

Which, if Toel had been a demon rather than a vamp, would have fit his style. He was good at charades, good at mocking others for his own benefit, and all the while appearing harmlessly goofy and completely sincere.

But he wasn't harmless, and he hadn't made king status because he was an expert surfer. "My plan isn't to kill him," I told Hone. "But I'm making one real sweet example of him."

Hone clapped his hands and rubbed them together. "You wouldn't be takin' personal revenge, now, would'ya, Kali?"

"You know me better than that." I flashed him the folded-up decree. "This is Bridge business."

Hone jerked his head in Rad's direction. "He helpin' with this Bridge business?"

Until then, I'd been putting off deciding what to do with Rad. Knowing him, he wouldn't sit this out, but I didn't want him in the line of fire, either.

Which annoyed me. I didn't want to feel protective of him, and besides, he'd demonstrated his ability to take care of himself quite effectively with both Lilith and Cole. There was no good reason to tie his hands.

I still didn't like the idea of him coming in with me. Stepping a little closer to Hone, I lowered my voice. "Can you read his mind?"

Hone stared off at Nudra's compound, going utterly still for a long moment. Then he shook his head. "Nothin'."

Damn. "He's half human. Why can't you read him?"

The big guy shrugged. "Too many blocks. Too much chaos in there for me to get a beat on anythin'."

There were all kinds of different mental blocks. Even the chaos itself was a type. "Are the blocks tangible?"

"Ho, yeah. He's been trained."

The Noctifectors at work again. I squeezed Hone's arm. "Thanks for trying. Get an earpiece from the tall black guy at the tail of the Escalades. I'll let you know when I'm ready to breach the compound. I want you on my left when I walk in, okay?"

"You got it."

I left Hone and moseyed over to Rad. "Is there anything I can say to make you stay out here when I go in?"

His arms were crossed over his chest, and he leaned on the Land Rover. Shadows covered his face. "Looks like you've got plenty of backup. You don't need me."

Wait. Was he willing to sit this one out? I narrowed my eyes. What was up with his sudden change of heart? "Vamps make you nervous?"

He didn't laugh at my half-hearted joke, nor did he deny my accusation. Instead, he motioned me to get in the SUV with him. "We need to talk."

As usual, Rad's timing sucked. "I'm about to go head-to-head with a vamp king. Now's not the time to talk about the past."

My protest went unheeded. He got in the driver's side, shut the door, and stared at me through the windshield. In the dim recesses of the car, his mouth moved. "Get in."

Looking around, I noticed Cole was the only one watching me. The others were all engaged in checking their weapons, testing mics, and strapping on ropes and other gear.

I walked around to the passenger side and climbed in. "Did you know Nudra was high-jacking teenagers at the concerts and turning them?"

One of Rad's hands hung over the top of the steering wheel. He tapped his fingers on the dashboard. "Nudra was my latest Noct assignment. I was investigating his various business transactions. You killed him before I got anything concrete."

I settled myself in the seat, straightened my skirt. Noctifectors didn't discriminate. Vamps, demons, shifters, we were all evil. They killed anything not human. "He was a vamp. Why didn't you just stake him?"

Rad turned his head to face me. His gold eyes reflected the small amount of light coming from the street. In their depths, I saw guilt and desire. Guilt for not taking out Nudra or guilt over still wanting me after all these years?

"Despite the twelve Noctifector tenets I've broken in the past twenty-four hours over you, I usually follow orders and take my job seriously. My orders were to gather intel on Nudra, not kill him."

"You helped me kill him in the torture chamber."

"That assistance was personal, not professional. I'm sure it won't go unnoticed by my superiors."

He sounded so business-like, so professional. "Why are you here, Rad? Gathering intel on me now for your superiors?"

Once more, his eyes flashed with desire and guilt. He wanted me, and he wanted to be a good soldier. No way he could have his blood and drink it, too.

"You're not a killer," I said. "How did the Noctifectors manage to turn you into one?"

He looked away, staring out the windshield. What he was seeing, though, was far removed from this suburb of Chicago. "Are you going through with this vampire coronation thing?"

I sat back and sighed. "I don't have any choice. A demon with blood slaves can't work for the Council, and in fact, is considered to be a ticking bomb. Damon's willing to cut me some slack, but it involves me making nice with the Undead."

"He's blackmailing you."

It wasn't a question. "If I don't go through with this, he'll be forced to kill my blood slaves."

Rad tapped his thumb on the dashboard, then cut his eyes to me. "Does he know I'm your blood slave?"

"No, and I plan to keep it that way, but the bond has to be severed one way or the other, or I can't work for the Council. It's either the slaves or..." I took a deep breath and let it out slowly. "Me."

Rad chuckled without humor. "He won't kill you, Kali. You're too valuable to him."

Snorting, I shook my head. "One thing I've learned over the years is everyone's replaceable. Even me. Damon taught me that."

188 of MISTY EVANS

"You're valuable to the Bridge Council, but that's not what I meant." He searched my face for something I didn't understand. "Damon has plans for you that go beyond the Institute."

I started to ask him what he was talking about, but my car door opened, and Cole stood there, holding out one of his hands. In the palm was an earbud. "Madison's discovered something. She wants to talk to you."

Taking the minuscule equipment, I slipped out of the Land Rover, a surge of adrenaline shooting down my legs. "I'm here, Maddy," I said as I stuck the receiver in my ear. "What's up?"

"I'm in the basement. Actually, in a tunnel below the basement. There's a hidden room or something. The door's locked, and I can't get in."

The torture chamber. The memory of being strapped to Nudra's dissection table, him leaning over me with that silver dagger, sent a shiver down my spine that had nothing to do with the November wind blowing up my cape. "Don't worry about that room. I know what it is. You don't need to get in there."

"You don't understand." Her voice was strained, barely above a whisper, but I could hear noise in the background. "There are people in there. Humans. They're trapped, and I can't get them out."

TWENTY-EIGHT

Toel had brought humans to the party. To turn them or use them as an entree?

Why would he do that? I stared at Cole for a second, brain cells clicking together like magnets.

To get to me. Toel had kidnapped humans and stuck them in the torture chamber to get to me. Whether he and his friends turned them into vamps or feasted on them tonight didn't matter. He was again thumbing his nose at the Bridge Council and me in particular.

Bastard. "Hang tight, Mouse."

I removed the earbud and flicked the switch off. "Did she give us any other intel?" I asked Cole. "Do we know how many are in there?"

"Seven vampires in the study, playing pool and partying it up. Three staff in the kitchen. The staff members aren't Undead. Most likely blood slaves. The rest of the place appears clear."

"No one watching the cameras?"

"Madison couldn't find the control room, but she cleared the fence in the back and got in without raising any alarms."

Vamps could jump anything and become nearly invisible in the night. Either the girl was as covert as she claimed, or Toel didn't have anyone on security detail. "Is your squad ready to crash this party?"

"At your signal, Madam Enforcer."

I opened the connection to Maddy. "We're coming in. Stay out of sight. I'll let you know when it's clear."

Cole took out his gun, double checked the clip and chamber. "What's your plan?"

My weapons were securely stashed in my cape. Volante was coiled on my wrist, vibrating with anticipation. "Send the tree squad in now. Have a couple stay in the trees and keep eyes on all exits. The rest go in from the roof. Tell them to stay out of sight and double-check the upstairs. I don't want any surprises. The rest of your squad should take up positions around the perimeter and restrain anyone who comes out until I give the okay to release them. You, me, and Hone are walking in through the front door."

Rad left the Land Rover, gave me a sad smile, and started walking away.

So he was going to leave just like that? Not tell me what he was referring to about Damon and his plans for me? Not even say goodbye?

I told myself it was for the best, but my heart pinched hard inside my chest. What Rad and I'd shared in the past few hours had been nice, but we were enemies. No matter the desires burning inside us, nothing good would come from hanging out together.

Cole saw Rad walking away and shot a questioning look at me. I shrugged, and he called out softly, "Hey, Guitar Boy. Where are you going?"

Rad stopped short, stuck his hands in his pockets, and slowly faced us. He seemed to be fighting with himself, giving up after a few seconds. "You got a spot for me?"

Cole didn't, but I did. "Can you take care of the humans we send out?"

He strolled back, curiosity evident on his face. "What humans?"

Rad hadn't heard Madison's report. "Toel has humans stashed inside. He's either planning to use them to make me look bad, or he's offering his friends inside a little incentive to join the coup he's staging against me. Either way, if I don't free those humans, they'll be vamp food by morning."

"What do you want me to do?"

"When we get them out, they'll be freaked. I need you to calm them down, ensure they weren't already bled or bitten, and find them a ride home." I handed him a stack of my Bridge business cards. "Give them one of these and tell them to contact the office if they want to file charges against any of the vamps inside."

"In other words, I'm on coffee duty again."

Demons and their egos. "This is far more important than getting coffee."

"Yeah, Guitar Boy." Cole drew an extra earpiece from his pocket and tossed it to Rad. "Besides, you got to hog all the fun with Lilith while I sat on the sidelines. Now it's my turn to get some action."

"Fine." Rad fingered the equipment and gave me a guarded look. "If you need any real help, say my name. I'll be inside in a flash."

There was heat in his eyes. Not sexual, but something that looked more like love. Which was ridiculous. But I knew this was personal, again, between him and me. "Drive us up to the entrance?"

He stuck the earpiece in his ear and nodded. "Let's rock and roll."

"Hey." I punched his arm. "That's my line."

Cole whistled to his squad and made a circular motion with his index finger in the air. His soldiers fell into line. He handed out orders while Rad and I climbed in the Land Rover as half of Cole's squad headed around back. The other half spread out over the front.

"Thank you," I said.

I don't know why I said it; the words popped out of my mouth before I could stop them. That iceberg in my chest had melted a lot in the past day, and Rad had been there for me through everything. He'd even stood up to Lilith with me.

After this job, though, I had to send him on his way. We'd crossed clearly defined personal and professional lines and thrown ourselves into dangerous territory. If anyone at the Bridge Institute found out I'd knowingly slept with a Noctifector, I'd be executed before I saw another sunrise.

Hone climbed into the backseat, interrupting my thoughts. His cell phone was glued to his ear, and he placed a beefy hand over the mouthpiece. "How long this gonna take, Kali? Renee wants to know when I'll be home."

I checked my watch. "You should be out of here before midnight."

He relayed my message, Cole got in, and Hone tucked his phone away.

"We ready?" I asked.

Everyone nodded.

"No matter what happens between me and Toel, nobody touches him but me. Got it? I'm going to egg him on because I want to see what he's got."

Cole harrumphed. "Why do you get to have all the fun?"

I adjusted my cape and smiled into the night. "I'm going to give Toel Chase a dose of his own medicine. After tonight, no one in the Undead world will mess with Kali Sweet again."

TWENTY-NINE

"Cali-for-ni-a," Toel said, dragging out the syllables like he'd done at our earlier meeting. The surfer accent was absent, though. He motioned at me and my two bodyguards. "Come in, come in. We've been expecting you."

Eight words and not one "dude." I liked him better this way.

Just like I'd assumed, Toel had left the front gate open, wanting me to find him. He probably knew Madison was inside, and I had over a dozen Bridge soldiers on the grounds. What was he up to?

Much like the torture chamber under the basement, Nudra's study boasted old-world amenities. Heavy on the leather, wine-colored drapes, and masculine furniture. Dark wood trim with Jodhpur carvings embellished the door and window frames. The desk was embellished with fat curved legs, carved elephants, and palm leaves. Above the sofa, a gold leaf Budda-head sculpture looked down on all of us.

None of the vamps in the room looked like they belonged there, but I felt the pull in my blood. There were indeed seven, including Toel. He strode around the pool table, cue in hand, and took a dead ball shot at a stripe. The cue ball barely moved but sent the stripe into the side pocket.

I sized up each of the other vamps, assessing their threat level more than their features. Four males, three females. All three women were artificially enhanced clones. They appeared to be stoned. None of them paid me the slightest bit of attention as they hung on two of the Undead males seated on a sectional leather sofa. The third male vamp stood near a window overlooking a garden outside. He was younger than his friends on the sectional.

The male vamps were dangerous, all of them sizing us up as fast as we did them. Vamps high up in Nudra's hierarchy or Toel's minions—I couldn't be sure. But the way they'd made themselves at home suggested they'd been here previously. The way their blood tugged at mine, they had to be Nudra's. I felt nothing from Toel except the usual Undead powers combined with sexual desire and blood lust.

While staking him was preferable to playing nice, I had a different plan in mind. I strolled up to the pool table and shifted one hip so it rested against the polished wood. "What are you doing here, Toel?"

His eyes took a leisurely stroll up my boot-clad legs to the short skirt and rested there on my bare skin before he moved around the table to set up his next shot. "Doing a little business in Nudra's place until the new king is crowned."

I pretended interest in the shot he was lining up, casually caressing my fingers along the pool table's edge as I walked around the corner. My new vantage point allowed me to see Hone, whose hands hung at his sides, and put me directly across from Toel's focused attention. "What kind of business?"

Toel didn't like the distraction of my short shirt in his line of vision. Or, rather, he liked it a little too much. The sex and power radiating off him grew thicker, heavier.

He blinked and fought it, sending another stripe in my direction. Right before the ball could drop into the pocket, I snatched it off the table. "Answer my question."

Anger flashed in his eyes, and his vampire power smacked up against my protective magical barrier.

Short temper, this one.

He straightened to full height, the cue loosely held in his right hand. "Why do you care?"

"This house is mine now." I removed the Bridge papers from my cape and tossed them on the pool table. "Nudra's business is also mine. You have no right to be here and no reason to undermine my authority unless you're looking for trouble." Toel liked playing games, so I leaned forward on the pool table and discreetly licked my lips. "And if trouble's what you're after, you've found her, buddy boy."

A low chuckle came from his chest, sounding confident and slightly intrigued, but he didn't move. One of the women sidled up to him, molded her body against his as she ran a hand over his chest. She gave me a *back off* glare.

Toel grabbed her hand and shoved her away none too gently. While equal amounts of lust and power drove most vampires, his primal supernatural magic was driven by the need for supremacy and dominance. "The vampire world is not your concern, no matter what Rafael and Juliana have led you to believe. You're a demon, not one of us, and we don't want you meddling in our affairs."

He saw me as being beneath him. Many vamps, especially the latest generation, who hadn't been around as long as their older counterparts, viewed demons the same way. Toel had big plans, and no one was going to get in his way, especially not some measly vengeance demon.

I could have cared less about Undead affairs. If I wiped the entire vamp population off the face of the planet, there wouldn't be any affairs to worry about, and my job would be a lot easier. Killing this entire room of vamps would have been a good start, but maybe the best way to bring down the vampire nation was from the inside.

And upsetting Toel was fun. "You threatened one of my employees. Were you afraid to confront me face to face?"

He stepped toward me, insouciant and sure of himself but determined to take me down a peg. Cole and Hone tensed, so I made a slight motion with the hand holding the ball to stop them. I'd warned them I was going to provoke Toel so I could see how he reacted. I wanted to know exactly what he was capable of, and pushing him to the extreme was the only way to find out.

With my boots on, he was only a few inches taller than me, maybe five-six or -seven. I hadn't realized he was so short in the conference room, but I'd been distracted at the time. Now he invaded my personal space and stared me down, cue stick still held nonchalantly in his hand. His eyes were cold and hard, their light blue color tinged with red.

He was hungry.

And I was about to become the meal.

Or so he thought.

"You have two choices," he murmured. His power orbited around me, tickling my protective barrier as it searched for a way in. The sensation reminded me of poison ivy vines creeping up my legs, over my arms, encircling my neck. "Leave now and forfeit your nomination to be queen of the Central American Vampire Kingdom, or stay and prove yourself worthy to rule."

Radison Beaumont wasn't the only demon who liked a challenge. Purposely lowering my protective magic, I closed the few inches of distance between us and turned my face up to his like I was going to kiss him. "Oh, I'll stay. But fair warning... I'm blistering good at pool."

He grasped the end of my ponytail between his fingers, rubbing the hair. "We're not playing pool, Cal-i-for-ni-a."

I batted my lashes and looked innocent. "We're not?"

"No."

He flipped me on my back, jamming the cue stick across my larynx and pinning down my body on the green pool table felt with his.

Several things happened at once. Cole and Hone both yelled, the other male vamps jumped up as if to intercept them, and I held up the hand with the stripe ball out of Toel's sight to signal my bodyguards to stand down.

I couldn't breathe, couldn't swallow with the hard wooden cue stick crushing my larynx. Through the sudden dots in front of my eyes, Toel's face was contorted with satisfaction and greed. His lust for my body and blood surfaced, mixing with his need to dominate me. He was going to hurt me and rape me in front of the others to prove his superiority.

As if I'd let that happen.

My right hand held the stipe ball, my left, the handle of my whip. Choices, choices...

Since he was such a dick, I decided to use both.

I smacked his temple with the ball first, and when he flinched, the tension on my throat eased a fraction, allowing me to breathe. I expanded my chest, flicked my whip out, and smacked him across his back.

Volante cut through his clothes and made a satisfying crack against his skin. He didn't cry out, but his body arched in response to the pain. Not as much as I'd hoped, but enough to lift his upper body off mine marginally. I dropped the ball and, with another quick, although much lighter flick of my wrist, sent the end of Volante's leather arcing over the back of his neck. I grabbed the end with my right hand and wrapped my legs around Toel's stomach.

The boots I wore were custom-made by one of my favorite designers. Four rows of tiny spikes ran down the inside, outside, front, and back, making them fashionable and functional in the hardware department. I tightened my hold on him until I heard a satisfying grunt of pain.

Fighting both my restraints and the pain, Toel regained his self-control surprisingly fast. His upper body crashed back down on mine, shoving various weapons inside my cape into my chest and lungs. Air whooshed out of my lungs.

Ignoring the discomfort, I looked into his eyes as the cue stick once more bore down on my throat. He couldn't get the leverage he'd had before since he was only using one hand to hold the stick. The other pinned down my whip hand.

Putting his vulnerable upper body so close to me was stupid, but he probably didn't realize that since he thought so highly of himself and so poorly of me. The demon inside me laughed.

"You bitch," he spit in my face. "You're going to pay for that."

As he spoke, I discreetly wrapped the end of the whip around my right hand, clasping it tight. I also tightened my leg grip around his stomach, digging my knees and the spike-lined boots into the sides of his ribcage. Again, he arched, raising his head, and that was all I needed. Two quick turns of the whip around his neck, and I jerked the finely crafted leather hard.

Toel's body went rigid at the shock of being strangled. His eyes bulged. He released his hold on the cue stick, and a new rush of adrenaline sped through me, along with the air I sucked in.

The red in the vampire's eyes darkened as he called up his

supernatural power to fight back. Turnabout's fair play, so I called up my own magic and made another rotation of my hand around the whip's leather, increasing the tension on his neck. Toel's tongue flopped out, fingers clawing at Volante's hold on his trachea, and his magic succumbed to mine.

No matter what the Undead tell themselves, demons are at the top of the food chain.

He gurgled and continued to fight, the swimming and surfing he'd done over the years magnifying his vamp strength to Hulk-like levels. My muscles shook with the effort to continue choking him into submission without killing him. Volante could have decapitated him, but I didn't want him dead. I just wanted him unconscious.

Behind me, I heard the sounds of scuffling and fighting. "Don't kill them," I yelled to Cole. After all, if we killed Nudra's midlevel managers, who would spread the news about what a badass I was?

I gave Toel's ribs another dig with my knees and heard bones snap. A second later, his eyes rolled up in his head, and his body went limp. He could've been playing possum, so I didn't ease up on the whip's tension while I rolled us both off the pool table and onto the floor. I exerted another thirty seconds of pressure and then released him.

Cole's squad of soldiers swept into the room. Cole and Hone had Nudra's managers subdued. The three of them sat on the sectional, bloodied and bruised, gazes darting between me and their fallen leader.

I stood over Toel's body, keeping an eye on him. Vamps healed almost as fast as demons. I probably had less than two minutes to secure him in the torture chamber before he woke up. "You three." I motioned at the male vamps. "Carry him downstairs, shackle him in the silver manacles on the west wall." Making eye contact with Jimmy, the jiu-jitsu expert, I motioned at the Undead males. "Secure them down there too. I'll be down in a minute to talk to them."

"What about us?" one of the female vamps said, swaying on her feet.

"Leave."

The one that had hung on Toel rushed me from the corner, one hand raised as if to slap me. "Bitch," she screamed.

I caught her hand in midswing and snapped her wrist. She cried out and fell to the ground as if I'd mortally wounded her. I shook my head. "You guys really need to expand your repertoire of curse words."

In my ear, Madison and Rad were asking me if I was all right. "I'm fine," I answered, but my voice didn't sound fine. It sounded rough and scratchy.

Jimmy was rousing the vamps from the sectional. The young male who'd been standing near the window protested. He was thinking hard about the torture chamber, and his fear was evident. "We just came here to hear Toel's proposal. We didn't know he was planning on killing you."

Right. "What proposal?"

The three looked slightly abashed. The young one spoke again. "He wanted us to object to your nomination and rally our citizens against you. At the coronation, he wanted us to stage a protest and let the Prince know we wouldn't be led by a demon."

"But did this protest involve killing me?"

The male vamps exchanged a look. "We never agreed to anything," the young one said.

The adrenaline was slipping away, and my nerves twitched. My brain was twitching, too. Vamps. Undead and deceitful as hell. "And what did Toel promise in return?"

He looked at me, perplexed, and shrugged. "His help. To rule the Central Region."

"Did Toel tell you that the Prince is the one who wants this deal between the Bridge Council and the Undead nation? Did Toel say he would personally step forward at the coronation and defend you to the Prince? Did he offer to take the blame if the plan failed?"

His flat stare told me the answer.

I motioned at him and the others to grab Toel's arms and legs. "Toel wanted the Central Region for himself. After you and your citizens started the riot, he would have stepped in and subdued you, thereby gaining the Prince's favor and making himself look like a hero. With me out of the way, he'd have the three of you killed for insubordination, and his path to this kingdom would be a slam dunk."

More of Cole's soldiers joined us, bringing Maddy and Rad with them. As the vamps carried Toel out and the females were shown to the front door, I sank down on the sectional and wound Volante around my wrist. She hummed with energy, itching for more action.

Rad sat on one side of me, Maddy on the other. Both spoke at the same time.

"Are you hurt?"

"Are you okay?"

"I'm fine," I answered.

Rad placed a hand on my back, looked me over. "You don't sound fine. You sound like shit."

"That happens when a pool stick ends up embedded in your larynx."

"Rad and I got the humans out, and they're all okay," Maddy said. "None of them had been bitten, so Rad gave them your card, and we sent all of them home."

Cole wandered over. "You gonna interrogate the vamps?"

Hone brought me a glass of water and the three servants who'd been hiding in the kitchen. I took a drink, eyed the servants, and sniffed the air. They smelled like moldy carpet and had teeth marks on various exposed patches of skin. Dark bruises under their haunted eyes. It was my job to interrogate the vamps downstairs, and I wanted a crack at Toel when he came to, but I was tired and still had a full plate of things to do. "All in due time. I need to go through Nudra's desk and this house."

One of the slaves lifted her face. She didn't look directly at me but somewhere in my midsection, showing deference. A natural redhead, her hair was now a dull copper color, held taut in a bun at the base of her skull. "Are you going to kill us?"

"Nudra's dead, which breaks your bond to him. You're free. Why are you still here?"

Her green eyes dropped to my boots, and for the first time, I noticed her freckles. She was in her early twenties, if that. Like all old vamps, Nudra liked them young. "We have nowhere else to go."

"No family? No friends?"

She shook her head, looking for the world like I had when face to face with Lilith. Head bowed, eyes downcast, my flight instincts screaming at me in full self-preservation mode.

Beside me, Maddy eyed the blood slave with equal amounts of disgust and desire. She could smell the slave's blood, and it was turning her on even after her rich dinner in my car. "Blood slaves are chosen for the very reason they have no one who cares about them. No family who comes looking for revenge on the master or makes a big stink with the cops."

I sipped my water. The three slaves were human in essence, but no longer able to live like normal beings, thanks to their Undead sugar daddies. If I kicked them out, they'd end up hooking or stripping or finding another vamp who wanted them. If I left them to their own devices, sure as shit, all three would be dead before Christmas.

On the other hand, I wasn't a social service agency, and, as I'd been repeatedly told that day, the Bridge Institute wasn't accepting human boarders. They needed someone to teach them how to be human again, and I didn't have the time or, quite honestly, the patience.

What I did have was Aphrodite. Not only did she live to play matchmaker, she enjoyed taking in lost causes. She was forever boarding handicapped dogs, cats, birds, and other animals no one else wanted and showering them with love until she found the perfect home for them.

"Here's the deal," I told Nudra's slaves. "You can stay here until I figure out what I'm doing with this house. Could be tomorrow, or next year, but eventually, I'll sell this place or turn it over to the Bridge Council, so don't be surprised when it happens. If you want to leave, I'll give you a severance check from Nudra's accounts. If you want to stay, you must abide by my rules and allow my friend Di to help you figure out what to do with your life."

The redhead perked up, but she kept her gaze cast down. "We can stay here for now, though?"

"If you agree to talk to Di. She'll clean you up, get you healthy, and help you find a job. A real job."

"You mentioned rules. What kind of rules?"

Clever girl, asking for the details before she committed to anything. Nudra had probably liked that cleverness as well as her once-pretty looks. "What's your name?"

"Corina."

I stood, set the empty water glass on the coffee table, and straightened my cape. "Well, Corina, we'll get to that later. Right now, I want you to give me a tour of the house."

"Where would you like to start?"

Cole and Rad both answered before I could. "The weapons room," they said in unison.

Sounded good to me. "The weapons room it is."

Corina nodded. "There are three, one on each floor. Which one do you want to see first?"

Three? My pulse quickened with unease. Glancing at Cole and Rad, I saw their faces reflecting the same surprise and suspicion.

What had Nudra been doing in this compound?

THIRTY

The main floor's weapons room was impressive. Most supernaturals had at least one type of weapon they preferred to carry that worked with their personal magic. Like me with Volante and stakes. The older generations preferred knives, swords, clubs, and other close-combat defenses. Younger generations gravitated to handguns and assault weapons. Many took commercial-grade weapons and endowed them with magical spells and unique enhancements that worked on particular species, especially their enemies. Cole and his holy water bullets were a prime example. Two taps to the forehead or heart of almost any supernatural, and you could take them out.

Because of Nudra's East Indian roots and his age, I expected to find a room of ornate swords, thick daggers, assorted knives, and archery equipment. He didn't disappoint. Three walls of the rectangular room were filled with exactly that.

But the fourth wall was decked out in military-grade assault weapons and munitions. Rifles, handguns, sub-machine guns, and grenades, along with assorted range finders, compasses, video cameras, and thermal sights that could be attached to the guns.

"What the hell?" Cole ran a hand over a black, tubular thing almost as long as I was tall. He stared at it like it was a thing of beauty. "Why would a vamp have a Stinger?"

"A Stinger missile?" Maddy said, eyes wide.

Rad lifted a similar weapon from its supports. This one was shorter, and he set it on his shoulder and looked through the scope with an ease and familiarity that made my skin crawl. "Not much need for rocket launchers or surface-to-air missiles in Naperville, Illinois."

My throat was healing from Toel's abuse but nevertheless felt too tight. "Either Nudra had a weapons fetish, or he was expecting trouble of the helicopter and tank variety."

Corina stood off to the side, still doing her submissive servant routine. The other two blood slaves had disappeared. For good, I suspected.

"Why did Nudra have all these weapons?" I asked Corina. "Was the freak really into weapons, or was he expecting some kind of war?"

She bit her bottom lip as if at war with herself over whether to tell me the truth. Her master was gone, but she was still loyal to the bastard.

"Rule one," I snapped my fingers at her. "I ask a question, you answer it. Truthfully."

"He was preparing for a war."

I exchanged a glance with Cole. "A war with who?"

In the back of my mind, I heard Kirill correcting my lousy grammar. I ignored him.

Corina shuffled her feet. "The Prince."

"Of the Undead?"

Another head bob. "King Nudra planned to take out the

other American rulers, then the Canadian and Mexican king and queen."

Ambitious prick. "So he'd have North America totally for himself."

"Doing so would put him on equal standing with the Prince."

It was too bad the Undead didn't rise up against each other and annihilate the whole kingdom. Would save me a lot of work.

A war of the Undeads, though, would spill over everywhere else. Innocent humans, as well as other supernaturals, would end up collateral damage. The Bridge Council would never allow that to happen.

And neither would the Prince of the Undead.

Toel wasn't quite smart enough to win a duel between him and Prince Vlad. After all, Vlad had been a vampire since the thirteenth century, giving the term vengeance new meaning. While Toel was clever, he was no match for the vamp who'd started it all. The Prince of the Undead had been challenged numerous times since selling his soul and still impaled his enemies on wooden stakes with hideous delight. He'd eat Toel alive.

I looked over the collection of weapons again. There was no stun baton, which disappointed me, but I didn't need one to cross-examine Nudra's minions or Toel. Eyeing the assortment of swords and daggers, I thought it a shame not to put any of them to use.

I took down a handsome Khanda sword, drew it from its sheath, and watched the overhead lights bounce off the metal. It was heavy in my hands and not conducive to up-close torture, but it looked intimidating. I suspected Nudra's minions wouldn't be any more willing to talk than Toel, but I didn't want to stake them. Not yet, anyway. I had to play it cool, be the Bridge enforcer, and not simply a vengeance demon who didn't like their kind. Without my threat of staking, I needed something more persuasive. My whip would work if I wanted to keep my distance from vamp scum. The khanda would work if I wanted to get a little closer.

I turned and smiled at Rad and Cole. "I think it's time to see if the asshat is ready to talk. Anyone want to come with me?"

Maddy grabbed a dagger and held it up. Her gaze was steady as it met mine. "I'll help."

Rad returned the missile launcher to its supports and helped himself to a bamboo cane meant to beat someone bloody. "Me, too."

Cole rolled his eyes, but he drew his gun from its holder. "Let's get this over with. I'm hungry."

My stomach felt empty, too. "Corina, make us some sandwiches while we're gone."

"Yes, master," she said, ducking her head.

"Rule two, Corina, don't call me master. Ever."

"Yes...Kali."

Finally, someone got my name right. I patted her on the shoulder and motioned for her to leave ahead of me. "We're going to get along just fine."

Maddy huffed beside me as we left the weapons room and walked down the plush carpeted hallway. "I thought rule one was to never give away more information than you were asked. And rule two was..."

"The rules change on the hour, kiddo." I gave her my best Italian grin. "Try to keep up."

THIRTY-ONE

Hone met us outside the torture chamber. He and Jimmy were talking in low voices. They stopped when they saw me, and Hone threw a thumb over his shoulder. "Lot of mental anguish goin' on in there. Shouldn't take much to get the info you want from Nudra's squad. The other one, Toel? He's not so easy to read."

"I already know what he's up to, but I want to have some fun with him. You got time to help me out?"

Hone checked his watch. "I gotta few."

Inside the chamber, Toel was manacled to the wall in silver restraints. The skin of his neck sported several bright red stripes, white skin peeking between them, reminding me of the pool ball I'd used on him upstairs. His shirt was torn and bloodied from my boot spikes, and his hair was a tangled mess. Very surfer dude meets revenge of the demon.

The power flowing off him was intense, making the hair on my arms rise in warning. He'd completely vamped out, and his sharp incisors hung over his lips as he lunged at me against the restraints. Nudra's minions did the opposite, backpedaling against the stone wall in matching manacles.

Rad took up a position near Toel; Cole stayed by Nudra's minions. Maddy casually strolled around the chamber, examining various instruments and the jars of blood on the shelves.

Let the fun begin.

"Sorry I don't have time or the proper equipment for an official *tortura* session," I said, unsheathing the Khanda and twisting it back and forth to catch light came from the sconces. The threat of torture was as frightening to some as the actual deed itself. "Rad, here, destroyed the willow death bed Nudra had set up. I needed one of the branches to stake him, which is kinda funny if you think about it. I dusted him with a piece of his own death bed."

Curly willow branches still lay scattered over the floor. Rad kicked one into the air with his boot and sent it in my direction. I sliced the air with the Khanda, and the blade made a soft *snick* as it sheared the wood in two.

Everyone's eyes watched the blade dissect the thick wood with ease. Nothing changed in Toel's expression. The others cringed.

"So I guess we have to do this standing up."

Toel swore, continuing to lunge at me as if he could wear out the silver wrapped around his wrists and ankles or pull the heavy chains from the wall. Nudra must have expected prisoners to attempt just that. Reinforced steel anchored the manacles to the ancient stones.

"You cocksucking bitch," Toel yelled at me. Or tried to. His voice box wasn't functioning correctly yet. "When I get my hands on you..."

Rad, a few feet away from the vamp king, smacked Toel across the nose with the bamboo pole. The vamp jerked back. Blood gushed from his nose and into his mouth.

"Shut the fuck up," Rad said. "You're starting to get on my nerves."

Cole snickered. If he'd been closer, he would have high-fived Rad.

Seeing Toel's blood gushing over his mouth and chin and dripping onto the floor, I was momentarily transported into the past and another torture chamber. Queen Maria's laughter rang in my ears. My stomach clenched...

I'd been a girl then. A demon girl, yes, but still a girl. Demon or human, nine years old was too young to know better. Too young to fully understand what I was doing and why I was so desperate for the queen's love and affection that I would twist and cut and screw flesh and bones until they gave under my assault. It was all for her. For a woman who never loved anyone but herself.

Shaking my head, I pushed the memory away. Once again, I was torturing others to prove myself, but it wasn't for love this time. Nor was I a girl anymore. If there was some big cosmic scale in the universe, I'd more than made up for the atrocities I'd performed for Queen Maria, and the four vamps in front of me weren't human. In fact, they were almost as far from human as I was.

"Ms. Sweet." Nudra's young vamp leaned toward me. "The three of us will pledge our allegiance to you right here, right now, if you let us go."

I hadn't even made the first cut, and we were already getting somewhere.

Calling up the training Cole had given me in swordplay, I swung the sword in several arcs, spinning my body in choreographed circles of a familiar routine until I stood close to the young male. The sharp edge of the blade sliced through his silk shirt as easily as a silver knife through demon skin. "You'll also round up the members of your vampire packs and insist they pledge allegiance. Tomorrow night at midnight, I expect all of you to attend the coronation and bow to me."

I didn't intend to go to the coronation, but I hadn't yet figured out how to avoid being crowned queen. Something would come to me. It always did.

The three vamps nodded their heads vigorously, and Toel, through the blood, called them traitors. Quick as a heartbeat, Rad smacked the bamboo across Toel's throat, hitting one of the red stripes left from Volante. "I told you to shut up."

Toel coughed and spit blood. "Go to hell, you piece of shit."

Rad's mouth quirked to one side. "Already been there."

Did he mean that literally? I gave him a look, but he was staring at Toel. This wasn't the right place to ask, so I cut my eyes to the young vamp. "We have a deal or not? If not—" I slid the blade along the vamp's neck, opening his skin. "I'll bring your body, impaled on this sword, to the coronation."

He nodded, careful not to brush against the blade. I eyed his companions, and they all nodded as well. I motioned at Jimmy to release them, and as he did so, each of the vamps bowed on one knee and pledged their fidelity and loyalty to me. When I gave them the word, they scrambled out of the torture chamber, nearly climbing over each other in their haste. Maddy smiled at me, and I smiled back.

Jimmy ordered several of his squad to follow the vamps out. Then, he excused himself to return to standing guard at the chamber's door.

Hone's face had taken on a far-off expression. He was reading somebody's mind, and I doubted it was mine. I refocused on Toel. "Thought you'd be the hero at the coronation tomorrow night, didn't you? Prove to the Prince you could handle both your and Nudra's territory? Make it look like you'd already won over Nudra's constituents?"

He spit again but didn't say anything. That was his tell. He was a powerful vamp—the power radiating off him was still prickling my skin—but he was also a lot of bluster. He'd never expected little ol' me to overturn his carefully crafted plans.

"Newsflash, *dude*." I threw the word at him. "Not only are you incapable of running the central corridor, you're not even capable of outsmarting me, a lowly vengeance demon."

He grinned then, showing me his teeth. There was blood on them, and a repulsive shiver slid down my spine. "Go ahead and torture me, bitch. I'll never bow to you or any of your kind."

My kind. Hm. I eyed the sword and considered shoving it into his stomach. But a sudden thought emerged...that's what he wanted.

His power, magic, and blood lust filled the room with such intensity because he wanted to take one for the team. The more we hurt him, the stronger his case would be against me when he finally got back to Rafael and Juliana and convinced them I was a sadistic psycho.

Hone's arms were still by his side after Toel's declaration. No surprise. I didn't expect Toel to be easy to break, nor did I believe he'd grovel at my feet. It would have been like expecting Nudra to show deference. Fat chance, a cold day in hell, and all that.

Hone looked pained, though. Toel had something going on inside his brain that troubled the psychic. Something I was sure was going to upset me, too. I leaned against a nearby cabinet that held various clamps, weights, screws, and dissection tools, sure I already knew why Hone's face was pinched. "You deserved what I did to you tonight, and it was within my rights as the enforcer for the Bridge Council. You harassed and stole from my human assistant. You threatened him, and I have no doubt you planned to threaten others in my life to dissuade me from becoming vamp queen. But if you wanna run back to mommy and daddy and tattle, be my guest. You attacked me here tonight, and I was defending myself as well as revenging my assistant."

Toel's eyes narrowed, but he kept his mouth shut. Definitely his tell. I spoke the truth, and he knew it. He also knew this game of torture was about to end. I couldn't take it further without becoming the sadistic psycho he wanted me to be.

Toel was good at playing games. But I'd learned from the best at nine years of age.

I set the sword down and took a leather blindfold off a nearby hook. "You know, if you'd just come to me at the start, I might have worked something out with you. I have no desire to be vamp queen. No desire to take any of Nudra's territory or assets for myself. We could have made some kind of deal that would have benefitted both of us, but messing with my friend and associate was a serious mistake. Now you're my enemy, and I never let my enemies rest."

"You can't take personal revenge on me, demon."

I smiled, tossed the blindfold to Rad, then caught Cole's eye and tapped my finger against my temple. "I don't have to."

In one long stride, Cole stepped up to Toel and slammed the butt of his gun into the vamp's head. The blow knocked him out and then some. His body slumped, the power he'd been emitting seized, and then it dissipated. Rad fitted the blindfold over Toel's eyes and snugged it tight

"Oh, man," Maddy said, coming to stand beside me. She beat her dagger against her jean-clad leg. "I didn't even get to cut him."

"Next time," I promised, secretly hoping there wasn't a next time.

Hone rubbed his fingers across his forehead, jerked the hat off his head. Sweat shone in his close-cropped hair. He took a deep breath, let it out slowly before meeting my eyes.

"What is it, Hone?"

"You ain't gonna like it."

"Tell me anyway."

He pointed his chin at Toel. "He and Nudra had plans. Big plans. They wanted to take out those other two regional managers and control all of North America."

Since Corina had already told us Nudra had been vying for America's top vampire, I wasn't surprised. That he would work with Toel, though, did surprise me. "Guess we put a stop to that."

Hone's eyes were anxious, and he shook his head. "But there's another reason Toel didn't want you at that coronation tomorrow night."

"What's that?"

He paused and shook his head again as if he couldn't believe what he was about to say. "Vlad, the Impaler, will be there."

Again, nothing I didn't already know. "And?"

"He's looking for a bride, Kali." Hone's face was a mess of distress. "And the Bridge Council has promised him you."

THIRTY-TWO

I t's difficult to shock me to the point I'm speechless. Hone's announcement did just that. I stood there for a second with my mouth hanging open in pure, unadulterated shock. Anger followed.

Half a second after the anger hit, the walls of the room closed in on me, suffocating my lungs and closing off my throat.

I ran.

Out of the torture chamber, through the basement, past the movie room, up more stairs to the first floor, my boots thwacking on the carpet, clicking on tiles. I sped past Corina, who was emerging from the kitchen with a tray of sandwiches, and ran the length of the hall until I hit the main foyer with its double staircase and crystal chandelier. I flung open the front door, startling the guards posted there, and bent over at the waist on the porch, sucking in the cold night air.

My legs shook, and I dropped down onto the top stairs. Emotions collided inside me like my body was suddenly a particle accelerator, spinning everything at high speeds, trying to break atoms apart. A sense of irony bubbled up inside me, and I laughed out loud.

Me, the bride to the Prince of the Undead? Yeah, right.

Throughout history, Vlad had always taken human wives, some two hundred in all last I'd heard. He turned each one into a blood slave, produced a kid here and there, and then when the wife died, he'd live like a bachelor for a while until he got the bug to marry again. To think he'd consider marrying a demon was ludicrous.

To think I'd be crowned queen of the Chicago vamps was just as ludicrous and, as far as I could tell, that had a distinct possibility of coming true.

I fumbled in my cape for my cell phone. The screen was dark, but the face lit once my thumb brushed over it. Toel's all-star wrestling moves hadn't broken it.

Cole's guards watched me surreptitiously, so as I hit the speed dial button for Damon, I walked down the steps and climbed into the Land Rover. The night was black, but Nudra's mansion had plenty of decorative landscape lights.

I shut the door and listened to Damon's phone at the Institute ring once, twice, three times. My anger simmered hot, ready to bust out. Where the hell was he?

"Kali," he answered after the fourth ring. "What's happening?"

I sat forward, elbows on my knees, and stared at my feet. "Did you think I wouldn't find out what you and the Council were up to?"

There was a long pause. "Please clarify. I don't understand what you're asking."

"With the Prince of the Undead, you archdemon ass. The deal you made with him over me."

In the background, I heard Yasmin asking Damon a question. She wanted to know what I was saying. Damon covered the phone with a hand and said something to her that sounded like, take a seat, *and I'll be with you momentarily*. Bet she loved that.

Damon's voice came back on the line, firm. "You were in the conference room when I struck a deal with Juliana, Rafael, and Toel. You know the guidelines of that deal. What is the problem?"

"You didn't make a sideline deal with Vlad to marry me?"

Damon's voice now boomed in my ear. "What?" Without waiting for my answer, he broke out laughing.

Any other time, I would have enjoyed hearing the archdemon laugh. It was rich and melodic and reminded me in some ways of my dad's laughter...full of the elements of a long and mysterious meaningful life.

That night, however, it sounded a touch mocking. As if I'd just claimed to have straightened the tower of Pisa without using magic. It reassured me, though. If Damon was laughing at the prospect, it couldn't be true.

I waited for his laughter to subside. "Are you done?"

A few more chuckles. Once more in the background, Yasmin questioned him. He ignored her. "Are you serious?"

"I have it from a credible source that the Bridge Council made a deal to marry me off to Vlad at the coronation ceremony tomorrow night."

"Your source is not as credible as you think. I assure you there is no deal of that magnitude between the Bridge Council and the Prince of the Undead."

A new thought dawned. "What about the European Bridge Council? They couldn't make that kind of deal without getting your okay first, right?"

Damon's voice lost its humorous edge. "Of course not."

The driver's side door opened. Maddy slipped into the seat. Time to wrap up my conversation. "Do me a favor and put out some feelers. I don't like being blindsided, and I want to ensure nothing wonky is going down at the coronation."

"Wonky?"

Hell's blood, I needed to get him out in the real world more. Yasmin spoke in the background, this time closer to the phone. In my mind's eye, I saw her standing by Damon's desk, arms crossed and brows knit because he wasn't sharing. "Whatever you do, do not tell Yasmin about this."

I snapped the phone shut. "Sorry, I ran out like that. I had to make a call."

She knew I was lying but nodded her head. "I had no idea about the whole marry the Prince thing. Never heard that on the street before I went to your place. The only thing on the vamp grapevine was about you becoming the Central Region queen and Toel wanting to stop the coronation."

Her voice was earnest. She played with a ring on her right hand, twisting it in circles until I thought she'd rubbed it raw.

Damon's laughter and denial seemed genuine. So did Maddy's declaration. But Hone was never wrong about the thoughts he read, so what was the real truth?

"I believe you." I pocketed my phone. "Either Toel knows something the rest of us don't, or he made it up. I've got a twenty that says he made it up."

And the only reason he'd do that was to screw me again. Was it possible he realized Hone was a mind reader?

The psychic in question appeared on the top steps, Cole and Rad beside him. Rad was the tallest, all muscle, strong hands, and conflicted interests. Hone was the broadest, a bighearted beefcake. Cole, in between, was scarred physically and mentally and exuded more attitude than I did, but his loyalty was so solid that I could cut my teeth on it.

All of them looked as strung out and unhappy as I felt. Their presence, though, was a balm to my raw emotions. The three stood tall and unmovable, looking like nothing could topple them.

With everything spinning out of control, it was surprisingly nice to have them grounding me. Since the age of seventeen, and even before that in Queen Maria's court, I'd had to look out for myself. Sitting there in the Land Rover, even Maddy's presence calmed me. Aphrodite, JR, and Neve were my family now, but the group with me that night was a tangled mess of friends and enemies I trusted even though I shouldn't have.

As I'd explained to Damon, trust wasn't something I handed over easily, but each of these people had earned it.

"You gonna stick around and help?" I asked Maddy, looking out at Nudra's well-manicured lawns. *Not Nudra's. Mine.* "I want to look at the rest of the house, see what Nudra's hiding besides weapons of mass destruction."

"Can I keep the knife?" She held up the dagger she'd lifted from the weapons room.

"If you agree to let Cole teach you how to use it."

Her gaze shifted to look at Cole on the front steps. "He's a demon, isn't he?"

"One of the best."

She sighed in a way that reminded me she was a teenage girl. "Can Radison Beaumont show me some moves?"

I surprised myself by laughing. "Take my advice. Stay as far away from Rad as you can."

Her eyes cut to me, curious and jealous at the same time. "You and him...hooked up?"

I glanced at Rad, who was still zeroed in on me. He didn't like waiting, evidenced by the way he kept tapping the bamboo stick against his leg, but he was giving me space. Trying not to rush me or push me or be annoying. A first.

Hooked up. The phrase always reminded me of a fish caught on a hook, being dragged out of the water to die and then be eaten. Seemed like a fitting term. "Yeah, we hooked up. A long time ago."

Maddy tilted her head. "And now?"

"I don't know what we are. Friends. Enemies. We have a lot of history. None of it good."

"That sucks. He's sick."

She meant sick in the uber-cool way. Sick, to me, though, was how I felt when I remembered the Noctifector tattoo between his shoulder blades. I stepped out of the Land Rover, ending the conversation. "Hone?"

He shuffled down the stairs, the white bandage glowing on his dark skull. "You okay?"

I patted his arm to assure him. "Is there any way Toel knew you were a mind reader?"

"Don't think so. Never seen the dickwad before."

Rad and Cole came down the stairs and gathered around Hone. The tension leaking off all of them tickled my nose. "Is it possible Nudra told him? You did work for Nudra on occasion."

"Nudra hired me for security, nothin' else. He didn't know about my mad skills."

Cole leaned a hand on the SUV. "What are you thinking, Kali?"

"That Toel knew Hone reads minds, so he planted false information in his to throw me off. Damon says there's no deal with the Prince about me being his bride."

"You trust Damon?" Rad asked. Skepticism tinged his voice.

"With something like this? Yeah. He's manipulative but does what's best for the Bridge Council, Institute, and the supernatural world. He wouldn't want to lose me or my services to Vlad."

Maddy got out of the Land Rover and sidled up to Rad.

"Who's Damon?"

"My boss."

Hone stuck his hat back on his head and snugged it down. "What do you want me to do, Kali? Hang around 'til the vamp regains consciousness? See if I can get any more out of him?"

Checking my watch, I noted it was nearing midnight. "Nah. Go home. Hug Renee. Tell her I'm sorry for dragging you out here tonight, but as always, you were invaluable."

A jerk of his chin confirmed he appreciated my compliment. "I'm comin' to that coronation," he said. "Just in case."

Having Hone at the coronation afforded me several advantages, the least being his mind-reading capabilities. "I don't know where the ceremony's being held yet, so I'll have Damon call you with the details once I get them."

He threw his beefy arms around me in an unexpected hug. "You take care, here? I'll see you at the coronation."

The sensation of being squeezed in a warm, nonsexual, non-fighting way took me off guard. It was a rare day when someone hugged me with plain old affection and nothing else. "Thank you, Hone."

I wasn't sure if I was thanking him for helping me out at Nudra's, hugging me, or promising to attend the coronation ceremony. Didn't matter, I guess. Hone seemed satisfied. He smiled big and took off for his car.

What a teddy bear.

"What now?" Cole asked.

I skimmed the mansion. I wanted to see the rest of the weapons rooms and have a gander at the other rooms as well, even though it would take hours to go through them all. Lilith's job weighed heavy on me, but I could do nothing about her witch until daylight. Once morning came, I'd be in Eden to follow the witch, do some recon, and determine the best place to cause her problems before exacting revenge for Lilith. And while doing that, I'd try to figure out a way to send the queen back to hell in case she decided not to return on her own.

Stomach growling, I started up the steps. "I say we eat, check out the remaining two weapons rooms, and have a look at Nudra's office. I bet he has at least one safe, and from the intel JR gave me, he's got a harem of pretty cars we should inventory."

Silence behind me. I looked over my shoulder and saw Rad and Cole exchange a guy look. Cars. The magic word.

"We could do that," Rad said, shifting the bamboo stick to rest on his shoulder as he lightly shuffled up the stairs next to me.

Maddy snagged the insulated case with her bottled blood from the back of the Land Rover. "Can I have a car?"

"No," we all responded.

She stuck out her tongue, pointed at Cole and Rad. "Why do they get to have all the fun?"

"Rule four." I held up four fingers and grinned. "Demons always get the spoils."

"Yeah, well, demons suck ass, and so do your rules."

She jogged up the stairs past us, and we all chuckled. Entering the house, Rad held the door for me and Cole. As we passed the threshold, I lowered my voice for Cole's ears only. "Satan screw me, but if I end up Vlad's bride, I'll slit my wrists with a butter knife."

Cole patted my back. "I'll kill you before he can lay his hands—or his teeth— on you."

He said it in a kidding manner, but I wasn't so sure he wouldn't take me out if I asked him. "Promise?"

He winked at me. "Promise."

THIRTY-THREE

B y three a.m., we were all tired. We'd scoured the house from top to bottom and found six safes and more over-the-top weaponry in the second-floor and basement weapons rooms. I'd been through hundreds of paper and computer files in Nudra's office. The best thing I'd gotten my hands on all night was Corina's superb chicken salad sandwiches on sour-dough bread.

While I logged time with Nudra's files, accounting records, and notes on various Undead members of his organization, Cole and Rad took turns test driving the vamp king's cars. Toel regained consciousness sometime before two, but I only heard his yelling if I ventured down to the basement.

Which I didn't. Being alone and wearing a blindfold in a torture chamber that reeked of death and blood seemed like a fitting punishment. I toyed with the idea of embarking on another session of questions and answers but doubted I'd get much valuable info out of him, and I wasn't interested in any of his threats.

My neck cramped from leaning over Nudra's desk, and my ass ached from sitting in his leather chair. And I still had over a two-hour drive to Eden staring me in the face.

I'd culled over the info, sorting the paperwork into three piles. The first pile had to do with Nudra's actual job at the Madhouse and didn't interest me, although I bet it might be to the management team to find out Nudra'd been skimming money and taking bribes from bands for favors. The second pile contained his personal information: other houses he owned, his net worth, which was hefty even for a vamp king, and other essential documents. All of it would be transferred to my name.

I neatly gathered the third and final pile and shoved it into a bag. His vamp business papers with lists of blood slave constituents he worked with throughout the United States, Mexico, and Canada, along with his contacts, his minions and their job duties, and his dealings with the other vamp royalty. I'd copied numerous files from his computer to a USB and tossed that in the bag, too.

Maddy was watching TV, some music video channel that showed more reality TV than videos. I tapped her on the back of the head. "I'm heading to Eden, Illinois, to handle some Sweet Investigations business there. I'll probably be gone all day. You stay here, find some clothes, clean up, and wait for me to return. We'll go to the coronation ceremony together if I haven't figured out how to get out of it by then."

She nodded, lost in her show.

So young.

In the garage, I hailed Cole. "Road trip. Let's go."

Rad, looking at home behind the wheel of Nudra's Porsche, was driving in.

Cole stood to my right, eyes fixed on the Porsche's tires. "How'd she drive?"

The Chaos demon grinned, shifted into park, and unfolded himself from the seat as if leaving the car pained him. "Smooth as silk, man."

Cole glanced at me and waved a hand at the lineup of high-end vehicles. "Which ride do you prefer for this road trip? I haven't driven the Porsche or the Bugatti yet."

They were all beautiful, and I felt cheated that Cole and Rad had gotten to drive them before I did, but the trip we were about to take needed to be covert and comfortable. I dangled my keys in front of Cole's face. "The Land Rover. And you're driving so I can read."

He snatched the keys out of my hand. "Fuck."

Rad looked surprised but grinned. "So I'm not the driver this time?"

"You're not coming," I said and turned to leave.

"Wait." He caught up to me, matching my strides. "Why not?"

Because I couldn't stand the thought of being trapped in a car with him for two hours. Because I knew one of us would say something, and the terrible truth about our feelings for each other would spill out. Or the past would surface like it always did. I couldn't avoid the landmines piling up on all sides. "I work alone."

"But you're taking him?"

I'd known blowing off Rad wouldn't be easy, but it annoyed me he was making it complicated. "Cole's assigned to me until we get through the coronation. Otherwise, I'd go alone."

Rad followed me in silence to the front entrance. "What if Lucifer's with the witch? What are you going to do then?"

The thought had crossed my mind, but it was a question I couldn't answer yet. Avoiding him was the best idea. One way or the other, I was going to pay the piper. Either Lucifer would strike me down for messing with his lover, or Lilith would strike me down for not doing my job. "What I always do. Figure it out."

Emotions were pumping through him with alarming speed, causing my chest to tighten in response. "This is suicide, Kali, and you know it."

Standing there, close enough to see the desire in his eyes, to hear the blood throbbing in his veins, to feel the left-over excitement of driving the Porsche rolling off his skin, my legs trembled. "Well, at least we'll finally be free of each other."

Hurt flashed in his eyes. He started to say something, closed his mouth.

For the second time that night, I wanted to run. "Next time you're on stage, sing that song. The one from the other night."

His brows dipped. "It's not finished. It's only half a song."

"So finish it."

"I can't."

"Why not?"

"I don't know how it ends yet."

Like most good things in my life, in my version, it would end bloody. Someone's heart would be ripped in two. "Goodbye, Rad. Good luck with your upcoming tour. I'll bank some blood for you at Chloe's."

I shuffled down the steps. Cole was waiting for me in the Land Rover. Behind me, Rad half-hummed a few words from the song under his breath. "After all this time, after all the wrongs...I still care..."

Hopping in the car, I shut out the rest of the song, shut out Rad's emotions coursing through me. Cole had the GPS up and working, but his broad-tipped fingers kept hitting the wrong buttons on the touchscreen, and he swore at it. Rad's fingers, nimble and agile, would have skated over the touchscreen's buttons with ease. I smacked Cole's hand away, feeling awkward that we were still sitting there while Rad watched. "Just drive. I'll figure this out."

I pretended to be busy with the GPS and didn't look at Rad as we drove away, hating myself for being such a coward but telling myself I was doing this for Rad's own good.

THIRTY-FOUR

"Why didn't you let Guitar Boy come?" Cole asked once we were on the highway.

This time of early morning, there were few cars. The speedometer hovered around ninety. I played with the passenger side light above me to focus it on the papers in my lap. "Why would I?"

"He's handy to have around."

"I don't need him, and he's been around too much already."

We both knew that wasn't why I didn't want Rad there. Cole accepted my flimsy excuse, though, and we fell into a comfortable silence.

The words on the papers in front of me blurred. Initially, I'd planned to use Rad to help me with Lilith's witch. The only way to break Lucifer's hold was to recondition the human. Rad could create chaos whenever Lucifer was near her, or any time she sought him out—my own version of Pavlov's dogs. If Amy encountered something bad when Lucifer was around, she'd get gun-shy and decide he wasn't worth the trouble.

While that approach allowed me to stay covert with my

work, the type of conditioning necessary to change a human's psyche required months, sometimes years, to effectively sever the human's ties to the supernatural. I didn't have months or years on this assignment. I had hours.

Rad's ability to cause chaos might still have been useful as a distraction if things went wrong with Lucifer. I couldn't imagine things would possibly go well. But if the situation went bad, as I suspected it would, Rad would end up in the pit with me, enduring Lucifer's punishment.

I fingered the papers and stared out at the dark countryside. We'd left the city limits and were in farm country. White two-story houses rose ghost-like from flat stretches of land, dark barn counterparts shadowing them. Here and there, fences, cows, horses. Beyond them, harvested fields of corn, their stubby stalks marking rows like ragged soldiers.

Cole drove silently, giving me the space I needed to think. Rad wouldn't have done that. Rad would have tried to keep up a steady stream of conversation. He would have asked questions I didn't want to answer, probed into the past, and tried to talk about what had happened between us. Even if he'd steered clear of the most painful subjects, there was no way around discussing our lives that wouldn't somehow lead back to that day all those years ago.

Or the fact he was a demon killer.

When Cole finally broke the silence, he was there in the moment with me, planning for the immediate future and not thinking about the past. "How can you take revenge on Lucifer without getting your ass fried?"

"I can't."

"So this is a suicide mission?"

"Ye of little faith."

He snorted. "You made it through the encounter with Lilith. You took down Raj Nudra and handled Toel Chase like he was nothing more than an annoying fly. If anyone can handle Lucifer, it's you."

I appreciated his confidence. My phone rang, caller ID showing me Di's face. "Hey, Di. Everything okay?"

Her voice was light and cheery. "The Blackstone is perfection. Nice of your boyfriend to lend it to me. Will you thank him again?"

"Thank him yourself. You'll see him before I will."

"JR told me you were at Nudra's house together."

"*Were.* I'm on the road now. Out of town business."

"And Rad's not with you?"

Amazing how in such a short time, we had seamlessly become a couple in the eyes of everyone else. "No, he's not. He's probably on his way back to the Blackstone."

Her voice hardened. "Please tell me you didn't break up with him already. He's good for you. You need to stop living in the past."

If only it were that easy. "If it wasn't for Radison Beaumont, Nudra's Merc demons would never have gotten the jump on me."

"If it weren't for Rad, you'd still be Nudra's blood slave."

Point to the goddess. "Speaking of slaves, a young female at Nudra's compound needs your help. I told her she could stay at the compound for now if she let you work with her on regaining her human life. Can you go see her?"

"Of course. Now stop changing the subject."

"There's also a young vamp there who could use a friend. Her name's Maddy. Maybe you can help her, too."

"Kali, what are you doing?"

"I'm heading to a small town near the Mississippi River to break up a romance between Lucifer and a witch."

"JR told me. And while I'm not digging the idea, that's not what I'm talking about, and you know it."

Another sigh threatened to surface. I shoved it down. "Unless I figure out how to break up this relationship and send Lilith back to the pit, what I'm doing with my life, and Rad's place in it, won't mean jack squat."

Silence dangled between us as she thought it over. "So what's your plan to break up the witch and Lucifer?"

There was no plan. Not yet. Once I got eyeballs on the witch and watched her for a while, something would come to me. "I'm working on it."

"You can't break up true love. Temporarily, yes. You can throw a kink in their relationship. But long term? You can't stop them if they're meant to be together."

Everything in Di's book was about love. "He's Lucifer. He's had hundreds of women, maybe thousands, both human and supernatural, at this beck and call for millions of years. Why is this witch special?"

"Exactly." Her voice was no-nonsense. "After millions of years and all his affairs, why is Lilith worried about this one?"

JR's notes said Lucifer and Amy had been together for seven years before the witch broke up with him for sleeping with her sister. They now appeared to be back together.

Seven years was a microscopic speck in the history of time. Lucifer, while not as prolific in wives and children as Vlad the Impaler, still had infinite women through the years. Di was right. Why was Lilith losing her cool over this one? "You may have a point."

"I always have a point. He's met his soul mate, and nothing you or Lilith do will change that."

"Soul mates can be separated."

"Sure, if you're Shakespeare and write tragedies. Or you're a god, and the Stretchers mess with your life." *Stretchers* was goddess slang for the Titans, deities that overstretched their powers to screw with lesser gods and goddesses, as well as humans. "In the overall scheme of the universe, however, true love always wins out. It can't be pushed aside, suffocated, or damaged beyond repair."

Might have been my imagination, but I suspected she was talking about my relationship with Rad as much as she was Lucifer's with Amy. "You don't think I can break them up?"

"You're a conniving demon—I mean that in a good way— and you always manage to find the perfect weakness to exploit in order to gain revenge, but in this case? Even if you turn the witch against the fallen angel, he'll never go back to Lilith, and that's what Lilith truly wants."

I slouched in the leather seat, staring up at the starry sky through the moon roof as I walked through the scenario out loud. "It's not enough to remove Amy from the picture. I have to get Lucifer to desire Lilith and want to be with her."

Cole shot me a look and shook his head in a *you are so fucked* smirk.

Di made eating noises. "You should have brought me along. I could have sensed whether Lucifer and his witch are soul mates." She bit into something and moaned softly. "Damn, that's so good. *Cordero lechal.* Have you ever had it?"

"I don't even know what that is."

"Lamb in red Catalan curry sauce. Mm-mmm." She licked her fingers. "I'm Rad's guest, so I get room service whenever I want. He has connections at this hotel, let me tell you. That boy has a special charm."

"Rad's been charming the pants off women for centuries. Doesn't mean anything."

"Kali! Why can't you admit he's a nice guy and you love him?"

"Mind your blood pressure." *And your own business.* "You don't know him like I do."

She fell silent, but I could hear her chewing. Funny how she could convey irritation even with her mouth closed.

My stomach got tight whenever Di was mad at me, and I didn't like that feeling. I drummed my fingers on my thigh. "So what should I do with Lucifer?"

There was a superior tone in her voice when she answered, but she loved it when I asked her advice. "I doubt he wants Lilith roaming the streets of Chicago any more than you do, and if he's truly in love with this witch, he'll go to any means to protect her."

My brain worked at the problem, poking it from different angles. Various ideas and options arose, and I discarded all but one. "I should form an allegiance with him."

Di's smile conveyed through the phone as easily as her earlier irritation. "Make him an offer he can't refuse. You'll leave his witch alone if he helps you eliminate Lilith."

"If I double-cross Lilith, I'll pay for it when I die and go to hell."

"So don't die."

Easy peasy. *Not.* "Thanks, Di. This plan might work."

"Any plan that focuses on keeping soul mates together will work. Trust me, I know."

We disconnected. Cole glanced at me, one brow raised. "Seriously? You're going to double-cross Lilith?"

The more I thought about it, the better it sounded. Not double-crossing Lilith per se, but asking the fallen angel for assistance in disposing her back to hell. "Even if Lucifer destroys me, Lilith won't stop trying to harm his witch or break up their relationship. Di's right. He'll do whatever it takes to protect Amy, which means getting rid of Lilith."

"But if Victoria raised her once, what's to stop her from doing it again?"

I smiled at my bodyguard. "Me."

THIRTY-FIVE

Eden was a small river town in the Midwest. Off the highway, the streets narrowed, the trees became more numerous, and a combination of businesses and residential properties jostled each other for space along the main road.

It was just after five in the morning, and heavy clouds covered the November moon. The houses, a combination of ranch and two-stories, were dark. We met a patrol car as we drove by the Welcome to Eden sign, population 3,800.

The town sat low and flat compared to Chicago's overpopulated skyscrapers. To the west was the downtown area and the Mississippi River. Flat prairie land stretched like syrup to the south, flowing around copses of trees, random farmhouses, and the highway. North, limestone bluffs rose like dark sentinels in the distance.

Three minutes after we entered the township's eastern limits, we exited on the northwest side...and two four-way stops had slowed us down. Small town, indeed.

"Bet they don't have vampires here," I said, already liking the place.

"Hell, they don't even have a McDonalds."

Cole turned the Land Rover around and took a right at one of the intersections. We drove over a hill and down, down, down into the heart of town. The business district was laid out in a square with a courthouse, a couple of bars boasting dollar draft beer and pizza, a library, a florist, a gas station that looked like it doubled as a used car lot, a lawyer/chiropractor combo and a tourist attraction center.

And, of course, there was Amy Atwood's ice cream shop, Evie's.

Except for the stately-looking courthouse, the other buildings housed apartments on their second stories. Amy's shop had new construction on the second floor. JR's notes mentioned her apartment had burned up back in the summer. The new apartment looked almost complete, and once they added a brick façade to match the rest of the Victorian-era buildings, no one would guess it was new.

What bothered me as I stared at it was the faint glow coming off the building. Not from the streetlights reflecting against the shop's large plate glass windows in the front or security lights scattered around the building in a few places. This light was ethereal, unearthly. Human eyes couldn't see it, but I could. The glow sent a warning straight to my brain and central nervous system.

Angel light. *Merde.*

Just because Lucifer had rebelled against God didn't change his angelic stripes. He was an angel. His presence still had the ability to protect and defend if he so chose to use it that way. That didn't mean I couldn't enter the shop, but I suspected the moment I touched the building, he would know.

There was something off about the light, though. Something...too white, too heavenly about it for Lucifer.

I called JR, set the phone in a cradle, and hit the speaker

button so Cole could hear. "Does Lucifer live at the shop with Amy?"

"How should I know?" The words were pissy, but his tone was bored. "It's not like he runs Satan's blogspot or gives interviews to *People* magazine."

Satan's blog. Funny. "I've got angel light coming from the building, but I don't think it belongs to the fallen angel."

The tapping of computer keys filtered through the line. "One of the employees lives there. A Gabriel, no last name. That's it."

Cole faced me, eyes wide. "As in *the* Gabriel?"

"*The* Gabriel?" JR echoed. There was a pause, and when he spoke again, all traces of boredom and sarcasm vanished. "Holy shit. The *archangel* Gabriel?"

Holy shit was an understatement. I rubbed my forehead. "Can't be. Archangels don't vacation on Earth. Why would he be here?"

Silence met my question.

Too bad Satan *didn't* have a blog. "See what you can find out, JR. Call local supernaturals if you can find any and get the scoop."

"You'd be better off to find the town's gossip and ask her."

He had a point, but I wasn't sure if the humans knew about the supernaturals in town. "We'll look into it. Call if you find out anything in the meantime."

Lost in our separate thoughts, we cruised the main drag. Vehicles were typical American trucks and mid-sized cars. A few blocks north, there was a fire station. A few blocks south, a bridge led over the river and into Iowa. A dike separated the town center from the Mississippi.

Cole parked in a designated spot, and we walked the footpath up the dike to see the river. The water flowed dark and cold under the cloudy sky. I bet the sight was beautiful during the day, especially in the fall. Trees turning colors along the bluffs, the tall spires of churches peeking through here and there. The river, with its barges and boats, creating a serene and historic postcard image.

But on a cold, cloudy November morning, the barren trees sported ugly limbs, and the church spires glowed a ghostly gray. The river whispered eerily, and the sparse lights of the dike seemed unable to fight back the dense darkness.

Just like in Chicago, a lot of evil had been done here. Humans and supernaturals had gone to war with each other, and not many on either side had lived. Their blood soaked the ground, and it slithered up from under the dike's path, worming its way into my demon nature. It was happy to see me. Starved, in fact, for dark magic. It wanted to be fed so it could reanimate itself. Wanted my blood to strengthen it.

Whatever war had been fought, the good guys had won, sequestering the evil. That didn't mean the evil had left. It had simply sunk back into the ground and bided its time. My presence excited it, made it believe I had come to resurrect it.

Cole felt it, too. He bounced on his feet, sticking his hands in his pockets and giving me a concerned look. He wanted to get back to the Land Rover. Posthaste.

Interesting was the fact Lucifer's witch lived here when she could live anywhere in the world. As his mistress, she could have whatever she desired, but she chose to live in this town and run a simple ice cream shop.

To me—a demon filled with lust and greed—that didn't compute.

Even when I put on my human thinking cap, it still didn't add up.

Mimicking Cole's actions, I tapped down the evil under my feet and motioned for us to head back to the SUV.

He cranked the heat the instant we were inside. Cold

rarely bothered me, but I rubbed my hands together and blew on them to warm them up. "This would be a good place to hide."

"I was thinking the same thing."

Cole and I often thought alike. "What would Lucifer's witch be hiding from?"

"Lilith?"

"Nah. She doesn't even know Lilith's here."

He shrugged. "Maybe Amy's not hiding. Maybe she likes it here. Small town, family, friends. The American Dream."

I tended to think everyone had a devious reason behind their choices, but Cole was right. The ice cream shop had been in her family for several generations. She didn't have any family except her sister. This was home to her.

Home. Rome would always be my home. In the twenty-first century, it was Noctifector territory in a way it had never been before. They lived to drive all supernaturals from the world, and most definitely from their hometown.

Cole shifted into reverse, interrupting my revelry. "Can't believe they don't have a fucking McDonalds. I need caffeine and some greasy food."

I'd noticed a ma and pa restaurant across the square from the ice cream shop. "Before we eat, let's get a closer look at the witch's place."

There were two police cars parked in front of the courthouse. I didn't want the patrol car that had seen us earlier returning to the station and noticing us sitting on the street. "Squeeze into the alley behind the shop."

As we drew closer, the white light glowed brighter. The power coming off of it didn't reach out, though. It simply vibrated around the building.

We parked and got out. "Consecrated ground?" Cole asked.

The consecrated ground inside my church didn't glow. It hummed and pulsed with energy like an electrified fence. "I don't think so."

"Touch it. See what happens."

"You touch it."

Cole grinned at me. "Fine," he said. He raised his demon magic and stuck the toe of his shoe into the light. Nothing happened.

We exchanged a look. I shrugged.

"Any other security system?"

"According to JR, she has deadbolts on the doors."

"That's it?"

We examined the back door located near a dumpster. Sure enough, there were two locks, one a deadbolt. Not much call for high security in this town. The place was growing on me.

No fallen angel showed up from our breach of the light either.

"Amy's living with a friend until her apartment is done." I was talking to myself as much as Cole. "And she has the Mark of Cain on her forehead, so even if she were here, Lucifer's not worried about anyone attacking her."

"How are you going to convince him to help you send Lilith back to hell if Lil baby can't hurt Amy?"

Stepping back from the door, I leaned on the SUV. "No one can harm Amy directly. Doesn't mean Lilith won't make her life miserable. That's why she hired me. To exact revenge on Lucifer by screwing with Amy."

Cole drew a lock pick from his jacket. "Wanna take a peek inside?"

I did, but caution held me back. Lucifer wouldn't be as likely to listen to my offer if he found out I'd broken into the witch's building. "Not yet. Let's watch the place for a while, grab breakfast, and see if we can dig up some scoop before we charge in."

A look of disappointment crossed Cole's face. "Not a lot of good surveillance spots around here."

And the Land Rover did not fit in on Main Street. "You notice that cemetery on the bluff north of the fire station?"

The tone of his voice was wary. "Yeah."

"Good a place as any, and I bet Officer Small Town won't be cruising through there at sunrise."

"We can't see the shop from that far away."

I patted the Land Rover's door with one hand. "I have binoculars."

Defeated, Cole climbed in. I did the same. A minute later, he maneuvered the SUV up the steep, winding hill of the cemetery, swearing softly at the sharp curves and potholes big enough to swallow small animals. "The cops can drive a thirty-thousand-dollar patrol car, but the city can't fill in the ruts in the boneyard?"

Cemeteries didn't score high on the budget list for any town, Chicago included. Once we parked on the hill, giving us a view of downtown, I rummaged in the back for two sets of binoculars. There wasn't much to see at that time of the morning, so mostly I sat and stared at the river in the distance. I thought about turning on some music, but it seemed wrong to disturb the quiet of the night and that place.

Cole shifted in his seat, binoculars glued to his face. "So you and Damon..."

He let the sentence trail off, his tone vague and accusing simultaneously.

"Me and Damon, what?"

"He can read your mind." He continued to hide behind the binoculars. "What's up with that shit?"

What indeed. "Wasn't my idea. He just..."

The binoculars dropped from Cole's face, and he met my gaze, the skin tight around his eyes, lips pressed together in a tight line. "Did he force himself on you?"

"He kissed me, that's all."

"Bastard." He set the binoculars on the dash. "Should I kill him for you?"

I punched Cole lightly on the shoulder, trying to lighten the mood. "You're just jealous."

Staring out the windshield, he nodded his head. "I am."

Cole had a different woman every week. Sort of like Di with her boy toys. Maybe I should get them together. "You ever date a goddess?"

His gaze swung to me, and his eyes told me he knew what I was thinking. "No. Way."

"Di's an incredible person and drop-dead gorgeous."

He laughed, and the sound echoed in the car. "I'm a demon, Kali, in case you've forgotten."

"Di's not prejudiced."

"Everybody's prejudiced."

I tsked. "So jaded."

"Me? What about you and Guitar Boy? What's the story there?"

"You know, you and Di are more alike than you realize."

He chuckled softly. "You never bought me that steak. You owe me. Spill."

I didn't talk about the past to anyone. Not Di, not Neve, certainly not the people I worked with in the Bridge Council. Rehashing old history didn't change it. And if I couldn't change it, what was the point?

Sitting there in the Land Rover with the river flowing strong and apathetic before us, the thought of letting the story out seduced me. *Letting it out* was exactly the way it felt. As if I'd been holding it in, imprisoning my history like I imprisoned my demon and refusing to set it free for all these years. Sure, Damon and the Council knew the facts in my file, but no one knew exactly what I'd been through with Rad. After Rad. The secrets I was keeping.

The idea that I could suddenly set them down here in this rundown cemetery and free myself had a strange and frightening appeal. I stewed it over for several minutes and decided to let go of a few facts and see how it felt.

"Rad came to Queen Maria's court as a French ambassador and had no trouble charming all of us in her inner circle. I fell for him immediately, but so did Maria. He took a particular interest in me, and I was young and stupid and gave in to his advances. We kept our affair secret, but Maria learned of it. She tried to bed him, but he politely refused, and that angered her. She forbade me to see him and threatened to kick him out of the Roman Empire, so Rad devised a plan. He didn't want to leave me, so he became more solicitous toward her and continued to steal away when he could to meet me in private.

The years fell away, and I was back in court. "Maria wasn't stupid. My family's business began to fail, my father's creditors suddenly came calling for their money. My mother was no longer invited to attend the balls and other upper-class doings in Rome. All because Maria no longer favored me. She kept me at court, mostly to ridicule me."

My chest felt both lighter and heavier as I relived the days of my youth. Cole sat quietly, not prompting or rushing me.

"Rad was sure the queen would destroy me and my family. He devised a plan to get us out of the Empire and take us to France with him. Not only was he a trusted advisor to the king there, but his family had connections all over Europe, and he could help my father secure a position of prestige and wealth for us.

"My father would only leave Italy if Rad agreed to marry

me. The date was set, and I was overjoyed. But on the day of our secret wedding at my parent's estate, Rad never showed. I was sure Maria had discovered our deception and had one of her mercenaries kill Rad, so I went out searching for him. I never found him, and when I finally gave up, I returned home to find my family dead. Murdered. My mother, father, and four-year-old sister."

Cole had been staring out the windshield. Now he cut his eyes to me. "Maria killed them."

That's what I'd believed until I'd seen the Noctifector tattoo on Rad's back. "I sought revenge, but it didn't work. I ended up in the dungeons, where I was tortured by Maria's new pets, a couple of young female demons she'd trained to take my place. I was held there until the ruling parties changed."

"Maria was a demon?"

"Half demon, half human, and all psychotic." All those years later, I could still see the craziness in her eyes. "I escaped, made sure Maria never hurt anyone again, and went to Spain. That's where Damon found me."

Cole shifted in his seat. "What'd you do to get on his radar?"

"His wife hired me to take revenge on him for an affair. I didn't realize who he was when I accepted the job."

Cole laughed again, and I could almost forget the knot in my stomach. "That's rich. Taking revenge on an Archdemon. Wish I could have seen that." He rubbed his jaw with his knuckles. "What happened with Rad?"

Ah, yes, Rad. "I thought he was dead, but I searched for him anyway. I heard rumors about various Chaos demons, but none ever led to him. Damon eventually sent me back to England to work for the Bridge Council there, and then I followed him to America in 1910. I gave up searching for Rad and tucked all that horrible time into a deep, dark hole. A couple of years ago, my friend Neve shared a bootlegged video of a band she'd seen in a rundown bar outside of Milwaukee. I didn't have to see his face. I heard his voice and knew it was him."

"So he deserted you? Or blackmailed you to Maria?"

He'd blackmailed me, all right, but not to the queen.

The sky was steel-colored, the sunrise muted by storm clouds moving in from the southwest. "The café's open. What do you say we grab some breakfast?"

While Cole pushed my buttons in the gym to make me fight harder and longer, he knew when not to push, too. He started the Land Rover, shifted into drive. "I could eat a water buffalo."

After my confession, I felt lighter. "I could eat one too."

THIRTY-SIX

"How will we know when Lucifer enters the shop?" Cole asked, digging into his Hungry Man Three Meat special.

Good question. Even if we hadn't stood out in Eden like black spots on a white dog, Lucifer probably didn't use the front door of Evie's to drop in for a visit. I stared out the plate glass window of the café, across the street to the witch's building. "I've got a jones for a waffle cone."

The waitress appeared at our table, carrying two coffee carafes, one with an orange ring and one without. She poured the caffeinated version into Cole's cup and eyed my red cape for the third time. "Evie's don't open 'til ten."

Her name tag read "Jan." She'd already asked if we were from out of town, although the look she gave us when we walked in suggested she knew the answer to that question.

My coffee needed a reheat, so I slid the cup toward her. "What happened to the upstairs of the ice cream shop, Jan?"

"Burned down a few months back. Amy's lucky the shop didn't go with it."

"Anyone hurt?" Cole asked.

"Nah. She wasn't home. Her cats were, though. One of her boyfriends rescued them. He was a real hero."

One of her boyfriends? "How many boyfriends does she have?"

"Two or three guys over there all the time, hanging around. The one that saved the cats seems to be pulling ahead of the others." She looked Cole over from head to toe. "Women like a good hero."

Cole sent me a *holy shit, help me out here* look. I just smiled and winked at him as Jan strolled off, ignoring my cup. "Looks like you've got an admirer."

He threw a triangle of toast at me. "Shut up."

We ate, bought a local paper from a stack on the counter, and proceeded to drink coffee and read. Jan didn't seem happy about us taking up her table, but she liked looking at Cole, so I forced him to make small talk whenever she swooped by with her coffee pots. The café got busier, and soon she paid us little attention.

Finally, at ten o'clock, I saw lights go on inside Evie's. The witch raised the shades, unlocked the doors, and flipped the Closed sign over.

Time for business.

THIRTY-SEVEN

C ole paid the bill, and for the first time since we'd entered the café, Jan didn't stare at him like he was a prize steer. Instead, she kept glancing out the front window.

"Storm's coming," she said, handing Cole his change. "You two might want to get on the road before it does."

For a second, I thought I was in a Stephen King novel or a B-grade movie, and she was issuing some portent for the audience. But when I looked at her face, there was no indication she was stating anything other than plain fact. This was the Midwest, and a nasty storm was moving our way. We were city folk; driving these hills and plains in a winter storm was difficult even for those accustomed to it, so she was kind and warning us to get on the road.

Cole gave her a hefty tip, and I thanked her for the advice. We left the café, and I told Cole he didn't have to go to the ice cream shop with me or stand guard while I confronted Lucifer. After all, someone had to tell Damon what happened if the devil vaporized me.

Cole told me to shut the hell up. He wasn't letting me go in alone.

The downtown square wasn't big, so we crossed the street on foot, passed the courthouse, and took the sidewalk to Evie's Ice Cream Shop. The sharp wind blew my cape around helter-skelter, and I grabbed the edges and tucked them close to my body.

When we entered, a bell tinkled above our heads, and two things struck me at the same time: the smell of waffle cones, which I love, and the fact that Amy Atwood had the palest blue eyes I'd ever seen on a human or a supernatural.

A side effect of sleeping with the devil?

In Chicago, my get-up turned heads, but I was one in a thousand unique-looking people. Here, I stood out like Little Red Riding Hood in a sea of Bo Peeps.

Amy took in my hair, red cape, and spiked boots, and then her gaze swept over Cole. She pegged us, just like Jan, as out-of-towners. Unlike her neighbor across the street, Amy gave me a big smile. Red Riding Hood was cool, not weird.

"Hi, folks." She glanced again at my legs. "Nice boots."

Preparation is the key to any successful plan. Although it occasionally happens, I don't like being surprised when I'm on a case. I don't like flying by the seat of my skirt, but that happens, too. Face-to-face with the devil's mistress, all the prep-ping, planning, and digging into her life seemed silly. Lilith's anxiety was a bunch of overblown drama.

Amy Atwood appeared harmless. Although she was pretty, she was no beauty queen and didn't exude any particularly powerful magic. She was friendly, open, genuine, and, well... ordinary.

Except for those eyes.

Under the delicious smell of waffle cones and chocolate ice

cream, she smelled like the wind outside, cool and fresh. Her magic element was obviously air.

My skin crawled with a warning. Air witches could fool you. On the surface, they resembled a light breeze caressing your skin. Underneath, they were the hard, driving wind of an ice storm, freezing you to the bone.

Whatever I did, I would not underestimate her. Problem was, I liked her on sight. And not just because she dug my boots.

The special of the day on the menu board above her head said a Mocha Cappuccino Chiller was five bucks. I pointed at the board. "Does the special come with whipped cream?"

She grinned. "Whipped cream *and* shaved chocolate." She glanced out at the square where the flag on the flagpole strained in the wind. "If you'd prefer a hot cappuccino without the ice cream, I can make that too. That's three-fifty."

"I'll take the chiller. I've heard your ice cream is the best in this part of the state."

Her eyebrows lifted a fraction, but she took the praise in stride and grabbed a large paper cup in one hand and a metal scoop in the other. "Chiller it is."

She went to work scooping first vanilla and then chocolate coffee bean ice cream into the cup. After adding chocolate syrup, she placed the cup under a machine with a drill-like mechanism, flipped a switch, and the machine stirred the ice cream and syrup into a frothy mixture. She tapped the cup several times, added more syrup, and let the machine mix it again.

The whole time, Cole stood off to the side, eyes scanning every exit and potential weapon in the place. He kept his back toward the side wall so he could keep an eye on both the front entrance and a hallway in the back. War demons. Always on the defensive.

Amy squirted whipped cream on the top. "How about you, sir? Can I get you anything?"

Cole glanced at me, and I nodded, telling him to order something. "Coffee."

I made a face. *That's it?*

Reading my expression, he shrugged. "We just ate. I'm not hungry."

"You're always hungry. How can you pass up ice cream?"

Amy smiled as she shaved pieces off a chunk of chocolate over the whipped cream. "One coffee, coming up."

While she poured Cole's coffee, I laid a ten on the counter. No reason to get down to business until I'd had a chance to suck down my chiller, and I wanted a waffle cone as well. Hey, what can I say? I'm a bottomless pit, and planning face time with Lucifer made me nervous. Besides, it might be my last meal. Might as well make it a good one.

"Jan over at the restaurant said your upper story burned down in the summer. Didn't touch the shop?"

Amy handed me a straw and spoon, her eyes avoiding mine as she snagged the ten and rang us up. "No."

Okay. She wasn't much of a conversationalist unless it came to boots or ice cream. I spooned whipped cream from the chiller, dug down further, and grabbed some mocha cappuccino ice cream. "Wow. This is excellent."

And it was. I was having a waffle cone before I butted heads with her boyfriend.

Her gaze met mine again. "Thanks."

I took my change, dropped a few bills in her tip jar, and motioned for Cole to follow me to a table near the back. The booth was tucked into a corner, allowing us visibility of both entrances and the street.

Amy busied herself behind the counter for a few minutes, playing with a commercial-grade espresso machine. On top, there was a big, hand-written sign touting the shop's new coffee bar selection of hot drinks. Like most places in the Midwest, ice cream probably wasn't a big seller during the winter.

I forced small talk with Cole as I simultaneously sipped and spooned at my ice cream and watched Amy try to make two espresso shots. Cole played his part well, still acting like a SEAL instead of my boyfriend, but what could I do? You can take the warrior out of the war zone, but you can't take the warrior out of the demon.

After a couple of minutes, when it was apparent Amy had no idea what she was doing, I took off my cape and made my way over to the counter. "Need help?"

She used an arm to brush bangs from her forehead. "Trying to expand my business, so I bought this espresso machine from a gal who runs a restaurant up the street." She chuckled and brushed at her shirt, now dotted with dark coffee stains. "Still haven't gotten the hang of it."

The Mark of Cain was faint, but I saw it before her bangs covered it again. The demon inside me surged back. "Maybe I could help."

"You know how to use one of these?"

"I worked in a barista in California back in the day." Back in the day being the 1950s and the barista being The Med on Telegraph Avenue in Berkeley. We didn't have fancy machines back then, but the overall construction and design of the espresso machine had changed little since La Pavoni started producing them in 1905 in Milan.

Amy motioned me behind the counter and offered a hand. "I'm Amy."

Her fingers were delicate but strong. "Kali. And that's Cole." I tipped my head toward my bodyguard. He lifted a finger in a pseudo wave.

"Where you from?"

"Chicago."

"Just passing through?"

"Yes, if the storm doesn't ground us."

I checked the portafilter and saw she had packed the coffee grounds too tightly. Her witchy strength was high. "There's your problem." I smacked out the hard disc of coffee, refilled the basket, and tamped down the grounds with a medium force. "You want to match your grind to the brewing method, and since you're making espresso, the grind should be fine. Then you have to perfect your tamp. Tamping is an art. Too tight, water can't flow through. Too loose, the espresso turns watery."

She was a fast learner. A few minutes later, she made espresso shots like a pro. She was also making conversation. As I returned to my ice cream chiller, she told Cole and me about the shop's history and how lucky she was that it hadn't burned down with the apartment. She mentioned her friend Keisha and confirmed that Gabriel worked there part-time.

I just hoped Gabriel wouldn't show up and turn me to demon dust before I could talk to Lucifer.

I needn't have worried.

Lucifer entered through the front door as if he were a normal human being. Rain had begun to fall outside, and his blue-black hair was dotted with tiny drops. Dressed in worn jeans, a leather jacket, and heavy black boots, he looked like one of Eden's townsfolk, although edgier. I doubted anyone living there realized there was something just a little off about him.

He was as tall as Rad, maybe taller, and as broad as Cole. Power, magic, and an energy I'd never felt before radiated off him. His body, his eyes, and the very pores of his skin exuded superiority—like Damon times a thousand. The air around him vibrated with preeminence and incomparability.

Danger. My brain cells registered threat level red. The fine hairs on the back of my neck rose and the natural flight instinct hard-wired into my demon brain kicked in.

And dammit, I hadn't had my waffle cone yet.

Although humans throughout time had associated the fallen angel with hell, demons associated him with heaven. He was the ruler of our domain, but he wasn't one of us. We were peasants in hell's kingdom, and peasants never looked on the king.

He paid no attention to us, but his body tensed ever so slightly as he registered our demonness. We'd kept our magic suppressed to not tip him off, but we couldn't conceal the very thing that made us supernatural.

He greeted his witch, and the two embraced and murmured low to each other for a minute, his back to us. All the while, Amy's face shone with love and adoration. I couldn't see Lucifer's, but his protective, loving energies filled the room.

My heart pinched, and an image of Rad singing softly to me on the steps at Nudra's house flashed through my mind. I wanted to embrace the image, but this wasn't the time or place.

Amy went to work peeling a banana. Apparently, the devil ate banana splits for breakfast. I glanced at Cole, trying to catch his eye, but he was staring intently at Lucifer, his Adam's apple working in his throat.

My own throat had a lump the size of a basketball in it. I sucked at my chiller, but the flavor tasted flat and artificial now.

While Amy continued to work on the banana split, Lucifer turned to face us. I straightened as he moved in our direction. A soft glow of white light outlining his body.

Hell's blood. He was handsome beyond words. The most beautiful creature I'd ever seen, and I'd seen my share of extraordinary ones in three hundred years. I might have groveled at his feet if the warning siren in my head hadn't been going at top decibel.

Lucifer stopped a short distance away, keeping the perfect amount of distance between us. "What do you want?" His low voice sent a heated flush over my skin.

Danger, my brain screamed again. My demon echoed the sentiment. *Get out.*

At war with the warnings was my desire to stay in the presence of one so beautiful, so heavenly. Lucifer had been the chief in the hierarchy of heaven, foremost in beauty, power, and wisdom. His sin was pride, a sin I understood.

I didn't dare move, except to lower my gaze as I'd done in Lilith's presence. He saw me as a threat, and the slightest movement could cause my destruction.

Amy noticed he was talking to us and walked over. "This is Kali and Cole. They're from Chicago." She held out his banana split. "Kali, Cole, this is Luc."

Luc? The king of hell allowed the witch to call him by a nickname? How...human. Not only was the fallen angel willing to do anything to protect his witch, he was also willing to do whatever it took to blend in with humanity for her.

Di would say it was love.

He was still staring at me, ignoring the banana split. The heat rippling over my skin intensified. "I need to speak to you," I said. "About Lilith."

Amy blanched. "Lilith?" She stepped back, fear registering. "Did she send you here?"

So the witch knew about her competition. Interesting.
"Yes."

Lucifer didn't move a muscle, didn't even blink, but in the next second, I was jerked from the chair, hauled through the air backward, and thrown up against the far wall by an invisible force. Vertebrae in my back cracked. My hands were pinned against the wall with the rest of me, so I couldn't touch my fingers together to call up my protective magic. It was pointless against the fallen angel, anyway, and I had hoped keeping my defenses down would show him I meant no harm.

Cole jumped up, ready to defend me. Big mistake. Lucifer glanced his way, and Cole's head snapped to the side, producing a popping noise. Lucifer had broken his neck.

"Cole!" I yelled, but it was no use. His body fell to the floor, lifeless.

There were no curse words strong enough, but I looked Lucifer in the eye and belted out a few Italian ones anyway.

Amy dropped the banana split, splattering ice cream and banana slices across the black-and-white tiles. "Luc, what are you doing? You promised no magic."

His attention never left my face. "What do you want, demon? What about Lilith?"

Amy returned her focus to me. "Did she hire you to poison me? To burn me up? To take me to hell again? Well, guess what? Been there, *not doing it again*. I took down the other assassins and can take you down, too."

She was a feisty one. I liked that...even though I had no idea what she was talking about.

Although it wasn't hard to figure out. Lil had already tried getting to Amy, and the witch had outsmarted whatever Merc demons Lilith had sent and was quite proud of herself. She was ready to take me on.

But pride went before a fall. The devil's mistress should know that.

I wasn't a common Merc demon, and if I'd had time to structure a plan, I could have worked around the Mark of Cain and made the witch's life miserable. And if Lucifer destroyed me here and now, Lilith would find someone else to do the job.

The pressure on my body was intense. I could barely

breathe. "Not here...to kill you. Work...for...the Bridge Council."

Lucifer still didn't move, but something changed in his eyes. "The Bridge Council has no business in my affairs."

Wasn't that everyone's story? "Not yours." The heat he'd ignited inside me was burning me up. My head pounded with pressure. The room swam before my eyes, hot tears pouring down my cheeks. "Lilith's. She walks...the Earth."

Outside, the rain had turned to sleet. It pinged against the glass windows. He stepped closer, the fine lines around his eyes tightening. "That's not possible."

Blood trickled out of my nose and ran into my mouth. The sharp metallic taste of my blood caused bile to rise in my throat. I searched for my demon, thinking I might have to use her, but she was AWOL for once. "It's true," I whispered.

A sharp spike of pain hit my lower spine, making me cry out. The pain flared into my hip joints and lower intestines. A second later, my lungs filled with fluid, and I started to cough.

"You're lying," Lucifer said.

"No." I shook my head as much as I could. "She hired me... to take revenge...on you."

The bell over the door tinkled, and the sound of roaring wind and driving sleet filled the shop. Amy whipped around, fear evident on her face that a customer had entered to see Cole dead on the floor and me pinned against the wall, hemorrhaging out.

She raised her hands and started toward the customer. "We're closed. The storm's bad. No ice cream today."

"She's telling the truth," a familiar, dangerous-sounding voice said. Let her go."

Rad.

Damn him to the fires of hell.

He walked around Amy and into my view. The look on his

face was angry and full of determination, and it was the best sight I'd seen in a good long time.

But the damn fool was going to get his neck snapped, and what good would that do me?

He stopped a few feet from us and looked Lucifer straight in the eyes. "A witch in Chicago raised Lilith from hell. I saw her. I was there when the queen of hell commanded Kali to take revenge on you. If not for the Mark of Cain, she would come after your witch herself."

And then he told Lucifer precisely what I'd been thinking. "Killing Kali won't stop Lilith. The only way to stop the queen of hell is to send her back to her kingdom."

The invisible pressure pinning my body against the wall eased. I took a breath, but the fire and pain ramming my internal organs and joints did not let up. I bit my bottom lip to keep from crying.

Rad sensed my distress. The wildness of the storm outside intensified. The door and windows on the front of the building rattled. The overhead lights flickered. "Let her go. Let her talk. She has a plan, but she needs your help."

That he had such faith in me was heartening. I would have enjoyed it more if I hadn't been fighting for my life.

The fatal pressure on my body evaporated without warning. I slid down the wall and crumpled into a heap on the floor next to Cole.

His neck was broken, but it would heal. That level of injury would take a while, though, to mend itself. Lying on my stomach, I coughed up blood and eased my fingers over to touch his arm. He was going to kick my ass for getting him killed if we survived this.

"There is no witch alive who could raise Lilith from the pit," Lucifer said.

Rad crossed to me, bent, and helped me sit up. The cracked

bones in my back screamed in pain. He brushed hair from my eyes and wiped blood from my chin. In his gaze, he silently willed me to tell Lucifer the truth.

The truth. I blinked and tried to remember my plan. Pain burned in my lungs, stomach, back, and hips. I could barely stay conscious, much less conduct an intelligent conversation.

I'd had plenty of time on the road trip to think about Victoria and her abilities. Taking another breath, I swallowed hard and cordoned the worst of the pain behind a mental blockade. "The witch has latent talents, probably from a genetic throwback in her bloodline. There's demon blood in her ancestry, I'm sure of it." The black and white tiles seemed to turn 3-D on me, my blood rising up and hovering over the checkerboard pattern even as it spread. "She ingested potent supernatural blood, which, combined with her latent magical gene pool, was enough to get the job done."

There was silence, as Lucifer considered it. He still didn't believe me, but he was watching my blood, and I wondered if he saw it levitating like I did. "Whose blood did she ingest?"

Admitting it was mine was embarrassing and didn't lend credibility to my story. My blood was powerful, and so was Nudra's, but powerful enough to raise the queen of hell? No one would believe it, especially not Lucifer. "Does it matter?"

"Whose blood?" he repeated, anger deepening his voice.

"Mine," I squeaked. "And a very old vampire's."

"Why would you let her drink your blood? You're not a Child of the Night."

And thank the universe for that. "The vampire wanted me to join his organization. I refused. He created blood slaves to keep me connected to him. Victoria, the witch, was one of them."

Lucifer stepped toward me, and Rad tensed. The front

door blew open, and wind and sleet poured in, rattling the window blinds.

Amy ran to shut it, and Lucifer narrowed his eyes at Rad. "Enough, Chaos demon. I want to have a better look at this one."

Rad didn't relax, but the wind died enough for Amy to close and lock the door. Lucifer reached out and lifted my chin, forcing me to meet his gaze. Rad's fingers dug into my arm as if he would whip me away from the fallen angel if Lucifer tried anything.

The moment Lucifer touched me, my body jerked in response. Once again, my base instinct told me to run away. At the same time, I wanted to throw myself into his arms. I suddenly felt light, as if my organs had turned to feathers, my blood to air. Staring into his eyes, I saw the fires of hell in them right before my mind went blank.

He laid his other hand on my forehead, and a flood of memories swept through my frontal lobe. My immediate past, then the distant past, flipped fast in reverse. Rad, Cole, Di, and my other friends. Damon and the Council. All the humans I had saved over the years. Before that, the ones I had tortured at Maria's request. My family.

The memory of my little sister lying in her own blood broke my paralysis. I lurched away from Lucifer's touch. "Stop," I whispered, losing my balance and falling.

Rad caught me. Tears trickled out, and I damned my weakness. Rad's arms encircled me as Lucifer frowned. He seemed surprised and annoyed I could break free from his grip. I was surprised myself.

His voice was soft and almost reverent. "My God, do you not know who you are?"

Cole moaned beside me. His eyes fluttered open, and I

could see him struggling to remember where he was and what had happened. Relieved, I patted his arm.

The lightness I'd felt while Lucifer touched me evaporated, and I coughed again, blood filling my mouth. I turned my head and spit, not caring how rude it was.

Amy, being human, and a compassionate one at that, grabbed napkins from one of the table dispensers and handed them to me. The witch who was going to go ten rounds with me five minutes ago now felt sorry for me.

Humans. Gotta love 'em.

I thanked her for the napkins, cleared my throat, and firmed my voice. "Of course, I know who I am—Kali Sweet. I run Sweet Investigations and work as an enforcer for the Bridge Council."

Lucifer sat back on his haunches, staring at me as if I'd grown horns or was shooting tracker beams from my eyes. The intensity of his gaze unnerved me. "*Spiritu sancto.*"

By the Holy Spirit wasn't exactly what I was thinking. Of course, who knew what a fallen angel had in his head. "Look, Lilith is eating souls even as we speak. We need to send her back to hell, pronto. I had hoped she might return on her own once I did this job for her, but now I doubt it. There's a cemetery on my property in Chicago that will work for the exorcism. It's private, inconspicuous, and a portal between worlds. I'll get her there. All I need you to do is perform the exorcism."

For some reason, this seemed to amuse him. "Why do you not kill the witch who raised her?"

"Because she's human, just like yours." I glanced at Amy before returning to Lucifer. "I don't kill humans."

"So I see. Do you know why you are compelled to protect humans? Why you were blessed with an aptitude for vengeance and have used it so competently all these years on Earth?"

I shook my head, not giving a rat's ass about the psychology lesson. I ached all over, and my lungs continued to gurgle with blood.

Cole tried to sit up and failed, landing face down. His eyes were cloudy, and he was in pain. Lilith's ability to torture and torment was unequaled by other demons, but Lucifer's went way beyond that.

The one stabilizing factor was Rad's strong, solid presence behind me. He kept me propped up, his arms around me—not in a suffocating manner but in a supportive one. This hero complex was annoying, but I sort of liked it.

"I'm a freak," I admitted to Lucifer. "A demon who would rather help humans than take them to hell."

While he didn't smile, I could still see amusement in his eyes. What was so damn funny?

"You are one of the *vitiums* of Mary Magdalena."

Rad sucked in a breath and swore softly. His supporting arms sagged for a second, then firmed once more. I didn't know what it meant, but I did know Lucifer was smoking angel dust. "You saw my memories. I'm not that old. Mary Magdalena was way before my time."

"Do you remember anything before you were born to your earthly parents?"

"Do I remember hell? No."

"Souls do not come from hell."

Of course not. Souls came from heaven. "I'm a *demon*. I don't possess a soul."

"Seven demons possessed Mary Magdalena. They were exorcised from her by Jesus Christ. She then became the most beloved disciple Jesus had on Earth." He rose, removed a pen from the inside of his jacket, grabbed a napkin, and wrote something on it with broad strokes. Holding the napkin in front of my face, he gave me another one of his intense looks. "Do you recognize this symbol?"

My pulse skittered erratically under my skin. Two Vs, one inverted over the other, formed a rough diamond. He'd drawn an eye in the center. I opened my mouth to answer, but my voice was gone.

Rad spoke. "It's her family's coat of arms."

There was more to my family's coat of arms than the diamond-all-seeing-eye symbol—the sun, moon, and nature's elements. A rendition of the whip coiled around my arm, along with my mother and father's personal family symbols.

"What about it?" I asked Lucifer.

"These" —he motioned to the two V's— "represent Magdalena and The Christ." He shifted the end of the pen to point at the all-seeing eye. "And this represents their bloodline. *Spiritu sancto.* You."

Amy frowned at me, then at Lucifer. "You mean, Jesus and Mary Magdalena did the nasty and had a baby? A *demon* baby?"

Cole had finally managed to rouse himself from the floor. He gave me a perplexed look. Whether it was from the current conversation or over how he'd ended up on the floor next to a whole lot of blood, I wasn't sure.

"Jesus cast the *vitiums*, the vices, from Mary Magdalena with the purest form of heavenly magic possible." Lucifer eyed me again with what seemed like scientific interest. "Kali is not a demon. At least not in the way Lilith has created them. As she stated, she's a freak of nature. An extremely potent mix of good and evil."

A shiver ran from the back of my neck to my toes. The room swam again. My voice came out a whisper. "I don't know what you're talking about."

Lucifer tossed the napkin and pen on the table. "It's not

within my powers to send Lilith back to hell, but you don't need my help. You can handle her on your own."

I would have laughed if I'd had the energy. First, I was Jesus' magical offspring, and now I didn't need help sending Lilith to hell. Lucifer had gone off the deep end. "If I perform the exorcism, I'll wipe out any demon in the area, including myself. I'll be in hell *with* her, which works great for you, but sucks for me."

"You won't go to hell, Kali. The best way to fight the queen of hell is by asking the queen of angels and the powers of heaven for assistance. They'll help you."

A large man walked into the shop from the back room, not seeing us as he headed for the ice cream freezer. A glamour had been placed over his wings, making them invisible to humans. They were massive, rippling and pulsing like a heartbeat. He glowed like Lucifer, only ten times brighter. I flinched and shielded my eyes, and the warning siren in my head went into full panic mode again.

Gabriel.

Rad and Cole recognized the Archangel's eminence as well. Both stood, drawing me up between them, even though Cole wasn't any steadier on his feet than I was. "Time to go," Rad murmured in my ear.

Damn. I didn't want to leave without securing Lucifer's help, but I didn't want to stay either. I was going to fail at sending Lilith back to hell unless I went with her, and it pissed me off that Lucifer was playing psycho angel when I needed him.

My cell phone rang, the notes of *Bad to the Bone* identifying it as Damon. Gabriel's head snapped up. Seeing us, he froze, one hand digging out ice cream in the freezer, the other holding a large plastic bowl. "How dare you," he said.

But he wasn't looking at me. He was looking at Rad and Cole.

His wings rippled with a warning. "How dare you stand in my presence, demons?"

Amy and Lucifer moved simultaneously, one to Gabriel's left and the other to his right. "They were just leaving," Amy said. "No harm, no foul."

Right. She wasn't spitting blood.

I thought it would be a cold day in hell before I begged a fallen angel for assistance, but what do you know? Hell had frozen solid, just like Eden outside the shop's front door. "Please, Lucifer. I'm begging you. I cannot handle Lilith alone."

Gabriel narrowed his eyes at me. He lifted a hand and pointed at me, but Lucifer placed his hand on Gabriel's and pushed it back down. "And you won't have to if you call on the powers of heaven."

Rad and Cole awkwardly secured my cape around my shoulders. Cole grabbed me by the elbow and started forcing me toward the door. "Let's go."

No, I wanted to say. *Not until Lucifer comes with us*. But I knew it was hopeless. I turned hard eyes on him. "I won't forget this."

Threatening the fallen angel was sheer stupidity. I didn't care.

For the first time, he seemed to see me as the vengeance demon I was and not one of his imaginary beings. His black eyes locked with mine. "*Dominus vobiscum, et cum spiritu tuo.*"

The Lord wasn't with me or my spirit; apparently, neither was his enemy, the devil. I started to flip Lucifer the bird, but Rad caught my hand and marched me out the ice cream shop's door.

The storm had turned the sidewalks and roads into an ice rink. The strains of an electric guitar competed with the sound of sleet slapping the ground as Damon's ringtone went off again. Lifting out my cell, I almost punched the "ignore" button.

"Yeah," I said, knowing he'd just keep bugging me.

"Where are you? You haven't checked in for hours."

The GPS on the Land Rover had a tracking system that allowed Damon to keep tabs on me. Another reason, I usually drive my own vehicle. My joints ached, and the metallic taste in my mouth made me nauseous. Standing in a sleet storm, I wasn't in the mood to play games. "You know where I am. What's the problem?"

His voice was stern but edged with genuine concern. Or maybe the connection was sketchy out here in the storm. "The coronation is a little over twelve hours away, Lilith is on the loose, you have a vampire king chained up in a torture chamber, and you're in some small town on the other side of the state pissing off Lucifer. Where do I begin?"

Pissing off Lucifer? What about him pissing *me* off?

Rad, Cole, and I started to cross the street. I ducked my head and ignored the blood on my cape. "I've got everything under control," I said.

"Lilith has gone underground. Her current location is beneath a primary school."

So maybe I didn't have *everything* under control. "Kids souls make a nice snack, but why isn't she after larger game?"

"Ask your boyfriend. He knows more about her than I do."

I glanced at Rad, who watched Cole and me to ensure we were still recovering from Lucifer's TKOs. "Do whatever you have to about the kids. Call in a bomb threat or a gas leak or whatever. Get them out of that school."

"What's your plan for handling Lilith in the long term?"

"Still working on it."

"What?"

His indignation stung. "Lucifer's a no-go. He told me to call on the powers of heaven, whatever the hell that means."

Silence. We made it to the Land Rover and Rad crawled into the back with me. Cole climbed into the driver's seat.

Damon sighed heavily. "Means we're screwed."

"No, Damon." I shook from head to toe, a combination of adrenaline, lingering pain, and the ice storm. "I'm the one who's screwed."

THIRTY-EIGHT

I got off the phone with Damon, promising I'd be back in town in a few hours. Rad was staring at me, and Cole was staring out the windshield. The windows were covered in ice, but I had the feeling he hadn't noticed.

I'd never seen Cole silent, not even when I rescued him from the Erinyes. "You okay?" I asked.

He looked at me over his shoulder and gave me one brief downward nod. "You?"

Hell, no, but neither of us would admit we were messed up. "Yeah. Fine."

"Kali." Rad said my name with that *we need to talk* tone.

I was so tired I could barely sit up. "Start the car, Cole. We need to get back to Chicago before Damon strokes out."

But Cole kept looking at me, his face conveying the same thing as Rad's tone. "Kali, about what Lucifer said..."

I hate it when I'm outnumbered, but it doesn't stop me from arguing or fighting. "Lucifer was messing with us. You know who I am. *What* I am. The *testa de cazzo* doesn't want to sac up and confront his ex, so he's leaving me to clean up his damn mess." I wiped cold water off my face and pushed my wet hair back. "Which is exactly what I'm going to do. Now, start the damn car."

Cole didn't look happy, but he acquiesced. "You riding with us?" he said to Rad.

"No, he's not." I made a *get out* motion with my hand. "You can follow us in whatever vehicle you came in."

He ignored my hand and my command to get out. "I took one of Nudra's cars. We can leave it."

"Which one?" Cole was suddenly back to normal. "The Lamborghini?"

"Sweet car, but drives like shit in this weather."

Cole started the Land Rover, put the defrost fan on high, and met my eyes in the rearview. "We'll send one of your new Undead minions to get it tomorrow."

My minions. Funny how that had become the least of my problems. "If I live to see the coronation."

"Lucifer seemed certain you can handle Lilith," Rad said.

"Did you see him?" I shook my head and stopped when it felt like my brain was banging against my skull. Pressing my fingers to my temples, I shut my eyes for a second. "He's whipped by that witch and acting like a normal human being. Hard to believe he was once an Archangel."

The windshield wipers began to loosen some of the ice. Cole dug under the seat and found an ice scraper. "Be right back," he said.

He dove out of the car and began chipping at the ice on the various windows to speed things along. I was all for that, except for the fact I was now alone with Rad.

He opened his mouth, and I raised a shaky hand. "Don't start. I just survived a round of bubonic plague. I don't want to talk. I want to sleep."

I laid my head against the cold window and closed my eyes. That lasted all of two seconds.

Rad's warm hand gripped mine, startling me. I resisted, but he held firm. "The Noctifectors crucified your parents and little sister. It wasn't Queen Maria, although she was the one who told them where to find your family. She told them you were all demons."

Crucified. The ugliest word in the human language.

The memories of my mother and father nailed to makeshift crosses flashed across my mind. My baby sister's tiny body spread-eagled on the floor, spikes driven into her small hands and feet. The blood...

Hot, angry tears filled my eyes. "Stop. Please."

"You need to hear this. You need to know what happened that day."

"The past can't be changed." I shook my head as if I could shake loose the memories. "It was my fault. Their deaths. I should have been there."

The words came out herky-jerky between breaths. Rad drew me close. He hugged me, and his warmth was a balm to my injured body. "It was not your fault. It was no one's fault."

Of course, he would say that.

I struggled against his comfort, trying to wrench free of his strong arms. Here I was, remembering my murdered family and allowing my sworn enemy to comfort me while he admitted his deceit.

His hands tightened, trapping me against him. "The Noctifectors kidnapped me a few hours before our marriage ceremony, Kali. Maria had told them about me too. I didn't betray you or your family. Maria sold us both out."

I stopped struggling. Hearing Rad confirm the fact the Noctifectors had murdered my family because of Maria's betrayal made my skin crawl. "*Porca miseria.*"

"They knocked me out, hid me inside the catacombs under one of the basilicas. They tortured me for several centuries, brainwashing me to turn me into a tool they could use against other demons." He squeezed my arm. "I was told you were dead. That they'd killed you along with your family. It was one more way for them to break me."

Cole was chip, chip, chipping away at the windshield, and two small circles of ice had melted. He caught an edge with the scraper and tore a large chunk free. A modicum of light filtered through.

However, the storm continued to rage around us while a different storm raged inside me. "That's why I couldn't find you."

Rad's thumb rubbed my arm in slow, comforting motions. "When the Noctifectors finally released me, I returned to your house. I searched for your grave. There was nothing. No evidence that you and your family had ever existed. How did you survive their attack?"

Wiping tears off my cheeks, I sat up. This time, he released me. I stared at the ice-covered window, seeing my dark past. "I was out looking for you. When I returned and found my family dead, I thought Maria had sent some of her mercenaries to kill all of us. You included. I burned with revenge and went to confront her. She caught me and imprisoned me. Tortured me."

To his credit, Rad didn't force a hug or other comfort on me this time. "How did you escape?"

I stared at the seat in front of me, shutting down my emotions even as I opened up and spilled the facts. "The king was killed, a coup staged, and Maria was forced to leave. Her successor ordered all the prisoners killed, but I was able to call up enough magic to break free and escape before they could behead me. I hunted Maria down. She was living in a convent in Milan. I took revenge on her. For all the things she had done. Then I went to Spain."

Cole was working on the ice on my side of the car. Rad shifted forward and caught my eye. "You can't take personal revenge, Kali."

"I didn't take revenge for me." The ice on my window cracked and fell off. I glanced down at my hands, magic rising from them as my thumbs and ring fingers touched. "I took it for everyone else Maria had ever betrayed and hurt. All those humans she made me torture."

Such a dark place. A place I never wanted to go again.

Above all, though, I was a vengeance demon, and justice had to be served. I'd released my demon on her and repaid her for many, many wrongs.

Raising my gaze, I met Rad's with it. "I made her feel all the pain and despair she'd dished out on the rest of us all those years. She died screaming and begging me for forgiveness. But forgiveness wasn't mine to grant."

We sat that way for a long minute, staring at each other, the outside noise of the sleet and Cole's ministrations fading into the background.

Rad's gaze was heavy, weighted. Was he reevaluating me? "I didn't know you were alive until I came to America. I was shocked and relieved and..."

The heater was pumping out more air than I needed. Sweat broke out along my hairline. I released the hold I had on my magic and let it dissipate. "And what? You couldn't pick up the phone and call?"

"No. I couldn't."

"Why not?"

The driver's side door opened, and Cole flung himself into the seat, slamming it quickly behind him. His brown hair was plastered against his head. "God's balls, it's fucking cold out there."

Talk time was over, and Rad seemed relieved. I slouched in the seat and closed my eyes. My head pounded again, and my throat was tight with unshed tears. "Take me home, Cole. Wake me when we get there."

Cole put the Land Rover in drive, and beside me, Rad blew out a long-suffering sigh. Tough. He still had some explaining to do, but really, what did it matter? He was marked as a Noctifector. He may have been forced into it, but he'd had to prove himself to get that tattoo between his shoulder blades. And that meant he'd hunted and killed demons and other supernaturals without distinguishing good from evil.

Demons like me and my family.

As ice and sleet crunched under the Land Rover's tires, I let a tear escape down my cheek.

THIRTY-NINE

I woke sometime later, sprawled out across the backseat, warm and relatively comfortable, considering I wasn't home in bed and my head was in Rad's lap. Facing his crotch.

One arm was slung over my shoulder, a hand resting against my back. The other hand was buried in my hair at the top of my head. He'd removed his coat and made a pillow for me.

A soft snore expanded his chest. I thought about what he'd told me. About the Noctifectors kidnapping him, telling him I was dead. Torturing him until he agreed to become one of them. My face heated with shame for giving him such a hard time.

I'd built a solid, impenetrable wall around my heart. It wasn't easy letting it down or admitting maybe I was being stubborn not to trust Rad again.

Why hadn't he come to me, though, after he'd found out I was still alive? Why hadn't he contacted me in some form until now?

All the years I'd thought he was dead, my heart in shreds,

and then the more recent years, knowing he was alive but thinking his love had been a farce...my heart had shredded all over again.

Now, it squeezed off kilter, sending that familiar pain flooding my chest. Just like his song said, so many wrongs.

I eased out of his hands and sat up, wanting to say I was sorry, although I wasn't sure for what. For not saving him from the Noctifectors? For not contacting him after I realized he was alive? For not believing he wasn't out to kill me and every other demon on the planet?

He continued to sleep like the dead, head thrown back and tilted toward the door, the cords in his neck fully exposed. I'd never really looked at his neck before, but now I did. It was a sturdy neck, tan and virile. If I'd been a vamp, I'd have wanted to sink my teeth into it.

As a demon, I still had the urge simply because he was so human. So alive.

And this might be our last day on Earth together.

We'd left the ice storm behind. Viscous clouds still hung in the sky, making the afternoon seem like twilight. The Land Rover ate up the interstate miles, and we passed a highway sign that said Rush Medical Center was a few miles away.

Dread mixed with relief in my gut. I was home, but for how long?

I climbed into the front seat next to Cole. He kept his eyes on the road and his voice low. "You and Guitar Boy have a heart-to-heart?"

Typically, I would have told him it was none of his business. Instead, I nodded.

"You all cozy again?"

"Why? You jealous?"

"Just wanna know where things stand."

If only I knew. "How's your neck?"

He rubbed a hand around it, shrugged. "Never had my neck broken before. Everything else on my body, but not that. Weird feeling."

"Try having the plague. Not exactly a walk in the park."

Traffic grew heavier. Cole took an off-ramp. "Institute or your place?"

"I get a choice?"

He flicked his gaze to me, and there was something leaden in his eyes. "For now."

He'd heard enough of Lucifer's lies to make him question who I was. "I'm just a demon, Cole. Nothing more, nothing less."

His gaze returned to the road. "Didn't say you weren't."

He might not have said it out loud, but his body language spoke volumes.

Not much I could do about it at the moment. "My place first so I can get cleaned up. Then, the Bridge Institute. I'm sure Damon wants a full report in person."

"Damon wants a lot of things."

Wasn't that the truth.

My phone went off, JR's ringtone loud inside the cabin. Before I could answer, Rad stirred in the backseat. His hair was slightly mussed, and he stretched like a giant, dangerous cat, meeting my gaze with bedroom eyes. A little thrill went through me.

I squashed the thrill and answered my phone. "Hey, JR. What's up?"

JR's voice on a good day is high-pitched. At that moment, it was almost shrill. "Where are you?"

"We're near Rush. Everything okay?"

"Your blood slave, the witch, is here. She's clawing and banging on the doors, demanding I let her in. Wants to know where you are."

I put the phone on speaker, so Cole and Rad could hear. "Why does Victoria want to know where I am?"

"Says she's hungry. Guards ran her off a couple of times, but she keeps coming back. What do you want me to do?"

I shuddered at the thought of Victoria drinking my blood. "Anyone else with her?"

"No. Nobody."

Interesting. Lilith had loosened the leash on the human holding her here. Could be good, could be bad. "Leave Vicky outside, but tell her to hang tight. I'll be there in about twenty minutes."

"She's a freak."

"A dangerous freak. Don't let her in, okay?"

"Hurry, will ya? She's driving me nuts."

I disconnected and looked back at Rad. He'd jammed a hand through his hair, and tufts stuck up at odd angles. His neck, though no longer vulnerable, still looked incredibly sexy, and I bit my lower lip.

His gaze dropped to my lips, and instant desire flashed through him. I know because I felt it. He was hungry again, just like Vicky, but it wasn't only for my blood.

Needing to put some distance between us, I reached for the radio button. Metallica screamed from the speakers, and Cole winced. I couldn't physically get away from Rad in the small confines of the Land Rover, but music at high decibels could work as an invisible barrier.

Early afternoon traffic was thick, but Cole loved the challenge. We arrived in my neighborhood seventeen minutes later, after three near accidents. Rad laughed all the way. Me, I tried not to stroke out.

Vicky paced the parking lot like a caged animal. Her kinky hair stood out in a disarrayed hive around her head. Her long skirt was dirty. The jacket she wore was mis-buttoned and ripped on one elbow. When she saw us pull in, she ran for the car, eyes wide and feral.

I raised my protective magic. She might be human, but she was out of her mind with blood lust like a vampire, and only my blood would calm the beast inside her.

She reached for my door handle before the car came to a stop. The auto locks were engaged, and she couldn't open it. She smashed a hand against the window and tried to see past the tinted glass. I exchanged an eye roll with Cole. Out of all the humans to be tied to, why her?

Cole shifted into park, got out and played bodyguard, forcing Vicky away from my door.

"Are you going to feed her?" Rad asked from the backseat, his voice low but piqued with jealousy.

Like I had a choice. "Yes, I'm going to feed her. Do you need to eat again?"

"Need?" He chuckled low in his throat.

The sound raised gooseflesh on my arms. I turned to look at him and saw his eyes, half-lidded and filled with lust. No, he didn't *need* more of my blood, but he wanted it. Wanted blood and sex and a hundred other things I couldn't give him.

I swallowed hard, opened my door, and slid out. Leaning back in, I met his gold stare with my brown one. "Wait for me upstairs."

FORTY

In the kitchen, I slit a wrist and bled into a glass while JR gave me a status update. Nothing had changed while we were gone. No visitors, except for Vicky. Di continued to enjoy herself at the Blackstone. Arman, my werecat blood slave, was still in the wind.

But if Vicky was this strung out, Arman had to show soon. Unless his cheetah side tempered my blood's call to him.

Blood slaves. So high maintenance.

Vicky's need was so strong that Cole had to restrain her while my blood dripped into the glass. I'd thought she was freaky before, but now she was downright scary.

I thanked JR, sent him back to his tech cave in my office, wrapped a dishtowel around my wrist to stop the bleeding, and handed the glass to Vicky. "Where's Lilith?"

She grasped the glass with both hands, but I drew it back an inch before she could raise it to her lips. "Answer the question."

Her body shook from head to toe. "I don't know."

"What do you mean, you don't know? Where was the last place you saw her?"

"At a school. Underground."

That matched Damon's report. I let Vicky drink for a few seconds and dragged the glass away again. "Why'd she let you come here without her?"

Vicky licked her lips, eyes glued to the blood. "She said she'd follow me here but never showed up."

JR poked his head in. "Kali? We've got a visitor in the cemetery."

"Lilith?"

"Can't tell. I see movement on the cameras, but there's so much overgrowth in there and a fuzzy haze all the time. I can't make out what or who it is. Could be an animal. Could be a person."

Could be the queen of hell. Unlikely, she'd hang out in the boneyard, though.

Cole drew out his gun. "Want me to take a look?"

"It's probably a raccoon or possum. Let's stay inside and see if it comes to us or leaves on its own. If it's not out of there in a few minutes, I'll check it out."

JR disappeared. I let Vicky drink some more. The shakes began to subside, and her body relaxed a bit. "Why do you want Lilith here?" I asked her. "On Earth?"

Her gaze lifted, a quizzical expression in her eyes. "She is my god. Why wouldn't I?"

"She'll destroy all of humanity. You and everyone else."

"She'll bring us freedom. Lilith is unbound desire, sexual equality, and power. She'll raise women up where we should be and give us control over the world."

The creativity I so admired in humans often brought about their destruction. Vicky and her followers had been drinking the Lilith-is-a-misunderstood-goddess Kool-Aid and creating a savior in their minds.

But doctrine and religious beliefs were harder to change than converting a Cubs fan to a Sox fan, so I didn't argue. Didn't bother telling her about the repercussions Lilith's freedom brought with it.

Before I sent Lilith back to the pit, though, I had to figure out how to get Vicky to stop playing with demon worship. As Rad had mentioned, she would do it again if given the chance.

And what could I do about it? There was no way to stop her unless I killed her.

Rad was going to have to wait for his afternoon fix. I grabbed the kitchen phone and dialed Damon.

He answered on the first ring. "Where are you?"

"You need a better opening line. I'm at home."

"I've got something to help you call on the powers of heaven for the exorcism. I found a spell in an old Yezidic text on angels. I've translated it and am faxing you several pages along with the spell now."

"Yezidic? Is that some magical language only Archdemons know?"

"It's an ancient religion in the Middle East. I'm also sending you a standard Judeo-Christian prayer for angelic help."

"You can't be serious."

"What will it hurt?" He cleared his throat and lowered his voice. "Kali, if you want me there when you do this, just say the word."

Facing the enemy and certain death makes you long for your friends and family to gather around you. It lessens the fear somehow. But this was my fight, and I wasn't taking anyone along for the ride. If I failed, Damon and the others would have to rally and continue to fight Lilith however they could.

"I'm good." Vicky finished my blood and laid her head on the table. I moseyed out of the kitchen and away from her hearing. "You don't happen to have a super-charged exorcism in any of those books of yours, do you?"

"Actually," he hesitated. "I wrote a new one specifically for this occasion. There aren't many rituals, ancient or modern, that involve sending Lilith back to hell, so I sort of mixed and matched several exorcisms into one."

The nerd in me thought that was pretty cool. The demon in me didn't. This wasn't a science experiment. "Will it work?"

"Probably."

"Probably?"

"It's included with the other material in the fax. When are you going to perform it?"

"As soon as my guest arrives."

"You're going to do it there? At your house?"

"Cemetery. The portal there will help. I've kept a tight hold on all these years, so I'll have to reverse my magic and open it instead. Just so you know, I'm not sure what might sneak through. You should be prepared."

"I'll handle it." He paused. "Be careful, Kali. I'll see you at the coronation."

"See you, Damon."

But I was pretty sure I wouldn't.

FORTY-ONE

Two hours later, Lilith still hadn't shown up. I'd kept Victoria against her will, finally allowing Cole to give her a love tap on her temple and knock her out when her ranting became too much. Rad tried to coax me into sex upstairs, but once I read all the information Damon sent, my libido went south. Instead, I called Di to say goodbye without really saying goodbye, and also Neve. I told JR he rocked as a tech guru, and he looked me in the eye and blushed. Then I called Nudra's house in my stupid emotional state to talk to Maddy.

Corina answered on the first ring. "Mistress Sweet's residence. May I help you?"

Mistress Sweet? I sounded like a madam. "It's Kali. Let me talk to Madison."

"She's in the basement. May I take a message?"

"What the hell is she doing down there? She's not torturing Toel, is she?"

"No, mistress. She's chained up. Master Chase is gone."

Oh, fuck. "Corina? How did Toel get out?"

"His friends came and released him. They killed the guard that was still here and chained Miss Madison up for befriending you. Oh, and Master Chase told me to give you a message."

"And what was that?"

"He said to tell you...let me get this right...oh, yes, he said to tell you, 'you're dead, dude.'"

That moron. "Is Maddy hurt?"

"No, Mistress. She is simply chained up."

"Well, go unchain her, Corina."

"Do you wish to hold while I do that?"

"Yes."

I paced off the seconds while I waited for Maddy to come to the phone. Finally, I heard her bitching out Corina before she grabbed the receiver and started ranting to me about Toel, the douchebag, and what she was going to do to him.

"Maddy, shut up for a second. Is Jimmy dead?"

That took the edge of her hysteria. "Yeah. I'm sorry, Kali."

I was, too. Jimmy had been a good demon and a damn fine soldier. I swallowed my anger. "You hurt?"

"They roughed me up a bit, but I'm already healed."

She was tough. "How fast can you get back to my place?"

Vamps had super speed, even on foot. "I can be there in a few minutes."

"Good. Lock up the house and tell Corina she is not to let anyone in except me, you, or someone from the Bridge Council."

"Got it."

We disconnected.

Cole lounged against the doorway "Did that piece of shit take out my soldier?"

I rocked in my chair. "'Fraid so. I'm sorry."

Cole clenched his jaw and shook his head. He felt about Jimmy and the other soldiers like I did about Hone.

"According to Corina, he also threatened to kill me."

"Ooooh." Cole made a face. "Bet you're scared now."

"He shows at the coronation, and I'm staking him flat out. No matter what Damon and the Council do to me, it'll be worth it to kill that SOB."

"Gonna be a lot of vamps at that thing tonight. We could take out more than Toel Chase."

"We could."

He gave me that leaden look again, as if he wished we could go back a few days and rewrite what had happened. Like he wanted to say goodbye because he knew I wouldn't make it to the coronation.

"Cole, when this goes down with Lilith, you, Rad, and your guards must be long gone. You know that, right?"

"I'm not leaving you, Kali."

"Me, neither." Rad appeared in the doorway behind Cole. "I'm staying right here."

I shuffled the faxed papers on my desk and pointed to the top one. "I can't pick and choose who gets sucked into hell when I do the exorcism. It's a heavy-duty mother and will take out any demon within a dozen yards of the portal. You both have to leave."

"Much simpler to just take out Victoria." Cole tapped the barrel of his gun against his forehead. "She's a danger to all of us, human and supernatural alike."

I'd already been over all the options when it came to her. "I'll take care of Victoria. Her days as a witch are over."

Rad arched a brow. Cole smiled, thinking I was going to kill her. Which I was, but not in the way he thought.

Cole said, "I'm still staying."

Bullheaded bastard. I shook my head. I was just as bull-headed. "No."

"You'll need someone in hell to cover your six."

A sudden rush of emotion made my eyes tear. "I'm not taking you to hell."

"I'm going willingly."

Rad was eyeing us both with a bemused expression. "Nobody but Lilith is going to hell."

I sat up straight and made a production out of looking through the papers Damon had faxed to me. "All right, then. I guess we better go over my plan before Lilith shows up."

The two men came all the way into the room, and Cole took the only chair before Rad could get to it. Never easily daunted, Rad made himself at home on the edge of my desk, his jean-clad thigh invading my personal space to such a degree that my pulse tripped under my skin.

I cleared my throat. "The cemetery is a portal. If I can lure Lilith in there and reverse the magic I have on it..."

For the next ten minutes, I explained my strategic plan, showed them the spell, prayer, and exorcism, and answered their questions.

Rad shook his head as he read over Damon's notes. "This is much too complicated." He picked up one of my finely sharpened pencils and began scratching things out. "You won't have time to call on all these heavenly entities. Lilith will figure out what you're doing and stop you before you get halfway through the first set."

The musician in him began rearranging words, scribbling notes in the margins. The pencil tapped against his thigh as he reread his arrangement.

Damon was no slouch in the spell department. I might have worried about Rad hacking up the spell and prayer if I thought they'd work. Since I didn't, I let the Noctifector, who knew more about Lilith than I did, do his thing.

Maddy showed up while Cole and I mapped out places around the cemetery for him, Rad, and the others to hide. I kept a set of plastic green army men in my desk, and Cole was having a blast lining them up and pretending to blow the smithereens out of Lilith.

"Did I miss anything?" Maddy asked, eyeballing the toys with mock teenager disgust.

I swiveled my chair to get a good look at her. Her color was good, and her eyes were bright and clear. She was hungry but not famished. Perfect.

"I have a critical job for you, assistant."

"Cool. Are we picking out your ball gown for tonight?"

"Ball gown?"

She saw the confusion in my eyes. "A queen has to look the part at the coronation. Very important. You need something showy but modern to send the right message."

Going to hell held sudden appeal.

"We'll get to that later. First, I need you to handle a little problem for me."

Maddy bounced on her toes, eager to help. "What's that?"

Victoria staggered in, rubbing an egg-shaped lump on her temple. "Is Lilith here yet?"

"Not *what*," I told Maddy, smiling at the witch. "Who."

FORTY-TWO

The cemetery sensed I was up to something. The suppressive magic I'd placed on it hummed with electrified energy, zinging into my legs as I walked through the brambles and overgrowth. The energy would hit, bounce off, and hit me again.

A few feet above the ground, the magic hung on me like a cloying perfume, coating my hair, face, and hands. I didn't raise my protective magic but walked around the headstones and checked the air for any sign of Lilith. I'd asked Victoria to mentally call to her and ask her to come to the graveyard. Since they were linked mentally and magically, they could tap into each other's thoughts. Lilith, of course, kept a tight rein on hers so Victoria couldn't read her mind, but I was sure Lilith was reading Vicky's mind with ease.

Which was one of the reasons I had kept the witch in the dark about my plans. She thought I wanted Lilith to come to the cemetery because I had news about Lucifer. I'd made up a story about the devil's desire to reunite with Lilith, and he was willing to meet her. She was to show up at sunset. Vicky was more than happy to pass on the information.

The weather had turned wintery, fog rising from the ground as cold rain drizzled from the clouds. In a few hours, it would turn to the sleet storm we'd left behind in Eden.

As I walked the property, I kept to a pentagram pattern. It was easy to do since the grave markers were laid out in that exact pattern. Multiple pentagrams, in fact, increasing in size, surrounded a small one in the center. That small pentagram earmarked the portal to other worlds.

The pattern wasn't easy to see on the ground, but I'd had a bird' s-eye view from the church's roof every morning. The pattern looked like a magical bulls-eye.

I'd also walked the outline every year, tracing containment magic over the portal. Now, I walked the opposite way, reversing the spell and diffusing the restrictive energy. I wasn't ready to delete it altogether—no telling what monster would be passing by the portal on the other side and decide to pay a visit —but I did lower the concentration so the portal was pliable from my side. If something tried to come through, I could push it back. And when I was ready to send Lilith packing, I could push from this side hard enough to break the remaining barrier.

Above and around me, my army of guerilla soldiers hid in various spots outside the pentagram's boundaries. Cole and Rad were at the cemetery's edges and hopefully out of range of the exorcism's reaches. The two Merc demon bodyguards, whom I'd given the option of leaving and who had both declined, were stationed on the rooftop of my house, sniper rifles loaded with two different varieties of demon-repelling bullets.

Vicky stood over the portal, my willing—if oblivious—bait for the trap. Maddy lurked behind a large gravestone a few feet away, ready to do her part on my signal. The exorcism would not affect her, and I'd done my best to talk Victoria out of her Lilith fangirl mindset, but the witch had stuck to her guns as I'd suspected she would. She was one human I couldn't save.

Walking the pentagram surrounding Vicky and the portal, I whispered Rad's revised invocation spell under my breath. White or dark, magic only worked if you believed it would. I couldn't say anything would work at that moment, but the chanting calmed my nerves.

The words made little sense to me, but Rad assured me it was all part of the ritual. "Sole Almighty Creator of heaven and Earth, Thou hast neither feathers, wings, arms, voice nor color. The morning stars joyfully cry out your name, and the Earth shouts in applause."

"What are you saying?" Vicky asked.

"I'm clearing the energies here for Lilith and Lucifer."

She seemed pleased by the lie. Her face lit up. "I could help."

She was going to help, but not in the way she intended. "You've done enough."

I continued walking and whispering. "I invoke thee through the mediation of the Holy Seven. Shamseddin, Fakreddin, Nasreddin, Sijeddin, Isa, Backram, Kahdirrahman. I invoke thee through the mediation of Mother Mary, the queen of angels. I pray for deliverance from evil. I invoke your protection from evil. I..."

A twig snapped behind me. The air filled with the scent of smoke and burning fires. Heat breached the barrier of my clothes and licked over my skin. My earpiece came alive with Cole's voice. "Mama demon, three o'clock."

A smart ass to the end.

I moved toward the center of the pentagram. Dark earth magic tugged at my feet, weighing them down as it climbed up my legs. Vicky felt it, too, and closed her eyes in euphoria.

The sensation, compelling and seductive, made me shiver. Is this what Lilith felt all the time? Did the magic feed her like a constant ecstasy drip into her bloodstream so she never came down from the high?

Magic was a drug to humans. The more they tasted of it, the more they wanted. Problem was, they weren't born to handle magic long term any more than they were built to handle drugs. The high came at a terrible price, and those like Vicky, who allowed magic into their systems daily, became addicted. They no longer saw the world the same way, and once addicted, they couldn't turn back. Like a blood slave who had to have their master's blood to live, humans addicted to magic had to have a regular dose of it to stay functional. Eventually, the magic would eat them up.

"*Alciscor.*" Lilith emerged out of the fog and drizzle in front of me. The beautiful mink coat was perfectly dry, and the rain seemed absent where she stood. Dry heat radiated off her, chasing away the fog around her feet.

She glanced around, an expectant look on her face. "Where is Lucifer?"

Vicky took a step forward, ready to fall to her knees at Lilith's feet. I stopped her by placing a hand on her wrist and sending some magic up her arm. She jumped and frowned, but I smiled and squeezed her wrist tighter, drawing her closer to me. For my plan to work, she needed to stay out of Lilith's reach. "He's on his way," I said.

"He said twilight, and it is twilight." Her voice was superior. "Where is he?"

How she could tell it was twilight with the heavy cloud cover and fog was beyond me. "He'll be here."

I stepped back and dragged Vicky with me. My magic confused her, dampening her thoughts. She stepped back with me instead of fighting me, and Lilith stepped forward as if drawn to us without even realizing it.

Perfect. Two more feet to the portal.

I looked over my shoulder, turning my body eastward so Vicky again had to step away from Lilith. I acted as if I were keeping an eye out for Lucifer. Mentally, I finished the invocation prayer and continued to turn my body to the four points. *Yehowah. Adonai. Eheieh. Agla.*

Then I let go of Vicky, who had moved out of the portal's circle and closer to the gravestone Maddy hid behind. I spread my arms as if stretching, but in fact, I was forming a human cross. The act made me sick as I couldn't help but think of my parents and sister being forced into the same position before being crucified.

Ah, the past. Constantly popping up at the most inconvenient moments.

"Before me, Raphael," I whispered, shoving my memories aside. "Behind me, Gabriel." I cringed at that one, remembering the Archangel and his righteous anger at the ice cream shop. So not someone I wanted to tangle with. "On my right, Michael. On my left, Uriel."

In my earpiece, Rad said the prayer with me. His voice ran over my outstretched arms like a peaceful stream over a rock, calming me. The magic leaching up my legs halted. The cloying air slipped off my skin and flung itself away from me.

Lightning zig-zagged across the sky, and a breeze rose, making me think of the flap of an angel's wings.

I took a deep breath. *This might work.*

Lilith moved closer, squinting her eyes and staring into my face with disturbing intensity. "What are you saying, demon of mine?"

She stood directly over the portal. It was now or never.

"For about me flames the pentagram," I said out loud, and

through the drizzle, flames did indeed rise around us. Small flames at first and then growing more significant as I continued. "And in the center stands the evil one."

Lilith's eyes went black as night, flames flaring to life in the orbs. Not reflections from the pentagram. The fires of hell.

"What have you done?" she screamed at me.

"Now," I yelled at Maddy. The young vamp jumped out from behind the gravestone, her preternatural movements so fast that she was a blur. She grabbed Vicky from behind, tilted her head to the side, and sank her fangs into the witch's jugular.

Vicky didn't even have time to cry out.

She'd already sold her soul to Lilith, was already bound for hell. There was nothing I could do to save her from that. Being Undead offered her a life on Earth while cutting her ties to witchcraft. No more raising demons. No more playing with the queen of hell. She was already my blood slave and a pretty shitty one at that. Turning her into a full-fledged vamp wasn't ideal, but it was better than the alternatives.

Thunder boomed overhead loud enough to make my ears ring. Lilith's eyes widened, and I was suddenly locked in a vice grip. I tried to keep speaking, but my vocal cords were paralyzed.

Damn it. Hadn't thought of that.

I started the exorcism anyway, using my mind.

Rad had tossed out the one I'd planned to use and substituted a Latin one. He was saying it in my earpiece, urging me to join him. My Latin was rusty, and I stumbled over some of the words in my head, trying to keep up with him. As Lilith lifted my body from the ground without touching me, I switched to English.

Way easier.

We exorcise you, impure spirit, satanic power, incursion of the infernal adversary. Thus, cursed demon, we adjure you.

Cease to deceive human creatures, and to give to them the poison of Eternal Perdition.

Searing pain ripped through my ribcage. I jerked in response, and blood ran from my eyes.

Rad's voice continued, unwavering. I took up the chant again.

Go away, Lilith, mother of demons, deceit, and enemy of humanity's salvation. Be humble under the Powerful Hand of God. Tremble and flee from the Queen of Angels.

My limbs suddenly bent at weird angles, bones breaking. I didn't feel it, though. Wind swirled a blinding mass of leaves around us. The ground under Lilith's feet sank.

She lost her balance, and my limbs righted themselves. I still hovered off the ground, but something was working to open the portal door and take her to hell. Either Vicky was close to death, or the heavenly powers were listening.

My vocal cords worked again. I yelled over the thunder, lightning, and wind. "I invoke by us the Sacred Name at which those down below tremble. Mother Mary, full of grace, help me. Angels on high, hear my words and lend your grace."

At that moment, I dropped to the ground in a heap near Lilith's feet. She raised her hand, and my body rolled toward her, magnet to steel.

The ground opened.

God help me.

That last part was not part of the exorcism. It was solely my addition.

The portal became a black swirling mass of nothingness under me, the ground turning into a slide. Rad and Cole screamed my name in my ear as I grabbed for purchase, digging my nails into the wet grass and weed-covered ground. Soil gave under my weight, the grass slipping right through my fingers. I slid down, down, down.

Dirt blew into my eyes, the wind sucking oxygen from my mouth and nose. My legs swung uselessly below me. The black magic, the tainted souls sacrificed to Death, clamped hands around my ankles to drag me down with them.

Out of nowhere, hands gripped my wrists. For a second, I stopped falling. Maddy's face appeared above me.

"Get back," I yelled at her, but she shook her head, gripping me tighter as the wind whipped hair across her eyes. Below us, the souls lost in the portal shrieked and screeched. Fires burned.

She should have listened to me. A second later, the portal sucked both of us in with Lilith.

I'd always loved roller coasters, the free-falling sensation when dropping hundreds of feet in the air at high speeds. This was similar. My stomach went up in my throat, my body turned weightless. I twisted in circles, tumbling over and over. No longer attached to the ground or Maddy, screams erupted from my mouth from the brutal hit of adrenaline. I wasn't flying over a rollercoaster hill. I was flying off a cliff.

Volante's handle slid into my hand. I flicked my wrist upward, sending her reaching for a gravestone. She hit something, tried to wrap herself around it. Failed.

Over the screeching noise of the portal and my own screams, I heard a voice. A voice that had brought millions of women and probably a few men to their knees. A voice that had rocked the world. Had rocked *my* world.

Rad spoke with force and conviction in my ear. "Sole Almighty Creator of heaven and Earth, Thou hast neither feathers, wings, arms, voice nor color. The morning stars joyfully cry out your name, and the earth shouts in applause."

I had brushed against Death a few times but always survived. This time, things were different. I could feel it at my core. The demon in me knew it was a lost cause, and whatever else was in me did, too. All was black and evil energy around me.

But that voice...that voice was my lifeline.

I didn't want to die, didn't want to go to hell. I wanted to live.

I took up the chant, more to savor that last connection to Earth than believing it had any power in this deep hole between worlds. "I invoke thee through the mediation of the Holy Seven. I pray for deliverance from evil. I invoke your protection from evil. I summon thee for help. Mother Mary, help me!"

White light blinded me. At the edges of my corneas, blue lightning bolts flashed. Searing pain pierced my heart, my organs. It felt like I was being turned inside out.

A sharp jerk stopped my somersaults and reversed my trajectory, catapulting me up, or at least I thought it was up. I didn't have time to figure it out. The light seared my retinas, and my mind went blank.

FORTY-THREE

I was lying on the wet ground when I woke, staring up at the foreboding night sky. Sleet stung my face.

Blue lightning bolts danced around the peripherals of my eyes, and I tried to blink them away. It didn't work. Above me, Rad, Cole, Maddy, and Damon stared down at me, their shadowy faces displaying a mixture of relief and concern.

My vocal cords worked, but they were in bad shape. "You okay, Maddy?"

Her head bobbed, and she smiled wider. "You. Kicked. Fucking. Ass."

Running my hands over my various body parts, I found everything whole and in the right places. My cape was still tied around my neck. Volante was on my wrist.

I was alive. Maddy was alive. Rad, Cole, and Damon were okay.

Damon. Where had he come from? "What the hell are you doing here?"

He slanted his eyes at Maddy. "I came to reprimand you for

breaking another Bridge law. Really, Kali. Turning Victoria into a vampire?"

His words were severe and chastising, but his tone was light. I thought he was joking, but I wasn't sure.

"Did it work?" I asked.

"She's alive and sleeping it off." Maddy looked over her shoulder as if to check on Vicky and returned her gaze to me. "I gave her some of the AB neg. Hope that's okay. I didn't want her drinking my blood and being tied to me when the change is complete."

Smart girl. I glanced at Cole and Rad. "The portal's closed? Lilith's gone?"

The two of them grabbed my arms and helped me sit up. "Looks that way," Cole said. "The pentagram was burning with fire when you all went down. Then the flames disappeared, you and Maddy hurtled out of the hole, and the pentagram burned with white light. Maddy was fine, but you've been unconscious for about ten minutes."

Vertigo hit. I was soaked, and my teeth chattered. "Get me off this damn wet ground."

They lifted me, and I managed to stay on my feet, hanging onto their arms for support. The blue flickering lightning bolts continued to go off in my peripheral vision. I saw a body on the ground outside the circle. Vicky. When she came to, she was going to be one pissed-off vamp.

As luck would have it, I was pretty good at handling pissed-off vamps.

Cole and Rad walked me toward the church. "Wait. I have to make sure the portal won't open again."

"I'll do it," Damon said. "You go inside and clean up. The coronation is at midnight sharp, and we're meeting with the Prince and a few of his officials beforehand, including the

Master of the House. They want to go over your duties and responsibilities."

Duty and responsibility. My calling cards. Justice, however, was still mine. "Does the Prince know about Toel?"

Damon gave me a nod. "He knows." The disgust on Damon's face told me Vlad knew very well what his West Coast Regional Manager was up to and didn't care.

"Just so we're clear. If Vlad doesn't rein in Toel, I will."

Not waiting for his reply, I started walking—tottering really —toward the church. Maddy took Cole's place next to me, and he lifted Vicky and carried her. With every step, my internal organs trembled as if I were on a floating boat launch, trying to keep my balance during a storm. My ears rang. The aftereffects of the portal were a bitch, but at least I wasn't coughing up blood.

Remembering the experience, I gritted my teeth. The white light. The whisper of angels' wings. Heavenly intervention sounded like the weirdest of weird ass reasons for me to still be standing, but I wasn't about to look a gift horse in the mouth. Maybe Lucifer wasn't as crazy as I'd thought.

A few steps from the edge of the cemetery gate, a dark figure shot out from a gravestone, moving with feline-like grace. I should have smelled him before I saw him, but my senses were off.

All of us froze. Even in the darkness, his numerous spots and long tail gave him away. The cheetah stood tall and stream-lined, all lanky limbs and slender body. His ears flattened when he saw me, and he bared his teeth, white teeth flashing in the darkness.

I slid my whip handle into my hand. "Arman."

His predatory stance didn't change. His tongue flicked out and back in, and he dropped his head and eyed me more intently.

"Return to your human form, and I'll feed you."

"It's too late," Maddy said. "He needed to feed before the cheetah took over. Shifter blood slaves are that way. Once they go into animal form, they can't shift back on their own."

Damn. "My blood was supposed to stop him from shifting."

"But he's running on empty. Your blood was only a short-term solution."

I'd faced many predators in my time as an enforcer. I knew the look on Arman's face, even if he was a cheetah. There was no getting out of this situation without taking him down. "Sorry, Arman. I have no choice."

I flicked my wrist, and Volante wrapped around his front legs, taking him off his feet. He snarled and fought against the restraint. I removed a stake and threw it at his head. The blunt end hit him solidly in the center, knocking him out.

Rad carried Arman, Cole carried Victoria, and Maddy supported me. Inside, I reopened the wound on my wrist and bled into a fresh glass. I forced Arman's cheetah lips apart and poured some down his throat. Then I left the rest in the fridge and trudged upstairs alone.

I threw myself into the shower and washed my body twice, the feel of the water and the smell of the soap washing away the last of the portal's aftereffects. Once I'd walked out of the cemetery, I no longer saw the blue flashes of light. As I let hot water cascade over me, bone-deep relief mixed with a certain amount of satisfaction made me giddy. Going through the vampire coronation was small peas compared to besting Lilith. Whatever the night held, I'd handle it.

After the shower, I climbed into bed, thinking I'd take a short rest. The only sleep I'd had in the past twenty-four hours was the two-hour nap on the way home from Eden. I'd used very little magic then, but my body was worn out from the stress.

I woke up a few hours later when someone slapped me on the butt. Hard.

"Ow," I said, sitting up too fast. The room tilted, then righted itself as my brain caught up to the sudden movement.

Yasmin was staring at me, arms crossed over her chest. She was dressed in a long, flowing green gown that sparkled so much, I looked away. "I can't believe you're sleeping. You're not dressed, your hair is..." She made a disgusted sound in the back of her throat. "Get up. Now."

I was naked under the sheet, so I shifted around carefully, keeping my assets covered. "What are you doing here?"

"Damon insists we all go to the coronation together. Isn't that delightful?"

Her tone was spiteful, but I sort of understood it. I had no desire to go with her either. "Okay, I'm up. You can leave my bedroom now."

Maddy swooped in, wearing one of my Marchesa dresses that had been stored in a spare room. The hand-pleated pale pink silk tulle was embroidered at the neckline and hung in a cascade from her breasts, the hemline ending in a fluffy wave around mid-thigh. She looked better than I did in it. "That's my dress."

"I have to wear something nice. It is a formal affair, you know." She'd piled her hair on top of her head and had cute, messy ringlets falling around her face. "I can't go to the coronation ceremony in my jeans, but I'm much too young for" —she cut her eyes to Yasmin and back—"ballroom dresses."

Holding up a bone-colored flowing dress in front of Yasmin, she waved a hand over it. "How about this one for Kali?"

It was another Marchesa—one that Di had picked, as evidenced by the goddess vibe it emitted. Yasmin shook her head. "It needs to be classy and sophisticated but with an edge to it. It should say business but not office."

"Have you seen her closets?" Maddy grabbed Yasmin's hand and, to Yasmin's horror, hauled her toward the door. "They're amazing but completely unorganized. I have no idea how to find the right dress."

As they went out, I called after them. "Can't I just wear my usual skirt and turtleneck?"

"No," came their replies in unison.

While they were gone, I threw on a tank top and sweat-pants. While I'd always loved getting dressed up, I hadn't worn something fancy in a long time. The coronation was a formal affair—hell, anything the vamps did was a formal affair—but dressing up held little appeal. I would be surrounded by the Undead, including the Master himself. I wanted my fighting clothes on.

Yasmin and Maddy returned, Yasmin carrying a midnight blue, almost black, strapless silk dress with a tasteful swatch of tulle in the front. It was stunning and suggested elegance without overdoing it. I'd bought it several years ago to wear to a Bridge party and never worn it because I'd had to work that night on short notice.

Eyeing the beautiful dress, I thought it would definitely make a statement, but I preferred making statements with actions rather than clothes. "I was thinking more leather. Less silk."

She huffed and removed the dress from its protective bag. "This will show off your arms."

"And I want to show off my arms because?"

"They're your best asset."

I'd always thought my legs were my best asset. "The only assets I plan to show the vamps are my whip and stakes."

Yasmin gave me a tight-lipped frown. "Really, Kali. This is a serious commitment from the Bridge Council to join the

Undead Nation. It's beneath you and the Council for you to act so immature."

I took umbrage at her condescending tone, but in some ways, she was right. Like it or not, I had to step up and act like... well, Damon. In control, serious, and able to handle whatever the vamps handed me. It was time to call up my rules.

Don't take anything personally.

Don't get emotional.

Shutting down every ounce of emotion I felt, I snagged the dress from Yasmin's hands. She wanted me to act mature and handle this like she would? Fine. Only, I'd handle it even better than she would. "I'll meet you downstairs in fifteen."

Her frown eased as she saw the hardness in my eyes. She glanced at my hair. "No ponytails."

Once she walked out, Maddy gave me a wide-eyed look. "How do you do that?"

"What?"

"You just went Terminator on her. Like you did to me in the parking lot."

"I didn't even touch her."

"It's your eyes." She visibly shuddered. "They go black, and your face...you become a machine."

Machine. Enforcer. Vampire queen. Bridge Council pawn. All one and the same. "Can you do something with my hair?"

Maddy's face brightened. Then, she mimicked Yasmin. "Classy and sophisticated with an edge to it. You bet."

In the bathroom, I sat at my dressing table, working on my makeup while the flatiron heated. Maddy picked out a sparkly charcoal eye shadow and showed me how to glam up my eyes. I left the rest of my makeup natural. Pale cheeks with a hint of shimmer on the bones, nude lips tinged pink.

Maddy straightened my already reasonably straight hair and grabbed one section in the center to tie at the back of my head with a crystal comb. Very mod 1960's and emphasized my bold eyes.

Because of the elegant dress, boots were out. The dress hit me mid-thigh, so I chose a pair of nude heels with tiny crystals decorating the tops. They made my legs look longer, and I liked the stiletto heel. The overall effect in my full-length bathroom mirror was impressive. I didn't look like Kali Sweet any longer, but I still had a badass air to me. It was the eyes, I decided. Maddy was right. My eyes were hard and flat. Commanding, confident.

I wrapped Volante around my wrist, making her look like a leather cuff. There was nowhere to hide a stake inside the dress, so I strapped on a knife holder to my upper thigh and slid a stubby, flat stake in the shape of a dagger into the pocket. In a pinch, it would do.

"Wow," Maddy said on a breath.

I tossed her a small silver, two-bladed axe. It wouldn't take a vamp's head off cleanly, but it would stop them cold if you embedded it in their skull. "A girl's gotta be prepared."

She hiked up the tulle skirt and slid the axe into a pocket I had sewn inside the fabric. "I love the way you think."

The church didn't have a grand staircase, just an old one running along the east wall from my upstairs loft to the main living area. Maddy went down ahead of me and gathered the troops.

As I descended, a hush fell.

Damon was dressed to the nines in a modern Armani tux. Single button front, silk lapels, fitted to perfection. A black shirt, dark gray vest, and tie. With his Basque coloring, it all blended into a dark, dangerous package.

Our eyes locked, and I saw him catch his breath as he drank me up. His eyes flashed with desire. Commanding as mine had been in the bathroom mirror. He would have swept me off the stairs and kissed me again if we'd been alone. I knew it as if the image playing out in my mind had already happened in the past.

Me. Damon. Coming together, intense, carnal, needy.

His wood smoke scent filled my nostrils. For half a second, there was pressure in my head. My ears rang as if I were in a vacuum. *Definite weak spot.*

Get out of my head, I replied. I wasn't in the mood to flirt. I kept my gaze level, calm, and detached. He tensed ever so slightly and lost the carnal look. He hadn't outright proposi-tioned me, but I'd turned him down anyway, and he didn't appreciate the rejection. His ego, though, was well controlled. He simply nodded, as a boss would to an underling who had at least left the rubber band out of her hair.

To his left was Cole. His outfit was less fashion-oriented but no less strategic. A charcoal gray wool suit coat emphasized his broad shoulders. Black jeans stretched over his muscled legs. White shirt, opened at the collar, showed off a patch of his collarbone. He'd pulled his brown hair back in his usual low ponytail, highlighting his face and crooked nose.

He wore a ponytail and looked classy. I wore one and looked like a pubescent teen. Life wasn't fair.

Yasmin and Kirill stood off to the side, Yasmin's green dress a flashy, almost mermaid-esque companion to Kirill's matching green vest. The two looked like prom dates standing next to each other—not exactly sophisticated, but what did I know?

In the sunken living room area near the fireplace, Arman, back in human form, and Victoria, now a vampire, sat with distant expressions as if they didn't quite recognize me. Then something clicked, probably my blood calling to them, and Arman stood and gave me a goofy grin. Vicky narrowed her eyes and rose as well, balling her hands into fists.

Yep, she was pissed.

Couldn't say I blamed her. I'd be pissed, too, to wake up and discover I was a vamp, but I'd deal with her fallout in a minute.

My eyes scanned the rest of the lower level. The one person missing was Rad.

Cole whistled low under his breath and held a hand to me as I descended the last few stairs. "Damn, Kali, you clean up nice."

His hand was warm and supportive in more than a physical way. The two of us had been through many harrowing situations in our work together, but the past few days had cemented our friendship in a deeper kind of trust and kindredship. "You're looking pretty hot yourself, War demon."

Arman jumped the stairs from the sunken area and rushed to me, throwing his arms around my neck. "Thank you for the blood. For not killing me, and well...for everything," he gushed. Then he whispered in my ear. "I know why you're doing this vamp queen thing. Thank you."

The human in him was so tangible at that moment I wanted to hug him back. This was one of the things that made my job worthwhile. Appreciation and gratitude were no small things.

I untangled his arms from my neck and forced him back a couple of steps. "You're welcome. Next time, as soon as you feel the blood lust rising, you need to find me. Better yet, you should keep a few bottles of my blood at your place so this doesn't happen again. Okay?"

Arman nodded vigorously. "I'd attend the coronation tonight, but you know how vamps are about shifters."

Shifters were too territorial. Vamps were too political. Put them in a room together, and someone would end up dead. "Yeah, I know. Don't worry about it. Did you drink all the blood I put in the glass?"

He nodded.

"Good. Go home, be human, and I'll have more delivered in a day or so. Until we figure out exactly how long you can go between meals, let's stick to a glass every two to three days."

Vicky came up behind him. Her eyes glowed bright red. She pushed Arman to the side and shook a fist at me. "How dare you turn me into a vampire! How dare you send Lilith back to hell!"

She drew the fist back to strike my face. I understood her anger and didn't blame her for the attack—hell, I would have come up swinging, too, if I'd been turned against my will—but I couldn't let her screw up my makeup or hair. I dodged, and Cole lifted one beefy arm and clotheslined her across her throat. She went down on her back, choking and staring up at me.

"What do you want to do with her while we're gone?" Cole asked.

Maddy stepped forward and stared down at Vicky. "She needs to be chained up until the first wave of blood lust is over. Otherwise, she'll start attacking every human in sight."

I considered the options and discarded all but one. "She's coming with us."

Reaching down, I held out a hand to help her up. "Come on, Vicky. Time to meet your new family."

She gripped my hand with newfound vamp strength and tried to jerk me down. I twisted her hand at a wrong angle, and she cried out, swearing at me.

Guess it was time to set a few ground rules. Hauling her to her feet, I grabbed the front of her dress's collar and brought her face to mine. My voice came out low and dangerous, and the moment she heard it, she stopped struggling and went very still. "You're not human anymore, Victoria, so watch your step. I didn't want to turn you into a vamp, but you gave me no choice. Suck it up and deal. Otherwise, I'll stake your sorry ass, and you can join Lilith in hell."

She swallowed visibly and made a slight acquiescing nod.

With things squared with her, I released her and faced Damon. "Is Hone meeting us there?"

Damon shook his head. "I asked him not to come. He's human, and we don't need more issues with humans than we currently have. Taking him into an Undead coronation is asking for trouble."

He was right. "Let's get this show on the road then."

Maddy handed me a black lynx fur coat that had been stuffed in one of my closets along with the Versace dress Lilith had stolen. Damon took it from her outstretched hand and held it open for me. "Allow me."

The heavy wood smoke scent enveloped me once more. There was a flicker of something I couldn't quite name in Damon's eyes again.

Merde. It was going to be a long night.

Slipping my arms into the coat, I asked, "Where's Rad?"

Cole smirked. "Guitar Boy said there was something he had to do. Left about an hour ago."

My heart sank. Guess I knew he wouldn't walk into a nest of vampires, but still, it rankled that he'd deserted me.

JR shuffled in. There were dark shadows under his eyes and his shoulders sagged more than usual. "Hey, boss. You need me tonight?"

"When was the last time you slept, JR?"

He slanted his attention to the ceiling and wiggled his fingers as he counted back the hours. "Couple of days."

Loyalty was a priceless thing. I wanted to send him home, but Toel was still on the loose. I expected he'd be busy with me at the coronation, but the damn vamp had shown me up one too many times. "We'll be gone most of the night. Grab a blanket and a pillow out of the upstairs linen closet and get some sleep. After tonight, things should return to normal, and you'll be safe at home and Sweet Investigations."

He yawned and dug a piece of paper out of his pocket. "Rad asked me to give you this."

I took the note while the others put on their coats. Rad's familiar, elegant handwriting took my breath away. The last note I'd had from him had been in Rome all those years ago, the words professing his undying love. Was this another love note?

Not hardly. The message was short, sweet, and entirely confusing.

Watch your back at the coronation tonight. When things go bad, get out. RB.

I fixated on his initials, caressing the end of my whip absentmindedly. There was no *Love, RB.* No *See ya later, RB.* Just *RB.* All business.

*When things go bad...*what did that mean?

The answer whispered in my head. Bad equaled Noctifectors.

Rad was bringing a group of Nocts to wipe out the vamps.

I whirled around and faced Damon. He was watching me with a keen interest, and for a heartbeat, I wondered if he was reading my mind. "Where is the coronation taking place?"

"Carpathia in Lake Forest. Their upper-level managers all live there."

The Carpathia house was the region's private Undead hangout. A mansion that made Nudra's place look like a Barbie house. Uber private...most of the supernatural world didn't even know where it was located. Hell, I didn't know exactly where it was. "Did you give Rad the address?"

"No. Why?"

The Noctifectors probably knew the address. I waved him off, another thought surfacing. "Nudra didn't live there. He had two other residences. A condo downtown and that mansion outside of Naperville."

Damon shrugged, glanced at the paper in my hand and gave me a questioning lift of one dark brow. "Nudra bucked the system and did what he wanted most of the time. But he did stay in Lake Forest at least half of every month as dictated by vampire canon."

Vampire canon. What else did it dictate? I was sure I didn't want to know. "I'm not living in some prissy vamp house in Lake Forest two weeks out of every month."

Damon heard the teeth in my statement. Decided not to push it. "Duly noted."

Three black, aggressive-looking SUVs were waiting in the parking lot for us—my Land Rover and a couple of caddies. From the way the Council was dressed, I kind of expected limos, but I preferred what was there. Like my charcoal-lined eyes, the three SUVs would make the right statement—sophisticated with a *don't mess with us* edge.

The sleet had stopped, and a fingernail moon lazed in the sky. As we hustled to the waiting vehicles, drivers dressed in black suits and caps opened doors for us. Lower-level demons, they were accustomed to servicing the Bridge Council and did so with blank faces and skilled hands.

Maddy climbed into my Land Rover, and I passed Victoria off to Damon. He gave me a *don't be ridiculous* look. "You ride with me. We have a strategy to discuss about tonight. Things you need to know."

Cole stepped to my side. "Then I ride with you too."

Damon shook his head. "Kali will be safe with me. You ride with the two vampires."

Victoria's head went back and forth, watching the verbal tennis match with interest.

Cole put his hands on his hips. "I'm Kali's bodyguard. I don't leave her side."

"Boys." I held up a hand and stepped between them, facing Damon. "I have a strategy, thank you, and I'm riding with Cole and Maddy."

Victoria seemed pleased with my decree and sidled up to Damon, looping her arm with his. Witch or vamp, she was drawn to power. I couldn't wait to put her in a room with Toel.

Damon drew a patient breath. Pressure filled my head. *You owe me, demon.*

I was pretty sure sending Lilith back to hell had me way up in the who-owed-who department.

Pissing match over, Cole and I climbed into the backseat of my Land Rover. Maddy rode up front. I handed Cole Rad's note as the driver pulled out of the lot.

Using the overhead light, he read it. Read it again. Looked out the window in thought.

"What does it mean?" I asked, keeping my voice low.

"Guitar Boy knows something we don't." He looked at me, suspicion evident on his face. "Anything you want to tell me?"

That's when I should have confessed my insider knowledge and told my bodyguard the truth about the tattoo between Rad's shoulder blades. "Like what?"

"What your boyfriend does in his spare time?"

"He's a singer in a rock band. I assume the old axiom is true. Drugs, group sex, and hotel room trashing."

He held my gaze for a long moment before looking away. We rode the rest of the way in silence, the trust we'd established over the past two days strung taut.

FORTY-FOUR

Like mansions everywhere, the Lake Forest vampire house was ostentatious. Once our IDs were checked and names crossed off the visitor list, a gate opened and allowed us onto the grounds. Victoria and Maddy were allowed in as my special guests.

Bilateral symmetry, check. Veranda covering the front porch, check. Rotunda domes flanking the ends, arches and columns, check and check. A water fountain spouting blood-colored water in the front. Gross.

Undead guards stood at the French doors. They didn't make eye contact, but both murmured "queen" under their breaths as they allowed me to pass. The single word rang with sarcasm.

The entry hall was marbled and two stories with a *giganto* chandelier that would crush multiple vamps if I severed the chain holding it. Double staircases bookended the foyer, and I saw stars twinkling through a skylight as I looked up.

We were greeted by Undead servants in dark suits who

took our coats with downcast eyes. The French doors to the grand ballroom were closed, but no noise came from the other side. Fresh blood and grave dirt scents accosted my nose. The most prestigious vamps in the Central United States were waiting for us on the other side of the walnut doors.

In utter silence.

Trap, my gut said. My brain echoed the sentiment.

I grabbed Damon's forearm as two male servants prepared to open the doors. "I don't like this."

He patted the top of my hand. "The Bridge Council will be with you every step of the way."

He thought I was worried about myself. In reality, I was worried about all of us. Inviting the leaders of Chicago's Bridge Council here under the guise of crowning me queen suddenly seemed like the best underhanded plan I'd heard of in a while. We were sitting ducks.

Before I could state the obvious, Damon's voice filled my head. *Show no fear. Act like an equal.*

How did he know my mantras?

I didn't have time to figure it out. The servants threw open the doors, and the oldest one, who looked severe and gaunt in his tux, made an announcement. "The vampire queen-elect of the Central United States."

The grand ballroom sported multiple chandeliers hanging from the ceiling, stone walls, marble floors, and a fireplace large enough for three people to stand upright in. A hundred or more vamps stood around in groups, dressed in their finest duds and holding crystal glasses of blood. They turned their gazes to us, taking me in before they bowed their heads, fell back to open a path to the front of the room, and repeated in unison, "My queen."

Standing at the front, one male's head—covered with thick

brown hair and jelled to messy perfection—didn't bow. The glass the male vamp held was filled with bubbly champagne rather than blood. His gaze ignored my entourage, his eyes instead doing a slow slide up my legs with heart-stopping intensity. They followed the shape of my hips, skipping over the gathered tulle at my stomach and landing on my cleavage. He scanned my whip bracelet, the muscles in my arms, the pulse beating at the base of my throat.

Finally, he raised his gaze to meet my dark-rimmed eyes, giving me a full-on challenge.

My perusal of him was quicker, less blatant, and more about his weaponry than his body proportions, although those were quite nice. Black leather was his choice du jour from the jacket to the pants and barely concealed the line of the sword he carried at his waist. His feet were encased in thick black boots, steel-toed no doubt, and a wide belt with two rows of sharp studs—similar to the ones on my special-made enforcer boots—hugged his waist. A plain white t-shirt peeked out from under his leather jacket and was most likely the only piece of clothing on his body not concealing a weapon.

He regarded me with a mix of rebellion and magnetism. It wasn't a glamour, just the stature of a confident vamp very high up in the food chain with a chip on his shoulder. He could have been trying out for axe man in the Chaos Demons or one of the endless pretty actors who appeared on the CW or ABC Family TV shows.

"Your new queen has arrived. Finally," he added in a tone of mock regard. His deep voice echoed off the stones. "And she is a double rainbow of demon, isn't she folks?"

That's Alexandru, Damon said. *One of Vlad's sons. Weapons expert and Carpathia House Master and protector.*

Weapons expert. That explained the armor. Master and

protector of the house explained the attitude. *Impertinent little vamp.*

Damon chuckled beside me. *Make nice, Kali.*

I snorted. This could only be described as one of my worst nightmares—being the center of attention in a room full of Undead and expected to *be nice.*

Worse, I found Alexandru likable and not just because he was a pretty boy. The renegade attitude was done to perfection, from his clothes to his bored, half-lidded eyes and deriding tone of voice. A vamp, yes, but an interesting one.

Releasing Damon's arm, I signaled Cole to stay put and sent Alexandru a calculating smile. I strolled toward him, and as I did so, the watching vamps on each side of me dropped one by one to their knees, reminding me of a crowd of sports fans doing a reverse wave. As they bent down, they murmured "my queen" again under their collective breath. Apprehension and reluctant respect rolled off them as I continued my approach to Alexandru.

The only ones who didn't show respect were three males off to one side. Toel's buddies from the previous night. Apparently, they'd forgotten their vows to me already. Guess I'd have to teach them a lesson before the sun rose.

I stopped directly in front of Alexandru and tipped up my chin. He gave me a curious return stare, waiting to see what I would say or do. Not wanting to leave him in suspense, I plucked the champagne glass out of his hand and took an exaggerated, lingering sip.

His eyes widened ever so slightly, his magic reaching out to tease mine. It was intense and virile, clawing at the cage surrounding it. The cage, however, was secure, reminding me of my own.

Hmm. What would it take to make him lose control?

Licking my lips, I loosed my magic, allowing it to reach out and play with his. His pupils expanded, grew darker. Ah, yes, there it was. Lust. Desire. Power. Those things I could manipulate with or without magic.

I swirled the champagne in the glass, bubbles rising to the top in a frenzy. "I appreciate the warm welcome, Dru."

The use of a nickname, probably one he hated, got him. But he didn't get mad as I'd expected. Instead, he gave me a cocky, pulse-skipping grin and lowered his voice. "I'll show you my weapons if you show me yours."

I gave him my Bambi eyes. "What weapons?"

His grin widened. He raised his voice for all to hear. "The queen-elect wishes you all to return to your drinks and conversation until the midnight hour."

Murmurs rose around us as the Undead did as instructed, reforming into groups intent on gossiping and drinking. Alexandru and I stayed eye-locked in a mental showdown. From the corner of my eyes, I saw vamps shooting us curious stares. Toel's minions glared openly.

In my head, Damon chastised me. *I said play nice, not undermine Alexandru's power in front of his house.*

This was why I hated Damon looking over my shoulder in the field. He understood power in the political arena he worked in inside the Institute's walls. Street power was a foreign language. But it was a language I was pretty comfortable with, especially when it came to a hard-ass vamp who needed a little challenge in his life.

However, I wasn't up for a mental showdown with Damon during this foray. I wanted him off my back, and acting like a humble employee was the best way to achieve that. *Sorry, boss. I'll do better.*

There was more grumbling in my head, and then he told me he and the rest of the Council had been asked to meet in private with Vlad, Rafael, and Juliana. The Prince of the

Undead was staying in his chambers until the official ceremony. They'd be upstairs for an hour or so.

Behave yourself, he added. *You represent the Bridge Council.*

I represented the Council, but not enough to know the secret handshake that got me into their meeting. And so much for him staying with me every step of the way.

Be careful, I told him, miffed that I wasn't invited and concerned that being in this house surrounded by vampires was still a bad, bad idea.

He told me not to worry, and the Damon-invoked pressure in my head cleared.

I was still invading Dru's space and should have broken eye contact and stepped back, but he was so damn cute I couldn't resist. His magic continued to tease mine, which I rather liked.

The grin on his face teased me as well. "Nice play, demon, but I do have to ask you to surrender your weapons."

"No dice." I sipped the champagne. It was the real stuff, not just sparkling wine. "This is delicious."

"The devil's wine," he said, retrieving the glass and taking a drink. There was something intimate about the way he sipped from the opposite side, his gaze never leaving mine. "I imagine you have a refined palate for the stuff."

"I grew up in the Roman Empire at the feet of Queen Maria. My refined palate is thanks to her, not the devil."

He gave a tilt of his head. "Touché." Handing me the glass, he snapped his fingers at a passing servant who hustled over to refill it. "Now, about your weapons."

Cole wormed his way closer, Maddy his petite shadow. "I never go anywhere unarmed."

"You're safe here. No one will harm the queen-elect."

"I'm not worried about the vamps in this room." That was a lie, but he didn't need to know my imagination was running wild with worst-case scenarios. "I'm worried about outside intruders."

"You have enemies who would breach the House of Carpathia to get to you?"

"Currently, Toel Chase heads my list of enemies. Not hard for him to breach your doorstep."

Dru's hand went to his sword's hilt. His fingers dug into the pommel.

No love lost between those two. That worked to my advantage. "He's caused me quite a bit of grief in the past few days, killed a Bridge employee, and his last message was a direct threat to my life."

Another squeeze of the pommel. "He will be dealt with after the coronation. You have my word."

"Do you know where he is?"

"Let's walk, shall we? I'll show you the house's security. It'll make you feel safer."

Didn't answer my question. Irritating, but I allowed him to take my elbow and guide me through the throng of people.

Magic buzzed from his fingertips into my skin. A pleasant sensation set up camp in my stomach.

Cole and Maddy fell into step behind us. Dru leaned over, lips close to my ear. "We're being stalked."

"My bodyguard and assistant."

"Even with a bodyguard, you carry weapons?"

"How do you know I'm carrying?"

He squeezed my elbow and a zing of magic laced its way up my arm. "X-ray vision."

Right. "A man of many talents."

"Many," he agreed with a smirk.

The crowd parted before us, and the vamps bowed again. I took it in stride. This time, there was less resistance in the air as I passed. Dru's acceptance earned a bit of respect.

Approaching the doors, I noticed Victoria standing by herself, chewing on a fingernail.

"Do you have anyone who might take a newly turned vamp under their wing?" I asked, motioning my chin at Vicky.

Dru hesitated a second, snapped his fingers at someone in the crowd. A female hurried over. He whispered in her ear and she went off to introduce herself to Vicky. The new vamp gave me a half-grateful look as we passed by. She was still pissed, but she was awed by the fancy digs and power radiating throughout the room. If she had to give up being a witch, this was the next best thing.

We moved into the foyer, and Dru led me toward one of the matching grand staircases. "This is usually the point where my sire gives the history of the house and its significance to the Undead dynasty to visiting guests. Do you really care?"

I didn't. I'd lived enough history for three demons and never found much point in hearing about more. But his voice was pleasant, and I wanted him on my side later if the Noctifectors showed up. "How about the highlights?"

With each step up the plushy carpeted stairs, he reiterated a fact about the house, its construction, inhabitants, and place in the Undead hierarchy. In some ways, it mimicked the Institute, providing housing, training, and resources for its brand of supernaturals. At the top of the stairs, we faced a wide hallway with crimson-colored doors on both sides. Hand-painted portraits of various important vamps hung in elaborate gold frames.

I recognized dark brows and haughty eyes in one as we passed the first crimson door. "Is that you?"

"Linen ruff and all." He released my elbow and opened a door with a gold nameplate labeled Security Operations. "I hated those damn neck chokers."

"At least you didn't have to wear a corset."

REVENGE IS SWEET   321

His eyes flashed, pupils darkening as his gaze grazed over the exposed skin of my décolletage. The strapless dress required a bra that pushed my meager assets to new heights, and I could see Dru imagining me in nothing but a fine-boned corset.

Dream on, buddy boy. I had no intention of pursuing anything more than Dru's allegiance, but flirting with him was fun and entertaining. Flirting was also the fastest way to secure a bond.

Cole and Maddy walked several steps behind us, and Dru cut his eyes from my chest long enough to give Cole a look that suggested he wasn't welcome in Carpathia's security control center.

Cole's return look said, *fuck you.*

"Your minions must wait outside," Dru said to me, still locking eyes with Cole. The magic seeping from his body had shifted from sexy and flirty to edgy and challenging.

"My bodyguard goes where I go."

Maddy raised a hand. "Me, too."

Dru positioned himself between me and them. He looked down at me, his eyes for once serious. "No one goes into the security room unless they have spoken an oath to my sire and pledged their allegiance to this house."

Oaths. Dangerous stuff. Would have been nice if Damon had mentioned that little fact. Probably one of the things he'd wanted to discuss with me on the way over. "Then why take me in?"

"You're queen-elect. At midnight, you'll swear your fidelity to my sire. An oath to protect this house and our family."

A champagne revolt ensued in my stomach. Really should have found out about that oath stuff beforehand. "What if I change my mind and don't swear my fidelity to your dad?"

Dru let out a sad breath. "Then I'll have to kill you."

I thought maybe he was kidding in that *I'd tell you, but I'd have to kill you way,* but he still seemed dead serious.

All righty, then. He could try to kill me, but he'd fail.

Of course, if I didn't take the oath, Damon would find me in contempt of Bridge law and do something nasty to me and my blood slaves. Vicky was no longer a problem, but Arman and Rad were. I had no doubt Damon would eventually find out Rad was tied to me, just like Arman.

"What happens when my temporary reign as queen is over?" I punched him lightly on the arm, trying to ease the tension. "Will you have to kill me then?"

Dru's dark brows slanted down. "Temporary?"

"Yeah, you know. I'm only doing this queen gig until you find a qualified candidate to take Nudra's place. By the way, I don't recommend Toel Chase."

My attempt at snarky humor failed. His frown deepened. "There is no 'temporary' oath, demon. If you pledge to be queen of the Undead of this region, it is for life."

For half a second, I wondered if I could hurry the Noctifectors' surprise attack along. No way was I pledging permanent allegiance to the Prince of the Undead. It was one thing to defend a nest of vamps against our common enemy, the Noctifectors. Another to bend over and take it in the ass from Vlad the Impaler.

Damon and I were definitely having a heart-to-heart before midnight.

I laid a hand on Dru's arm to calm him and spoke to Cole. "I'll be fine. Stay out here and wait for me."

Cole's expression never changed, but he nodded. He was pissed at being left behind, and I didn't want him that far away from me if things went wrong, as Rad had suggested they might, but I needed to see what kind of security Carpathia had. If the Noctifectors were going to hit, they'd do it at midnight during the ceremony. That was their best chance to take the vamps—and us demons—by surprise. I had an hour tops to scope out the grounds and house and develop a defense plan.

"Come on, Alexandru." I tugged him across the threshold into security command central. "Show me your weapons."

FORTY-FIVE

The moment the door closed behind us, Dru backed me against the wall, raised the skirt of my dress, and slid his fingers over my outer right thigh, landing on the stake secured there.

"Tsk, tsk," he muttered, his face an inch from mine as he drew it out of the holder. "What do we have here?"

I could have fought him, and I suspected he'd make a formidable opponent. Now wasn't the time to prove my superiority. "Is this how you treat all your queens?"

"You're not my queen, and the only vampire I answer to is my sire."

The Undead hierarchy was a confusing mess of titles that made no sense to me, and I'd been around to see many kingdoms come and go. "The stake is for personal protection. You wouldn't deny me that, would you?"

He stuck the sharpened wood in the waistband of his pants at the small of his back and trailed fingers over other parts of my body, searching for more weapons. "And the whip? That's simply for adornment?"

Cheeky. "What can I say? I know how to accessorize."

His laugh was low and deep. Satisfied I wasn't carrying anything else, he stepped back, righted my skirt, and didn't try to take Volante. Smart vamp. "Why would you agree to become queen of this House, Kali Sweet?"

A top-level vampire who called me by the correct name— that earned him a kernel of truth. "The Bridge Council believes this arrangement will be mutually beneficial to both of our groups."

"Do you always do what the Bridge Council wants?"

"Do you always do what your father wants?"

He conceded with a smile. "Come on. Let's look at my security system."

The room was well-lit and almost homey. Hardwood floors, bookshelves, and a flatscreen on all four walls. In one corner, a dorm-size fridge, microwave, and sink. Across from it was a lounging area with sofas, end tables, and a stack of magazines on a coffee table.

The bulk of computers were centered in the middle of the floor, with comfortable chairs at each station. Minions in black pants and white shirts wore headsets and watched the screens in front of them along with those on the TVs. Views of the mansion, inside and out, as well as the grounds, flashed on their displays.

Dru walked me through the room, introduced me to his people, and gave me a laundry list of specs about the cameras, ground patrols, sentries, and tripwires. He talked logistics and staffing with the same ease as I talked vengeance. The whole layout was impressive—almost as impressive as the Institute's.

More impressive was the Master Vamp's love of this part of his job. His voice and body language told me he enjoyed being the point man in protecting the House. He loved being in charge of security, weapons, and soldiers. He was proud of his kingdom and would defend it until the last breath left his body. He was Cole in Undead form.

"So you see, queen-elect, you're in good hands inside Carpathia."

Except that I had an ass full of vampires. So far, though, they'd all been on their best behavior. If they'd planned some underhanded assassination of me and Bridge Council, they'd probably already done their worst. Since I was still standing, odds were I was simply paranoid. The only vamp going to cause me trouble was Toel, and only if he somehow managed to slip past the guards. Even the Nocts were going to have a hard time sliding under the radar in a sneak attack.

I wondered what Damon, Yasmin, and Kirill were doing with the Prince. "Any chance, as Master of this house, you could walk me through the ins and outs of the coronation cere-mony before it goes down? All that oath stuff?"

His dark brows descended. "You have no idea what you're getting into, do you?"

Trouble. That's what I was getting into. Nothing new about that. "I don't have to drink anyone's blood, do I? Or bathe in it?"

"Only the blood of your followers."

The muscles in my jaws tightened involuntarily as if I were going to hurl. "The vamps who kneeled in the ballroom? All of them?"

"There are only a hundred or so. They represent the different districts in the Central region. They expose their necks in an act of submission, and you drink from them."

Only a hundred or so. Gaw. "But I'm not a vamp."

"You have teeth, don't you?"

"How about we shake on it instead?"

His laughter came slow and light, then deepened into belly laughs. "You should see your face right now." He chucked my chin with his fist. "Priceless."

"You're yanking my chain."

He wrapped an arm around my shoulders and led me to the door. "An outdated ritual, but one my sire still employs. He likes bloody ceremonies. This is America, however, and Carpathia is my House. If you don't want to drink directly from your subjects, you don't need to. They do have to swear allegiance to you, but it can be a handshake if you so desire."

We stepped into the hall and Cole immediately zeroed in on Dru's arm around my shoulders. He gave me a questioning glance, and I winked at him. "Anticlimactic, I imagine, for your father."

"After almost six centuries, he's a bit pompous. I'll back you up."

He steered us deeper into the second floor's interior, stopping outside of a pair of wooden French doors stained almost black. A gold sign on the wall next to them announced this was Dru's office. A touch of his hand and the doors swung open in a grand gesture.

Magic. It made even the little things fun.

Cole and Maddy followed us inside, and Dru made no move to stop them.

The office, if you could call it that, resembled a swanky living room in an upscale European hotel. But where the rest of Carpathia was heavy on formal furniture and vintage trappings, Dru's office was the height of modern casual. Chocolate leather sectionals, the latest gaming system hooked up to an enormous flatscreen, Linkin Park coming from the speakers overhead. His desk, a chrome and glass concoction, was littered with sports drink bottles and candy bar wrappers.

At the sectional, he dropped his arm, strolled over to a built-in bar, and opened a cabinet door to reveal a refrigerator. "Drink?"

More sports drinks, cans of soda, and bottles of water. Not a container of any size or shape filled with blood.

Curioser and curioser.

Maddy dropped onto the sectional next to me. "I'll have a root beer."

Cole, hanging around the door and doing his warrior evaluation of the room's strengths and weaknesses, shook his head.

Dru gave Maddy a disapproving look. "The queen-elect is served first, vampire. And she sits alone."

Maddy stuck her tongue out at him but rose, gave an exaggerated curtsy, and flounced over to the other end of the sectional. "Root beer, please," she said, giving Dru a false smile.

He ignored her impertinence, for which I was grateful. "Kali? Anything?"

"Just the details about the coronation."

Dru handed Maddy her soda and grabbed a red sports drink for himself. He took a swig, leaned back on the cabinet, and began peeling the paper off the outside of the bottle. "It's rather like...a requiem. Formal. Father says his lines; you say yours. You agree to help guard, protect, and lead the House and the Undead citizens of the Central region in following our rules and regulations. The vampires of the house come forth one at a time and pledge their allegiance to you and reaffirm their allegiance to my father. There's a lot of archaic bullshit that no one actually holds you to, but Father insists we go through the motions. It's over in a matter of minutes."

"What exactly are my lines?"

Dru set down the drink and walked across the room to a bookcase loaded with row after row of nearly identical leather-bound books. They resembled volumes of legal precedents in a lawyer's office. He perused one shelf with a long finger and found the tomb he sought.

Returning to me on the sectional, he flipped open the book

and thumbed through the beginning pages. "Here," he said, holding the book out to me. "Memorize these."

Sure enough, there was a script for the coronation detailing Vlad's lines and mine. Kings and queens, although of the same rank in the House, had different responsibilities to the members and to the Master and his sire. A queen's vows differed from a king's and were quite sexist, but we were dealing with a leader who'd grown up in the Middle Ages.

I flipped the page, skimming the promises I would verbally make to the Prince and his Undead nation and vaguely committing them to memory in case we got that far during the ceremony. For grins and giggles, I flipped through the following sections describing my duties once the vows were over. I stumbled upon a section titled *Servicing Your Master*, and my flipping finger paused.

Although I was pretty sure I didn't want to know what that entailed, I still couldn't divert my curiosity. My throat tightened as I read. 'Servicing' was part of the job description for both king and queen and was defined as giving the Master of the House whatever he wanted, whenever he wanted it, to make his life easier.

I tapped the section and raised my eyes to Dru. "This is one of those archaic bullshit sections you were talking about, right?"

He didn't even read the title; he simply smiled at me, pupils darkening. Magic enveloped me, heating the exposed skin at my throat and going lower. Taking the book from my hands, he tossed it on the coffee table and drew me off the couch.

"That policy, my sweet demon, is still in effect." He leaned forward and laid a gentle kiss on my cheek. "And I intend to explore it fully with you once you're queen."

FORTY-SIX

I stared into his eyes, magic swirling around us, and thought, *maybe in another time and place*. But there was no way. Not here. Not now. Not when he was a vampire, and I was a mixed-up mess over Rad.

Besides, I was pretty sure he was yanking my chain again.

A knock on the door saved me from replying. Without taking his gaze from me, Dru called out, "Enter."

A female servant in a black dress and white apron opened the door and bowed her head. "The Prince is ready."

Dru took a step back, held out his arm. "Shall we?"

Vlad might have been ready, but I wasn't. The time was finally here but there was no way I could go through with being vamp queen, regardless of the servicing stuff. I hated vamps, Dru and Maddy the current exceptions.

Out of all the supernaturals I'd ever faced, vamps were my favorite to dust. I would have been more than happy if all of them, my two new friends the exceptions, were wiped off the planet. But here I was, about to become vamp queen.

Damn Nudra. This was his fault. Even in death, he was still screwing me over.

Turning back wasn't an option. I'd given my word to Damon that I would do this in order to save my blood slaves and my job. I would act as the Bridge Council's tool to bridge—there was no better word for it—the chasm between the Council and the Undead nation, making us both stronger. I wouldn't have to fight vamps anymore. Once this group swore fidelity to me, they also swore it to the Bridge Council, just like I was swearing allegiance to the Prince.

A new chapter was about to unfold in the supernatural world, and I was making it happen.

I won't lie. Pride swelled inside my chest as I rested my arm in Dru's. Besides the pretty boy being Master, and an entertaining challenge at that, there was a perk to becoming queen. Toel Chase was going to eat his grave dirt.

I smiled at Dru. "You'll help me deal with Toel after the coronation, right?"

"My pleasure."

"Well, then, lead the way."

My entrance into the ballroom was once again received with bowed heads, bent knees, and a fresh flute of champagne. A raised dais had been uncovered on the north side with three royalty-worthy chairs propped on it. The largest sat in the middle on a second platform, raising it considerably above the other two. Vlad's, I supposed, but he was nowhere to be seen.

Damon and company were on the right side in a second set of ornate chairs. To the left, Juliana and Rafael sat in full view of the crowd with an empty chair between them—Toel's.

I whispered in Cole's ear to stay near Damon and keep eye contact with me. He took Maddy's arm, and the two of them skirted the outside of the crowd.

I wanted to talk to Damon a moment before it all went

down, so as Dru led me toward the dais, I told him I needed to do so. He dropped me off in front of Damon and walked up the stairs to sit on the right side of Vlad's chair.

Upon my arrival, Damon rose, and I tugged him off to the side. "How was your meeting?"

"Fortuitous. And your time with Alexandru?"

Fortuitous. Such a Damon word. "The same, although I have some deep reservations about what they're asking me to agree to in order to be queen. You are going to come to bat for me and get me excused from some of the archaic bullshit, right?"

"One day at a time, Kali. Let's get through tonight first. Tomorrow, we'll tackle your reservations. Remember, what you're doing is historic and requires tact and compromise. A touch of humility would be welcome as well."

Humility? Right.

His lips pinched. "We both know you lack interpersonal skills and common sense. Perhaps tonight, you'll school yourself in both."

Ouch. "I have interpersonal skills. They may not be polished like yours, but that doesn't mean I have none. In fact, I've made quite a good impression on my new friend over there."

We both glanced at Dru, who was watching me closely. One edge of his mouth tipped up.

"I can see that," Damon replied, tone dry as vamp dust. "But the real test is yet to come in the form of Alexandru's sire."

"I was thinking about that. What if I stake Vlad instead? Wouldn't that solve a lot of our problems?"

Damon closed his eyes for a long moment, digging for patience. When he reopened them, his eyes were hard and flat. "This is no joking matter, Kali."

Who was joking? "Did Rafael, Juliana, or Vlad mention their black sheep?"

Damon shook his head. "They haven't seen Toel since our meeting at the Institute. They wouldn't admit it, but they're worried he's gone rogue."

Rogue vampire. My favorite.

A loud chiming echoed through the room, signifying midnight was upon us. Vamps scurried into rows, some vying with others for a better view. Damon gave me a slight push in the small of my back toward the dais and resumed his seat.

Okay, I told myself, swallowing hard as I headed for the chair waiting for me. The clock gong echoed loudly in my head. *Let the nightmare begin.*

Dru gave me another pulse-tripping grin, and I forced myself to smile back. Behind Damon, Cole watched me and nodded ever so slightly to let me know he wouldn't let anything happen to me or the Council. Maddy smiled wide and gave me a thumbs-up.

Lifting my eyes to the elongated windows on the second story, I prayed that Rad and his Noct friends came to my rescue, and at the same time, I prayed they'd steer clear of tonight's doings.

Because even if they crashed the party before I took my vows, I would defend the Undead to the bitter end.

FORTY-SEVEN

One of the Disney theme parks had lost a pirate.

Vlad, the Prince of the Undead, was over six feet tall with a strange bulbous stomach. Long, thin hair hung in ringlets around his face, and a mustache sat under his thin, fleshless nose. Skinny arms and legs gave him a definite cartoon character appearance.

He wore clothing that emphasized his odd body shape— flashy gold and black duds, white socks up to his knees, and black pointed shoes. Around his neck, a large gold cross. I didn't think it was possible for a vampire to be unattractive, but the head of the vamps was ugly even in demon terms.

Serendipitously, I glanced at Dru. While his father stood in the doorway, pausing for everyone to get a good look at him, all I could wonder was how Vlad had sired such a beautiful son.

Dru rose to his feet, as did the rest of the crowd. I followed suit. As Vlad strolled down the aisle, passing his vamp minions with his nose in the air, they went to their knees like they'd done for me. Toel's crew of followers knelt as well, but when they rose again, daggers shot from their eyes, all aimed at me.

Aw, wasn't that sweet.

I shot a few back for good measure.

Vlad stopped and chatted with Damon, then walked across the aisle to acknowledge Juliana and Rafael. It all reminded me of the President before a State of the Union address—handshaking, back slapping, and preening for the home audience.

After the final exchange with his regional managers, Vlad faced us. Dru went down on one knee, and taking my cue from him, I did the same. Maybe it was the dress or perhaps the rebel in me, but I went down slowly. The dais's marble floor was hard and cold.

Pressure filled my head. *Very nice, Kali.*

Since Damon had a backside view, I wasn't sure if he was referring to my supplicant position or my ass. Better not to ask.

Vlad took his seat. Dru rose, helped me to my feet. Then he took my hand and turned me toward his father. "My sire," he said, his voice again carrying throughout the room and bouncing off the stones. "I present the queen-elect for the Central United States of America."

I met Vlad the Impaler's eyes and ice rushed down my spine. This vampire had tortured thousands of humans, created a whole race of blood-sucking Undead. Everything in me wanted to remove him from the Earth. Send him straight to hell, where he belonged.

Easy, demon.

It was rare for Damon to purposely remind me of who I was. In this case, his words did two things: first, they reinforced that I was a demon and, as such, the highest predator on the food chain in this room. Second, they made me his enforcer, subject to his and the Council's decisions.

In other words, he put me in my place with one word.

So, while I *could* exterminate the big bad vamp, I would do so at great cost, jeopardizing the Council's safety and my own demon life.

I bowed my head slightly at Vlad but refused to break eye contact.

He wasn't called the Prince of the Undead for nothing. Tainted magic filled the air and sucked my breath away. A creepy-crawly sensation ran over the back of my neck and a sharp pain burst inside both ears.

I flinched but still refused to break eye contact. I touched my fingers and thumbs together and raised my protective shield, bouncing Vlad's tainted magic back at him.

The vamps in the room felt it, and their gasps broke the silence. He didn't react except for the thin line of his lips firming.

I expected Damon to yell in my head. Instead, he said, *careful. Don't give away too much.*

Damon didn't want Vlad to know just how powerful I was. Interesting.

I stepped forward and gave the Prince a confident smile. "Kali Sweet at your service."

"Kali Sweet, queen-elect." Vlad's Romanian accent was heavy and thick. "You are pledged to the Undead of this region to be their queen. To honor, protect, and lead them in accordance with my wishes. Do you accept this role with gravity and the respect due it?"

Merde. I opened my mouth; nothing came out. Damon's voice prompted me. *I do.*

What was this a marriage ceremony? "I'll do my best," I answered honestly.

Vlad stared his dead-eyed stare. Guess my best wasn't good enough.

So I lied. "Yes."

"Kali Sweet, queen-elect, do you accept your Undead brothers and sisters with open arms?"

Open arms and a sharp stake. "I do."

"Do you submit your will to mine?"

Hell no. Again, my lips parted to answer, but the word I needed to say wouldn't come out.

Please, Kali. Do this for me.

'Please' from Damon was another unusual event. I rubbed my temple, took a deep breath, and considered all he had done for me through the years. I would never submit my will to Vlad, but I owed Damon.

It took every bit of willpower to open my mouth, but I did it, looking Vlad squarely in the eye and leaving no doubt I was doing this for the Bridge Council. "Yes."

For a second, all was silent. Vlad studied me, looking for deceit in my face, my tone, anything. Again, I maintained eye contact, knowing I dared not look away and give him an excuse to doubt me. We held each other's gazes, me attempting to look honest. It worked.

He gave a minuscule nod to Dru.

Dru's hand grabbed my arm and swiveled me toward the audience. "My brothers and sisters, I present the queen of the Central United States of America."

Reserved applause filled the room. They were no happier to put me in this position than I was to find myself there. However, a pang of compassion gave me pause. Maddy and Dru had opened my eyes to the fact there were a few decent vamps around. Maybe more than a few. There were Undead servants and blood slaves who hadn't asked to be turned and had had their human lives taken away from them. Perhaps in my new role as queen, I could ferret out the evil vamps and help the not-so-bad ones.

I nodded to the group, acknowledging them, and the

applause escalated a fraction. I bowed my head and smiled to myself. I would make this work—for them, for the Council, for me.

But I froze when I looked up again at my new Undead brothers and sisters.

At the back of the room, standing in the doorway looking every bit the California surfer dude, was Toel Chase.

FORTY-EIGHT

He paid me a mock salute.

"How did he get in here?" I murmured to Dru.

The answer came when the two guards who'd flanked the outside door walked in behind Toel and stopped on either side of him, standing behind his lean body.

So much for security.

Toel wore a tux sans tie. Also, without proper shoes. Ragged flip-flops adorned his feet and smacked irreverently as he took a few steps forward. Without a word, he made eye contact with the three stooges in the back and they fell in behind the guards.

At the same time, I sensed movement to my left. Cole slid behind me, disregarding Vlad and skirting the empty chairs Dru and I had sat in. His chest was close enough to my back that I felt the heat coming off him. His magic tingled against mine.

Dru also shifted closer, his body in front of me but off to the side—not crowding me but guarding me, nonetheless. That he would do such a thing—make it clear to Toel and the others in the room that he stood with me—gave me pause. He hadn't made any vow to me, and yet he was willing to take on the West Coast King to defend me. That one action moved him into the potential friend category.

Toel strolled down the center of the room, more and more Undead falling in behind him. Didn't surprise me. He was a vampire, already a regional manager, and had made it clear to the general vamp population that he didn't want me leading them any more than they did. Rallying the troops was strategic to creating a strong showing in front of the Prince.

Vlad's voice boomed behind me, making me start as it filled the room. Dru may not have favored his father in the looks department—lucky for him—but the commanding voice was a dead ringer. "Toel," he said, clear reprehension in his tone. "You're late."

He sounded like a father who was aggravated that his kid was late for dinner, which was not exactly the reaction I was expecting.

Toel shrugged, gave me the stink eye. "Speed bump slowed me down, dude."

Great. We were back to surf talk and lousy acting.

Maddy maneuvered through the crowd behind Toel, edging closer and giving me a wink over his left shoulder. What was she up to?

Cole's breath warmed my ear. "Vamp or not, the guy's a douchebag."

I seconded that. "I thought your men were going to arrest him if he showed," I whispered to Dru.

He was gritting his jaw so hard that muscles jumped. "Seems that didn't happen."

Sounds of movement came from Vlad's direction. He appeared on Dru's right, walked past the three of us, and down the stairs, meeting Toel at the halfway point. Again, not the reaction I was expecting. The Prince meeting a renegade manager on the floor instead of making him bow at his feet? And why wasn't he demanding the houseguards take him into custody?

Did vamps take other vamps into custody?

"What's he doing?" I wondered out loud.

"Your stake." Dru shifted to his left, moving closer to me. "The one I took from you? Get it out of my pants."

For a second, I didn't understand what that had to do with Vlad and Toel. Then I did. Sort of. The details weren't clear, but the hum of magic coming off Dru's body and the tight jaw told me enough. Fighting was an option on the night's menu.

I slipped my fingers underneath his shirttail, fingertips skimming his naked back as I searched for the short stake he'd secured in the waist of his pants. He tensed ever so slightly at my touch, and our magics collided in a hot spark. I nearly jumped from the collision of magical electrons. For all his bluff and talk, he could back it up with the goods. He was as magically skilled as his father.

All eyes were on Vlad and Toel, but it wouldn't do for anyone to notice I was arming myself. I eased the stake out and covertly snugged it inside the gathered tulle on the front of my dress. I also let the handle of my whip slide into my hand. Volante hummed with anticipation, knowing she was going to spill blood—and soon.

Vlad towered over his manager as he grabbed Toel by the shoulders. He seemed oblivious to the group behind him, oblivious to any of the rest of us. "Toel, my son. It's good to see you."

The whole room sucked in a noisy breath of surprise.

I was a bit surprised myself. "My son?" I hissed in Dru's ear. "Tell me he means that in a sire-to-underling manner."

"Afraid not." Dru's mouth firmed before he spit out the next words. "Toel is my half-brother. My half-brother and the black sheep of the family whom my father never recognized until he gave him the Western Region. Vlad was making the official announcement that Toel is his son tonight."

My eyes rolled back so far in my head that I nearly fell over. The CW didn't have the market for vampire family dramas.

There were so many ways this meeting was about to go wrong I clenched my whip handle harder. "Is there an egress from this room other than those main doors?"

"Northeast corner. The servant entrance is hidden in the wall. Takes you to the kitchen."

Damon. I replayed the words in my head. *Did you get that?*

Pressure tightened the skin at my temples. *Leaving at this juncture would be rude.*

That's what he was worried about? Being rude? *It could also save your Archdemon ass. Now go.*

Not yet.

For fuck's sake. I reached back and touched Cole. A simple gesture between warriors. "If things go south, get them out of here for me."

Neither of us knew what exactly was going to happen, but we knew it wouldn't be a pleasant walk around Lake Michigan. He released a tight sigh, torn between me and them.

"Please," I said softly. "They're more important."

Knowing I was right, he said nothing and returned my touch with his own, giving my hand a firm squeeze.

Vlad embraced Toel. Over his father's shoulder, Toel smirked at me. Typically, I would have raised my middle finger, but it was better to play him, so I smiled back like I was enjoying the show.

The light in his eyes changed, going from muted and disinterested to too bright, too focused.

What the hell was he up to?

Toel wanted power, lots of it, and at that moment, he held

the ultimate vampire power in a close embrace. My breath caught as his audacious plan unfolded in my brain. According to Dru, this was his coming out party, so to speak. Toel planned to come out in a big, big way.

He who held Vlad, or Vlad s position, held the Undead world.

And I'd thought Nudra was an ambitious prick.

"He's not after me," I said, as much to myself as to Cole and Dru. "He's after the Prince."

Dru shot me a weird look, but I saw the idea didn't shock him. He ground his teeth together once more and reached for his sword.

I'd learned long ago to keep track of my enemy's hands. Their faces wouldn't kill you. It was the hands and the weapons they held that would do that. As Vlad leaned back, putting space between his and Toel's bodies, both of Toel's hands disappeared from my sight.

"Separate them," I told Dru. "Now."

Vlad raised his voice to the murmuring crowd and turned Toel to face them. "Here is my son, Toel Chase, who has honored my name in the Western Region of the United States and will secure the foothold vampires have established in the Northern Hemisphere."

Applause rang out, much heartier than the applause for me. Some vamps whistled and hooted. Others looked confused.

I was in the confused camp.

With cat-like precision, Dru moved near his father's right shoulder. As Vlad moved Toel in an arc, showing him off to the room full of vamps, Dru leaned in and said something in Vlad's ear.

The Prince of the Undead slowly raised his eyes to me. They were as black as Toel's tux and filled with hatred. How dare I try to ruin his party.

Damon, I questioned my boss, *should I intercede if Toel tries to take Vlad out?*

I waited for the pressure. Waited for the answer. It took so long to come that I nearly looked over my shoulder to see if Damon and the others had left as I'd requested.

Toel faced me, making his circuit under his father's guiding hands, his superior look taunting. He thought himself untouchable—above not only me but also the room of vampires.

One of his hands disappeared into his jacket.

Damon!

His voice finally appeared in my head. *Think before you act. We don't know what Toel is planning.*

Thinking took too long. Either I acted now while I had a clear shot, or my chance was over.

Volante slid off my arm to coil on the floor. I flicked my gaze to Dru. His hand was on his sword handle, and he gave me the briefest nod. He understood my conundrum and was giving me permission.

The demon in me prepared to strike. Then the weirdest thing happened...

I hesitated.

There were too many politics at play here. What if Dru was the one manipulating me? While I'd put him in my potential friend column, I hardly knew him or his underlying family issues. The political issues were all mixed in there as well. He'd known Vlad was going to publically acknowledge Toel. He didn't like Toel. My feelings for the *dude* aside, I didn't want to be played into taking out Toel to ensure Dru's standing if it initiated a war or plunked me face-first in the hot seat.

Toel drew a stake from his jacket. Vlad couldn't see it since Toel was facing away from him. Only twenty-four hours ago, I'd believed Vlad could eat Toel for lunch if Toel so much as stepped on the Prince's big toe. Now that wasn't the case.

While Vlad had no qualms about eating his young, he wasn't prepared for Toel to attempt such an outright defiant gesture as patricide.

This, however, was Toel. Two-faced, underhanded, and lousy at pool.

And I was no coward when it came to the hot seat.

"Dru!" I yelled, snapping my whip up at the same time.

Without hesitation, he grabbed Vlad's arm with one hand and shoved his father out of harm's way. The crowd gasped in shock.

The tip of Volante curled around the stake in Toel's hand, and I gave it a solid jerk, ripping it from his grasp. Dru extracted his sword with his other hand—a beautiful schiavona —and pointed it at Toel's neck.

Behind me, Cole grunted again and said, "Be right back." Then his body heat disappeared. I heard scuffling and knew he was rounding up the Council and forcing them through the servant's exit.

One last thing to worry about.

The stake flew into my waiting hand. After recovering from Dru's shove, Vlad righted himself, tugged on his pirate tunic, and yelled, "What is the meaning of this?"

Toel raised his hands, the tip of Dru's sword millimeters from the vulnerable spot at the base of his neck. "Yes, brother," he said, but his attention wasn't on Dru. It was on me. "What is the meaning of this?"

To his credit, Dru didn't even blink. "How dare you raise a stake to our father?"

Vlad's slit-eyed gaze raced between his two sons and the stake in my hand. I held it up for everyone to see. "Toel was going to stake you, Prince, and take your place."

There wasn't as much surprise as I'd expected. In fact, the group that had gathered behind Toel now surrounded him,

Vlad, and Dru. Most looked eager, ready to jump Dru and possibly Vlad at Toel's command.

I scanned the faces for Maddy. She'd been separated from the main group and held by a tall female guard at the back of the room—in plain view and yet out of my whip's reach. I'd been too focused on Toel to notice. The guard had one arm around Maddy's neck and a skinny, finely sharpened stake pointed at her heart. Maddy's eyes showed no fear as they met mine. Her bottom lip, however, trembled.

I adjusted the stake in my hand, tossing it up and flipping it end over end in a nonchalant manner. Letting the guard assume I cared little for Maddy's well-being. If she thought that, she'd be wrong, but it might make her look for a different way to manipulate me.

Toel's gaze flicked to Dru and Vlad before cruising around those nearest him. "As if! The stake was meant as a gift to my sire. It's the stake I used to cull nonbelievers from my ranks as West Coast regional manager." He stepped away from Dru's sword and turned his back on him to face his followers.

Ballsy, this one.

"Our members have been lax in what they'll accept for too long. Lax in what they'll tolerate because our numbers have been declining. But instead of this decline bringing us closer together, it's driving us apart. Every vamp for himself mentality leaves us open to attacks." He swung back around and faced me, lifting his head. "Leaving us vulnerable to manipulation by other supernaturals."

This from the master of manipulation. At least he'd dropped the surfer lingo.

Toel stepped up to his father, Dru's sword following his head. "Let me bring back order and control to the Undead of the United States. We don't need the Bridge Council or their ridiculous demon enforcer to restore our rightful place in the supernatural world."

Making a fist, he slammed it against his chest in a dramatic gesture that looked a little too Hollywood for me. "I will restore our power by returning to the old ways. The ways you, my sire, instituted over five centuries ago. We will carve up our enemies." He cast an openly hostile glance my way. "We will dance on their graves, eat their ashes. We..."

At this, he raised his fisted hands in the air and once more turned in a circle to rally his followers. "We will lead the supernatural world. And we...will...conquer humans!"

The noise was deafening. Applause, stomping feet, the cries of warriors running into battle. The hairs on the back of my neck stood at attention.

The female holding Maddy raised her stake in the air in a victory cry. Toel's arms were also still raised, Rocky-like. Two targets, one stake.

Decisions, decisions.

Odds were, I wasn't leaving the house alive. Maddy, though, had a chance.

While I hated Toel and wanted to dust him, Maddy deserved to live more than Toel deserved to die.

Decision made.

I met The Mouse's eyes and mouthed, "Get down!"

She couldn't go far with the female guard's arm still locked around her neck, but instead of fighting against the chokehold, she went limp, letting her full body weight drag the guard's arm downward.

Good enough. I hurtled the stake, and before the guard understood what was going on, the blunt end smacked her squarely in the forehead.

Her head snapped back, eyes rolled up, and she fell backward, taking Maddy with her. I lost sight of them in the crowd, but their fall went unnoticed.

Vlad's cry of "Stop!" rose above the crowd noise, but no one was listening. Dru and I exchanged glances. Then Dru exchanged a glance with his father. While we'd unarmed Toel, he was still a dangerous entity, even to Vlad. He was rallying the vamps in his own name, threatening the newly formed bond between Vlad and the Council. Worse, he was blatantly threatening to do harm to humans. No way could I let that slide.

But I was outnumbered more than usual. Even if Cole made it back, it would be him, me, Dru, and Maddy—and she was questionable since I still hadn't seen her come up for air—against Toel and a hundred vamps itching for blood.

Blood and war lust swirled like fog in the room, pricking at my skin, my hair, my magic. Volante hummed. My demon vibrated as well, picking up on the vamps' arousal for shedding blood and creating pain. She wanted in.

There was only one way to shut Toel down and save my friends. As he faced his father, he gave me a heartless grin. His too-bright eyes were rimmed in red.

He was hungry, so I needed to give him what he wanted.

A section I'd skimmed in the canon earlier surfaced in my mind. If Toel wanted a return to the old ways, I'd give it to him.

Clearing my throat, I stroked my whip, soothing her, and waited for the vamps to quiet. Vlad was saying something I couldn't hear and shaking his head at both sons. "Toel Chase," I called out loud and clear.

When he deigned to raise his gaze to mine, I smiled down at him. "As queen of the Central Vampire Region and acquiescing servant to the Prince of the Undead, I challenge you to a hand-to-hand combat duel. If you win, I'll submit to your will"

—I used phrasing I hoped would motivate him— "and concede to your right as ruler."

His brows furrowed. The previous day's fight was still fresh in his mind. But he snorted, refusing to let me see him sweat. "And if you win?"

The only way for me to truly claim victory was to kill him, and he knew it. "I'm surprised you would even consider the option."

He grinned malevolently. "Answer me, demon. What happens if you win?"

I couldn't give the Undead contingency in that room anything they wanted. Even if I could have promised them a rosy future, my popularity ranking was already in the negatives. There was no fixing that. "Don't lose, and you won't have to worry about it."

Challenges. Power-hungry vampires can't resist them.

"Let's Barney," he snarled.

I assumed in surfer lingo, that meant let's fight. If nothing else, I had to kill him just for the atrocious overuse of what was once cool slang.

Dru stared at me, mouth agape. I gave a no-big-deal shrug even though my palms were sweating. Surprisingly, Vlad continued to intercede, grabbing Toel's arm and trying to talk to him. Toel shook him off, wiggling out of his tux jacket and handing it off to one of his stooges. Then he stalked toward me, the *smack, smack, smack* of his flip-flops echoing in the room.

Seriously? He was going to fight me in those?

For all his prowess at getting the upper hand in politics, he wasn't much of a threat physically. However, he had more to prove in front of his peers and his father.

Still, my biggest concern was my dress. Not exactly fighting attire. I debated kicking the heels off, but like all my shoes and most of my accessories, they were weapons. A well-placed kick with the spiked heel and Toel could consider his membership in the Undead society revoked.

"Drop the whip," he said.

He was taking the hand-to-hand comment to heart. Even though she protested, I let Volante's handle fall. Fisticuffs were my least favorite form of fighting unless I was sparring with Cole, but nobody said I had to play fair.

"You're going to pay, demon bitch, for what you did to Nudra, what you did to me." He curled fingers in my direction, egging me on. "I'm going to show my brothers and sisters, as well as my father, what a back-stabbing donk you are."

I stood still, watching his theatrics and trying not to roll my eyes. "You gonna fight or talk me to death, butt crumb?"

A few snickers whispered through the crowd. As expected, Toel lunged, swinging a fist. Like I'd told Maddy, vampires were fast, but I was quicker. Even in heels.

I'd noticed he was left-handed when he was playing pool. Not that it mattered a whole lot, but I was ambidextrous with my fists and my weapons. That was an advantage. He would lead with his left, but I could lead with either. As he threw his first punch, I shifted just enough that the bulk of his fist skirted off my left shoulder. What did make contact stung, but it was a pleasant sting. A warm-up hit.

A hit that brought the vengeance demon inside to full attention.

The last time I let her out of her cage unrestrained was when I exacted revenge on Queen Maria. My demonness was nothing to mess around with. She was one of hell's top predators, and she had no preconceived notions of right and wrong, no moral quandaries, and no soul. She was power and magic rolled up tight with the seven deadly sins. Regardless of Lucifer's claims, her essence was evil. *I* was evil.

As Toel advanced for a second shot, this one aimed at my

head, I dodged, giving him a chance to make contact but not hurt me. The blow grazed my cheek, barely a love tap, but his flip-flops tripped him up, and he growled. He lost his balance and then righted himself. His fangs descended.

We circled each other on the dais, him tossing aside the chairs. They tumbled to the floor and were quickly shoved out of the way as the Undead surrounded the raised platform, turning it into a boxing ring.

Blood lust and dominance poured out of Toel, but I didn't bring up my protective magic, instead letting the swirling anger and hunger whet my demon's appetite.

I let him land a few more blows, giving him the rope to hang himself. He landed a solid punch to my stomach, and my demon roared her anger, my head snapping forward from the intensity of it. A tremor shook me from head to toe as she flooded my chest with a dark, deadly yearning. I stumbled on my heels, giving Toel an opening.

He was nervous about getting too close, but he was confident enough now to move in for the kill. He tackled me and took me down. His biggest mistake was pinning me on my back.

He liked to look his prey in the eyes and bare his fangs. To bask in his superiority and watch his prey cowering in fear. He didn't notice the change in my body, the demon staring back at him in my eyes. All he saw was someone weaker than himself. Someone he could dominate, humiliate, and kill.

A group of vampires had taken up chanting, "Toel, Toel, Toel." Over the top of that, I heard Maddy screaming my name, fear in the syllables. Had the female vamp or another of the guards grabbed her before she could escape?

If she was going to be my assistant, we would have to work on her survival skills.

"Yield," I said over the chanting.

Toel's eyes were completely red except for the black dot in

the center. He was so high on his own lust and pride at conquering me that his pupils had dilated to pinheads. "Why the fuck would I yield to you, you swamp donkey?"

The demon inside me laughed. She liked dirty talk.

Feeling inside the tulle Toel was smashing against me with his body, I suffered a long sigh. "Because if you don't, I'm going to ice you, *dude*."

He was too far gone to comprehend. He grinned, showing his teeth again as he lowered his head to skim the tips across my cleavage. With the stake in hand, I waited to see if he'd try to bite me. I held very still, my demon waiting with me, hate filling my chest, dark magic drawing up from the ground beneath it. The evil flowed through me like thick syrup, spreading to my limbs, fingers, and toes.

The moment Toel's fangs grazed my carotid artery, Dru raised his sword above us, willing to spear his own brother to stop my demise. My demon purred at the heroic move, but he needn't have bothered. With my left hand, I reached up, grabbed Toel's sun-bleached hair, and gave his head a tug. The movement exposed his neck to me, and remembering Dru's joking suggestion earlier that evening, I bared my demon teeth and sunk them into the donk's neck.

FORTY-NINE

Toel cried out as blood gushed from his throat. The taste disgusted me, but I hung on, wanting him to feel all the pain and fear and humiliation he'd inflicted on others. Dru, sword still aimed at Toel's back, froze, eyes going wide.

The demon in me found it all rather amusing, and I lifted the stake, prepared to stab the vamp through his back to reach his heart when the crashing sound of breaking windows stopped me.

Shouts, screams, and shrieks erupted around us.

Danger, my demon whispered.

I rolled Toel, sending him off the dais at the same time I came up on hands and knees, stake still in hand. Dru staggered and was swallowed up by a group of vamps. Vlad had disappeared, too, amongst the charging vampires, arms flailing as they pushed and shoved, trying to escape but creating chaos instead.

Chaos.

I looked around, noting flashes of red material amongst the vampires' black and white attire. Noctifectors. Their outfits were red with gold daggers embroidered on the front of their tunics. Black masks covered their faces.

And there I was on the raised platform, blood smeared on my face, stake in hand. I wiped the blood from my lips, grabbed my whip and stood, regardless of becoming a target. Where the hell was Maddy?

I didn't see her. What I saw instead curled my stomach.

Flashing blades caught the light from the chandeliers. Vampire heads rolled. Blood spurted and covered clothes, hair, and the floor. Screams rent the air.

A massacre.

My demon and my whip pulsed with delight, reveling in the blood and the screams. My stomach pinched in disgust. I'd dreamed about doing the same thing myself in the abstract, wiping the vampires off the face of the Earth, but that was before Maddy. Before Dru. Before I'd discovered humanity in their faces, their actions.

Continuing to scan for both of them, my heart tripped when I saw gold eyes on me from behind a Noct mask. Rad wove through the chaos and carnage, a dagger making swift work of the vamps who got in his way. After one fell at his feet, Rad raised his gaze and met mine again.

My demon went on high alert. She wanted him, even in the midst of battle. Her magic called to him across the expanse, and the demon in him answered. His eyes flashed with desire. My demon started moving in his direction, my blood calling to him like a sire vamp calling to an underling.

Reining in my demon when she's in full force is nearly impossible. She's an incorrigible child. An evil, incorrigible child.

I jumped off the dais, shoved a vamp out of my way, everything in me yearning, demanding I satiate the demon.

But the evil one recognizes danger as easily as she recognizes sin.

Noctifector. Run away.

Half-demon. Blood slave. Take him.

Torn in two, my logic, magic, and emotions at war with each other, I stopped. The room spun, the metallic smell of blood heavy in my nose. Vertigo sent me to my knees, the stake falling from my hand and spinning away when someone kicked it. Out of the corner of my eye, I saw a sword headed in the direction of my neck. I ducked, lost my balance, and fell into a set of legs.

I braced for the sound of steel cutting through the air, the feel of the blade slicing through my skin. Neither came.

Strong hands lifted me from the floor and sat me on the edge of the dais. Rad's masked face swam in front of my face, the flash of his dagger catching my eye. My chest tightened, and I struggled against his hold, the demon lashing out with her magic to push him away. Push the dagger away.

Or take it from him and bury it in his chest.

At the same time, the blood in my body sent a second flood of magic out, this time reaching for my lover. It grabbed him, jerking him closer and connecting a circuit.

Push, pull. Reject, entice. The tug-of-war continued. My head pounded, and my lungs refused to expand. Dark spots danced in front of my eyes. I grabbed the dagger in Rad's hand and tried to wrestle it from him. His demon—or perhaps the Noctifector in him—fought back, refusing to relinquish the weapon or surrender to me. We struggled, the blade swiping millimeters from my face, his throat

He forced my hand and the dagger upward, holding my arm captive in the air. "Yield," he demanded, echoing what I'd said to Toel only moments before.

Had he witnessed my fight with the vamp? Had he timed the Noctifectors' attack in order to interrupt it?

I strained against him, against the chaos he caused inside me. Gritting my teeth through the pain, I restrained my demon and pushed her down, down, down toward her cage. She laughed, throwing off my control, and a new wave of agony tore through my head.

Rad grabbed me by the shoulder with his free hand and shook me hard. "Yield, dammit!"

To him? Or to the demon?

Hell if I'd do either. "Never."

Looking into his eyes, a flash of sadness flipped some switch in my head. Emotions I couldn't name swarmed me. His own tug-of-war was playing itself out behind his eyes and I was at the center of it.

With my head splitting in two, my magic shredding into a thousand pieces, a spark of compassion warmed my chest. Compassion for Rad, who was trying to save me—not kill me—amid a slaughter. Compassion for the vamps dying all around me.

Compassion for myself, torn between two worlds, struggling to tame the evil inside me and protect humans. Struggling to *be* human when the only thing I would ever be was a raging demon.

But I was a demon who would fight for what I wanted. Fight for my friends. For the Council. I would fight for justice.

"Vengeance is mine," I whispered, touching my ring fingers and thumbs together.

My magic, old as time, flashed through me, shocking my demon into submission and jolting Rad with a powerful charge that would have sent most supernaturals to their knees. But he hung on to me and the dagger, nearly toppling us both.

Cole appeared, and with him, a group of trained Bridge

soldiers. Damon to the rescue, determined to make good on his promise to Vlad since I'd fulfilled my oath and become queen of the Chicago Undead.

A resurgence of fighting began as Cole came up behind Rad and assumed the worst. Who wouldn't when Rad was wearing that stupid Noctifector tunic, and we were wrestling with a silver dagger? Believing I was about to buy it from a Noct, Cole thunked Rad hard on the back of the head with the butt of his gun. Rad toppled, the blow enough to knock him out.

Surprised he hadn't killed the Noctifector, I chuckled. "Do you ever actually shoot that gun?" I was searching for a life preserver to bring me down from the magical tug-of-war I'd just undergone and snark was a good one.

Cole kicked Rad's ribs. "What, and waste a good bullet on Guitar Boy?"

So he'd figured it out. Figured out Rad was a Noct. I held out a hand for him to help me up and dropped the dagger on Rad's chest. Swaying on my feet, I took in the horror around me, the piles of formalwear, their owners reduced to ashes. Bodies missing heads. Blood everywhere and screams still ringing in the room.

My compassion for Rad notwithstanding, he'd brought this massacre to the Undead, to me. He was responsible for the deaths of all these vampires, some of his own Nocts, and possibly Bridge Council soldiers.

I shook with rage, magic overload, and adrenaline. "Where's Maddy?"

Cole fended off another Noctifector, finally putting the gun to its intended use. The bullet was filled with holy water and would only wound the human male, but it did stop him in his tracks. "We'll find her."

Still swaying on unsteady feet, I stepped over Rad and let Cole lead me away.

FIFTY

Two hours later, I sat in the Land Rover outside Carpathia House. The fighting had resolved shortly after Damon's soldiers arrived, the Noctifectors retreating and leaving behind a much smaller vampire population.

Vlad and Toel were missing. Maddy, too. Dru had been injured, but the gashes and cuts he'd received would heal. He stood on the front steps of his House, sword sheathed, and doled out instructions to the handful of guards who had not deserted him to join Toel's war. Rafael and Juliana stood behind him, lending their presence as support, even though they did nothing during the confrontation with Toel to make me think they cared one way or the other about Carpathia's loyalties.

Despite Cole's attempts to drive them away, Damon, Yasmin, and Kirill had never left the property. Damon had inserted Bridge soldiers in the area as a precaution—it would have been nice if he'd let me in on his strategic plan, but then again, I'd refused to ride with him, so it was my own damn fault for not knowing—and had called them in when things went wrong.

Two of the Noctifectors had been captured, but Damon wouldn't tell me what he planned to do with them. Neither of the Nocts was Rad, though. Either he'd regained consciousness shortly after Cole and I left him on the ballroom floor, or some of his peers had scooped him up and escaped with him.

My body, mind, and magic were shot. Cole had given me his coat, sat me in the Land Rover, and cranked the heat. The windows steamed up, and I had to continually wipe mine off with the sleeve of the coat to see out. I stared at the house, seeing Rad's face and the flash of the dagger. I switched on the radio, but all I heard were Maddy's screams.

Cole had searched the house and grounds three times but hadn't found her. There were endless piles of ashes inside the house, and as the hours passed, I was sure one belonged to her. The only hope I had was that no one had found a pale pink dress with weapons stored inside the tulle skirt.

Then again, most of the clothes left behind were covered in so much blood, who could recognize pink from white? Tulle from cotton? Everything was soaked crimson red.

One of the vamp guards emerged from the side of the house, joined Dru on the front steps, and spoke into his ear. Dru, already tense, went rigid. He sent the group gathered around him off in various directions before jumping down the steps and heading toward me and the Land Rover.

I rolled down my window. He put a hand on the car, leaned down. "We think we've found Toel's ashes. Thought you might want to see them."

Toel was dead. I let go of a sigh. "Damn right, I do."

I climbed out of the vehicle and followed Dru and the guard who'd brought the news. On the way past the house, I motioned at Damon and Cole, who joined our ranks. As they caught up to me, I told them the news. "Toel's ashes have been found."

Leaving the well-manicured lawn, we traipsed through undergrowth and woods to the south of the mansion. There was sort of a trail, but it was barely visible in the moonlight. After a few minutes of fighting through the trees and bushes, we came to a slight bend in the trail and a rocky outcropping. Here, the sliver of moon bathed the rocks in a white glow. One of Cole's soldiers stood guard over a pair of black pants, a white shirt, two flip-flops, and a pile of ashes.

My heart, which had been clenched from the moment Dru approached the SUV, did a hard thud in my chest. Why Toel had been dusted this far from the house was beyond me, but those stupid flip-flops were finally silent.

I gave Carpathia's Master an inquiring look, and he nodded. Together, we bent down and examined the clothes. The shirt collar was stained on the left side. The blood looked black in the moonlight.

I pointed it out to Damon. "I bit his neck."

Nonplussed, Damon gave me a *we'll discuss this later* look.

I stood. "Any way to confirm these ashes are his?"

Dru straightened. "Vampire forensics leave a lot to be desired. Vampires don't share DNA per se. We share blood, but without the blood running in his veins, we have nothing to identify him by except what he was wearing."

I kicked a flip-flop, stared at the bloodied collar. I knew that was his blood, but there was no way to compare it to the ashes.

The skin at my temples tightened as Damon's voice filled my head. *What's bothering you?*

What *wasn't* bothering me? *Just being thorough.*

You don't believe these are Toel's ashes?

I'd feel better if we had some way to prove he's dead.

It's been a long night. Have Cole drive you home. We'll debrief at the Institute at twenty-one hundred.

Nine p.m. Enough time for a hot shower and a day's sleep. *I'm not leaving until we find Maddy.*

Long, pregnant pause. *I'll have someone call you the moment she's found.*

Dru asked his vamp guard to bag up Toel's remains. We returned to Carpathia, and Cole deposited me back in the SUV, ignoring my arguments.

"I want to look for Maddy," I said, but I made no move to get back out of the car. The tromp through the woods in my stilettos had zapped the last of my energy.

Cole climbed into the driver's seat. "She's probably back at your place, raiding your closets and watching TV. Besides, Alexandru or Damon will call if they find her."

As the countryside gave way to gas stations, fast food joints, and early morning traffic, I stared unseeing out the window. Cole shot me worried glances, but his attempts at conversation fell flat in the car. I had no emotions left to hash over, no logic left to analyze what had happened. I was numb, and that was the way I wanted to stay.

"You hungry?" he asked, steering off the highway and heading toward a lit sign above a hamburger shop.

"No." My stomach turned traitor when I said it, though, and growled loudly.

"We haven't eaten since yesterday morning." He finagled the Land Rover around the side to the drive-through. "What sounds good?"

I closed my eyes and laid my head against the cool window. "Surprise me."

When we drove out of the lot a few minutes later, the SUV smelled like French fries. On our way to my place, we shared four bacon cheeseburgers, five large fries, two chocolate milk-shakes, and two fried apple pies.

Demons have high metabolisms and that whole gluttony thing going on.

The fat and salt euphoria lifted my mood. Cole asked to crash on my couch. I sent JR home, got out clean linens for the sofa, and tossed them at my bodyguard. "You don't have to stay with me, you know."

He grabbed me by the back of my neck and drew me close, hugging me in an awkward embrace. "You did good tonight."

I swallowed the lump in my throat. "Thanks."

He released me. "So Guitar Boy's a Noct?"

My shoulders tightened even though there was no accusation in his voice, no blame. Maybe a little curiosity, but nothing else.

"Yeah." I dug a toe into the rug. "He's one of my blood slaves, too."

"I figured." Cole started counting off on his fingers. "He left you at the altar, he's a Noctifector, and he needs your blood to stay upright. How many strikes does he get before he's out?"

I shrugged, and he chuckled. "Damn, you're getting soft in your old age, Kali."

There was only mockery in his tone, no condemnation. I wished I could be so light-hearted about it. "By rights, I know you have to inform Damon, but..."

I hesitated, not sure exactly what to ask for. More time? To do what? I'd given Rad a chance and he'd brought the Noctifectors down on Carpathia.

Cole grabbed the back of my neck again and gently shook me. "I'm not telling Damon a damn thing. You've taken it in the ass from the Council more times than I can count. If anyone deserves a free pass, it's you."

My shoulders relaxed. I gave him a reserved smile. "Thanks."

"Go take a nap. We'll figure out what to do with Guitar Boy tomorrow."

Upstairs, I stripped down, showered, and put on my Hello Kitty pajamas. I crawled into bed, prayed for Maddy, and fell asleep.

A loud blaring woke me. Twilight seeped through my windows. I'd forgotten to draw the shades but had managed to sleep through the sun pouring in anyway. Rolling over and covering my eyes with the blanket, I groaned, my lids sticking together like Velcro.

The phone on my nightstand rang again, and I stuck out a hand to locate it. Once found, I snatched up the receiver and drew it under the covers. "Hello?"

"I found my father's cross."

"Dru?"

"His cross, Kali. He never takes it off."

Forcing myself to sit up, I glanced at the clock. Half past five. I'd slept the day away even though it didn't feel like it. "Where did you find it?"

His answer sent chills down my spine. "Under Toel's ashes."

My depleted brain took a few seconds to piece the puzzle together. "Those weren't Toel's. They were your father's."

Dru seemed to be on the same page but didn't seem particularly upset. "He killed my father and faked his death. But why? He's not in line for the throne."

"Toel wants ultimate power over vamps. You heard him at the coronation. He intends to take over the human world as well."

A heavy, tormented sigh sounded on Dru's end. "I'm going to need your help to stop him."

Stop him? I would burn his ashes in my fireplace this winter and warm my hands by the fire. "My pleasure. I am a vengeance demon and the Bridge Council's enforcer" —*at least for now*—"after all."

"And Vampire Queen of the Central U.S."

"Going to hold me to that, huh?"

"Oh, yes."

With all these jobs, Sweet Investigations was going to go straight down the tube. "I'll be at Carpathia around midnight unless the Bridge Council has other plans for me."

"See you then."

We disconnected. I snuggled back down into bed and tried to sleep. My body was ready for another twelve hours, but Maddy's face kept hijacking my brain. Finally, I got up and went downstairs.

Cole was snoring like a bear on my couch, his gun on his chest. He'd stripped off his T-shirt and had one muscled arm thrown up over his head. His presence was comforting, and that annoyed me. I'd had far too much company in the past few days, but I'd miss him when he left.

I snuck past his sleeping form, entered my office, and saw that all the security cameras were working. Everything appeared back to normal. The grounds were quiet, the parking lot was empty, and the graveyard was foggy. I breathed a sigh of relief. At least on the surface, I could pretend nothing was amiss.

Remnants of JR's presence littered the desk and floor. I cleaned up the candy wrappers, threw them away, rinsed the soda bottles, and recycled them. The recycler came on Tuesday, but I couldn't remember what day it was. Didn't matter. JR's soda bottles were the only thing in the big plastic bin.

After I'd restored my office to order, I went to the shelves behind my desk and took down a brown leather journal.

I sat in my office chair, switched on the desk lamp, and rocked back and forth for a minute, running my hand over the worn leather cover. I opened it to the first page, blinked back tears.

Goffredo Dolce.

Rachele Dolce.

Pippa Dolce.

The three names, written in my flowing script, were the book's first entries. The ink had faded through the years and the paper had become crinkled and spotted from my tears. I touched the names with the pads of my fingers, tracing the letters.

Then I turned pages, reading off each name I'd entered in the book over the past two hundred and eighty-some years. Names of friends, distant family members, some human, many more demon or supernatural. Most had a capital N next to their name, designating they'd died at the hands of the Noctifectors. If they didn't have an N, it was only because I had no proof the group had assassinated them. My family had M's next to their names for Maria. I needed to scratch those out and replace them with an N.

No one close to me had died at the hands of the Noctifectors in years, so the last entry was dated shortly after I'd landed in Chicago. Taking an ink pen from my pencil drawer, I poised it over the paper. I wrote *M-a*, then stopped. My hand shook, and I brushed away the tears threatening to spill over my lashes.

I sat back, tossed the pen aside, and closed the book. I couldn't give up on her. Not yet.

Movement on one of the screens caught my eye. The sun had disappeared entirely, and the single lamppost spotlighted the empty parking lot. I stared at the screen, searching for what my tired eyes had picked up on. Saw nothing.

Beep, beep, beep. The security alarm blared from my computer speaker.

Someone *was* in the parking lot. I shot to my feet at the sight of long dark hair swept up in a messy bun and a tulle skirt flouncing haphazardly around thin legs. "Maddy!"

I yelled her name as I ran through the church, nearly giving Cole a heart attack. He jerked up from his sleeping position and waved his gun around, trying to find the target. I threw open the front doors and ran out into the November evening, feet bare and still in my Hello Kitty pjs.

She was covered in dirt and grime, the ringlets around her face now stringy. The dress was torn and missing some of the embroidery. One shoe on and one missing, Maddy bobbed up and down as she walked.

But she'd never looked better.

If anyone had told me I'd hug a vampire like she was my BFF, I'd have whipped them. Overcome with emotion, I did precisely that. "You're alive!"

She grinned. "The Mouse always makes it out alive. She's like a ninja. Never seen. Never heard."

I might have been overly emotional, but I still had to give her a hard time. "Is that why everyone in the three-state area heard you screaming last night at the coronation?"

She laughed, either from sheer exhaustion or my flair for standup. "Can I crash here for a few hours? I need a shower in the worst way."

The tang of sweat, old blood, and moldy grave dirt hung in the air. "You got that right."

I threw an arm around her shoulders and helped her limp to the church. Cole stood in the doorway, scratching his naked chest, gun hanging loose at this side. "Hey, kid."

"Hey," she said.

I took her upstairs, found her some sweats, and let her clean up in my bathroom. While she showered, Cole and I made eggs and waffles. Cole put his shirt on, which was kind of a shame but more appropriate for breakfast. I set three places at the kitchen bar and felt a homey pang in my chest. Usually, I didn't even set a place for myself. I ate in front of the TV or standing at the kitchen sink. Looking at the three plates, silverware, and napkins, I enjoyed the semblance of a family meal.

Maddy entered the kitchen, a comb in her hands and a snarl the size of a fist in her hair. She held out the comb. "Help me?"

I took the comb, my stomach clenching.

She saw the look on my face. "Kali?"

I shook my head and smiled at her. "Whenever I had a break from Court, I went home to my family. I used to brush my sister's hair every morning."

"What Court?" Maddy asked.

I sat her on one of the barstools and worked carefully on the knot. It came apart easily, and I wondered why she couldn't have removed it herself. "A long time ago in Rome. My little sister Pippa had super fine hair that would tangle while she slept. Poor thing. Sometimes, I feared I'd have to cut out the knots, they were so bad."

Cole slid a hot waffle fresh from the iron onto Maddy's plate. The scent of butter and vanilla filled the kitchen. She reached for the syrup, and I released my hold on her hair. The knot was out and I was running the comb through her tresses for the simple connection to my sister.

Once we'd all dug into our breakfast, Cole started prodding her for information. "How'd you escape? Where'd you go? Did you see Toel or Vlad leave the estate?"

She swallowed a mouthful of waffle, washed it down with milk, nodded. "They were together. I followed them into the woods, then lost them. And I wasn't the only one following them."

Cole and I both stopped eating. "Who else?" I asked.

She played with her fork. "Victoria."

Toel and Victoria. What an interesting couple they would make. I glanced at Cole. "Dru called earlier to tell me they found his father's cross under those ashes in the woods. It's possible Toel dusted him and then switched the clothes to fake us out." I faced Maddy. "Any possibility you saw that?"

She shook her head. "I barely saw Toel and Vlad once they entered the woods. I was hiding upstairs on the second floor and jumped out the window to go after them. When I got on the ground, Victoria ran out of the house and headed in their direction, so I followed her. Once or twice, I caught their scent, but she was making so much noise that they probably thought the Noctifectors were chasing them."

"Did she ever catch up to them?"

"At one point, they left the ground and went up in the trees, and that's when I lost them. I don't know where Vicky went."

We finished our breakfasts in silence. I had a couple of hours before I met with Damon, so I called Di. She was still at the Blackstone.

Toel may have been alive, but I figured he had more pressing matters than toying with my friends. "The threat level is yellow again," I told my best friend. "You can move back home."

"Oh." She sounded disappointed. "I was starting to like it here."

"Have you seen Rad?"

"No." Again, her voice rang with disappointment. "I assumed he was with you."

Rule number five: never assume. "My new vamp friend needs a wardrobe makeover. You up for the task?"

"Does it involve shopping?"

"Would I call you otherwise?"

She laughed, and the sound made me smile. "How did it go with Lucifer and his soul mate?"

"I'll tell you all about it when Maddy and I pick you up in half an hour."

"You're going shopping with us?"

A girl's night out. Such a human thing for a goddess, a demon, and a vampire. "Not if you're going to razz me about it."

"Lips. Sealed. Now get over here."

I disconnected. Cole was done cleaning up the kitchen—another gesture that left me with a case of family-itis—and he dried his hands on a dishtowel. "I'm heading to the Institute. Catch up with you later."

"What? And miss our shopping trip?"

"I have to coordinate Jimmy's funeral." He tossed the towel on the counter. "Be careful, okay? Toel's a douchebag, but he's a smart douchebag."

"If he's still alive," I said, trying to relieve his worries and feeling guilty over Jimmy.

"I can stay on as bodyguard if you want."

He could, and it wouldn't be such a bad thing. "I can take care of myself."

"Do me a favor?"

"Anything."

"Next time you have that douchebag in your grip, kill him. Once for me. Once for Jimmy."

I slid off the barstool and held out my hand. We shook. "Done."

FIFTY-ONE

For the first time in quite a while, I bought new clothes. Some for me, a bunch for Maddy. Skinny jeans, tank tops, nubby sweaters for the Windy City winter. Di styled both of us, and we laughed at some of the combinations of flowing peek-a-boo blouses and layered skirts that she favored, switching out the overly feminine choices for edgier ones.

We indulged in coffee and cheesecake before Maddy and I dropped Di off at her house and headed for the Institute. For two hours, I let myself forget I still had pressing concerns.

I'd had to drive the Land Rover since gnomes were the only ones who could fit in the TT's backseat. As I cruised through the security gates, Maddy leaned out her window to look at the spires, turrets, and overall imposing structure. "This place rocks."

"Wait 'til you see the inside."

I gave her a brief tour. The grand one would've taken forty-five minutes, but I was due in Damon's office in five, so I cheated her out of seeing the cafeteria, gym, and ops room. "I'll be in the meeting for an hour or so. Think you can find some-thing to do?"

Her gaze slid to the right. We'd spent the majority of the tour in the library, and she itched to get back there. It wasn't just full of books. Damon never did anything half-assed, so the library contained a movie room, music room, and game room, all interconnected with the extensive collections of ancient and modern texts.

"No problem. Take your time."

"Cole's in the basement, probably in ops or the gym if you get lonely. He can show you how to use your new weapon."

"He's hot."

I gave her an appraising look. "He's also old enough to be your great-grandfather sixteen times removed."

"Eww."

"Exactly."

She waved and half-skipped down the hall, looking over her shoulder at me when she reached the library's double doors. "He's a catch for you, though."

"How old do you think I am?" I said with mock indignation.

She giggled and waved again, disappearing into the library.

My good mood stayed with me until I entered Damon's office and found him scowling at his computer screen. "What's up?" I asked, flopping down on one of his chairs. Yasmin and Kirill were mercifully absent.

Damon peered at me from under dark brows and turned the screen so I could see it. The scene showed the ballroom and Toel, fists raised in the air. The angle of the shot suggested the camera had been hidden inside the fireplace. "Dru sent us copies of the security tapes from last night."

"And?"

He tapped a few keys on his keyboard. "Can you explain this to me?"

The tone of his voice hinted that he didn't need an explanation. That this was simply a formality.

I watched the screen, watched Toel's ringing endorsement for human domination and the sequence that followed. He and I in a stand-off, me letting go of my whip. The pathetic boxing match that ensued.

"Here," Damon said, watching me rather than the screen. "Were you baiting him?"

There was no pressure in my head for once, but I kept tight control over my thoughts just in case he came for a visit.

On screen, Toel punched me in the stomach. My head snapped back, and then I doubled over. Damon paused the tape. "What happened here when he punched you?"

Merde. No sense in lying. Even without skimming my mind, he knew exactly what had happened. "My demon woke."

He steepled his fingers together. "Why did you bait Toel into waking your demon? Why didn't you raise your protective magic and end this fight before it started?"

Because I hadn't wanted to. Because I'd been damned tired of Toel trumping me at every turn. I had wanted to make him suffer a little. To embarrass him in front of his father and the other vamps.

I blew out a breath and went for Italian flare instead of the truth. "I was trying to be a creative sadist."

My boss didn't laugh, didn't even crack a smile. His tone registered deep disappointment and mild condensation. "I don't need to remind you that waking your demon is dangerous."

My biological makeup was one hundred percent demon. But a part of me was separate, like a human's soul or spirit. I could call it to life when necessary.

I lived and breathed sin and magic, yet had been able to reign in my baser demon spirit so I could help humans and protect them rather than hurt them. To do that, I had suppressed the demon to the point of submission. Forced her to sleep unless situations precipitated her release.

Few demons could do such a thing, and even fewer were willing to. Those who did generally worked for the Council.

"There were no humans present, and I was one demon in the midst of a hundred vampires. Vampires who were cheering Toel's message of world domination. You and the rest of the Council were safe, Cole was gone, and Maddy was in trouble. Yes, I let Toel wake my demon, but it was out of self-preservation."

He started the tape again and paused it when the screen showed me clamping down on Toel's neck. "And this? Was this part of your self-preservation?"

I lowered my gaze, anger igniting in my stomach. Gripping the arms of the chair, I met Damon's accusing stare straight on. "If you have a problem with how I handled this situation, spit it out."

Damon tapped a key, waved a finger at the screen. "Keep watching. I'm particularly interested in this next part where the Noctifectors enter the room."

Had Cole told him about Rad? I sat frozen in place, wondering if there was any part of my job I could salvage once that truth came out.

Nope, nada.

On screen, I wrestled with a Noctifector. The dagger flew up, down, and at each of us in an almost comical display. "The Noct was going to kill me. I fought back. Cole knocked him out. The end."

Damon didn't appreciate my blow-by-blow analysis. "Was he honestly trying to kill you?"

"Well, yeah. Why?"

"Quite the opposite is what it looks like to me. If I didn't know better, I'd say he was trying to help you regain control of your demon. Why would a Noctifector do that?"

I swallowed hard and kept my face neutral. "You're seeing things. He was trying to kill me."

He stopped the tape, resituated the screen, and steepled his fingers. "Is there anything you'd like to tell me concerning that particular Noctifector?"

The moment of truth. Did I give Rad up? Ruin my career? Confirm my boss's suspicions and end up on the wrong side of his Archdemon magic. "No."

He reached into one of his desk drawers and drew a piece of paper. "Have a look at this."

It was a Most Wanted list. A Noctifector Most Wanted list. Guess whose name was in the number one spot?

Kali Sweet, aka Calina Dolce. Vengeance demon. Enforcer, Bridge Council, United States of America. Owner, Sweet Investigations, Chicago, Illinois.

At least they'd spelled my name right.

There was a warning under it. *Extremely dangerous to both humans and supernaturals. Use utmost caution. Wanted: dead or alive.*

Dead or alive, huh? That was an upgrade. So was being number one on their hit parade. The Nocts had been after me for years, but more in passing rather than all out hunting me down. There were far more bad supernaturals out there fucking with humans for them to focus on than me, who spent more time protecting humans than they did.

Still, a queasiness set up camp in my lower stomach. "Where did you get this?"

"A source."

I lifted a brow. "Inside The Catholic Church?"

"Inside the Noctifectors."

"No shit?"

He frowned at my crude language. "The point is, you're a wanted demon. The Noctifectors weren't after the vampires last night. They were after you."

All because of that rat bastard...I stopped myself before I could think a particular Chaos demon's name. "Who's your source?"

Damon stared at me, saying nothing. His eyes were flat and aloof.

"Are you sure you can trust them? Maybe that Most Wanted list is a joke, a red herring to scare us and keep me off my game. It won't work. I'm not running from this or hiding either."

"This is no joke, Kali, and I do not intend to treat it as such. You will move into the Institute tonight without further delay, and your enforcer duties will be minimized until further notice. I will personally sign off on those you are allowed to do."

"You've got to be kidding."

His eyes said, *try me.* "Your things are being moved here as we speak."

"What?" I shot up from the chair. "You can't do that!"

Damon stood, set his fingers on the desk, and leaned toward me. "I can, and I will."

"Kidnapping a Council employee violates Code 6A, Section Two."

"This isn't kidnapping. It's personal protection."

We stared each other down, my mind tripping over itself with options. Running away held appeal. I always kept an emergency bag stuffed under a floorboard in my closet for such times. I'd never had to use it, but my past had taught me to be ready to run at a moment's notice.

It wouldn't do much good, though. If the Noct threat was

real, I couldn't hide anywhere in the world safer than here. High-tailing it far also meant leaving everyone I cared about and everything I'd worked so hard for.

"I'm perfectly safe at the church. There are security cameras now and trip wires and my magical glamours keeping the place from human eyes and interference."

"Victoria found you, did she not?"

"Because she was my blood slave. She could feel the call in her veins even before she needed my blood. It's like a GPS."

Damon sat and stuck the Most Wanted Noct list back in his drawer. "You're staying here until further notice." He picked up a file and thumbed through it, effectively dismissing me.

Well, we'd see about that. I wheeled around and slammed his office door behind me. First, I'd grab Maddy and then head back to my place. Any demon who'd touched my stuff was going to get a whip pointed at his balls.

I found the girl in the library as suspected and she was none too happy about leaving, but we made it to the first floor doors without too much whining. There, however, two guards blocked the exit.

I ordered them to move; they refused. One of them spoke. "Director Soule requests you return to your quarters on the third floor."

"I don't have quarters on the third floor."

Yasmin appeared at my elbow. "Of course you do. Come with me."

"What about me?" Maddy asked.

Yasmin shrugged. "You're free to go."

I drew Maddy aside and whispered to her. "Stay at my place. I'll be home as soon as I can bust out of here."

She nodded, gave me a thumbs-up, and held out her hand. "Car keys."

"You're not driving my car."

"I have a learner's permit. Besides, I'm a vamp. My reflexes are better than the average Chicago driver."

That really wasn't saying much, but I handed her the keys. "Be careful. And keep that cell phone I bought you today charged."

We hugged. She left.

Yasmin held out a hand toward the elevators.

Sunrise the following day, I was holed up in an apartment suite on the Institute's third floor with a book, a soda, and most of my belongings. The movers had brought my bed, dresser, clothes, make-up, shoes, and weapons. I sat in the window seat in my Hello Kitty pjs, watching the night fade to gray and the sun peek over the horizon. My favorite blanket was wrapped around my shoulders. It was home, but it wasn't.

Much to Yasmin's dismay, the suite was directly across the hall from Damon's quarters. He was keeping a close eye on me, and she was keeping a close eye on both of us. She needn't have worried. I was so mad at him that I could hardly say his name without cursing.

I'd missed my meeting with Dru but had called him to explain the situation. We made new plans to talk at the Institute later in the week. In the meantime, he was hunting down leads, disciplining the guards who'd turned on him, and bickering with his older brothers about who would succeed Vlad. On a side note, Vicky had returned to the House. She claimed she didn't know what had happened to Toel or Vlad, and demanded Dru give her a job as a House guard. He'd refused but had her in training for kitchen duty.

A jarring *thud, thud, thud* sounded on the suite's door, jerking me out of my pity-party. Probably Damon doing his hourly check. He'd used his magic to secure the windows so I couldn't jump out. I was no vampire, and three stories was too high for me to jump without doing severe damage to my body, but I would have considered it if not for the magic bars.

There was no peephole on the door—another thing that annoyed me—but danger was unlikely to follow me here. I shifted the blanket higher on my shoulders, took a deep breath, and opened up.

Big mistake since danger was a relative term.

Rad held out a cup of coffee. "Hi."

I should have slammed the door. I should have. "How did you get in here?"

He reached inside his coat and drew out an envelope. "I have something for you. Damon said I could deliver it in person."

"Did he now?"

"It's highly sensitive material. It's also your key to getting out of here for a few hours of fun."

For half a second, I thought about marching him down to Damon's office and serving him up on a silver platter of betrayal. With him in tow, I could negotiate my release. Of course, then I'd have to admit knowing Rad was a Noct before the coronation ceremony and where would that leave me?

Locked up in the jail downstairs with the prisoners. "You shouldn't be here."

"Listen, about the coronation..."

I shushed him. Looked right and left down the hallway. Yasmin peered around the stairs at the end. She didn't even have the grace to look embarrassed.

Against my better judgment, I tugged Rad inside and shut the door. I opened my mouth to bitch him out, but he lifted a finger from the cup and overrode my pending tirade. "I had nothing to do with that ambush."

"Oh, that's rich, Rad." I paced away from him so I wouldn't smack the cup from his hand. "You must think I'm pretty damn gullible to believe that."

He followed me into the bedroom and set the coffee and envelope on my nightstand. "I didn't tell the group anything. Someone else snitched the information to the Nocts." His eyes flashed with seriousness. "Damon and I think the snitch is inside here. Inside the Institute."

I laughed. "You and Damon best buds now? He knows you're a Noct?"

He didn't answer. I shook my head, more than annoyed. "There's no one inside the Institute leaking information. You're making it up to cover your own ass."

His eyes dulled. "I know you don't want to believe it, but it *is* possible. There's an outside chance the snitch was a vamp, but that's not likely. Not even rogue vamps talk to humans, and the rogues wouldn't have known the exact day and time of the coronation. They're shunned. They're not in the vampire loop. No one but the upper echelon vamps and Bridge employees knew the date, time, and place. Oh, and Hone."

That he would suggest Hone was a snitch was even more ludicrous than suggesting a Bridge employee. "Any other fantasies you want to admit to? Strange hallucinations? Alien probes?"

"Look," he paced to the bed and back. "There are a lot of things you don't know, Kali. Keep an open mind and consider what you know and *who* you know. Damon's imprisoned you here for more reasons than keeping you safe."

My own imagination was all too willing to jump to conclusions where Damon was involved. "He's using me to draw out the snitch."

Rad stayed quiet, confirming my suspicions and letting me absorb that fact.

My legs went weak, so I shuffled past him and plopped on the bed.

He leaned over and gave me a soft kiss on my cheek. "I have to go. The concert's at seven. Damon said you could come. Meanwhile," he squeezed my arm, "stay safe and don't trust anyone. Not Cole. Not Yasmin or Kirill. Not even Damon."

After he left, my mind swam with his conspiracy theory and Damon's suspected deceit. Was Rad Damon's source inside the Noctifectors? Was there really a double agent inside these walls?

I picked up the coffee and took a sip. The warm, dark roast flavor slid down my throat with comforting ease. The white envelope tempted me. Inside were two tickets to a Diamonds and Denim charity event for one of the local children's hospitals. The event was for that night at the Blackstone Ballroom.

On one hand, it would get me out of my prison. On the other, it seemed strange that Damon would allow me to go after making such a big deal about my safety.

The door to my suite creaked open, and Damon stood before me, eyeing my pjs with mock concern. Either he didn't like Goth Hello Kitty, or he saw the consternation on my face. "I see you got the tickets."

I set them down and studied the Archdemon who could read my mind. "You hold me prisoner in the Institute, but you're willing to let me go to a rock concert at the Blackstone?"

"Not a rock concert, Kali. A job for the Council."

"You said you were limiting my jobs."

"I am. This job, however, requires special handling, and since I will be accompanying you, you'll be perfectly safe."

"Wait. You're going to the concert with me?"

He crossed his arms over his chest and looked amused. "Since you've been avoiding me, I thought this would give us time to discuss my plans for you."

I had the feeling his *plan* would be very tempting but very dangerous.

Rad's words rang in my head. *Don't trust anyone. Not even Damon.*

But who could I trust? Rad?

That was a dangerous plan indeed.

"I want my badge back, and I want Cole and Maddy to go with us."

Damon smiled, and the challenge in his eyes, as tempting and dangerous as his plan, made me swallow hard. "Done."

Toel was still out there, and I wasn't going to find him sitting inside the Institute. I had to get out, one way or the other.

Show no fear. Act like an equal.

I hopped off the bed and gave my boss, the Archdemon, a full-on smile back. "I'm in."

Ready to find out what happens next?
Click here to read **Sweet Chaos** so you can keep the romance and adventure going!

And be sure to sign up for my reader newsletter so you're the first to know about new releases, giveaways, and other cool stuff (including pet pics, crafts, and recipes)!
Sign me up! Misty's Newsletter!

Want to read the next story for FREE?
Join my VIP subscription community for bonus content, including deleted scenes, short stories featuring your favorite characters, recipes, pics of my doggies, and so much more!

GLOSSARY OF TERMS

Glossary of Terms

Alciscor – vengeance demon, based on Ulciscor, the Latin term for *to take vengeance for, avenge.*

Cupiditas – demon

Dominus vobiscum, et cum spiritu tuo – The Lord be with you, and your spirit also

Erinyes – Greek earth deity of vengeance

Errore colossale – colossal mistake

Fermati – that's enough

Giganto – gigantic, enormous

Giuro davanti a dio – so help me God

Il pistolino – dick, prick

Khanda – Indian double-edge straight sword used for hacking and cutting

Merde – shit

Noctifector – demon slayer belonging to the Roman Catholic Church's secret organization; slang term Slayer, Noct

Porca miseria – miserable pig

Psuhke – Greek derivation of Latin term "psyche" and means breath, life, soul

Spiritu sancto – by the Holy Spirit

Straordinario – exceptional

Stretchers - Titans, deities that overstretched their powers to screw with lesser gods and goddesses as well as humans

Tempter – demon who tempts other supernaturals

Testa de cazzo - dickhead

Ti voglio bene – I love you

Tortura – torture

Vitiums – vices

Volante - flying

Vaffanculo – fuck you, fuck off

VISIT MY STORE

Did you know you can buy directly from me? When you do, the retailer doesn't take a cut and I can pass on the savings to YOU!

https://mistyevansbooks.com/shop

Benefits:

You can find ALL my books in one place

SAVE money

EARLY access to new releases

Special Collections, Boxed Sets, and Limited Editions

Support a small business

Why Buy Direct?

When you purchase a book by your favorite author, electronic or print, on retailer platforms, the company keeps 30-70% of the sale, leaving the author with little to no profit (after the company deducts delivery fees, taxes, and other fees).

Buying directly from the author means that more goes to them so they can keep turning out stories for you. Every published story, every book, requires cover art, editing, and hours and hours of the author's time simply to create it. Not to mention overhead costs, such as websites, newsletters, writing software, graphics programs, advertising, taxes, etc.

In addition, one of the big-name retailers requires exclusivity, and all of them have terms of service and rules and regulations that make it challenging and time-consuming for an indie author to navigate the publishing world.

Most of us would MUCH rather spend our time creating more stories for YOU, rather than trying to jump through the hoops at the retailers. Buying direct from your favorite authors (where available) helps ensure that an author you love is not subject to unexplained account closures, withholding of royalties, censorship, and other issues that can affect their livelihood.

I've experienced ALL of these. By buying direct, you help put control of my work back in my hands - and I can continue to write more.

Either way, thank you for supporting me! I understand buying direct doesn't work for everyone and even if you use the retailers to buy my books, I appreciate you!

Happy reading,

Misty

https://mistyevansbooks.com/shop

THRILLING ROMANTIC SUSPENSE & MYSTERIES

Don't want to miss a single release? Click here to join my reader list!

SEALs of Shadow Force Series

Fatal Truth

Fatal Honor

Fatal Courage

Fatal Love

Fatal Vision

Fatal Thrill

Risk

SEALS of Shadow Force Series: Spy Division

Man Hunt

Man Killer

Man Down

Covert Affairs

Covert Tactics

Covert Obsession

The SCVC Taskforce Series

Deadly Pursuit

Deadly Deception

Deadly Force

Deadly Intent

Deadly Affair, A SCVC Taskforce novella

Deadly Attraction

Deadly Secrets

Deadly Holiday, A SCVC Taskforce novella

Deadly Target

Deadly Rescue

Deadly Bounty

Deadly Betrayal

Deadly Threat

The Super Agent Series

Operation Sheba

Operation Paris

Operation Proof of Life

Operation Lost Princess

Operation Ambush

Operation Contraband

Operation Sleeping With the Enemy

Operation Heist

The Justice Team Series (with Adrienne Giordano)

Stealing Justice

Cheating Justice

Holiday Justice

Exposing Justice

Undercover Justice

Protecting Justice

Missing Justice

Defending Justice

SCHOCK SISTERS MYSTERY SERIES w/Adrienne Giordano

1st Shock

2nd Strike

3rd Tango

The Secret Ingredient Culinary Mystery Series

The Secret Ingredient, A Culinary Romantic Mystery with Bonus Recipes

The Secret Life of Cranberry Sauce, A Secret Ingredient Holiday Novella

PNR & UF BY MISTY/NYX HALLIWELL

The Accidental Reaper Series

Grim & Bare It, Book 1

Reaper's Keepers, Book 2

In too Reap, Book 3

Killin' It (short story for newsletter subscribers only)

The Vampire's Kiss (an exclusive short story available in Misty's Store. *Intended for mature audiences 17+*)

Grave Girl

Grave Magic

Grim Vows

The Kali Sweet Series

Revenge Is Sweet, Kali Sweet Series, Book 1

Sweet Chaos, Kali Sweet Series, Book 2

Sweet Soldier, Kali Sweet Series, Book 3

Sweet Curse, Kali Sweet Series, Book 4

Witches Anonymous Step 1

Jingle Hells, WA Step 2

Wicked Souls, WA Step 3

Dark Moon Lilith, Witches Anonymous Step 4

Dancing With the Devil, Witches Anonymous Step 5

Devil's Due, Witches Anonymous Step 6

Dirty Deeds, Witches Anonymous Step 7

Wicked Wedding, Witches Anonymous Step 8

Soul Survivor, Moon Water Series, Book 1

Soul Protector, Moon Water Series, Book 2

COZY MYSTERIES (WRITING AS NYX HALLIWELL)

Sister Witches Of Raven Falls Mystery Series

Of Potions and Portents

Of Curses and Charms

Of Stars and Spells

Of Spirits and Superstition

Confessions of a Closet Medium Series

Pumpkins & Poltergeists

Magic & Mistletoe

Hearts & Haunts

Vows & Vengeance

Cupcakes & Corpses

Tea Leaves & Troubled Spirits

Haunted Honeymoon

Wedding Bells & Psychic Spells

Phantoms Are Forever

Sister Witches of Story Cove Series

Cinder

Belle

Snow

Ruby

Zelle

Sister Witches of Story Cove Complete Set

***

Witchy Candy Shop Mysteries

Tricks and Treats

Candy and Creeps

Gum and Ghouls (releasing 2025)

MEET MISTY

USA TODAY Bestselling Author Misty Evans has published over ninety novels, as well as nonfiction inspirational journals. She loves writing urban fantasy, paranormal romance, and mystery/suspense. Under her pen name, Nyx Halliwell, she also writes supernatural cozy mysteries.

When not reading or writing, she enjoys music, movies, and hanging out with her husband, twin sons, and three spoiled rescue dogs. She's a crafter at heart and has far too many projects to finish.

Visit www.mistyevansbooks.com to check out her online store and sign up for her newsletter.

LETTER FROM MISTY

Hello Beautiful Reader!

Thank you for reading this story! It is an honor and a privilege to write books for you. I'm an indie author and every fan is important to me. I pour my heart into each story and do my best to bring you an escape from the real world.

Readers are the key to my success - not a traditional publishing deal (had four), an agent (had two), or a publicity team (yep, you guessed it, had several of those as well.)

Those of you who read my books, love my characters and worlds, and then tell others about them are the best of friends. I adore you and will keep writing if you keep reading!

If you'd like to learn about my other books, sales, and special promotions, please sign up for my newsletter at **www. mistyevansbooks.com**.

You'll get coupons to download starter packs for FREE, whether you love my suspense or my paranormal.

Support me directly (no retailer taking their cut), grab

special edition box sets, and get new releases before they are out at retailers by visiting my store **https://mistyevans books.com/shop**.

I have sales and offer NEW RELEASES early! Check it out.

Last but not least, if you enjoy clean, cozy mysteries, visit my pen name **www.nyxhalliwell.com** to see those books.

Thank you, and happy reading!

Misty

www.ingramcontent.com/pod-product-compliance
Lightning Source LLC
Chambersburg PA
CBHW020254030726
47499CB00001B/195